Dan Rosen

203-221-7127

THE HEPTAMERON
Selected Tales

THE HEPTAMERON
Selected Tales

MARGUERITE, Queen of Navarre

EDITED BY **STANLEY APPELBAUM**

DOVER PUBLICATIONS, INC.
Mineola, New York

Bibliographical Note

This Dover edition, first published in 2006, is a new selection of forty stories
from *The Heptameron; or, Tales and Novels of Marguerite, Queen of Navarre,* as
published in 1905 by George Routledge & Sons, Limited, London, and E. P.
Dutton & Co., New York. The original edition was privately printed in 1886, presumably in London. For information on the French original, see the Introduction.
The selection and the new Introduction to the Dover Edition are by Stanley
Appelbaum.

Library of Congress Cataloging-in-Publication Data

Marguerite, Queen, consort of Henry II, King of Navarre, 1492–1549.
   [Heptaméron. English. Selections]
   The Heptameron : selected tales / Marguerite, Queen of Navarre ; translated
by Arthur Machen ; edited by Stanley Appelbaum.
     p. cm.
   A new selection of forty stories from The Heptameron; or, Tales and novels of
Marguerite, Queen of Navarre, as published in 1905 by George Routledge &
Sons, Limited, London and E.P. Dutton, New York. Now with a new introduc-
tion.
   ISBN 0-486-44763-4 (pbk.)
   I. Machen, Arthur, 1863–1947. II. Appelbaum, Stanley. III. Title.

PQ1631.H3E5 2006
843'.3—dc22

                                      2005055019

Manufactured in the United States of America
Dover Publications, Inc., 31 East 2nd Street, Mineola, N.Y. 11501

Contents

The Arabic numbers are those of the 40 stories in this new Dover selection.
The Roman numbers are those of the stories in complete editions.
The story titles are those given by the translator, Arthur Machen.

Introduction to the Dover Edition

Marguerite de Navarre

She has been called "one of the most outstanding figures of the French Renaissance," one who "dominates the first half of the 16th century in France." Marguerite's biography explains why she is also known as Marguerite de Valois, Marguerite d'Angoulême, and (more rarely) Marguerite d'Alençon. Valois was her broader family or clan name; the Valois (named for a district in the Parisian basin) ruled France from 1328 to 1589. The Angoulême title derived from her father; those of Alençon and Navarre, from her two marriages. She was born at Angoulême in central western France in the memorable year 1492. Her father was Charles I de Valois, count of Angoulême (1460–1496), who, in one of the dynasty's innumerable loveless marriages of convenience, had wed the daughter of the duke of Savoy,[1] Louise de Savoie (1476–1531). This intelligent, cultured woman, who left behind notable memoirs, and to whom some poetry is attributed, had as her (Latin) motto *Libris et liberis* ("for books and [my] children"). Her second child, François d'Angoulême, was born at Cognac, not far from Angoulême, in 1494. Widowed two years later, she devoted herself to her offspring, giving them an excellent education and preparing them for the highest situations. Young Marguerite learned much more than most girls of that epoch; she was particularly adept in languages. Louise and her children were now living in the Loire valley.

---

1. Western parts of this then independent duchy were successively ceded to France between 1601 and 1860.

By 1508 the siblings, who remained very close for decades, were residing at the royal court of Louis XII, of the Orléans branch of the Valois (born 1462; son of the great poet Charles d'Orléans [1394–1465]; reigned 1498–1515). In 1509, the king married Marguerite off to a royal prince, Duke Charles IV of Alençon (a section of Normandy); their court was held sometimes in the city of Alençon, sometimes in nearby Argentan; the duke was far from learned, and Marguerite was disappointed. But things were going very well for her brother: in 1514 he married his cousin, the king's ugly, lame daughter Claude (1499–1524), who inherited the duchy of Brittany in that year.[2] In 1515, Louis XII died without a male heir, and François (a Valois of the Angoulême branch) became the renowned François I of France. He immediately rekindled the dormant "Italian wars," French expeditions into northern Italy in pursuit of hereditary claims to the duchy of Milan and the kingdom of Naples, and in that very year of 1515 he won a resounding victory at Marignano, near Milan. (Also in 1515, he made Angoulême a duchy for his mother; it reverted to the French crown when she died in 1531.)

The years from 1515 to 1525 were a glorious era for Marguerite. Her brother, as king, bestowed on her and her husband the duchy of Berry (in the center of modern France), where Marguerite fostered the recent university at Bourges, and the small county of Armagnac (roughly midway between Bordeaux and Toulouse); the duke of Alençon was now the second most powerful man in France. Marguerite and her dearly loved brother were closer to one another than he ever was to Claude, who became merely an heir-bearing machine. By 1517, the year of Luther's 95 theses, Marguerite had become interested in church reform; though she never converted to Protestantism, she subsequently leaned very far in that direction and was to welcome Calvin at her court in the future. By

---

2. Her mother was the political pawn Anne of Brittany (1477–1514), daughter of the last duke of that region (which was finally ceded to France in 1532). When Anne married Louis XII, she was the widow of his predecessor, Charles VIII (born 1470; reigned 1483–1498).

1519, when the eminent poet Clément Marot (1496–1544) entered her service, she had become one of the chief patrons of scholars, theologians, writers, and artists living in or visiting France.[3] Two of her many other famous protégés were the poet Antoine Héroët (1492–1568) and François Rabelais (c. 1483–1553), who dedicated his *Tiers livre* (Third Book [in the Gargantua and Pantagruel series]) to her in 1546. She also founded hospitals and religious houses, and has been called the "prototype of the modern woman in social service." By 1524, she was doing writing of her own, influenced by Italian humanism and Neoplatonism (with its emphasis on divine and human love), as well as by Evangelism (the moderate church-reform program of the day).

The year 1525 spelled disaster. After 1519, when Charles V (Charles I of Spain) became Holy Roman Emperor (François had been a candidate), France was encircled by Hapsburg-held territory, and the "Italian wars" became pan-European (the French wars against the Empire over Italy went on intermittently until 1544 in the lifetime of François I, and until 1559 thereafter). The 1525 battle of Pavia (in Lombardy) ended in a defeat that dealt a heavy blow to the French royalty and nobility: the loss of Milan, the death of many lords (including the subsequent death from wounds of Marguerite's husband, who was said to have run away from the battle), and, worst of all, the capture and imprisonment of her brother the king. Marguerite herself journeyed from Lyons to Madrid, where she nursed him back to health (he returned home in 1526) and helped to negotiate a treaty less harsh than the one first proposed. (The chief French mastermind of this treaty was Louise de Savoie, whom François had left behind as regent of France both in 1515 and

---

3. Her brother, François I, was also a great patron of the arts, renovating royal châteaux at Fontainebleau and at Blois and Amboise, on the Loire; inviting Leonardo da Vinci and Benvenuto Cellini to France (he failed to lure Erasmus); and establishing a venue for lectures in Paris that would eventually become the prestigious Collège de France.   4. Whereby France was to desist from its pretensions to Italy, and the Empire from its claim to Burgundy; François I broke this treaty in 1539. (Burgundy, earlier an extremely powerful independent duchy, had been attached to the French crown in 1482.)

in 1525; in 1529 she was to negotiate the Treaty of Cambrai,[4] known as "the ladies' peace" because the other chief negotiator was Margaret of Austria, aunt of Emperor Charles V.)

In 1527, Marguerite was married again, this time to the eleven-years-younger Henri II d'Albret, count of Béarn and king of Navarre (in substance, this was Lower Navarre, now the extreme southwestern corner of France; the house of d'Albret had begun to rule Navarre in the late 15th century; the main portion of Navarre, around Pamplona, became part of Spain in the early 16th; Henri's capital was at Pau, whereas Marguerite's base in Navarre was Nérac, southeast of Bordeaux). In 1528, Jeanne, the only child of Marguerite's to outlive infancy, was born.

In 1531, Marguerite wrote the meditational poem *Le miroir de l'âme pécheresse* (The Mirror of the Sinful Soul); when it was published, together with other works, in 1533, it was banned by the Sorbonne (the Parisian theological faculty). In England, it was translated by the future Elizabeth I when she was eleven. Marguerite wrote many other poems, which are highly regarded today (an entire English-language volume is devoted to an analysis of her poetry, which is said to have pioneered the personal lyric in France), as well as plays both religious and secular, not to mention a voluminous correspondence.[5] Her chief claim to literary fame, of course, is the *Heptameron*, which is discussed at length in the following section of this Introduction.

Ever since his return from Spain, François had been moodier and more distant, and he reacted with violent repressive measures to the *affaire des placards* ("affair of the broadsheets") in 1534, when Zwingli-oriented pro-Protestant leaflets were widely disseminated clandestinely; Marguerite, known for her sympathy with the Protestants, had to withdraw from the royal court to Navarre and "lie low." (Though François was always the principal object of her affections, she progressively lost favor and influence with him, but she was still participating in royal policy-making later in the 1530s.) In 1541, the king imposed a particularly brutal forced marriage between Marguerite's

---

5. Two other important French women poets of Marguerite's day were Louise Labé (c. 1520–1566) and Pernette du Guillet (c. 1518–1545).

daughter Jeanne and the duke of Cleves (Kleve, a pivotal small state on the border between Germany and the Netherlands.)[6] (Jeanne's marriage was annulled in 1545, and in 1548, again unwillingly, she wed Antoine de Bourbon [1518–1562]; see story 38 [LXVI] and the commentary thereon in the last section of this Introduction.) Marguerite was largely reclusive in the 1540s. In 1547, the year of her brother's death, she published an anthology of some of her poems and plays called *Les Marguerites de la Marguerite des Princesses* (The Pearls of the Pearl of Princesses). She died in 1549 in the castle of Odos in the Bigorre district (around Tarbes, in the Hautes Pyrénées). Upon her death, the duchy of Alençon reverted to the French crown.

The *Heptameron*

Marguerite's magnum opus was the *Heptameron,* which has been termed "a considerable literary achievement and an invaluable evocation of life in Renaissance France," and which has won her a place just below Rabelais and Montaigne as a master of 16th-century French prose. It is indisputably the best French short-story collection of the century, and a landmark in the development of European short prose fiction.[7] Surely

---

6. Anne of Cleves had become the fourth wife of England's Henry VIII in 1540. 7. Ancient Greco-Roman brief prose narratives were usually embedded in longer works, such as the werewolf story in the *Satyricon* and the Cupid and Psyche story in *The Golden Ass.* The prose short story in Europe (apart from the hard-to-date Irish examples) is basically a medieval innovation, though verse remained the chief vehicle for narration until the late 15th century. In French, the first collection of stories in the modern sense is the *Cent nouvelles nouvelles* (Hundred New Stories), compiled at the court of Burgundy not later than 1467. Other important story collections in 16th-century France include: *Le grand parangon des nouvelles nouvelles et délectables* (The Big Model-Book of New, Delightful Stories) by Nicolas de Troyes, written c. 1535, not published until 1866; the *Nouvelles récréations et joyeux devis* (New Pastimes and Merry Sayings), attributed to Bonaventure des Périers, another protégé of Marguerite's (1510–c. 1544), written c. 1538, published 1558; and two collections by Noël du Fail (c. 1520–1591), the *Propos rustiques* (Rural Conversations; 1547) and the *Baliverneries* (Silly Trifles; 1548).

planned as a 100-story collection like the Italian *Decameron*
(c. 1350) by Giovanni Boccaccio, which it lovingly emulated (in
the early 1540s, Marguerite commissioned a new French translation of the *Decameron* which appeared in 1545), the
Heptameron as we have it consists of 72 stories (it is uncertain
whether the rest were lost or never written).[8]

At least seventeen manuscripts of the *Heptameron* (not to
mention certain other fragments) are extant; they vary considerably among themselves, some of them even lacking the discussions by the fictitious storytellers after each story. The first
printed edition, 1558 (nine years after Marguerite's death),
edited by Pierre Boistuau and published in Paris by G. Gilles,
contained only 67 stories in a random order and not divided into
days; it was called *Histoire des amans fortunez* (Story of Lucky
Lovers) and had no author credit.[9] The book (more or less) as
we know it wasn't published (Paris, J. Caveillier) until the following year, now attributed to Marguerite and called the
Heptaméron des nouvelles; its editor, Claude Gruget, included
72 stories (though he made substitutions for three scabrous
ones) and divided them into days; he also included the lengthy,
summarizing story titles that appear in French-language
editions.[10]

In Boccaccio's *Decameron,* the fictitious storytellers flee to a
country villa from the plague in Florence. Marguerite, in her
Prologue, has her characters visit the spa in Cauterets (close to
the Spanish border, in the Hautes Pyrénées); dispersed by
floods, bandits, and a wild bear, they meet and, while awaiting
the construction of a bridge, tell their stories at an abbey, the
provisos being that the stories must be historically true and nar-
rated unpedantically. Indeed, many of the tales have a factual

---

8. The *Decameron* (Greek *deka*, "ten," and *hemera*, "day") is told by ten fictitious characters over a period of ten days, each one telling one story per day.
The *Heptameron* as we have it, with its ten speakers, covers seven full days
(Greek *hepta*, "seven") and 2/10 of an eighth day.   9. This has led a number
of critics over the years to question Marguerite's authorship and to put forward
some unlikely candidates; most scholars in recent days accept her authorship,
though some believe that she may have been merely the "general editor" of a
collective effort by her courtiers.   10. Apparently he didn't invent them,
because they are to be found in at least one manuscript dated to 1553.

basis in history, and the events can be dated to Marguerite's life-time or shortly before;[11] only a few have more or less direct sources in earlier literature (see Commentary, below).

The ten aristocratic speakers (in the order of their appearance in the Prologue) are (using Machen's spellings): Oisille, a pious elderly lady; Hircan, a hedonist and a decided male chauvinist; Parlamente, Hircan's wife, a moderate feminist who suggests the storytelling; the witty widow Longarine; the gallants Dagoucin and Saffredent; the sprightly ladies Nomerfide and Ennasiutte (or Ennasuitte); and the gentlemen Geburon and Simontault. These fanciful names, elaborate punning anagrams, cloak real people, though some identifications are disputed.[12] Parlamente is surely the author herself, with puns on "parlia-ment" and "pearl" (the meaning of the name Marguerite), whereas Hircan stands for her second husband, the king of Navarre, Hircan being an anagram of Hanric (Henri) with a strong connotation of "goatlike." For some four hundred years it was an article of faith that Oisille (an adapted anagram of "Loise") stood for Louise de Savoie (though the character's Protestant-tinged piety didn't quite fit), but more recently some scholars have plumped for the lady-in-waiting Louise de Daillon, mother of Anne de Vivonne ("Ennasiutte"); Anne de Vivonne and François de Bourdeilles ("Simontault") were the parents of the famous raconteur-historian Brantôme (Pierre de Bourdeilles, seigneur de Brantôme [c. 1540–1614], author of the *Vies des dames galantes* and other biographical works. The rest of the storytellers were also highborn ladies and gentlemen of Marguerite's court in real life.

The announced subjects (not rigidly adhered to) of the eight extant days of storytelling are: (1) bad turns done by women to men, and vice versa; (2) the first striking thing that comes to

---

11. Marguerite's acquaintance with many parts of France, evident in the sto-ries, was due not only to travels, but chiefly to her life in various residences (every French court was mobile). Her journey to Madrid in 1525 gave her a personal introduction to Spain. She no doubt learned detailed facts about central and southern Italy from diplomats and legates.   12. At least one full-length English-language volume has been dedicated to the *Heptameron* story-tellers.

mind; (3) honorable ladies and hypocritical monks; (4) patient women and prudent men, in wooing and marriage; (5) virtuous, wanton, or simpleminded women; (6) deceits practiced by men and women; (7) people who have done what they least desired; and (8) cases of lechery.

A notable feature of the *Heptameron* is the inclusion after each story of a moral, or practical application, drawn from it by its teller, as well as a brief or lengthy discussion, or even lively dispute, among the others concerning its social implications, especially in the field of sexual politics. In the course of these discussions, Marguerite sometimes hints that the story may have been told with a bias or slant that was not to her own liking.

Marguerite's style, once condemned as flat, is now generally regarded as varied and carefully crafted. Much of the dialogue is easy and natural, whereas in the occasional long set speeches and soliloquies, the Greco-Roman rhetorical background of Renaissance literature is clearly in evidence. Current Italian elegance is to be found side by side with extensive remnants of medieval "crudity" such as appear in the scatological tales and those inspired by *fabliaux* (the risqué, humorous verse narratives of the 13th and 14th centuries). New, Protestant-flavored ideas are embodied in the numerous antimonastic tales. Renaissance philosophy, theology, and psychology pervade the work. Almost every story concerns love or sex, ranging from truehearted self-sacrifice to seduction and rape. Indeed, in later centuries, down almost to the present, the *Heptameron* was often considered and marketed as a salacious, "naughty French" book.

There have been at least eight English translations of the *Heptameron* between 1597 and 1984. This Dover selection of stories is based on the 1886 translation (privately printed, presumably in London) by Arthur Llewellyn Machen (Welsh; 1863–1947), best known for his tales of horror and the supernatural which began appearing in the 1890s (he had arrived in London in 1880, and had been cataloguing occult books). Machen had good reason to consider his rendering as the first complete English translation of the *Heptameron*; he worked from the best-edited French text available to him (and still a standard, though not the only one). He chose consciously to "give the work a thoroughly English dress," and to use an archaizing style, even though Marguerite's language was not archaic in her day. He considerably abbreviated the story titles, but, even so, some of his titles unfortunately reveal the ending. He prided himself on his accuracy, but was rather cavalier with regard to proper names, both personal and geographical, and used a few Victorian Anglicisms that might disconcert a 21st-century American reader (explanations, rectifications, and further identifications of people and places are offered in the Commentary, below, which also supplies material for dating the events in the stories).

The present Dover edition, based on the Machen text, has been abridged in order to be priced attractively. It emphasizes the stories themselves (each story included is complete, and all ten storytellers—named in the Commentary—are represented), and in order to fit in as many as possible—40 out of 72—it omits all of the "frame" material: the Prologue and the discussions after the stories. Also omitted is Machen's brief Introduction, which was concerned almost solely with bibliographical data and with attacks on earlier English translations. In the Dover text, table of contents, and Commentary, each story is referred to by a double numeral, such as "25 (xxxvi)"; the Arabic numbers (supplied for handy reference) are those of the 40 stories in this new Dover selection; the Roman numbers are those of the stories in complete editions (i–lxxii).

Commentary on the Individual Stories

1 (i); told by Simontault. Proctor (in the French original, *procureur*): a category of trial lawyer. Duchess and Duke of Alençon: the author and her first husband (the story takes place before his death in 1525). "Séez": Sées, near Alençon; its bishop was Jacques de Silly from 1511 to 1539. Lieutenant-general: vice-regent (or possibly: chief of police). Liberties of the Jacobins: asylum with the Dominicans. Brinon: Jacques Brinon (the chancellor was the minister of justice). Master of Requests:

the councillor who dealt with petitions. Regent: Louise de Savoie. The Provost of Paris (in charge of the Grand Châtelet tribunal) was Jean de la Barre (but if he served from 1526 to 1534, this would be an anachronism). "St. Blancart": the Baron de St. Blancard, general of galleys (prison ships).

2 (ii); told by Oisille. Amboise and Blois: royal residences on the Loire. The queen's son: Jean de Navarre, who lived for only two months in 1530.

3 (iii); told by Saffredent. King Alfonso of Naples: probably Alfonso V of Aragon and Sicily (born 1396; reigned 1443–1458); Naples was Aragonian from 1442 on.

4 (iv); told by Ennasiutte.

5 (v); told by Geburon. Coulon and Niort: in the center of far-western France. Grey Friars: Franciscans.

6 (viii); told by Longarine; apparently based on the *fabliau* "Le meunier d'Arleux" (The Miller of Arleux). "Alet": Alès, near Nîmes in southern France.

7 (ix); told by Dagoucin. "Coasts of" Dauphiné and Provence: lands on the border between those two southeastern French provinces (the Dauphiné is landlocked).

8 (x); told by Parlamente. Aranda: near Zaragoza in Aragon. Perpignan and Narbonne: cities in the Languedoc-Roussillon region directly north of Catalonia. The Spanish king and queen in the story are Ferdinand and Isabella. Fortunate Infante: Prince Alfonso of Aragon, born 1445. Duke of Cardona: a member of the Catalonian Ramón Folch family. Palamos: Palamós in Catalonia, near Gerona (or another place north of Barcelona?). "Nagara": Nájera, near Burgos in Old Castile. Salces: a fortress north of Perpignan. Leucate: near Narbonne.

9 (xi); told by Nomerfide. Thouars: north of Niort.

10 (xii); told by Dagoucin; this true story is that of "Lorenzaccio" (Lorenzino; "evil Lorenzo"), who murdered his cousin Alessandro de' Medici, duke of Florence, in 1537 (Alfred de Musset wrote a famous play about him in 1834). Emperor: Charles V. Portreeve: the official in charge of opening the city gates.

11 (xiv); told by Simontault. The duchy of Milan was inter-

mittently under French rule between 1499 and 1526. Grand-master of Chaumont: Charles d'Amboise, governor of Milan 1507–1509. Admiral Bonnivet: Guillaume Gouffier, seigneur de Bonnivet (c. 1488–1525); he was placed in command of the French troops in Italy in 1523 and was killed at Pavia. Mothering Sunday: Mid-Lent Sunday.

12 (xvi); told by Geburon. The unnamed hero of the story is said to be Bonnivet once more.

13 (xvii); told by Oisille. The count from the house of Saxony is Wilhelm von Fürstenberg. La Trémouïlle was governor of Burgundy from 1501 to 1525. Robertet: Florimond Robertet, who died in the 1520s, had also been treasurer in the two preceding reigns.

14 (xviii); told by Hircan.

15 (xxi); told by Parlamente. "A queen of France": Anne of Brittany, wife of both Charles VIII and Louis XII. Rolandine: a fictitious name for Anne de Rohan.

16 (xxii); told by Geburon; the details of the story place the events between 1530 and 1535. Marie: sister of the poet Antoine Héroët, a courtier of Marguerite's. Fontevrault: in the Loire valley. "Madame de Vendosme": a widow of the count (or duke?) of Vendôme (Vendôme is near Blois). La Fère: a town near Laon (in Picardy, northeast of Paris). Queen of Navarre: Marguerite. "Montavilliers": Montivilliers, in Normandy near Le Havre. Caen: in Normandy. Sisters-in-law: sisters of the king of Navarre. "Giy-juxta-Montargis": Giy near Montargis (not far from Orléans).

17 (xxiii); told by Oisille. Périgord: a former province in western France, east of Bordeaux. "Francis Olivier": François Olivier (1487–1560), named chancellor and keeper of the seal in 1545.

18 (xxv); told by Longarine; the enterprising prince is probably King François I. Sergeant-at-law (in the original French, *avocat*): a trial lawyer.

19 (xxvi); told by Saffredent. "D'Avannes": Gabriel, sieur d'Avesnes. Albret: Alain d'Albret. "Pampeluna": Pamplona, capital of (Spanish) Navarre. Monserrat: in the Catalonian

Pyrenees. "Oly" and "Taffares": Olite and Tafalla, in (Spanish) Navarre. *In manus tuas:* "Into thine hand (I commit my spirit)" (Psalm 31:5).

20 (XXX); told by Hircan. Georges d'Amboise was legate from 1500 to 1510; the legate of Avignon is Louis d'Amboise.

21 (XXXI); told by Geburon. Holy Roman Emperor Maximilian I (born 1459; reigned 1493–1519) held territory to the immediate east and north of France, as well as extensive Germanic lands in Central Europe; his grandson and successor Charles V added Spain to the encirclement of France.

22 (XXXII); told by Oisille; it seems not to have been observed up to now that this story is unmistakably adapted from one in the *Gesta Romanorum,* the most famous medieval Latin collection of moral-pointing tales (c. 1300?; compiled in England?). "John of Paris": Jean Perréal, who also worked for Louis XII and François I.

23 (XXXIII); told by Simontault. Charles d'Angoulême: Marguerite's father. Cognac: near Angoulême; birthplace of François I and a childhood home of François and Marguerite. "Village hard-by Cherves": "village hard-by, Cherves," is the correct reading. *Corpus Domini:* the Lord's Body, the consecrated host.

24 (XXXV); told by Hircan.

25 (XXXVI); told by Ennasiutte. Grenoble: city in the Dauphiné, southeastern France. "A president": a presiding judge (the indefinite article makes it less likely that the head of the local assembly is meant).

26 (XXXIX); told by Saffredent. "Grignaulx": Grignols, near Périgueux (the capital of old Périgord). "Esquire of the Body" (in the original French, *chevalier d'honneur*): the principal household official.

27 (XL); told by Parlamente; connected with an earlier story in the *Heptameron,* 15 (XXI). The father is Jean II de Rohan (died 1516).

28 (XLII); told by Parlamente; the hero is said to be François I (thus, his sister would be Marguerite herself).

29 (XLIII); told by Geburon.

30 (XLV); told by Simontault. Giving the Innocents: on Innocents Day (December 28), people played pranks; young men could beat women who slept late. Duke of Orléans: Charles, the third son of François I (died 1545).

31 (XLIX); told by Hircan. The King Charles is Charles VIII. Astillon: Jacques de Châtillon, killed at Ravenna in 1512; Durassier and Valnebon are fictitious names for two other historical noblemen-soldiers. "Closet" (in the original French, *garderobbe*): a small room (clothes-storage room, dressing room, etc.).

32 (LII); told by Simontault.

33 (LIII); told by Ennasiutte.

34 (LV); told by Nomerfide.

35 (LVI); told by Hircan. Raphael and Tobit: in the book *Tobit* of the Old Testament Apocrypha. *Dominus vobiscum:* "The Lord [be] with you." *Ite missa est:* the formula of dismissal at the end of a mass.

36 (LX); told by Geburon; details of the story indicate 1515 as the year of the events. Claude: first wife of François I. The Regent: his mother.

37 (LXI); told by Saffredent; details indicate 1515 or 1522 as the year of the events. Autun: in Burgundy (central eastern France).

38 (LXVI); told by Ennasiutte; the wedding took place in 1548. My lord of Vendôme: Antoine de Bourbon. Princess of Navarre: Marguerite's daughter Jeanne d'Albret, who succeeded her father on the throne of Navarre, reigning as Jeanne III from 1555 to 1572. The son (1553–1610) of Antoine and Jeanne succeeded his mother as King Henri II of Navarre, and became the famous Henri IV of France in 1589, changing the royal line from the Valois to the Bourbons. Guienne (or Guyenne): a former province in southwestern France, with Bordeaux as its capital. "Prothonotary": protonotary, a title of certain ecclesiastical dignitaries.

39 (LXVII); told by Simontault. "Robertval": Jean-François de La Roque de Roberval (1500–1561), who became lieutenant-general of Canada in 1541; the designation "island" connotes a

New World colony (cf. the island that Sancho Panza longs to govern in *Don Quixote*). La Rochelle: France's chief Atlantic port at the time; on the central west coast.

40 (LXX); told by Oisille; this is a very close prose retelling of the mid-13th-century narrative poem *La châtelaine de Vergi* (or *Vergy;* "The Lady of Vergi Castle"), which was otherwise widely imitated in the 14th to 16th centuries (there had already been a prose version in the 15th). The lady in question was the wife of the seneschal of Burgundy. Duke of Burgundy: Hugues IV (ruled 1218–1272). *Angustiae sunt mihi undique:* from verse 22 of the apocryphal Old Testament book of *Susanna* (in the Latin Vulgate Bible it constitutes chapter 13 of *Daniel*); the New Oxford Annotated Bible translates this as "I am completely trapped." Argilly and Le (not "La") Vergier: small places in Burgundy. The footnote in the text is Machen's.

THE
HEPTAMERON
Selected Tales

1 (I)

The misdeeds of the wife of a certain proctor, who had a bishop for her gallant.

Fair ladies, I have had such a poor reward for all my long service that, to avenge me on Love, and her whose heart is so hard toward me, I am about to recount to you the misdeeds done of women on us poor men; and I will tell you nothing but the whole truth.

In the town of Alençon, in the time of the last Duke Charles, there was a proctor named St. Aignan, who had for wife a gentlewoman of the country. And she, having more beauty than virtue, and being of a fickle disposition, was courted by the Bishop of Séez, who, to gain his ends, handled the husband in such fashion that he not only did not perceive the wickedness of the Bishop, but did even forget the love he had for his master and mistress, and at last had dealings with wizards, that thereby he might compass the death of the duchess. For a long while did the Bishop have dalliance with this evil woman, who received him not for the love she bore him, but because her husband, being greedy of money, so charged her. But her love she gave to a young man of Alençon, son of the lieutenant-general, and him she loved to madness; often obtaining of the Bishop to send her husband away, that she might see Du Mesnil, the son of the lieutenant, at her ease. And this fashion of life lasted a long while, she having the Bishop for profit, and Du Mesnil for pleasure, for she told the last that all the pleasaunce she did to the Bishop was but for his sake, and that from her the Bishop only got words, and he might rest assured that no man beside himself got aught else.

One day when her husband had to go on some charges of the Bishop, she asked him to let her go into the country, saying that

1

the town air was hurtful to her; and having got to her farmstead, she straightway wrote to Du Mesnil, enjoining him not to fail in coming to her at nine in the evening. This the poor gallant did; but at the porch he found the maid who was wont to let him in, who thus addressed him: "Go farther, friend, for here your place is taken." And he, thinking the proctor was come, asked her how they fared. The serving-maid, having pity on him, for that he loved so much, and was so little loved in return, and seeing, moreover, that he was comely, young, and of an honourable address, showed to him the frailty of her mistress, believing that when he heard this the flame of his love would be somewhat quenched. And she told him how the Bishop of Séez was hardly come, and was now in bed with her mistress, though it was appointed that he should not come till the morrow; but having kept the proctor at his palace, he had stole away by night to privily visit her. Who then was in despair but Du Mesnil; yet scarcely could he believe the tale, and hid himself in a house hard by, where, remaining till three hours after midnight, he then saw the Bishop come out, not so well disguised as not to be more easily recognized than he desired.

And in this despair he made his way back to Alençon, whither this evil woman having returned, she came to speak to him, and would fain have fooled him in her old fashion. But he told her that she was too good, since she had touched holy things, to speak to a poor sinner like himself, whose repentance, nevertheless, was so great that he hoped ere long his sin would be forgiven. So when she perceived that her case was known to him, and that excuses, oaths, and promises availed nothing, she made complaint of him to her Bishop. And after having well pondered the matter with him, this woman came to her husband and told him that she could no longer live in Alençon, since the son of the lieutenant, whom he had accounted for a friend, did incessantly lay assault to her honour, wherefore she entreated him to take her to Argentan, to do away with all suspicion. To this her husband, who let himself be ruled by her, agreed. But they had been but a short while at Argentan when this evil one sent to Du Mesnil, saying that of all men in the world he was most wicked, and that she was well advised of his publicly speaking ill of her and the Bishop of Séez, for which she would labour to call him to account.

The young man, who had spoken to her alone on the matter, yet fearing to get into disfavour with the Bishop, went forthwith to Argentan with two of his servants, and found his mistress at evensong at the Jacobins. He, kneeling by her side, spoke thus: "Mistress, I am come to this place to swear to you before God that I have spoken against your honour to no one save you yourself; and so evilly have you entreated me that what I told you was not the half of what you deserved. And if there be man or woman who will say that I have so spoken, here am I to give them the lie before your face." She, seeing that much folk were in the church, and that he had for companions two stout serving-men, constrained herself to speak to him in the most gracious sort she could, saying she made no manner of doubt but that he spoke the truth, and that she esteemed him too honourable to speak evil of any man, much less of her who had for him so great a love; but some tales had got to her husband's ears, on which account she would have him make declaration before her husband, that he had not told them, and believed them not at all. This he freely granted, and thinking to accompany her home, he would have taken her by the arm, but she told him that it would not be well for him to come with her, since her husband might suppose she had put the words into his mouth. And taking one of his servants by the sleeve of his doublet, she said, "Leave this man with me, and when it is time I will presently send him for you, but meanwhile do you go and rest in your lodging." And he, who knew not that she conspired against him, did as he was ordered.

To the servant she had taken with her, she gave supper, and when he often asked her if it was not time to look for his master, she told him that it would shortly come. And when night had fallen she privily sent one of her own serving-men to seek Du Mesnil, who, not knowing the evil that was to befall him, went with bold face to the house of the aforesaid St. Aignan, where his mistress still kept his servant, so that he had only one with him. And when he came to the door of the house, the man who had brought him told him the lady wished much to speak with him before he came into the presence of her husband, and that she awaited him in a room with only his own servant with her, and that he would do well to send the other to the door in front. This he did, and whilst he was going up a small and gloomy stair, the proctor, who had laid an ambush in a closet, hearing the noise of his steps, called out, "What is that?" And they told him that it was a man privily endeavouring to enter his house. Whereupon a fellow called Thomas Guerin, an assassin by trade, who to this intent had been hired by St. Aignan, rushed forth and dealt the young man such blows with his sword that, for all the defence he might make, he fell dead between their hands. His servant who was with the lady said to her, "I hear my master talking on the stairs, and will go to him." But she held him back, saying, "Be not troubled, he will shortly be here." And a little after, hearing these words in his master's voice, "I am gone, and may God receive my soul," he would fain have succoured him. But she held him back, saying, "Be not troubled, my husband does but chastise him for these follies of his youth; come, let us go and see what is being done." And leaning against the balustrade of the stairs, she asked of her husband, "Is it finished?" And he said to her, "Come and see, for in this hour I have avenged you on him who has done you so much shame." So saying he gave with his dagger ten or twelve strokes into the body of him whom, when alive, he durst not have encountered.

After that the murder was done, and the two servants had fled to carry the news to the poor father, the aforesaid St. Aignan considered how the thing might best be kept secret, and perceived that the two servants could not be admitted to bear witness, and that none in his house had seen it done, save the murderers, an old serving-woman, and a young girl of fifteen. The old woman he was fain privily to put away, but she, finding means to escape, took refuge in the liberties of the Jacobins. And her witness was the best on the matter of the murder. The young girl stayed some days in his house, but he, having caused one of the murderers to bribe her, put her in a stew in Paris, to the end that her witness might not be received. And, better to hide the murder, he had the body of the dead man burnt; and the bones which the fire had not consumed he made mingle with the mortar that was being used in building. This done he sent with great speed to court to ask for pardon, letting it be understood that he had many times forbidden a man whom he suspected to enter his house. And this man, who would have dishonoured his wife notwithstanding that he was forbidden, had come secretly by night to speak to her, wherefore having found him at the door of her room, and wrath casting out reason, he had slain him. But for all his haste he was not able to dispatch this letter to the chancellor's before the Duke and Duchess, who had been advised of what had taken place by the father of the murdered man, likewise sent to the chancellor, that pardon might not be granted him. This wretch, seeing that he could not obtain pardon, fled beyond seas to England, and his wife with him, and many of his kinsfolk. Yet before he set out, he made known to the murderer who had dealt the blow that he had seen express letters from the King, to take him and put him to death. And since, in return for the service he had done him he would gladly save his life, he gave him ten crowns for him to fly the realm. This he did, and has not been found to this day.

This murder was so confirmed by the servants of the dead man, by the old woman who had fled to the Jacobins, and by the bones which were found in the mortar, that the case was begun and brought to an end in the absence of St. Aignan and his wife. Judgment went by default, they were condemned to death, to pay fifteen hundred crowns to the father of the murdered man, and the rest of their goods were escheated to the crown. St. Aignan, seeing that though he was living in England, in France the law accounted him dead, accomplished so much by his services to some great lords, and by the favour of the kinsfolk of his wife, that the King of England entreated the King of France to grant him a free pardon, and to restore to him his goods and his offices. But the King of France being assured of the enormity of his crime, sent the case to the King of England, asking him if such a deed deserved pardon, and saying that to the Duke of Alençon alone it pertained to grant pardon for offences done in his duchy. But for all these excuses he could not satisfy the King of England, who so earnestly entreated him that at last the proctor gained what he desired and returned to his home. And there, to fill up the measure of his wickedness, he called to him a wizard, named Gallery, hoping by this means to escape the paying of the fifteen hundred crowns to the father of the dead man.

And to this end, he and his wife with him, went up to Paris in disguise. And she, perceiving him closeted for a long while with the enchanter Gallery, and not being told the reason of this, on one morning played the spy and saw Gallery showing to him five wooden images, of which three had their hands hanging down, and of the two others the hands were raised. And she heard the wizard: "We must have images made of wax like these, and they that have the hands drooping shall be made in the likeness of those that are to die, but they that have the hands uplifted shall be made in the likeness of those whose love and favour we desire." To whom the proctor: "This one shall be for the King whose grace I would gain, and this for my Lord Brinon, the chancellor of Alençon." And Gallery said to him, "We must lay these images beneath the altar, where they may hear mass, together with the words that you shall presently say after me." And speaking of them that had the drooping arms, the proctor said that one should be Master Gilles du Mesnil, father of him who was murdered, for he knew well that as long as he was alive he would not cease from pursuing him. And another, that was made in the likeness of a woman, should be for my lady the Duchess of Alençon, the sister of the King; since so well did she love Du Mesnil, her old servant, and had so great a knowledge of the proctor's wickedness in other matters, that unless she died, he could not live. And the last image, that was also made in the likeness of a woman, should be his wife, since she was the beginning of all his evil hap, and he knew well that she would never amend the wickedness of her ways. But when this wife of his, who saw through a chink in the door all that was done, heard that she was numbered among the dead, it was her humour to send her husband on before her. And pretending to go and borrow money of an uncle of hers, named Neaufle, Master of Requests to the Duke of Alençon, she told him of her husband, and all that she had seen and heard him do. This Neaufle aforesaid, like a good old servant, went forthwith to the chancellor of the Duchy of Alençon, and showed him the whole of the matter. And since the Duke and Duchess chanced not to be at court on that day, the chancellor went and told this strange case to the Regent, mother of the King and of the Duchess, who straightway sought out La Barre, Provost of Paris; and such good diligence did he make that he clapped up the proctor and his wizard Gallery, who confessed freely the crime, without being put to the question, or in any way constrained. And the matter of their accusation was made out and brought to the King, whereupon some, willing to save the lives of these men, would fain persuade him that by their enchantments they sought nothing but his grace. But the King, being as tender of his sister's life as of his own, commanded that sentence should be given as if they had attempted his own peculiar person. Nevertheless, the Duchess of Alençon made entreaty for the life of this proctor, and for the doom of death to be changed to some other punishment. So this was granted her, and the proctor, together with the wizard, were sent to the galleys of St. Blancart at Marseilles, where they ended their days in close imprisonment, having time wherein to consider their sins, how great they had been. And the wife, when her husband was removed, sinned more wickedly than before, and so died miserably.

2 (II)
The wife of a muleteer had rather death than dishonour.

In the town of Amboise there was a muleteer who served the Queen of Navarre, sister to Francis the First. And she being at Blois brought to bed of a son, this muleteer went thither to be paid such monies as were owing to him, and his wife stayed at Amboise, being lodged in a house beyond the bridge. Now there was a servant of her husband who had for a long while loved her so greatly, that one day he must needs speak his mind to her. But she, being a woman of true virtuousness, so sharply reproved him, threatening that he should be beaten and sent away, that never after did he dare to address her. But he secretly kept the fire of lust in his heart, until one day when his master was abroad, and his mistress at evensong in the castle church of St.

Florentin, no short distance from her house. So, since she was living alone, he conceived the humour of taking by force that which he could obtain by none of his prayers or good offices, to which end he broke the boards that were between his room and that of his mistress. And this was not perceived when she, having with her a wench of eleven or twelve years, came to bed, by reason of the curtains that were hung by the master's bed on one side, and the servant's on the other. And when the poor woman was in her first sleep, the fellow came in by the hole he had made, clad only in his shirt, and with a drawn sword in his hand. But as soon as she was aware of his being in the bed with her, she leapt forth from thence, and implored him in such wise as an honourable woman would. And he, whose love was but beastly lust, better able to understand the noise of his mules than fair conclusions, showed himself more brutal than the brutes he had a long while tended; for seeing that so swiftly did she chase round a table that he could not take her, and that she had twice escaped from his very hands, he despaired of being able to rape her alive, and so gave her a shrewd stroke in the reins, thinking that pain would make her do what fear could not. Yet it had a contrary effect, for like a good soldier who, when he sees his blood flowing, is stirred up all the more to be avenged on his enemies, and gain for himself glory, so her chaste heart made her fly yet more swiftly from the hands of this wretch, making still more earnest entreaty to him, if haply he might see the wickedness of his purpose. But in such furious case was he, that to nothing of this would he give ear, and aimed at her more and more blows, to avoid which she still kept running as fast as she was able. And when, by reason of loss of blood, she felt death to be near at hand, she raised her eyes to heaven, and with clasped hands gave thanks to God, calling upon him as her strength, her virtuousness, her long-suffering, and her purity; beseeching him to favourably accept that blood of hers which she had poured forth for the sake of his Son, by whom she stead-fastly believed all her sins were blotted out from his sight. And saying: "Lord receive my soul, which by thy loving kindness hath been redeemed," she fell on her face to the floor, where the wretch gave her several strokes, and her tongue having lost speech and her body strength, he took that from her which she was no more able to defend against him.

And when he had appeased his evil lust, he fled forth in such hot haste that all pursuit was of no avail, for he was never found. The young wench who had been sleeping with the muleteer's wife had, for the fear she was in, hidden under the bed, but when she saw that the man was departed, she went to her mistress, and finding in her no speech or movement, called from the window to the neighbours to bring help. They, holding her in as good love and repute as any woman in the town, came presently to her, bringing with them chirurgeons, who made out that she had on her body five-and-twenty mortal wounds. All the aid they could give her was of no avail, and yet for more than an hour she languished on, showing by the signs she made with her eyes and hands, that she knew what was passing. Being asked by the parson in what faith she died, she gave answer by signs as plain as words, that she put the hope of her salvation in Jesus only; and so with glad countenance, and eyes lifted up to heaven, she gave up her soul and body to the Creator. And when she was being taken out for burial, the company thereto appointed attending, her poor husband came up, and saw the body of his wife in front of his house before tidings had been brought to him that she was dead. And the manner of her death being reported to him, he had then a double cause for lamentation, which he made in such grievous sort that he was well-nigh amort. So was this martyr of chastity buried in the church of St. Florentin, and at the burial of her all the honourable women of the town failed not to do her honour by their presence; thinking it no small thing to live in a place which had contained so virtuous a woman. And moreover, such women as were queans determined to live henceforth in amendment of life.

3 (III)
Of a lustful King of Naples, and how he met with his match.

Since, ladies, I have ofttimes desired to be a fellow in good-luck with him of whom I am about to tell you, I will declare to you that in the town of Naples, in the time of King Alfonso, to whom lust was as the sceptre of his kingdom, there lived a young gentleman of such honourable character and so fine an address, that for these merits of his an aged widow gave him her daughter to wife. And she yielded in nowise to her husband in beauty and graciousness, and there was great love betwixt these two. But on a day in Carnival time, the King, as his custom was, went masked about the different houses, each one striving to make for him the best fare and welcome. And when he came to the house of this gentleman aforesaid, he was received after a better fashion than anywhere else; so fine were the sweetmeats, so admirable the singing, and above all, the bravest lady the King had ever set eyes on. And she, at the end of the entertainment, sang a song with her husband in such sort that it did but increase her beauty. And he, beholding in that body of hers so many perfections, did not set such store on the good accord between her and her husband as not to ponder how he might best break it; but the difficulty lay in the great love that he perceived they bore one another, wherefore he kept this passion of his as secret as he was able. But in some way to ease it he gave many entertainments to all the lords and ladies of Naples, and at these the gentleman and his wife were by no means forgotten. And since a man believes what he desires, it appeared to him that this lady's eyes promised well for him, if it were not that her husband was present. So to try how he stood with her, he sent the husband on some charges of his to Rome, so that he might be away fifteen days or three weeks. No sooner was he gone than his wife, who had never before been without him, was filled with great grief, in which she was so comforted by the sweet remonstrances and gifts of the King, that not only was she consoled for her husband, but more than this was well content to live without him. And before the three weeks were come to an end she was grown so amorous of the King, the thought of her husband's return gave her as much discontent as before did his departure. And so, as not to be altogether shut out from the presence of the King, they agreed together that when the gentleman went a-hunting to his country house, she should advise the King of it, so that he might safely come and see her, and so privily that her repute, of which she was more tender than her conscience, should take no hurt.

In this contentment the lady kept herself, and her husband being returned she received him in such sort that, though he had been told that while he was away the King had had to do with her, he would not have believed it. But as time went on, that fire which so hardly can be concealed began to show itself, and in such fashion that her husband began to suspect her for a strumpet, and keeping close watch, was well nigh assured of it. But for the fear he had that he who had done him this great harm might, if he showed any suspicion, do him a worse, he determined to dissemble, thinking secret grief better than to make hazard of his life for a woman who loved him not. All the same, in the dolour of his heart, he was fain, if it might be, to cry quits with the King, and knowing that women, and notably those of noble mind, are more easily to be moved by grief than love, he made free one day, in speaking to the Queen, to tell her it was a mighty pity she was not better beloved of the King. The Queen, who had heard about the King and his wife, said to him: "One may not have both honour and pleasure at once. I am well advised that I have the honour, and another the pleasure, but she who has the pleasure has not the honour that appertains to me." He, understanding well to what intent these words were spoken, replied to her: "My lady, with you honour is inbred, for you come of such gentle blood that no title, be it Queen or Empress, can increase your nobility; yet your beauteousness and gracious ways so well deserve that you should likewise enjoy pleasure, that she who has robbed you of it hath done more ill to herself than you, since for a glory which is in truth her shame, she misses as much delight as you or any woman in the realm could desire. And I dare swear that, if the King's crown was fallen off his head, he could satisfy a lady no better than myself; and sure am I that if he would satisfy such an one as you, he would do well to change his complexion for mine." Laughing, the Queen replied to him: "Though the King be of more delicate complexion than you, yet I am so well satisfied with the love he bears me that I prefer it to any other." Then said the gentleman: "My lady, if it were indeed so, you would by no means move my pity, for I know well that the honourable love of your heart would content you, if there were in the King an equal love toward you; but God has wisely taken this from you, so that not finding in him that which you desire, you may not make him your god on earth." I confess to you," said the Queen, "that the love I bear the King is of such sort, that in no heart but mine can love be found like to it." "Pardon me," said the gentleman to her, "you have not sounded the depths of all men's hearts, for I say unto you there is one who hath toward you a love so great that your love for your husband beside it would show as nothing. And as he beholds the King's love failing you, his own grows and increases in such a fashion that, were it your pleasure, you would be paid in full for all your griefs."

The Queen began, as much from his words as from his countenance, to perceive that what he said was from the depths of his heart; and it came into her mind that he had longwhile striven to do her service, so that he was become sad and melancholic. And this she had thought to be by reason of his wife, but she was now well assured that it was for love of herself. And so love, that when it is not feigned is quickly to be discovered, let her know for certain that which had been concealed from all men. And looking upon the gentleman that he was by far more worthy of love than her husband, and seeing that he was forsaken of his wife as she was of the King, hard pressed by grief and jealousy of her husband, and by her love for the gentleman, she began to sigh forth with tears in her eyes: "My God, can it be that for vengeance' sake I shall grant that which no love could win from me." The gentleman, understanding well the intent of what she said, replied: "Vengeance is sweet, and sweeter when it slayeth not an enemy, but giveth life to a true friend. I think that the time is come for you to put away that foolish love for one who regardeth you not; and a true and reasonable love shall drive from your heart all fear, which never is able to dwell in a virtuous and noble soul. Let us lay aside the grandeur of your estate, and see in ourselves the man and woman who of all the world are most deceived, betrayed, and mocked of those whom they loved with a perfect love. Let us be avenged, not so much to give to our enemies their deserts, as to satisfy that love which, for my part, I cannot longer keep contained and live. And I think, if your heart be not harder than rock or adamant, you must feel within you some spark of that fire which I can no more keep concealed. And if pity for me, who am a-dying for love of you, do not stir in you some love for me, natheless love of yourself should do so. For so perfect are you, that you are well worthy of the love of every honest heart, yet you are contemptuously entreated and abandoned by him for whose sake you despised all others."

The Queen hearing these words was so confounded that, for fear of showing by her face the trouble at her heart, she took the gentleman's arm and went forth into a pleasaunce that was nigh her chamber, where for a long while she walked up and down without speaking a word to him. But the gentleman, seeing her to be half-won, when they reached the bottom of the alley where none could see them, made declaration of his love in a very effective sort of way, and finding themselves both at one on this matter, they played their mystery of *Vengeance*, and liked it better than the mystery of the *Passion*. And there it was agreed and determined that, whenever the King should be at the gentleman's house with his wife, he should be at the palace with the Queen; so the cozeners being cozened, they would all four have a piece of that cake which two thought to keep to themselves. This treaty executed, they gat them back, the lady to her room and the gentleman to his house, each with such a good satisfaction for what they had done that all old griefs were forgotten. And the mislike which they both had aforetime to the King's going to see the lady was turned to a good liking thereat, insomuch that the gentleman went more than his habit had been to his house in the country, which was distant about half-a-league. And as soon as the King was advised of his going away he straightway would go off to the lady; and the gentleman, when night was come, would go to the palace and enjoy the easements of the King's deputy with the Queen. And all this done so privily that none knew of it. Which going on some time, the King being of public estate, could not well contrive to conceal his share in the matter, and all the world was aware of it, and mighty compassionate toward the poor gentleman, so much so as to

make horns of derision at him behind his back, which he saw
very plainly. But, such was his humour, he took more delight in
these horns of his than the King's crown; and the King one day
seeing a stag's head in the gentleman's house, did himself take
occasion to say, with a laugh, that the stag's head was very well
placed. So the gentleman, who had as sharp a wit as the King's,
made write beneath the head in this wise:

> "These horns I wear, and plainly show it,
> But one doth wear them and not know it."

And the King, when he came next to the house, inquired of the
gentleman what was the intent of this, to whom he replied: "If
the secret of the King be hidden from the stag, it is not fitting
that the secret of the stag should be revealed to the King; but be
content to know that not all they that wear horns have their hats
lifted off thereby, for some are so soft, that they would distress
no one, and he carries them best who knows not that he has
them." The King easily perceived by these words that the gentleman knew of what passed between him and his wife, but not
a tittle did he suspect him and the Queen, for the better that she
liked the life the King led the more she pretended to the contrary. So for a long time they all lived in this fashion, till old age
took order with them.

4 (IV)

Of a young man who attempted the honour of a
princess, and the poor success of his adventure.

There was in the land of Flanders a lady of a most illustrious
house, who had been twice married and was now a widow without any children. In the time of her widowhood she lived retired
with her brother, who was a great lord, and married to a daughter of the King, and this brother loved his sister exceedingly.
Now this prince was a man somewhat enslaved to pleasure, having great delight in hunting, games, and women, as his youth led
him, but having to wife one of a peevish disposition, to whom
none of her husband's contentments were pleasing, he would

always have his sister with him, for she was of a most joyous nature, and a good and honourable woman withal. And there was in the house of this prince a gentleman whose beauty and grace did far surpass that of his fellows; and he beholding the sister of his master that she was joyous and always ready for a laugh, thought that he would assay how the offer of an honourable love would be taken by her. But her reply was by no means favourable to him; yet though it was such as became a princess and a woman of honour, she, seeing him to be a handsome man and of good address, easily pardoned to him his great boldness in speaking to her after such a fashion. And moreover she assured him that she bore him no displeasure for what he had said, but charged him from henceforth to let her have no more of it. This he promised, that he might not lose the delight he had in her company, but as time went on his love grew even more and more, so that he forgot the promise he had given. Not that he made a second trial of what words could do, for he had found out the manner of her replies; but he thought that since she was a widow, young, lusty, and of a pleasant humour, she might perchance, if he came upon her in a fitting place, take compassion on him and her own flesh.

To which end, he said to his master that hard by his house there was most excellent hunting, and that if in Maytime he would be pleased to come and chase the stags, he could promise him as good contentment as he could desire. The prince, as much for the love he bore him as for his delight in hunting, granted his request, and going to his house found it most bravely ordered, and as good as that of the greatest lord in the land. And the gentleman lodged his lord and lady on one side, and opposite to them he appointed a room for her whom he loved better than himself. And so bravely was this room decked out with tapestry above and matting below, that no one could discover a trap-door contrived in the wall by the bed, which led to where his mother was lodged. And she, being an old dame with an obstinate rheum, and troubled with a cough, had made an exchange of chambers with her son, so as not to annoy the princess. And before curfew-time in the evening this good lady would carry sweetmeats to the princess for her supper, in which

service she was assisted by her son, since being well-beloved of
the prince, it was not refused to him to be present at her *levee*
and *couchee,* at which times he got fresh fuel for the fire that
was in him. And so late one night did he tarry there that she was
well nigh asleep before he left her for his own room. And having put on him the finest and best scented shirt he had, and a
night-cap of surpassing device, he was well persuaded, on looking himself over, that there was not a lady in the world hard
enough to refuse a man of such a grace and beauty. Wherefore,
promising to himself a good issue of his adventure, he lay down
on his bed, hoping not to make thereon a long stay, but to
change it for one more pleasant and honourable. And as soon as
he had dismissed his servants he got up and shut the door
behind them, and afterwards listened for a long while if he
should hear any noise in the room of the princess. So when he
was satisfied that all was quiet, he was fain to begin his pleasant
travail, and little by little let down the trap-door, which, so well
was it carpeted over, did not make so much as the least noise.
And so he got into the room by the bed of the princess, who was
now asleep. And straightway, heeding not the duty he owed her
or the house from which she came, without with your leave, or
by your leave, he got into bed with her, who felt herself in his
arms, before she knew he was in the room. But she, being
strong, got from between his hands, and having required of him
who he was, fell to beating, biting, and scratching with such
hearty good will that, for fear of her calling out, he would have
stopped her mouth with the blanket; but in this he was foiled,
since the princess, seeing that he spared none of his resources
to rob her of her honour, spared none of hers to defend it. So
she called at the top of her voice to her maid of honour, an
ancient and prudent dame, who slept with her, and she, clad
only in her nightgear, ran to the help of her mistress.

And when the gentleman saw he was discovered, so great a
fear had he of being recognised, that as fast as might be he
departed by his trap-door; and in like degree, as he had been
desirous and well assured of a good reception when he was
going, so now did he despair as he went back in such evil case.
He found his mirror and candle upon the table, and beholding

his countenance, that it was all bloody from the bites and scratches she had dealt him, he began to say: "Beauty! thou hast received a wage according to thy deserving; for by thine idle promise I attempted an impossible thing, and which, moreover, in place of increasing my happiness, hath made my sorrow greater than it was before; since I am well assured that if she knew that I, against my solemn undertaking, had done this foolish thing, I should be cut off from that close and honourable commerce I aforetime had with her. And this I shall have well deserved, for to make my beauty and grace avail me anything, I should not have hidden them in the darkness; I should not have attempted to carry that chaste body by assault; but striven to gain her favour, till by patience and long service my love had gained the victory; for without love all the power and might of men are as nothing."

So, in such wise that I cannot tell, passed the night in tears, and regrets, and griefs; and in the morning, so torn was his face, that he made pretence of great sickness, saying that he could not bear the light, even until the company was departed.

The lady who had come off conqueror knew that there was none other in the prince's court who durst set about such an enterprise save her host, who had already had the boldness to make a declaration of love to her. So she, with her maid of honour, made search around her chamber to find how he could have made an entry. And not being able to find any place or trace thereof, she said to her companion in great wrath: "Be assured that it was none other than the lord of the house, and in such sort will I handle him on the morrow with my brother, that his head shall bear witness to my chastity." The maid of honour, seeing her so angered, said to her: "My lady, I am well pleased at the price you set on your honour, since the more to exalt it you would make sacrifice of the life of one who, for his love of you, has put it to this risk. But in this way one ofttimes lessens what one would fain increase. Wherefore, my lady, I do entreat you to tell me the whole truth of this matter." And when the princess had made a full account of the business, the maid of honour said to her: "Do you verily assure me that he had nothing from you but only scratches and fisticuffs?" "I do assure you," said the lady, "and if he find not a rare mediciner, I am much mistaken if to-morrow his face do not bear evident witness to what I say." "Well, my lady," said the maid of honour, "if it be as you say, it seems to me that you have rather occasion to thank God than to imagine vengeance; for you may conceive that since this gentleman had a heart daring enough to attempt such a deed, you can award to him no punishment, nay, not death itself, that will not be easier to bear than his dolour at having failed therein. If you are fain to be revenged on him, leave him to his love and to his shame, and from them he will suffer more shrewdly than at your hands; and if you have regard for your honour, beware lest you fall into the same pit as he, for in place of gaining the greatest delight he could desire, he is in the most shameful case that may hap to a gentleman. So you, good mistress, thinking to exalt your honour, may haply bring it to the dust; for if you make advertisement of this affair, you will cause to be blazed abroad what no one would ever know, since the gentleman, trust me, will throw but little light on the matter. And when my lord, your brother, shall do justice on him at your asking, and the poor gentleman goes forth to die, it will be noised abroad that he had his pleasure of you, and men will say that it is not to be believed a man could make such an attempt, if he had not before had of you some good matter of contentment. You are young and fair, living gaily amongst all, and there is no soul at court who has not seen your commerce with this man you have in suspicion, so all will determine that if he finished the work you began it. So your honour, which hitherto hath been mightily extolled, will become common matter of dispute wherever this story is related."

The princess, considering the fair conclusions of the maid of honour, perceived that she had spoken the truth, and that with just cause would she be blamed, since both openly and privily she had always given a good reception to the gentleman, and so would have her woman tell her what was best to be done. And she answered her: "Good mistress, since it is your pleasure, seeing the love from whence they come, to give ear to my counsels, I think that you should be glad at heart, for that the bravest and most gallant gentleman I have ever seen hath not been able to

turn you from the path of true virtuousness. And for this you
should humble yourself before God, confessing that it is not
your own strength or virtue, for women leading, beyond compare, straiter lives than you, have been brought to the dust by
men less worthy of love than he. And henceforth, do you avoid
proposals of love and the like, for many that at the first got off
scot-free, the second time have fallen into the pit. Be mindful
that Love is blind, and a causer of blindness, for it makes believe
the path is sure, when in truth it is most slippery. And it is my
mind that you should give him no sign as to what has taken
place, and if he say anything on the matter, feign to understand
him not, and so be quit of two perils; the one of vainglory for
your victory, the other of recalling to mind things that are pleasant to the flesh, ay, so pleasant are they that the chastest have
much ado to quench all sparks of that fire they are most fain to
avoid. And moreover, I counsel you, that he think not he hath
done you any sort of pleasure, that you do, by small degrees, put
a close to your intimacy with him, so he may perceive your misliking to what he hath done, and yet understand that so great is
your goodness that you are content with the victory God hath
given you, and desire no farther vengeance. And may God grant
you to abide in your virtuousness of heart, and seeing that all
good things are from Him, may you love and serve Him in better sort than afore." And the princess, determined to abide by
these conclusions, gave herself to a sleep as joyful as her lover's
wakefulness was sad.

And on the morrow, the prince being about to depart, asked
for his host, but they told him he was so sick as not to endure
the daylight, or to speak with any one, whereat the prince was
astonished and would have seen him, but being advised that he
slept, he went forth from the house without so much as good-
bye, and took him with his wife and sister. But she, hearing the
put-offs of the gentleman, and that he would see neither the
prince nor the company, was assured that he was the man who
had so troubled her, and would not show the marks she had
stamped upon his face. And though his master ofttimes sent for
him, he would by no means return to court till he was healed of
his wounds; save those indeed that love and shame had made

upon his heart. And when he did return, and found himself
before his victorious foe, he blushed; nay, he who was most
bold-faced of all the company, was in such case that, often in her
presence, he was struck dumb. At this, being quite persuaded
that her suspicion was truth, she by little and little severed herself from him, yet not by such slow degrees that he was not
aware of it, but could say nothing lest he should fare worse, and
patiently bore this punishment which he so well deserved.

5 (v)

How two Grey Friars were by one poor woman left in the lurch.

In the harbour of Coulon, hard by Niort, there lived a boatwoman, who, by day and night, carried people across the ferry.
And it came to pass that two Grey Friars of the aforesaid Niort
were crossing over by themselves in her boat, whereupon, seeing that the passage is one of the longest in France, they began
to crave love-dalliance, to which entreaties she gave the answer
that became her. But they, who for all their journeying were not
aweary, nor by reason of the water were acold, nor by her refusal
ashamed, determined to have her by force, and if she made an
outcry to throw her into the river. And she, whose wit was as
good and sharp as theirs was gross and evil, said to them: "I have
not so hard a heart as I seem to have, but I entreat you to grant
me two things, and then you shall perceive that I am readier to
obey than you to command." So the two Grey Friars swore by
St. Francis that she should ask nothing of them that they would
not grant, so long as she did them the pleasure they desired. "In
the first place then," said she, "I require of you that you advertise no man of this matter." This they promised with great will-
ingness. "And in the second place," she went on, "that you have
your pleasure of me by turns, for this would be too great shame
to have to do with the one before the face of the other.
Determine, then, which shall first enjoy me." This likewise they
deemed a reasonable thing, and the younger of the two granted
his companion the prerogative. So when they drew near a small
island she said to the former: "Holy father, do you tell your

beads and tarry here, while I am gone with your companion to
yonder island, and if, when he returns, he gives a good account
of me, we will leave him, and you and I will go apart together."
The young friar leapt on to the island, and awaited there his
comrade's return, whom the boatwoman took off to another
island. And when they had come alongside, the woman, making
pretence to fasten her boat to a tree, said to him: "Do you go,
sweetheart, and look for a place where we may dispose ourselves." The holy man got on to the island and searched about
for some nook fit for the purpose; but no sooner did she see him
on firm ground than she pushed off, and made for open water,
leaving these two holy fathers to their deservings, for all the
clamour they made to her. "Wait patiently, good sirs," said she,
"for an angel to come and console you, for to-day you will have
of me no pleasaunce."

Then the two poor friars, finding they were tricked, fell down
on their knees at the edge of the water, praying her not to
entreat them thus shamefully, and promising that, if she would
fairly bring them to port, they would ask nothing more of her.
But, rowing the while, she called to them: "Truly I should be a
thorough paced fool if, after escaping from your hands, I put
myself between them again." And when she had got to the village, she went to call her husband, and the constables, that they
might take these two wolves, from whose teeth, by the grace of
God, she had escaped. And so brave a company was made up
that none stayed in the village, either great or small, that was
fain to have a part in the delight of this hunting. But when the
poor friars saw such a sort of people coming against them, they
hid themselves, each one in his island, like Adam when he saw
that he was naked. For shame put their sin plainly before their
eyes, and the fear of what would befall them had made them to
tremble so that they were well-nigh amort. But nevertheless
they were taken prisoners, with many a flout and jeer from the
men and women. For the first would say: "These good fathers
preach chastity, and straightway attempt our wives," and the
second: "They are sepulchres whited without, but within full of
death and rottenness." Then another would cry out: "The tree
shall be known by his fruits." You may well conceive that all the

pleas of the Gospel against hypocrites were brought out for these poor prisoners, who were succoured by their warden; he coming in hot haste to this intent, and assuring the men of law that he would punish them in severer sort than if they had laymen for their judges. And to satisfy all he promised the friars should say as many masses as might be desired of them. The civil magistrate granted the warden's desire, and he, being an upright man, they were used by him in such fashion that never after did they pass over a ferry without making the sign of the cross, and recommending themselves to God.

6 (VIII)

Of one who on his own head engrafted horns.

In the county of Alet, there was a man named Bornet, who being married to a woman of honour, had for her good name such a regard as I suppose all husbands here present have for that of their wives. But though he was fain for her to be without reproach, yet this law of his did not press on husband and wife with equal rigour, for he loved his serving-maid, from whom he could get no more delight than that arising from a diversity of meats. Now he had a neighbour named Sandras, a drum-maker and tailor; and there was such friendship betwixt them that, except the wife, they had all things in common. So to this Sandras he made known the enterprise he had undertaken against the serving-maid, who not only thought well of it, but gave his friend all the aid in his power to bring matters to a conclusion, since he had good hope of dividing the spoil. The wench, who would by no means consent, seeing herself hardpressed on every side, went to her mistress, and prayed her that she might go home to her kinsfolk, since she could no longer live in such torment. The wife, who greatly loved her husband, and had before had some suspicion of him, was mightily pleased to hear this, thinking to show him that her jealousy was not altogether without foundation; and so said to the girl: "Do you, by little and little, entice my husband and then make appointment with him to lie with you in my closet, failing not to tell me the night agreed upon; and above all take heed that none be advised of this." All this the maid performed, and so much to the pleasing of her master, that he went to his friend to make known the good tidings. And he, since he had helped to fight the fight, entreated a share in the victory. This being granted, and the hour determined, the master went to lie, as he thought, with his maid, but his wife, who had renounced the authority of commanding for the pleasure of obeying, had put herself in place of the serving-maid, and received her husband not after the fashion of a wife, but like a timid and frightened girl. And this she did so well that her husband perceived nothing.

I cannot tell you which of the two had most delight, he at the thought of cozening his wife, or she at the thought of cozening her husband. And when he had remained with her, not according to his wish but according to his power, for he began to feel that he was an old married man, he went outside the house and found his friend, who was by far younger and handsomer than he, and boasting to him that a sweeter morsel he had never tasted, his friend said: "You know what you promised me?" "Come then, and quickly," said the master, "or she will have got up, or my wife may require her." His friend went, and found still there the serving-maid, who, taking him for her husband, refused him nothing he liked to ask. Much longer stay did he make than the husband, at which the wife was in amaze, for it was not her custom to have such work of nights; all the same, she bore it patiently; fortifying herself with the discourse she would have with her husband in the morning, and the jeers she would make at him. But a little while before dawn he got up from her, and in taking a last taste before he went, he snatched a ring off her finger, the same with which her husband had espoused her. And this ring of espousal the women of that country hold in high honour, and have in great regard the woman who keeps her ring even unto death. But on the other hand, if she loses it, she is held in no account, and esteemed as one who has given her faith to another than her husband. And she was glad to see him to take it, thinking it would be sure proof of the deceit she had laid upon him.

And when Sandras returned to Bornet, the latter asked of him, what his hap had been, to whom he replied that he had fared excellently well, and that if it had not been that the day was breaking he would have stayed still longer. And then they betook them to a most hearty sleep. But in the morning, as they were dressing, the husband perceived the ring his companion wore on his finger made in the exact likeness of the one he had given his wife at their betrothal, and so required of Sandras whence it came. But when he heard that it was snatched from the finger of the serving-maid, he was in great affray, and fell to knocking his head against the wall, saying: "Oddsfish! have I then made myself a cuckold, without the knowledge of my wife?" His companion, for his consolation, said: "Perchance your wife gave the ring to the wench for her to take care of it." To this the husband had nothing to say, but gat him home straightway, where he found his wife prettier, gayer, and more frolicsome than was her custom, as was indeed to have been looked for in a wife who had saved her maid's conscience, and sounded her husband to the depths, at the small price of a sleep-less night. He, seeing her with so pleasant a countenance, said within himself: "Did she but know of what has been done, she would have an otherguise visage." And making discourse on various concerns he took her by the hand, and perceived that she had not her ring, whereat in great affray, and with a tremor in his voice, he asked her: "What have you done with your ring?" But she, glad that he had brought that matter into discourse, from which it was her mind to draw out some points to his edi-fication, made this beginning: "O thou vilest of men! From whom, think you, did you ravish it? In good sooth from my maid, on whose behalf you poured forth more of your substance than ever fell to my share; for the first time you were bedded with me I judged you to be as vigorous as you were able. But after you had gone out and come back again you seemed the incarnate devil of concupiscence. Wretch! conceive your blindness in praising so much this poor body of mine, which you have enjoyed a year without placing it in any great esteem. It was not then the beauty or the breasts of the maid that gave you such great delight, but the deadly sin of lust which enflames your heart and so enfeebles your reason, that I verily believe in that mad heat of yours you would have taken a she-goat in a night-cap for a girl of surpassing comeliness. Of a truth, husband, it is time for you to cleanse your ways, and to be as content with what I can give you, in my proper person as a good wife and an honest woman, as you were when you took me for a naughty quean. This that I have done has been for the correction of your evil ways, and to the end that in our old age we may love one another with an honest love and a good conscience. For if you will still continue in your former manner of living, I had rather be severed from you than see from day to day before mine eyes the ruin of your soul, body, and substance. But if you will bring to mind the wickedness of your heart and live obediently to the law of God, faithfully observing his commandments, I will forget your sins that are past, as I trust God will forget my sin, who have not loved him as I ought." Who then was in despair but this poor husband? For he had abandoned this wise and chaste wife of his for a wench that loved him not, and, worse than this, had, without her knowledge, made her a strumpet, and caused another man to share in that delight which was for him alone. So well had he made him horns of everlasting derision. But seeing his wife, how wrath she was at his love for the serving-maid, he took good care to tell her nothing of the evil turn he had done her; and giving her back the ring, asked her pardon, and promised an entire amendment of his former iniquitous living. And he strictly charged his friend to tell no man anything; but since what is whispered in the ear is ere long proclaimed from the housetop, the whole truth became known, and making no account of his wife, all folk called him cuckold.

7 (IX)

A relation of a perfect love, and the pitiful end thereof.

In the coasts of Dauphiné and Provence there lived a gentleman whose riches stood rather in virtuousness, a brave address, and an honourable heart, than in gold or worldly gear. And he loved a maid, as to whose name I will say nothing, since she came of a most illustrious house; but be you none the less assured that my tale is the whole truth. And for that he came not of such gentle blood as she did, he was unwilling to make manifest his love to her, since this love of his was so perfect that he would rather die than cause her any dishonour. So perceiving that, compared with her, he was of low estate, he had no hope of marrying with her. Wherefore his love was bottomed upon this and this alone—to love her with all his whole might; and this he did, and for so long a time that at last she was advised thereof. And seeing that the love he bore her was honourable, and bore fruit in seemly and virtuous talk, she was well pleased to be loved by such an one, and carried herself so graciously toward him that he, who hoped for nothing better, was well contented therein. But malice, that suffers no one of us to be at rest, could not leave this goodly manner of living in peace, for certain ones must needs go tell the mother that it was matter of astonishment to them that this gentleman was made of such account in her house, that it was common talk that the daughter brought him there, and that she had often been seen to talk with him. The mother, who had no more doubt as to this gentleman's honour than that of her own children, was much troubled to hear his presence was taken in bad part, so that at last, fearing the scandalous tongues of men, she entreated him that for some while he would come no more to her house as his custom had been. And this he found tough matter of digestion, knowing that the honest talk he had with the maid deserved not this estrangement. All the same, to shut evil mouths, he kept away for some time, till the rumour was hushed, and then went as before, his love being in no wise lessened by absence. But one day, being in the house, he heard some talk of marrying his mistress to a gentleman who was not so rich as to rightly carry this point over him. So he forthwith took heart, and began to use his friends' offices on his behalf, thinking that if the lady had to choose he would be preferred. But the mother and kinsfolk chose the other man, for that he had the greater wealth, at which the poor gentleman took so much despair, knowing his sweetheart to be as much grieved as himself, that little by little, without any sickness, he began to consume away, and in a short time was so much changed that he seemed to have covered the beauty of his face with the mask of death, whither hour by hour he was joyously hastening.

Yet he could not restrain himself from going to speak as often as might be with her he loved so well. But at last, since his strength failed him, he was constrained to keep to his bed, not wishing his mistress to be advertised of this lest she too should have part in his woe. And giving himself up to black choler and despair, he left off both drinking and eating, sleep and rest, in such sort that for the wasting away of his countenance he could scarcely be known. And some one bringing tidings of this to the mother of the maid, she, being a woman full of charity, and liking the gentleman in such fashion that if the kinsfolk had been of her and her daughter's mind, she would have been better pleased with his honest heart than all the riches of another, went to see this unfortunate, whom she found more dead than alive. And perceiving that his end drew near, he had that morning made confession of his sins, and received the blessed sacrament, thinking to die without the sight of any one. But though he was within a span of death, when he saw her enter who was for him the resurrection and the life, he was so much revived that, starting up from his bed, he said to the mother: "What has brought you here, mistress, to visit him who has one foot in the grave, and of whose death you are the cause?" "How can it be," she said, "that you receive death from our hands, who love you so well? I pray you tell me wherefore you hold this manner of discourse." "Mistress," said he, "although I have, as far as lay within me, concealed the love I bore your daughter, yet my kinsfolk in speaking of our marriage have made too evident my thoughts. Hence I have lost hope, not on account of my privy pleasure, but because I know that at the hands of no other man will she receive as good love and contentment. Her loss of the best and most affectionate friend she has in the world does me more hurt than the loss of my life, which for her sake alone I was fain to preserve. But since it can now no more avail her anything, the loss of it is to me great gain." At this discourse the mother and daughter laboured to console him, the mother saying: "Take heart, my friend, for if it please God to give you back your health, I promise you my daughter shall be your wife. See! she

is here, and I command her also to make this promise to you."
And the daughter, with much weeping, laboured to assure him
of that her mother promised. But he, well knowing that if he
recovered his health, he could not have her to wife, and that all
this pleasant talk of theirs was only in some sort to revive him,
answered them that if they had said all this three months ago he
would be the stoutest and the most happy of all the gentlemen
in France, but that help had come too late to him, for whom
hope was no more. And when he saw that they still laboured to
persuade him he spoke as follows: "Since you, on account of my
feeble case, promise to me that which, even if you would have it
so, can never pertain to me, I ask you to grant me somewhat
less, which I have never had the boldness to require at your
hands." Straightway they promised, and confirmed their
promise with an oath, whereupon he said: "I beseech you that
you place her whom you pledge me for a wife between my arms,
and charge her that she both embrace and kiss me." The maid,
not accustomed to such dalliance, made some difficulty, but her
mother straightly charged her, seeing that the gentleman was
rather to be counted among the dead than the living, and she
went up to the bed of the sick man, saying to him: "Sweetheart,
I pray thee be of good cheer." Then this poor soul stretched out
his arms, all skin and bone, as well as he could, and kissed with
a fervent kiss the cause of his death, and holding her to his cold
and bloodless mouth kept her there as long as he could. And
furthermore he spoke to her: "The love I have had towards you
hath been so seemly and honest that I have never desired more
bliss of you than that I now possess, by which, and with which I
gladly commend my soul to God, who is perfect love, who
knoweth my soul that it is great, and my love that it is without
stain. And now, since within my arms I hold my desire, I entreat
Him in His arms to take my soul." And at this he pressed her
between his arms with such good will that his enfeebled heart
was not able to bear it, and was voided of its radical humours,
which joy had so used that his soul fled her seat and returned to
her Creator. And though the poor body had lain a long while
without life, and was therefore unable any more to hold fast its

treasure, the love which the maiden had always kept concealed was now made so manifest that her mother and the servants had much ado to draw them apart; but by force they took at last the living-dead from the dead, for whom they made honourable burial. And of this the crowning point was in the weeping and lamentations of that poor maid, who in like measure, as she had kept her secret while her lover was yet alive, so made it manifest when he was dead, as if in some sort to make satisfaction for the wrong she had done him. And notwithstanding that they gave her a husband for her contentment, never more, so the story goes, did she take any pleasure in her life.

8 (x)

Florida, hard pressed by her lover, virtuously
resists him, and on his death takes the veil.

In the county of Aranda, in Aragon, there lived a lady who, while yet in her first youth, was left a widow by the Count of Aranda, with a son and a daughter, the daughter's name being Florida. This lady aforesaid laboured to bring up her children in all virtuousness of living as appertains to those of gentle blood, and in such sort that her household was commonly accounted one of the most honourable in all the coasts of Spain. She often went to Toledo, where the King held his court, and when she came to Sarragossa, which was not far from her house, she would tarry a long while with the Queen and the Court, amongst whom she was held in as great esteem as might be. On one day going, as her manner was, to stand in the presence of the King where he was near Sarragossa in his castle of Jasserye, she passed through a village pertaining to the Viceroy of Catalonia, who was not used to stir beyond the coasts of Perpignan, for the great wars between the Kings of France and Spain. But it so fell out that at this time there was peace, wherefore the Viceroy and all his captains had come to do their suit and service to the King. And the Viceroy, being advised that the Countess of Aranda passed through his domain, went to meet her both for the ancient friendship that was between them and to do her honour as a kinswoman of the King. Now he had in his company many honourable gentlemen, who by the long continuance of the wars had gained so much glory and good report that any one who could see them and resort to them counted himself happy on that account. And amongst the rest there was one named Amadour who, although he was but eighteen or nineteen years of age, had so well-assured a grace, and so good an understanding, that he would have been chosen out from a thousand as worthy the office of a governor. True it is that this good understanding was conjoined with such beauty that no eye could do but look upon him, and though this beauty was of so excellent a kind, yet it was hard pressed by his manner of speaking; so that men knew not where to bestow the palm, to his grace, his beauty, or the words of his mouth. But that for which he was most of all esteemed was his surpassing bravery, notwithstanding he was so young, for in so many places had he shown the strength of his arm that not only in all the coasts of Spain, but also in France and Italy, were his virtues held in great account, and with good reason, since in no fight did he spare himself; and when his own country was at peace he would seek for wars in foreign lands, where likewise he was beloved as well by enemies as friends.

This gentleman, for the love he bore his general, came with him to his domain, whither the Countess of Aranda was arrived; and as he looked upon the beauty and grace of her daughter Florida, then about twelve years old, he thought within himself that she was the sweetest he had ever beheld, and that could he gain her favour it would do him more pleasure than anything whatsoever he might win from another woman. And after a long while fixing his regard upon her, he resolved to give her his love, although reason made plain to him that he desired impossible things, as much for that she was of a most noble house as for her tender years, which as yet were not fit to listen to the discourse he was fain to make to her. But against this fear he strengthened himself with hope, promising himself that time and patience would bring a happy issue to his undertaking, and from henceforth the great love that was entered into his heart assured him

of means of attaining thereto. And to surpass the greatest difficulty of all, that was the remoteness of his own land, and his few
opportunities of seeing Florida, he was resolved to marry, contrary to what he had determined while he was with the dames of
Barcelona and Perpignan, where he was held in such account
that few or none would have refused him. And so long had he
tarried in these coasts, by reason of the wars, that his speech
smacked rather of Catalonia than Castille, although he was born
near Toledo of a wealthy and honourable house, but being a
younger son, he had no inheritance. So, perchance, it came to
pass that Love and Fortune, seeing him abandoned of his kin-
folk, determined to make a masterpiece of him, and by means of
his virtuousness and courage granted him what he could not
obtain from the laws of his country. Such good skill had he in the
craft of war, and so well-beloved was he by lords and princes,
that he more frequently refused their employ than asked for it.

The Countess then has come to Sarragossa, and has been graciously received by the King and his Court. The Viceroy of
Catalonia often came to visit her, and Amadour never failed to
accompany him, only that he might have the delight of looking
upon Florida, for of speaking to her he had no opportunity. So
to make himself known in such good company he addressed
himself to the daughter of an old knight, his neighbour, whose
name was Aventurada, and who had such converse with Florida
that she knew what was in the depths of her heart. Amadour,
whether for the graciousness he found in her, or for the three
thousand ducats a year that was her dowry, determined to talk
to her as one he desired to marry. And willingly did she give ear
to him, but seeing that he was poor and her father rich, she
thought that he would never give her in marriage to Amadour
unless by the entreaty of the Countess of Aranda. Wherefore
she addressed herself to Florida, saying: "You have seen that
young gentleman of Castille often speaking with me, and I am
persuaded that his intent is to ask me in marriage. You know too
what kind of father I have, and that he will never consent
thereto, if he be not strongly entreated of the Countess and
yourself." Florida, who loved her as herself, promised that she
would lay this to heart as if it were for her own peculiar good;

and Aventurada accomplished so much as to present Amadour to her, who on kissing of her hand was like to have swooned away for joy. And he, who was accounted the readiest speaker in all Spain, was so affected in her presence that he stood dumb; and this was matter of great surprise to her, who, although she was but twelve years old, had well understood that no man in Spain could say what he wished more readily or with a better grace. So seeing that he said nothing, she begun thus: "The renown that you have won, my lord, in all the coasts of Spain is so great as to make you well known in this Court, and causes those who are of your acquaintance to desire to employ themselves in your service; wherefore, if there is anything wherein I can aid you, I am at your command." Amadour fixing his eyes upon her beauty was thereby possessed with such a ravishment, that he could hardly find words to give her his hearty thanks, whereupon Florida, astonished to find him thus dumb, but putting it down to some fantasy and not to the power of love, went from his presence without another word.

Amadour, perceiving the goodness which even in early youth began to show itself in Florida, said to her whom he intended for his wife: "Marvel not that in the presence of Mistress Florida I lost all power of speech, since the virtues and the wisdom which are contained in one of so few years in such wise astonished me that I knew not what to say. But, prithee, tell me, Aventurada, who know all her secrets, whether every heart at Court is not in love with her, for verily they who know her and love her not are either hard as rocks or senseless as beasts." Aventurada, who by this time loved Amadour better than all the men in the world, would not conceal aught from him, and so told him that Florida was beloved of all, but by the custom of the land few spoke to her, and still fewer—nay, only two—paid any court towards her. And these two were Spanish Princes, of whom one was the son of the Fortunate Infante, the other the young Duke of Cardona. "Prithee, then, tell me which she loves best." "She is so prudent," said Aventurada, "that she would never confess to having any will besides her mother's in the matter; natheless, as far as my wit goes, I am persuaded she loves the son of the Fortunate Infante above the Duke of Cardona.

But to her mother Cardona is most agreeable, since in the case of their being wed she would have her daughter always by her. And of such good judgment do I esteem you that this very day, if it is your pleasure, you may come to a conclusion, for the son of the Fortunate Infante is being nurtured in this Court, and is one of the bravest and most admirable young princes in Christendom. And if we maids had the disposing of the matter, he would be well assured of his bride, and we should have the fairest couple in all Spain. You must understand that, although they are both young, she twelve and he but fifteen, it is already three years since the courtship began, and if you would have her favour, I would counsel you to make yourself his faithful friend and follower."

Amadour was in great delight to hear she was in love with something, hoping that in time he might gain the place, not of husband but of lover, for it was not her virtue that he feared, but lest she should have no love whatever in her temperament. And soon after these passages he began to be constantly in company with the son of the Fortunate Infante, whose good graces he easily obtained, for in whatsoever pastime the young prince took delight he was well skilled, and above all in the practice of horsemanship, and in sword play, and to be short in all the games which it is becoming in a prince to know. But war broke out in Languedoc, and needs must that Amadour return with the governor, which indeed was great grief to him, since it took away the possibility of his seeing Florida; wherefore on his setting out he told a brother of his, who was chamberlain to the King, of the good match he had made in the person of Aventurada, and prayed him that in his absence he would do all that lay within him to forward the marriage, thereto employing the favour he had with the King and Queen and all his friends. The gentleman, who loved his brother not only for his kinsmanship but also for his excellent endowments, promised him to use his best endeavours, and moreover did so, inasmuch as the father, a surly old miser, laid by his natural complexion and paid some regard to the virtues of Amadour, which the Countess of Aranda, and above all Mistress Florida, took care to set before him. Also in this they were aided by the young Count of Aranda, who as he grew in years began to esteem brave men. So the marriage having been agreed upon by the kinsfolk on either side, the King's chamberlain sent for his brother, since a lasting truce had been made between the two Kings.

About this time the King of Spain betook himself to Madrid for the avoiding of the bad air that prevailed where he was, and at the advice of his Privy Council, and the request of the Countess of Aranda, he gave consent to the marriage of the Duchess of Medina-Celi with the young Count of Aranda, no less for their contentment and the union of their houses than for the love he bore towards the Countess; and so was pleased that the marriage should be solemnised in his castle at Madrid. And at the marriage feast was present Amadour, who used such good means on his own account that he was wedded to the lady whose love for him was beyond compare greater than his for her. But to be short, he held his wife only as a cloak to conceal his liking to another, and a means whereby he might be incessantly in Florida's company. After that he was married he entered into all the privity of the Countess of Aranda's household, where they paid no more heed to him than if he had been a woman. And though at this time he had not seen more than twenty-two years, yet so sage was he that the Countess would make known to him all her occasions, and enjoined her son to discourse with him and give ear to all his counsels. And having attained this high point in their esteem, he kept himself so prudently and coldly that even she whom he loved knew nothing of his thoughts. But since Florida loved his wife above all others, she trusted in him in such sort that she concealed from him nothing, and at this time opened to him all the love she had for the Fortunate Infante. So he, who sought but one thing, to gain her altogether for himself, talked to her always of the prince, for it mattered not one whit to him what the subject of their discourse might be so that it lasted a long time. There he stayed for a month after his marriage was concluded, and was then forced to go to the wars, whither he remained two years without returning to see his wife. And she lived all this while in the place where her nurture had been.

And during these two years he wrote often to his wife; but his

letters consisted for the most part of messages to Florida, who
on her side failed not to return them, and in every letter of
Aventurada's sent him some pleasant piece of wit, and this made
the husband unfailing in his writing. But with all this Florida discovered nothing save that he loved her as if he had been a
brother. Now and again he would come home, but in such sort
that in five years he only saw Florida for two months altogether;
yet in despite of estrangement and the length of his absence his
love did but increase. And it came to pass that he made a journey to see his wife, and found the Countess far removed from
the Court, for the King was gone to Andalusia, bearing with him
the young Count of Aranda, who was now beginning to carry
arms. The Countess had betaken herself to her pleasure-house
on the coasts of Arragon and Navarre, and was glad to see
Amadour return, since for nigh three years he had been away.
He was made welcome by all, and the Countess enjoined that he
should be used as if he had been her own son. While he was with
her she advertised him of all the charges of the household, and
for the most part took his judgment thereon, and so great
esteem did he win at this place, that whithersoever he would go
the door was opened to him, since they made such account of
his prudence that he was trusted like an angel or a holy man.
Florida, for the love she bore his wife and himself, sought him
out wherever he went, and had no suspicion of him, wherefore
she put no guard on her face, having no love to conceal, but only
feeling great contentment when he was by her. Amadour was in
great pains to escape the suspicion of those who can discern a
lover from a friend, for when Florida came privily to speak to
him the flame that was in his heart rose so high that he could not
hinder the colour rising on his cheeks or conceal the flashing of
his eyes. And to the end that nobody might observe all this, he
set himself to pay court to a mighty fine lady named Pauline
who, in her time, had such renown from her beauty that few
who saw her escaped her nets. And this Pauline, hearing that
Amadour had had some experience of the love-craft in
Barcelona and Perpignan, and had gained the affection of the
handsomest gentlewomen in the country, notably that of the
Countess of Palamos, who was accounted for the most beautiful

of all the Spanish ladies, told him that it was a great pity, after
such good fortune, to have taken to wife so ugly a woman. But
Amadour, understanding by her words that she had a mind to
help him in his hour of need, made as pleasant discourse to her
as might be, thinking that, if he could cause her to believe what
was false, he should thereby hide from her the truth. But she, of
keen wit, well tried in the service of love, was not to be contented with words alone, and being assured that such kindness
as he had for her did not suffice him, suspected he would fain
use her as a cloak, and on that account kept good watch on his
eyes. But these knew so well how to feign, that any suspicion she
might conceive was but dark and obscure, yet it was matter of
great toil to the gentleman, since Florida, ignorant of all these
plottings, used him in such familiar fashion before Pauline that
his eyes had a wondrous struggle with his heart. And for the
avoiding of this, one day he spoke as follows to Florida, while
they were standing by a window: "Prithee, sweetheart, tell me
whether is it better to speak or to die." And Florida presently
replied to him: "I would counsel all such as are my friends to
speak and not die, for 'tis a bad speech that cannot be mended,
but a life lost cannot be recalled." "You promise me then," said
Amadour, "that you will not only take in good part what I am
going to say, but even that you will not be astonished thereat till
I have made an end." To this she replied: "Say what you will, for
if you astonish me, none can reassure me." And so he began:
"Mistress, up to this time I have had no wish to speak of my love
towards you, and this for two reasons. In the first place, for that
I desired to be well tried by you, and in the second because I
doubted whether you would esteem it for an honour to be loved
by me, who am but a poor gentleman. And again, though I were
of as high estate as yourself, the steadfastness of your heart
would not allow you to listen to love-talk from any but him who
has gained your love, I would say the son of the Fortunate
Infante. But just as in war, necessity makes men sacrifice their
own possessions, and cut down their own corn lest the enemy
enjoy it, so I dare to risk gathering beforehand the fruit I hoped
to pluck much later, lest it profit our enemies and be to your
loss. Understand then that from your youth until now I have

been so given up to your service that I have never wearied in seeking to gain your favour, and for that cause alone did I wed her whom I thought you loved the best. And knowing the love you bore to the son of the Fortunate Infante, I have taken pains, as you are advised, to do him service and to be frequently with him, and all this because I fain would please you, and truly I have used to that end all my power. You know that I have gained the favour of your mother and brother, and all whom you love, in such sort that I am held in this house not as a servant but a son, and all the pains that for these five years I have taken have been to no other intent than that with you I may pass all my life. Understand that I am not of those who would pretend by these means to get anything from you to the hurt of your honour, for I know that I cannot take you to wife, and if it were in my power I would not do this thing against him whom you love, and whom I desire to see your husband. And so far removed am I from those who, by long service, hope for a reward against the honour of their ladies, and love with a vicious love, that I would rather see you dead than know you were less worthy of being loved, or that your virtue had, for my pleasure, been made of small account. For the end and reward of what I have done I ask alone one thing—that you be to me such a mistress as never to take your favour from me, that you continue me in my present case, trusting in me more than in any other, and being well assured that, if in any matter you need a gentleman's life, mine shall be with the heartiest good will at your service. And in like manner I would have you believe that whatever I do that is brave and honourable is done only for your sake. And if I have done for ladies of far less account than you things which have been thought worthy of regard, be assured that, you being my mistress, my bravery will grow in such fashion that deeds I aforetime found impossible shall become most easy to be performed. But if you will not accept me as wholly yours, it is in my mind to renounce arms, and the valour which helped me not in my hour of need. Wherefore, mistress, I entreat that my desire be granted me, for as much as your honour and conscience cannot fairly refuse it."

The maid, hearing this strange discourse, began to change

colour and let down her eyelids, as a frightened woman is accustomed. Natheless, since she was wise and prudent, she said to him: "Wherefore is it, Amadour, that you ask of me what you have already? To what intent is all this talk? I greatly fear that beneath your honourable words there is concealed some hidden evil to deceive the ignorance of my youth. Wherefore I am in great doubt what to reply; for if I refuse the honourable friendship you offer me, I shall be doing the very contrary to what I have always done, since I have trusted you above all men. Neither my conscience nor mine honour forbid your desire, nor yet my love for the son of the Fortunate Infante, for that is bottomed upon marriage, to which you make no pretence. I know nothing to hinder me from replying to you according to your wish, if it be not the fear I have at heart arising from the small need you had to ask all this; for since you have what you require, what need to ask for it?" Amadour, who was not without an answer, said to her: "Mistress, you speak according to wisdom, and do me so great honour by the faith you put in me, that if I were not content with this reward, I should not be worthy of any other. But know that he who would build a house to last for ever must take care first to lay a strong and sure foundation; wherefore I, who would dwell for ever in your service, must take care not only of the means whereby I may always be near you but also that none other be advised of my great love towards you. For though it be honourable enough to be proclaimed from the housetops, yet those who cannot discern the hearts of lovers often judge falsely concerning them, and thereby come evil rumours, of which the event is likewise evil. And she who makes me say this and manifest my love towards you is Pauline, who has strong suspicions concerning me, and knowing well in her heart that I do not love her, makes it her chief concern to watch my face. And when you so familiarly come and speak to me before her, I am in great fear lest I make some sign for her to bottom her suspicion on, and so fall into the pit I am fain to escape. Wherefore it has been my intent to entreat you that before her, and before others whom you know to be as malicious as she is, you come not so suddenly to speak to me, for I had rather die than any man should come to a knowledge on these matters. And had I not been so tender of your honour I would not have had this discourse with you, since I deem myself sufficiently happy in your love and confidence towards me, and ask of you nothing more than to continue them unto the end."

Florida, who on hearing this was exceedingly glad, began to feel a somewhat at her heart she had never felt before, and considering the fair conclusions he had laid before her, replied that virtue and honour answered for her, and granted his desire. And who that has loved can be in doubt as to whether Amadour rejoiced thereat? But Florida more straitly followed his counsels than he would have her, for she, being afraid not only in the presence of Pauline but everywhere beside, no longer would seek him out as she had been accustomed; and whilst they were thus estranged she took in bad part his often going to Pauline, whom she thought so pretty that she could not believe but that he loved her. And for the consolation of her sadness she had much talk with Aventurada, who began to be exceeding jealous of her husband and Pauline, and so oftimes made complaint to Florida, who comforted her as well as might be, she herself being stricken with the same plague. Amadour before long perceiving how Florida was changed towards him, thought that she did not merely follow his counsels, but had mingled with them some peevish imagination of her own devising. And one day, while they were going to evensong at a monastery, he said to her: "Prithee, mistress, what countenance is this you show me?" "I suppose that which pleases you," said she. Whereupon, having a suspicion of the truth, and willing to know if he was right, he began to say: "Mistress, I have so spent my days that Pauline thinks no more of you." To which she replied: "Than this you cannot do better, both for yourself and for me, for in serving your pleasure you preserve my honour." At which Amadour saw that she thought he took pleasure in parley with Pauline, and at this thought waxed so desperate that he could not contain himself, and wrathfully exclaimed: "Truly, mistress, these are early days to begin tormenting your poor slave and pelting him to death with bitter words, for I thought there could be no greater travail than to oblige myself to parley with one for whom I have no love. And since what I have done in your service is taken by

you in bad part, I will never again speak to her, come what will
of it! And that I may conceal my wrath as well as I have concealed my contentment, I will begone to some place hardby
until your fantasy is overpast. But I have good hopes while I am
there to get tidings from my general that will take me back to
the wars, where I will stay long enough to let you know that you
alone have kept me here." Thus saying, and without waiting for
a reply, he forthwith left her. At this Florida was filled with grief
and sadness, and love by its repulse began to show her all its
strength, in such wise that, knowing the ill she had done him,
she wrote again and again to Amadour praying him to return,
and this he did after that a space of some days had abated the
bitterness of his anger.

I cannot make for you a particular account of the discourse by
which they destroyed this jealousy. At all events, he won the battle, inasmuch as she promised him to believe no more that he
was in love with Pauline, and also that she was assured that to
speak with Pauline or anyone else, save to do her a service, was
a martyrdom hardly to be borne.

And when love had conquered this first suspicion, and the
two lovers began to take more delight than ever in talking with
one another, tidings were brought that the King of Spain was
drawing his whole army to Salces. Wherefore Amadour, who
was always in the van of battle, lost not this chance of winning
for himself glory, yet it is true that he went with a regret that was
not his custom as much for the loss of pleasure as fearing to find
some change on his return. And this because he knew that
Florida was sought in marriage by great princes and lords, seeing she was now come to the age of fifteen or sixteen years,
wherefore he thought that if she was married while he was away
he would no longer have any opportunity of seeing her, except
the Countess of Aranda should give her as a companion his wife
Aventurada. And so well did he manage his affairs amongst his
friends that the Countess promised that, let her daughter go
where she might, his wife should go with her. And though it was
intended that Florida should be married in Portugal, yet it was
determined that Aventurada should never forsake her; so on this
assurance, not without regret unspeakable, Amadour went away

and left his wife with the Countess. And when Florida found
herself alone after the departure of her slave, she set herself to
the doing of good works, whereby she would fain get as much
honour and repute as the most perfect women, and show herself worthy of such a lover as Amadour. And he, being arrived at
Barcelona, received from the ladies such welcome as he was
wont, but so changed did they find him that they would not have
believed that marriage had such power over a man as it had over
him. For it was plain that the things in which aforetime he had
taken delight now wearied him; and the very Countess of
Palamos whom he had loved so well could scarce find means to
draw him to her lodging, on which account he made but short
stay at Barcelona, being weary for the fight and the heat of battle. And when he had come to Salces, there began that great and
fierce war between the two kings of which I do not propose to
make any relation, not so much of the mighty deeds done by
Amadour, for if I did my tale would be long enough to suffice
for the entertainment of a whole day. But know that he far
excelled in glory each and all of his fellows. And when the Duke
of Nagera came to Perpignan, being captain over two thousand,
he entreated Amadour to be his lieutenant, who with this band
did such service that in every fight the battle-cry was *"Nagera!"*

At this time it came to pass that the King of Tunis, who for a
long while had waged war with the Spaniard, hearing that the
Kings of France and Spain were at odds together on the coasts
of Perpignan and Narbonne, thought that he could find no better occasion of doing a displeasure to the King of Spain. To this
end he despatched a host of light galleys and other ships to pil-
lage and destroy any badly-guarded place on the coasts of Spain.
The men of Barcelona, seeing a great number of vessels passing
in front of the town, advertised the viceroy of the matter; and
he, who was then at Salces, forthwith sent the Duke of Nagera
to Palamos. And the Moors, seeing the place guarded in such
sort, feigned to go away, but returned about midnight and sent
so many men on shore, that the Duke of Nagera was surprised
by the enemy and taken captive. Amadour, who kept good
watch, hearing the tumult, drew together as great a company as
he was able, and made such defence that the enemy, for all their

numbers, were for a long while unable to accomplish anything. But at last, knowing the Duke of Nagera to be taken, and that the Moors were resolved to set Palamos afire, and with it the house he held against them, he preferred to render himself up than to be the cause of destroying the brave men who were of his fellowship. Also he had hopes of being ransomed, and thus once more to see Florida. So he presently gave himself up to a Moor named Dorlin, governor to the King of Tunis. And this man took him to his master, by whom he was well received and better guarded, for the King, having him in his hands, thought he had taken the Achilles of the Spaniards.

And so abode Amadour nigh two years in the service of the King of Tunis. Now the report of this mischance was brought to Spain, at which the kinsfolk of the Duke of Nagera were sore grieved; but they who laid the honour of their country to heart esteemed the capture of Amadour to be the greater loss. And the news came to the house of the Countess of Aranda, where at this time lay Aventurada grievously sick. The Countess, who had great suspicion of the love Amadour bore her daughter, but suffered it and concealed it for the virtues she discerned in him, called her apart and told her these pitiful tidings. Florida, who knew well how to feign, replied that it was a great loss for the whole house, and above all for his poor wife, who was now in such evil case. But seeing her mother weeping exceedingly, she too let a few tears drop to bear her company, fearing that by feigning too much her deceit might become apparent. And from this time the Countess often spoke to her of him, but could never bottom her suspicions on anything in Florida's face. I leave untold the pilgrimages, prayers, and fasts which Florida discharged in due order for the safety of Amadour, who no sooner got to Tunis than he sent tidings thereof to his friends, and by a trusty messenger advertised Florida that he was in good health and hope of seeing her again. And this was the poor lady's only means of sustaining her anguish, so doubt not that, since it was permitted him to write to her, she in return did her part so well that her letters of consolation came to Amadour thick and fast.

At this time the Countess was commanded of the King to go

to Sarragossa, where he was come, and she found there the young Duke of Cardona, who so strongly urged the King and Queen that they prayed the Countess to give him her daughter in marriage. The Countess, who in nothing was disobedient to their will, agreed thereto, thinking that her daughter, who was still young, could have no will in the matter but her own. And when the agreement was determined upon she told her daughter that she had chosen as mate for her one she thought most fitting. And Florida, knowing that when a thing is done it skills not to give advice, said to her that for all things God was to be praised; and seeing her mother bear herself coldly towards her, she had enough to do to obey without much pity of herself. And as matter of consolation for her woes, it was told her that the son of the Fortunate Infante was sick unto death; but neither before her mother nor any beside did she ever make any appearance of grief. Indeed so strongly did she constrain herself that the tears driven inwardly into her heart caused such a flow of blood from the nose that her life was in jeopardy; and that she might be restored they gave her as wife to him, than whom she would far rather have received death. And after the wedding was brought to a close Florida went with her husband to the duchy of Cardona, taking with her Aventurada, to whom she privily made her complaints both of the rigour of her mother and the grief she had at the loss of the son of the Fortunate Infante. But of her grief at the loss of Amadour she said nothing save by way of consolation. And from this time she resolved to keep God always before her eyes; and so well concealed her sorrows that none of her people ever perceived that her husband was displeasing to her.

So passed a long time, Florida living a life scarce better than death. And of all this she failed not to send news to her lover, who knowing the greatness of her heart and the love she bore to the son of the Fortunate Infante, thought it scarce possible that she should continue to live, and mourned for her as one worse than dead. And by this dolour his own was increased, since he would willingly have continued all his days a slave, if Florida could but have a husband to her liking; so did he forget his own woe in that which his sweetheart had. And for that he heard, by

a friend he had at the Court of the King of Tunis, that the aforesaid King was resolved to give him his choice of impalement or
renouncing his faith, because he greatly desired for him to
become a good Mussulman and continue in his service, he persuaded his master to let him go on his parole. And this master
put upon his head so high a ransom as he thought could never
be found by a man of small means. So then, without speaking on
the matter to the King, his master let him go. And when he had
gone to Court and stood in the presence, he went forth amongst
all his friends to the intent that he might get together the ransom, and straightway betook him to Barcelona, whither the
young Duke of Cardona, his mother, and Florida had gone on
some charges. And as soon as his wife Aventurada had tidings
that her husband was returned from captivity, she bore them to
Florida, who rejoiced thereat, as if for love of her. But fearing
lest her joy upon seeing him might change the manner of her
countenance, and lest they who knew her not might take a bad
opinion of her, she withdrew herself to a window, that she might
see him coming from afar. And as soon as she perceived him she
went down by a stair so dark that no one could see her change
colour, and embracing Amadour she led him to her room and
that of her mother-in-law, to whom he was unknown. But he tarried there only two days, and in that time made himself as much
beloved by them all as he had been in the household of the
Countess of Aranda.

It is not my intent to tell you of all the talk that Florida and
he were able to have together, and the complaints she made to
him for the ills done her in his absence. After much weeping,
both for that she was married to one against her liking, and also
that she had lost beyond hope of seeing again him whom she
loved so well, she determined to draw some causes of consolation out of the love and firm trust she had in Amadour, though
she never durst declare it to him. But he, having some suspicions, lost neither time nor opportunity of letting her know how
great a love he had towards her. And just at that time, when she
was ready to receive him not as a servant but as a true and perfect lover, it fell out by evil hap that the King, by reason of certain weighty charges, commanded the immediate presence of

Amadour. And this so grieved his wife that, on hearing of the
news, she swooned away, and falling down a stair did herself
such hurt that she was not taken up alive. Florida, who through
this death lost all consolation, made mourning as one who weeps
for her father and mother and all her kinsfolk. But still more did
Amadour grieve, not alone that he had lost on his side one of the
best wives in the world, but also that he had lost all means of
seeing Florida; at which he fell into such sadness that he was
like to have died. The old Duchess of Cardona came often to
speak with him, and drew from the philosophical writings many
good and solid reasons for him to bear this loss with patience.
But this did not much avail him, for if death itself was torment,
love did but increase the agony. So Amadour, having beheld the
burial of his wife and having no more cause for delaying to per-
form the King's commands, was filled with such despair that his
brain wellnigh fell into some distemperature. But Florida, in
endeavouring to console him, spent a whole afternoon discoursing to him in the most gracious sort to the intent of diminishing
the extremity of his grief, assuring him that she would find better means of seeing him than he thought. And since he was to
set out on the morrow, and was so weak that he could hardly stir
from his bed, he entreated her to come and see him in the
evening after every one had done so, which she promised, ignorant that his love knew not bounds nor reason. And he, who
found himself in despair of ever seeing her again whom he had
served so long, and having had of her no favours except what I
have told you of, was so torn asunder by hidden love and the loss
of all means of being in her company, that he was resolved to
play at double or quits, to win or lose it all, and to repay himself
in one hour as he thought to have deserved. So he had his bed
decked with curtains in such fashion that those who came into
the room could not see him, and made more complaint than was
his custom, that the people of the house might not believe him
to have twenty-four hours to live.

After that every one had been to see him, Florida, her very
husband desiring her, went to him, intending as matter of consolation to declare her affection, and to assure him that, as far as
honour allowed, she would give him her love. And she sat her-

self down on the chair by the bedside, and began her consolation by weeping with him. Amadour, seeing her grief, thought that thereby he should more easily attain his ends, and raised himself from the bed, whereupon Florida, thinking that he was too weak, would have held him back. But he fell on his knees and began to say: "Must I for ever lose the sight of you?" and so let himself fall into her arms as one whose strength fails him. Poor Florida for a long time embraced and sustained him, doing all that lay in her power to console him, but the medicine she gave to cure his sickness did but increase it; for with the face of a man half-dead, and without a word, he fell to seeking for that which the honour of the ladies forbids. And though Florida perceived his evil intent, she could hardly believe it, having in her mind all his honourable conversation, and so asked him what he would do; but Amadour, fearing to hear her reply, which he knew well would be a chaste and virtuous one, persisted with all his strength in the quest of that he desired, whereat Florida, mightily astonished, suspected rather that he had taken leave of his senses than that he was attempting her dishonour. Wherefore she called aloud to a gentleman whom she well knew to be in the room, and at this Amadour, in the bitterness of his despair, threw himself back so suddenly upon the bed that the gentleman held him for a dead man. Florida, having arisen from the chair, said to him: "Go presently and get some vinegar." And this he did, whereupon Florida began: "Amadour, what fantasy is mounted to your brain? and what were you minded to have done?" He, who by reason of love had lost all reason, replied: "Doth so long a service as mine deserve so cruel a return?" "And where is that honour," said Florida, "which you have so often preached to me?" "Ah! mistress," said Amadour, "it is not possible to be more tender of your honour than I have been; for before that you were married I so conquered my heart that you knew nothing of my desire; but now that you are married, and your honour is in safe keeping, what wrong is this I do you in asking what is my own? For by the very force of love I have won you. He who first had your heart, made such poor assault on your body that he well deserved the loss of both. He to whom your body now belongs is by no means worthy of your heart, wherefore neither by right does the body appertain to him. But I, mistress, who for these five or six years have borne for your sake so many woes, you cannot deny that it is I alone who deserve both your body and your heart. And if you would call your conscience into court, be well assured that when love presses hard on every side, sin shall by no means be imputed. Those who in a fit of madness slay themselves are not to be accounted sinners for what they have done, for passion and reason cannot dwell together. And being love is the most unbearable of all the passions, and most of all blinds the senses, what sin would you impute to him who is carried along by its irresistible might? I am about to go, having no hope of seeing you any more. But if I had had before I set forth that security from you which my great love hath deserved, I should have gained strength to bear patiently the sorrow of this long farewell. And if it be not your pleasure to grant me my desire, you shall soon perceive that your hard heart has caused me a most miserable and cruel death."

Florida, no less grieved than astonished at such discourse from him, from whose lips she never thought to have heard the like, said weeping: "Alas! Amadour, is this the virtuous talk you had with me while I was yet young? Is this the honour and the good conscience you have so often counselled me rather to die than lose? Have you then forgotten your good examples of virtuous ladies, who made resistance to light love, and all your despising of wanton women? I cannot believe, Amadour, that you are so far from yourself that God, your conscience, and my honour are altogether dead within you. But if it indeed be as you say, I praise the Divine Goodness for that it has delivered me from the pit into which I wellnigh had fallen, and shown by your speech the wickedness of your heart. For having lost the son of the Fortunate Infante, not only because I am married, but also because I am advised he loves another, and seeing myself wedded to one to whom I cannot, take what pains I may, give my heart, I was resolved entirely and altogether to set my soul and my affections on loving you. And this love I founded on the virtuousness I perceived in you, and to which, by your help, I deem myself to have attained; and the manner of it is to love my honour and my conscience better than my life. Bottomed upon this rock of honour, I came here determined to make it yet more sure; but in a moment, Amadour, you have shown me that in place of pure and shining marble it would have been founded on a quaking sand, or a filthy mire. And though this my strong place, where I hoped to dwell for ever, has been in great part begun, you have suddenly brought it down, even to the dust. Wherefore you must now put aside every hope you had concerning me, and resolve yourself, in what place soever I be, not to address me by words or looks, nor ever deem that I can or will change this my determination. All this I say to you with great grief, but if I had so far gone as to swear with you eternal love, I know my heart, and am well assured that in that strife of the soul I should have died. And even now my sorrowful amaze for that you have deceived me is so great that I am persuaded it will make my life a short and sad one. And with these words I bid you farewell, but remember that it is for ever!"

I spare you the relation of the grief that Amadour felt at the hearing of these words, for it is not only impossible to write but even to conceive, except to those who have been in like case. And seeing that with this cruel conclusion she would leave him, he took her by the arm, since he well knew that if he suffered this bad opinion of him to remain in her, he would lose her for ever. Wherefore, having put on as solemn a countenance as he was able, he said to her: "Mistress, I have all my life desired to love a woman of honour, and since I have found but little of that commodity, I was fain to make trial of you, to see if you were as worthy to be held in esteem for your virtue as you are to be loved. And this I now know for a certainty, wherefore I give thanks to God, who has directed my love towards such perfection, entreating at your hands pardon for the folly of my endeavour, seeing that the issue thereof has been to your honour and my great contentment." Florida, who by his example began to perceive the wickedness of men, as she had been slow to believe the evil that was in him, so was now slow to believe the good that was not, and replied: "I would to God you spoke the truth! But I am not so simple that the estate of marriage in which I am does not let me know that the blindness of a strong desire made you do what you have done. For if God had slacked the reins, I am assured you would not have drawn in the bridle. Those who make search for virtue go on a different road to the one you have taken. But it is enough; if too lightly I believed in your virtue, it is time I should know the truth, which now delivers me from out of your hands." Thus saying, Florida went forth from the room, and while the night went on did nought else but weep, taking at this change so great grief that her heart had shrewd work to withstand the assaults of love and regret. For though, reason guiding her, she was resolved not to love him any more, yet the heart, which is lord over itself, would by no means allow this, so she was determined to satisfy her affection and continue to love him, and yet to satisfy her honour and never make any sign to him of her love.

And on the morrow Amadour went forth in such woe as you have heard; nevertheless his heart, which had not its equal in the world, would not suffer him to despair, but set him on some new means for seeing Florida again, and winning back her favour. Wherefore as he went to the King of Spain, who was at Toledo, he took his way through the county of Aranda, and came there one evening very late, and found the Countess in great sadness by reason of the absence of her daughter Florida. And when she saw Amadour she kissed and embraced him as if he had been her own son, as much for the love she bore him as for the suspicion she had that he loved Florida, of whom she made curious inquiry. And he told her the best news he could, but not all the truth, and confessed the love that was between them, which Florida had always kept secret, praying her to give him her help in having tidings of her daughter, and soon to bring her to Aranda. And on the morrow he continued on his journey, and having performed the charges of the King, went to the wars with so changed and sorrowful a countenance that ladies, captains, and all of his acquaintance scarcely recognised him. And henceforth black was his only wear, but of much coarser frieze than was due to his dead wife, whose loss served to conceal what was in his heart. So Amadour passed three or four years without returning at all to Court. And the Countess of Aranda hearing how Florida was changed, and that to see her was pitiful, sent to

her, wishing her to return home. But these tidings had the opposite effect, for when Florida heard that Amadour had made
manifest the love that was between them to her mother, and
that her mother, all good and virtuous as she was, held their love
for an honest one, she was in great perplexity. For on the one
hand she saw that if she told her mother the whole truth,
Amadour might get some hurt thereby, than which death would
have been preferred by her, for she felt herself to be strong
enough to punish him without calling her kinsfolk to her aid.
But on the other hand she perceived that if she concealed the
evil she knew of him she would be constrained by her mother
and all her kin to speak to him and show him a good countenance. And this she feared would but strengthen him in his
wicked purpose. But inasmuch as he was far away, she said nothing, and wrote to him when her mother charged her so to do; all
the same these letters of hers let him know pretty plainly that
they came from obedience and not good will, and so caused him
as much sorrow in the reading as aforetime tidings from her had
given him joy.

At the end of two or three years, having done so many and so
great deeds, that would scarcely be contained by all the paper in
Spain, he conceived a most daring imagination, not to win the
heart of Florida, which he held as lost, but to gain the victory
over his enemy, since it was in this manner she showed to him.
He put behind him all the counsels of reason, and even the fear
of death, of which he would thus make hazard, and this was his
fixed resolve. He made himself so esteemed of the Viceroy that
he was sent to speak to the King of a certain secret undertaking
against Leucate; and before that he had spoken to the King, he
declared the matter to the Countess of Aranda, to take her mind
upon it. And he came post haste to the county of Aranda, where
he was advised was Florida, sending a friend of his secretly to
the Countess to make known his approach, and praying her to
keep it in great privity, and for him to speak with her at night, so
that no one should be advertised thereof. The Countess, being
glad on account of his coming, told Florida, and sent her to
undress herself in her husband's room, to the intent that she
should be ready when the time was come and all others were in

bed. Florida, who was by no means recovered from her first
fear, made no sign to her mother, but went apart to an oratory.
There she commended herself into the keeping of our Lord,
praying Him to preserve her heart from all evil lust. And it then
came into her mind that Amadour had often praised her beauty,
which, though she had been for a long while sick, was by no
means diminished; so preferring to do hurt to this beauty than
to suffer the heart of so good a man by it to be kindled with an
evil flame, she took a stone that chanced to be in the chapel and
with it gave herself so hearty a blow that her mouth, nose, and
eyes were altogether put out of shape. And to the intent that
none should suspect that she herself had done it, she, when
summoned by her mother, let herself fall with her face to the
earth while she was going out of the chapel, and cried with a
loud voice. And when the Countess came she found her daughter in a pitiful case, and straightway had her face dressed and
bound up.

After the Countess had led her to her room, she told her to
go and hold discourse with Amadour until the company was
departed; and this did Florida, thinking there were others with
him. But finding herself all alone and the door shut on her, she
was as much vexed as Amadour was glad, since he conceived
that by persuasion or force he would get his desire. And when
he had spoken to her, and found her of the same mind as afore,
and that she would rather die than change it, maddened with
despair, he exclaimed, "I swear to you by God that the fruit of
my travail shall not be plucked from me by your nice points of
conscience; for since love, long-suffering, and humble prayers
have availed nothing, I will not spare my strength to gain that
without which I shall perish." And Florida saw his eyes and the
manner of his countenance that they were changed, and the
fairest face in the world was as red as fire, and his most sweet
and pleasant regard was so dreadful to look upon that a consuming flame seemed to blaze within his heart and on his face,
and in this phrensy he took within one of his mighty hands her
two hands most delicate and weak. She, seeing that all resistance
was of no avail, since she was thus straitly held a prisoner that
she could not fly, much less make defence, knew not what to do

save to seek if there were not in him some traces of his former love by the recollection of which he might forget his cruelty; wherefore she said to him: "Amadour, though you now hold me for an enemy, I entreat you, by the honourable love I formerly thought you had for me, to give ear before you begin your torture." And when she perceived that he gave ear to her, she went on with her discourse, saying: "Alas, Amadour, to what intent do you seek from me a thing whereby you will take no contentment, and will give me the greatest of all pains? You made so good trial of my mind in the time of my youth and beauty, by reason of which you might take some excuse, that I am astonished in this season of my age, and ugliness, and sorrow, you seek for what you cannot find. I am well assured you know my mind that it is not changed, wherefore you cannot gain save by force your desire. And if you look upon my face, and, seeing the manner of it, forget its beauty that was of old, you will not, I think, be wishful of approaching nearer. And if there are in you any remains of bygone love, I am persuaded that pity will conquer your madness. And to this pity, which I have found in you, I make my lamentation and pray for grace, to the intent that you will let me live to the end of my days in peace, and in that honour, over which, by your counsel, I am determined to keep watch and ward. For though the love you bore me is turned to hatred, and more for revenge than passion you would fain make me the most wretched of all women, I assure you that this thing shall not be, since against my desire you will compel me to make manifest your wickedness to her who believes you to be so good, and thereby your life shall be put in no small risk." Amadour, breaking into her words, said to her: "If I must needs die, then all the sooner shall I be quit of this torment; but your misshapen countenance, which I believe to be the work of your own hands, shall not hinder me from working my will, for though you were but bones I would hold them closely to me." And Florida, perceiving that sound reason, prayers, and tears availed nothing, and that in his cruelty he would endeavour to accomplish his wicked desire, called to her aid that help she feared as much as death, and cried in a sad and woeful voice for her mother. The Countess, hearing her daughter summon her in such a voice, had great suspicion of what was indeed the truth, and ran into the room as quickly as might be. Amadour, not being as near death as he would have Florida believe, so seasonably abandoned his enterprise, that the lady on coming in found him at the door and Florida far enough from him. Forthwith the Countess asked: "Amadour, what is it? Tell me the truth." And he, who was never devoid of invention, with a sad and solemn countenance, answered her: "Alas! mistress, into what case has Florida fallen? Never was I more astonished, for as I have told you, I thought to have had her favour, but now clearly perceive I have none of it. It appears to me that while she was with you she was no less wise and virtuous than she is now, but she did not then make it a point of conscience to speak with no one, and now that I would fain have looked upon her she would by no means suffer me. And seeing this change towards me, I was assured that it was but a dream, and required her hand that, after the manner of the country, I might kiss it, but this also she would not suffer me to do. I confess that I took her hand with a gentle compulsion and kissed it, and in this I did wrongfully and crave your forgiveness, but naught else did I ask of her. Yet she, as I believe, having determined my death, called you as you have seen; I know not wherefore, unless she feared some other intent, which I in truth had not. Natheless, mistress, however that may be, I acknowledge that I have done amiss, for though she ought to love them that serve her well, I alone, who am of all most devoted to her, am exiled from her favour. But I will still be towards you and her as I have always been, and I entreat you to continue me in your good will, since through no fault of mine I have lost hers." The Countess, who half believed and was half in doubt, went to her daughter, and said to her: "Wherefore called you me after this fashion?" Florida replied that she was afraid. And although the Countess made particular inquiry of her, she got no other reply, for Florida, seeing herself escaped from the hands of her enemy, held his ill-success sufficient punishment.

After that the Countess had for a long while held parley with Amadour, she made him stay with Florida to see what face he would put on it. But he said little to his mistress, save that he thanked her for not telling her mother the truth, and prayed at least, since she had driven him from out her heart, she would not let another man take his place. And to the first matter of his discourse she thus replied: "If I had had other means of defending myself except my voice, you would not have heard it; and you shall have no worse thing from me if you cease to constrain me as you have done hitherto. And be not afraid lest I love another, for since in the heart which I deemed the most virtuous in the world I have not found that I desired, I believe not I shall find it in any other man." Thus speaking, she bade him farewell. Her mother, though she carefully regarded his face, could come to no conclusion, save that henceforth she was well assured her daughter had no love for Amadour, and held her so void of reason as to hate everything she herself loved. And from that hour she behaved in such sort towards Florida that she spoke not to her but chidingly for seven whole years, and all this on account of Amadour. So during this time Florida turned the fear she had of being with her husband to a desire not to stir from him, because of her mother's rigorous entreatment of her. But finding this of no avail, she resolved to put a deceit upon Amadour, and, laying aside for a day or two her cold aspect, advised him to make proposals of love to a lady who, she said, had spoken to her of the love that was between them. Now this lady was in the household of the Queen of Spain, and was called Loretta. Amadour, believing this story, and thinking hereby to regain the favour of his mistress, made love to Loretta, who was the wife of a captain, one of the King's viceroys. And she, exceeding glad for that she had gained such a lover, set such store by him, that the rumour of it was blazed abroad, and even the Countess of Aranda, since she was at Court, was advertised of it, wherefore she ceased henceforth to torment Florida as had been her custom. And one day Florida heard that this warrior husband of Loretta's was become so jealous that he was determined, as best he might, to kill Amadour; and she who, despite her altered countenance towards him, could wish him no ill, presently advised him of it. But he, who easily took to his old paths, replied to her that if it was her pleasure to give him three hours of her company every day, he would speak no more with

Loretta; but this she would not grant. "Wherefore then," said Amadour, "since you are not willing to give me life, do you trouble yourself to guard me from death? Save, indeed, that you hope to cause me greater torments by keeping me alive than a thousand deaths. But though death escape me, I will seek till I find it, for the day of my death shall be the first of my rest."

About this time came news that the King of Granada had begun to make great war against the King of Spain, so that the King sent the Prince his son, and with him the Constable of Castille and the Duke of Alba, two old and prudent lords. The Duke of Cardona and the Count of Aranda were not willing to stay at home, and so entreated of the King to give them some command; and this he did according to the dignity of their houses. And for their safe keeping he gave them into the charge of Amadour, who during the war did such wondrous and mighty deeds as seemed to savour rather of despair than bravery. And to come to my story, I will show you how his great courage was proved by the manner of his dying; for the Moors, having made a show of giving battle, and seeing so large an army of Christians, feigned to retreat, whereupon the Spaniards began to pursue them; but the old Constable and the Duke of Alba, having a suspicion of their device, kept back against his will the Prince of Spain, so that he did not cross the river. But this, notwithstanding that it was forbidden them, the Duke of Cardona and the Count of Aranda did, and when the Moors perceived that they were pursued of a small company they wheeled round, and with one stroke of a scimitar the Duke of Cardona was slain, and so grievously was the Count of Aranda wounded that he was left where he fell for dead. At this Amadour came up so furiously enraged that he broke through all the press of battle, and made take the two bodies and carry them to the camp of the Prince, who grieved for them as if they had been his own brothers. But on searching out their wounds, the Count of Aranda was found to be still alive, and so was carried on a litter to his house, where he lay for a long while sick. And they bore to Cardona the dead body of the Duke. And after having in this manner rescued the two bodies, Amadour took so little heed for himself, that he was at last surrounded on every side by a host

of Moors, and no more wishing capture to be made of his body
than he had made capture of the body of his mistress, and not
to break his faith with God as he had broken it with her; knowing that, if he was taken to the King of Granada, he would either
be constrained to die a cruel death or renounce Christianity, he
was determined not to given his enemies the glory of his death
or capture. And so kissing the cross of his sword, and commending his soul to God, he drove it home so deeply that it
skilled not to give a second blow. So died Amadour, and the sorrow after him was that his valour deserved. And the news of it
was noised abroad through all the coasts of Spain, and Florida,
who was at Barcelona, where her husband had given command
he was·to be buried, heard the report thereof. And after that she
had made for him honourable burial, without speaking to her
mother or her stepmother, she became a nun of the Convent of
Jesus, taking for her spouse Him who had delivered her from
the burning love of Amadour, and from her weariness in the
companionship of such a husband. Henceforth she turned all
her affections to Godward, and, after for a long while living as a
nun, gave up her soul with such gladness as when the bride
goeth forth to meet the bridegroom.

9 (XI)

Of a very privy matter.

In the household of Madame de la Tremoille there lived a lady
named Roncex, who having one day gone with her mistress to
the Grey Friars at Thouars, was compelled there to visit a place
where she could not send her serving-maid in her stead. And she
took with her a girl named La Mothe to keep her company; but
since she was shamefaced she left the wench in a room, and all
alone entered a dark and gloomy privy. And this being held in
common by all the Friars, they had given such a good account
therein of all they had eaten, that the seat and the whole place
were covered with the lees of Bacchus and the corn of Ceres,
passed through the bellies of the Grey Friars. The poor woman,
being so hard put to it that she had scarcely time to lift her dress,

had the fortune to light upon the filthiest seat in the whole place, and found herself as well fastened to it as if she had been glued, with her thighs, dress, and feet in such case that she fell to crying at the top of her voice, "'La Mothe, La Mothe, I am ruined and put to shame." The wench, having heard tales of the Friars' wickedness, thought some to be concealed within the privy who would fain rape her, and so ran full speed, crying to all she met: "Quick! succour Madame de Roncex, whom the Friars would ravish in the privy." And these running there hot-foot, found the poor lady, who called for help to the intent that she might get some woman to clean her. And all her hinder parts were bare, for she feared to let down her dress, lest it too should be covered with filth. And on the entering of the gentlemen, they saw this sight, mighty pretty, but found no Grey Friar, but only the ordure on her thighs and fundament. And to them this was great matter of laughter, but very shameful to the lady, who, in place of women-servants, was groomed down by men, and seen of them naked in the worst case possible for a woman. And when she was well quit of this place of abominations, she must needs strip from top to toe, and change her whole dress before that she left the monastery, for when she saw the men she had let down her dress to cover her nakedness, forgetting the filth that was upon her in her shame at being seen of men. Very wrath was she with the help La Mothe had brought her, but hearing that the poor wench believed she was in even worse case than she was, she put aside her anger and laughed with the rest.

10 (XII)

A Duke of Florence would have his friend prostitute his
sister to him; but in place of love meets with death.

Ten years are now overpast since there bore rule in Florence that Duke who had for wife Margaret, bastard daughter to the Emperor. And for that she was so young, that it was not lawful for him to lie with her till she grew of riper age, he handled her mighty tenderly, for, while she slept of nights, he would talk to very good purpose with other ladies in the town. Amongst the

rest, he was amorous of a pretty, wise, and virtuous lady, sister
to a gentleman whom the Duke loved as himself, and whose
authority in his house was so great that his word was feared and
obeyed as if it were the Duke's. And the Duke had no secret he
did not declare unto him, in such sort that he might wellnigh be
named his second self.

And the Duke seeing his sister that she was so honourable a
woman that, after seeking every way, he could find no means of
declaring his love to her, came to the gentleman he loved so
well, and said to him: "If there were a thing in the world, my
friend, that I would not do for you, I should fear to make known
my mind to you, much less to ask your aid for the accomplish-
ing of my desire. But so great a love do I bear you, that if I had
mother, wife, or child, who could be effectual for the saving of
your life, I would so use them rather than let you die in torment;
and I esteem your love towards me is like to mine, and if I, who
am master over you, love you so well, you at least love me no
less. Wherefore I have a secret to manifest to you, from concealing which I am fallen into the case you now see, and from
which I hope amendment either through your offices or my
death."

The gentleman hearing this discourse of his master, and seeing his grief not feigned, and his face all covered with tears, took
so great compassion on him, that he said: "O, my lord, I am your
creature; all the contentments and all the honour I have in the
world come from you; you can speak to me as to yourself, well
assured that whatever is in my power is likewise in yours."
Whereupon the Duke declared the love he bore his sister, that
it was so strong and fierce that if he did not, by his means, have
the enjoying of her, he saw not how he could live any longer. For
he knew well that with her prayers and gifts would not avail anything. Wherefore he prayed the gentleman, if he loved as he was
beloved, that he would find some means of getting for him this
delight, which he never hoped to have in any other way. The
brother, loving his sister and the honour of his house better than
the pleasure of the Duke, would fain have made him some
remonstrance, entreating him to use him in all other straits, but
not to ask of him this abominable thing, the compassing the dis-

honour of his own blood, and saying that his heart and his honour alike forbade him take any part therein. The Duke, inflamed
with unbearable displeasure, and biting his nails, replied in
great wrath: "So be it then, and since I find no friendship at all
in you, I know how to play my part." The gentleman, well
advised of his master's cruelty, was afraid, and said to him: "My
lord, since it is your pleasure, I will speak to her and bring you
her reply." And the Duke returned: "As you love my life, so will
I love yours," and so left him.

The gentleman knew well what was the intent of these words.
And for a day or two he considered what was best to be done,
without coming into the presence of the Duke. On the one hand
there came before him all that was due to his master, the contentments and honours he had received of him; on the other, the
fame of his house, the virtuousness and chastity of his sister,
whom he was well persuaded would not listen to this wickedness, unless by some cozenage of his own finding she was overcome by force, and this such an infamous deed that he and his
would be for ever disgraced by it. And tossed from one side to
the other, he at last determined rather to die than do his sister,
one of the best women in all Italy, such an evil turn. But he
thought to do still better if he delivered his country from such a
tyrant, who would forcibly put this stain upon his house, for he
held for certain that if he did not slay the Duke his own life and
the lives of his kinsfolk would be in small security. Wherefore,
without parley with his sister or any beside on the matter, he
took counsel with himself how, by one blow, he might best save
his life and avenge his shame. And at the end of two days he
went to the Duke and told him he had used such order with his
sister that, after much toil on his part, she had at last agreed to
do him pleasure, if he would keep the matter so secret that
none, save her brother, should be advertised thereof.

The Duke, desiring to hear this news, easily believed it, and
embracing the messenger, promised him all he might ask for,
and entreated him presently to bring affairs to a conclusion, and
together they appointed a day. Whether the Duke was glad, it
skills not to ask, and when he saw that the long-desired night
drew near, on which he had good hopes of gaining the victory

over her whom he aforetime deemed unconquerable, he went
apart very early with the gentleman, forgetting not nightcaps
and perfumed shirts, and such like gear, the best that he had.
And when all were gone away, he went with the gentleman to his
sister's lodging, and entering in came into a bravely ordered
chamber. The gentleman having put his night-gear on him, and
laid him in bed, said to him: "My lord, I go seek one who will
not enter into this room without blushing, but before morning I
hope she will be assured of you." So saying he left the Duke and
went to his own room, where he found one of his people, to
whom he said: "Have you a heart bold enough to follow me
whither I would be avenged on my greatest enemy?" The fellow,
knowing not what he was called upon to do, replied: "Why, ay
sir, were it against my lord Duke." Whereupon the gentleman
led him away so suddenly that he had no time to take other
arms, but only a dagger, which he wore on him. And when the
Duke heard their return, thinking that the gentleman bore with
him her for whom he lusted, he opened wide both the curtain
and his eyes to look upon and receive the expected blessing; but
in place of seeing the preservation of his life, he beheld the
instrument of his early death. And this was a naked sword,
which the gentleman held in his hands, and with which he
struck the Duke, who was clad only in his shirt. But he, wanting
in arms and not courage, got behind the bed, and taking the
gentleman by the middle, said to him: "Is it thus you keep your
promise?" And having none other weapons save teeth and nails,
he bit him in the thumb, and by the force of his arm so defended
himself that they both fell on to the floor beside the bed. Then
the gentleman, not trusting overmuch in himself, called upon
his follower, who, finding the Duke and his master intermingled
so confusedly that he knew not which of the two to strike,
pushed them with his feet into the middle of the room, and
essayed to cut the Duke's throat for him. But he still defended
himself till loss of blood made him so weak as not to be able to
do any more, whereupon the gentleman and his follower threw
him on the bed, and there, with blows from the dagger, they
made an end of killing him. Then, drawing the curtain, they
went forth and shut up the dead body in the chamber.

And when he saw himself victorious over his great enemy, by whose death he thought to have freed the commonwealth, his work seemed to him but half done, if he used not in like manner the five or six who were kinsfolk of the Duke. To which intent he spoke to his follower, that he should go seek them one by one, and do on them like vengeance. But his follower replied, having neither courage nor folly for such an undertaking: "It seems to me that for this present time you have achieved enough, and would do better to think of saving your own life than depriving others of theirs. For if we take as much time to put an end to each one of them as we did to slay the Duke, the day will dawn upon our enterprise unfinished, even if we chance to find them undefended." The gentleman, whom a bad conscience rendered fearful, gave ear to his follower, and taking him alone, went to a Bishop, whose charge was that of Portreeve, to give authority for posting. To him the gentleman said: "This evening tidings came to me that my brother was at the point of death, and therefore I asked leave of the Duke to go to him, which he has granted me. So I pray that you give orders that I may have two good horses, and that the town gates may be opened to me." The Bishop, hearing his entreaty, and the command of the Duke his master, gave him forthwith a paper, by means of which the horses were granted him and the gates opened, even as he had desired. And in place of going to see any brother of his, he went straight to Venice, where he healed him of the bites the Duke had given, and after that journeyed to Turkey.

But on the morrow all the servants of the Duke, seeing how slow he was to return, had good suspicion that he was gone to see some woman, but since he tarried so long away made search for him in all the quarters of the town. And the poor Duchess, who began to bear her Duke great love, hearing that they searched and found him not, was exceeding troubled. But when the gentleman, his familiar friend, was seen no more than he, they went to his house and there sought for him. And finding blood at the door of his room, they entered in, but found no one who could give them any tidings. And following the trace of blood, these poor servants of the Duke came to the chamber

where he lay, and the door was shut. And when it was broken
open they saw the whole place that it was full of blood, and
drawing aside the curtain they found the body stretched out
upon the bed and sleeping its last sleep. Then were the servants
sorely grieved, and having borne the body to the palace, they
found there the Bishop, who told them how that the gentleman
had last night fled the town on pretext of seeing his brother.
Whereby it was clearly ascertained that it was he who had done
this murder. And it was also proved that his sister had not so
much as heard him speak of it, and she, although in great astonishment at what he had done, yet on account of it loved him all
the more, since he had not spared to make hazard of his life, that
she might be delivered from so cruel an enemy. And more and
more honourably and virtuously did she continue in her former
manner of living, for though by reason of the escheatment of her
goods, she was poor, yet did she and her sister get as honourable
and rich husbands as were in Italy, and henceforth have always
lived in good repute.

11 (XIV)

A very pleasant piece of cozenage done by my lord Bonnivet.

In the Duchy of Milan, while the grand-master of Chaumont
was governor, there lived a gentleman named Bonnivet, who
afterwards, for his merits, was made Admiral of France. Being
mightily beloved by the aforesaid grand-master and all others
for the virtues that were in him, he was often found at those
assemblies where ladies were gathered together, and was by
them more beloved than ever a Frenchman before, as much for
his fair speech, his grace, and his beauty as for the renown in
which he was held as one of the most brave and excellent warriors of his time. One day, at a masked ball during the Carnival
season, he led out in the dance the prettiest woman in all Milan,
and whensoever there fell a pause in the music he failed not to
make love to her, which it was confessed he knew as well as any
how to do. But she, who had no reply to his liking, brought him
to a halt by saying she neither loved nor would love any but her

husband, and, to be short, she would have nothing to say to him. For all this the gentleman would not hold himself beaten, and plied her vigorously up to Mothering Sunday. Notwithstanding his resolution, he still found her steadfast in her determination neither to love him nor anyone else, but to this he gave small credit, inasmuch as her husband was ill-favoured and she exceeding beautiful. So he was resolved, as she had used concealment, himself to use cozenage, and from that time he left off entreating her, and betook himself so well to making inquiries as to her manner of living that he found she loved an Italian gentleman, who was reported both prudent and honourable.

So my lord Bonnivet little by little became of this Italian's fellowship, and so pleasantly and craftily that the Italian did not perceive his intent, but liked him so well that he only came after his mistress. And Bonnivet, to arrest from him his secret, feigned to tell him his own—namely, that he loved a certain lady, of whom in truth he had no thoughts, praying him not to reveal it, so that they might only have one heart and one mind between them. And the poor gentleman, in return for this great love, made a long declaration of that he bore the lady on whom Bonnivet was fain to be avenged; and once in each day they met at a certain place to tell one another what luck they had had with their ladies, one telling lies and the other the truth. And the gentleman confessed to have loved his mistress for three years, without having had anything of her but fair words and assurance of her love towards him. Whereupon my lord Bonnivet showed him the means that might avail to accomplish his end, which he found so much to the purpose that in a few days she was ready to grant him whatsoever he might desire, and all to seek was the way to bring matters to a conclusion, and this, by the help of Bonnivet, was soon found. So one day before supper the gentleman said to him: "Sir, I am more beholden to you than all other men, for by your good counsel I hope to have that to-night which I have desired for so many years." "I pray you then," said Bonnivet, "tell me the manner of it, that I may see whether there is any cozenage or risk, and serve you as a friend." The gentleman told him that his mistress had found means to leave the chief door of the house open, under pretext of an illness of

one of her brothers, which made it needful to send to the town
on occasions at all hours, and so he might easily enter the court,
but was by no means to mount by the great stair, rather making
his way by a small one to the right hand, and thence entering
into the first gallery he came to where were the rooms of her
father-in-law and her brothers-in-law. He was to make for the
third door from the top of the stairs, and if softly pushing it he
found it shut, he must get him gone and know for certain that
her husband was returned, though she expected him not for two
days; but if he found it open he was to gently enter, and shutting
the door behind him to bolt it hard and fast. And above all he
was not to forget to wear felt slippers for fear of making a noise,
and to come not earlier than two hours after midnight, since her
brother-in-law, being very fond of cards, never went to bed
before one. To all this Bonnivet said: "Well done, my friend, may
you have good hap and meet with no mischance, and if my fellowship will avail you anything, I will spare nothing in my
power." The gentleman gave him his best thanks, but said that
in a matter of this sort one could not be too much alone, and
went to take order therein.

On his side my lord Bonnivet did by no means sleep, and perceiving that the hour was come for him to be avenged on this
cruel lady, he went early to his lodging, and had his beard cut to
the length and breadth of the gentleman's, and in like manner
his hair, that when she touched him she might not know the dif-
ference. Nor did he forget the felt slippers, and, to be short, had
all his dress after the fashion of the Italian's. And since he was
among the familiar acquaintances of the stepfather he was not
afraid of going early to the house, thinking, if he were perceived,
to go straight to the good man's chamber on some affair they had
together. So at midnight he entered the lady's house, and found
much folk both coming and going, but passed among them
unknown and got into the gallery. And on touching the two first
doors he found them fast, but the third was open. And when he
was in the room he bolted the door behind him, and beheld all
the room to be hung with white, and the ceiling and the floor
after the same manner, and in it there was a bed with a curtain
most admirably worked in white. And on the bed was the lady in

her nightcap and shift covered with pearls and precious stones; this he saw through a corner of the curtain without her seeing him, for there was in the room a great candle of refined wax, which made it as light as the day. And for fear of being known of her, he first blew out the candle, then doffed his clothes and got into bed beside her. She, believing him to be the man who had loved her so long, made for him the best cheer that she could, but he, knowing it was for another, would not say so much as a single word, and had no thoughts save of putting his vengeance into execution, that is to say, of taking away her honour and chastity without her will and favour. But she held herself so content with this vengeance of his that she thought she had made him a full return for all his services, till at last the clock struck one, and it was time to bid farewell. Whereupon in as low a voice as he was able he asked her whether she was as pleased with him as he with her. She, thinking him to be her lover, said that not only was she pleased but mightily astonished at the greatness of his love, which had prevented him for a whole hour from replying to her. At this he burst into a loud laugh, and said to her: "Will you then indeed refuse me another time, as has been your custom up to now?" She, knowing him by his speech and laughter, was made so desperate with grief and shame that a thousand times she called him *villain, traitor, deceiver,* and would have sprung from the bed to look for a knife that she might kill him, since it had been her fortune to lose her honour for a man who loved her not, and who, to make perfect his vengeance, might blaze abroad the whole matter. But holding her back with his arms he spoke to her gently, and assured her that he loved her better than the Italian, and that he would so conceal her dishonour that she would take no hurt thereby. All this the poor fool believed, and hearing from him how he had found out his scheme, and the pains he had taken to win her, swore to him that she loved him better than the man who could not keep her secret, and that she was now well persuaded that the common report as touching the French was false, since they were more wise, secret, and persevering than the Italians. Wherefore from henceforth she would forget the opinion her countrymen had of the French, and cleave to him. But she entreated him not to be present for some time at any assembly where she was save it was masked, for she knew well she should be so ashamed that her face would discover her to all men. To this he consented, and asked her, when her sweetheart came at two o'clock, to make good cheer for him also, but after this little by little to separate himself from him. At this she made so great difficulty that, had it not been for the love she bore him, she would never have granted it. And in bidding her farewell, he gave her such good matter of satisfaction that she heartily wished he could stay longer.

After he was arisen and had put on his clothes he went from the room, leaving the door as he had found it. And since it was hard on two o'clock, and he feared to meet the Italian on the way, he hid himself near the top of the stair, and soon after saw him pass by and go into the lady's room. Then he went home to his lodging to rest from his travail, which he did in such sort that nine o'clock in the morning found him still in bed. And while he was rising the Italian failed not to come and tell him his luck, though it was not of the kind he had hoped for. He said that when he entered the lady's room he found her out of bed in her dressing-gown and in a high fever, her pulse beating quick and fast, her face afire, and the sweat beginning to run adown it. In such case was she that she was fain for him straightway to begone, since she had more occasion to think of God than Cupid, telling him she was sorry he had run this risk, since she could not give him what he wanted in a world from which she thought soon to depart. At all this he was so astounded and grieved that his joyful heat was changed to most mournful ice, and he presently left her. And while he made this relation so bitterly did he weep that it seemed as if his soul would shortly follow his tears. Bonnivet, who was as fain to laugh as the other to weep, consoled him as well as might be, telling him that these long-lasting love affairs had always a difficult beginning, and that Love made this delay to the end that the enjoyment of her should be greater, and with this they parted. As for the lady she kept her bed some days, and when health was restored to her, gave her first lover his dismissal, founding it on her remorse and fear of death. But she kept in her favour Bonnivet, whose love lasted, as it was wont, as long as the flowers of the field.

12 (XVI)

A love persevering and fearless meets with due reward.

In the time of the grand-master of Chaumont there lived in Milan a lady esteemed one of the most honourable in the town. She, being the widow of an Italian count, lived in the house of her brothers-in-law, without any wish of marrying again, and kept herself so wisely and virtuously that there was in the duchy neither Frenchman nor Italian who did not hold her in great repute. One day, on which her brothers-in-law and her sisters-in-law made entertainment for the grand-master of Chaumont, although it was not her custom, she was constrained to be present, and when the Frenchmen saw her they mightily extolled her beauty and grace, and above all one whose name I tell not, but it will suffice to know that there was not a Frenchman in Italy more worthy of love than he, for he was fulfilled with every brave and knightly grace. And although he saw this lady, that she was clad in black, and sat apart from the maidens with old women all around her, yet fearing neither man nor woman he set himself to talk with her, taking off his mask and leaving the dances to be in her company. And all the evening he stirred not from her side, talking to her and the old women around, which he found more to his liking than if they had been the youngest and the fairest at Court, in such sort that when he must needs go, it seemed to him that he had scarcely sat down. And though he but held with the lady such common matter of discourse as was fit for the company to hear, yet she was well persuaded that he was desirous to be of her acquaintance, against which she was determined to guard as well as might be, and so neither at entertainment nor great assembly did he see her any more. Having made inquiry of her manner of living, he discovered that she went often to churches and convents, and he kept so good watch upon her that let her be as secret as she would, wherever she went he was there first, and would stay as long as he was able to see her, and all the while looking upon her in such a manner that she could not be ignorant of his love towards her. And for the avoiding of this she determined for some while to feign sickness and hear mass in her own house, at which the gentleman was sorely grieved, for he had lost the only means of seeing her. She, thinking to have put an end to that habit of his, returned to the churches as before, but love forthwith made it known to the French gentleman, and he became as devout as ever he was. And for fear lest she might a second time do something to his hindrance, or lest he might not have opportunity to make known his mind to her, one morning, when she thought herself shrewdly hidden away in a side chapel, he went to the end of the altar at which she was hearing mass, and seeing that she had no companions, just as the priest lifted up the Body of the Lord, he turned towards her, and in a gentle voice and affectionate, said to her: "Mistress, I will take Him whom the priest holds in his hands to my damnation if you are not the reason of my death, for though you deprive me of parley with you, yet you cannot be ignorant of the truth, since it is manifest in the languishment of my eyes and my face all amort." The lady, feigning to understand nothing, replied to him: "Thou shalt not take God's name in vain, but the poet say the gods laugh at the oaths and lies of lovers, wherefore ladies of honour should by no means be credulous or compassionate." Saying thus she arose and returned to her lodging.

Those who have had experiences like to this will be well assured that the gentleman was very wrathful. But he, whose heart never failed him, liked better to have had a bad answer than to have failed to declare his mind, the which for three years remained steadfast, and all the while he ceased not to pay suit to her by letters and by all manner of means, losing not so much as an hour. But during these three years he had no reply from her, since she fled from him as the hare from the wolf, not out of hatred, but for fear of her honour and reputation. And the cause was so plainly manifest to him that never before had he so vigorously pressed his suit. And after much refusal, pains, torments, and despair, seeing the greatness and perseverance of his

love, the lady took pity on him, and granted to him that which
he so much desired and had waited for so long. And when they
had come to an agreement upon the ways and means, the
French gentleman did not fail to risk his life by going to her
house, and the risk was indeed a great one, seeing that all her
kinsfolk were lodged in this same mansion. He, having no less
craft than comeliness, brought it about so well that he got into
her room at the appointed time, and found her lying by herself
on a most rare bed. But as he made haste to doff his clothes that
he might get into bed with her, he heard at the door a noise of
voices speaking low, and the clash of swords as they touched the
wall. His widow lady, with the face of a woman half dead, said to
him: "In good sooth now are your life and my honour in as great
peril as they can ever be, for I plainly hear my brothers, who
seek you out that they may kill you. Wherefore I pray you hide
yourself under the bed, that when they come and find you not I
may reproach them for alarming me without a cause." The gentleman, who never yet had known fear, said to her: "And what
manner of men are these your brothers to make an honest man
to be afraid? Were all your kin to be here, I am well assured that
they would not await so much as the fourth blow of my sword,
wherefore rest you in your bed, and leave me to guard the door."
And taking his cloak across his arm with his drawn sword in his
hand, he opened the door to the intent that he might see close
at hand the swords that made such a clashing. And when it was
opened he saw two serving-maids, who, with two swords in each
hand, had caused the tumult, and they said to him: "Sir, pardon
us, since we had commandment from our mistress to do this,
but from us you shall have no further hindrance." The gentleman, seeing then that they were women, did no more hurt to
them than that, sending them to the devil, he shut the door in
their faces, and got to bed with the lady as soon as he could,
since fear had by no means lessened his love, even forgetting to
ask the reason of all this, and thinking of nothing but the satisfying his desire. But seeing morning to be near at hand, he asked
her to tell him wherefore she had done him so many evil turns,
both in making him to wait so long and in this last affair of the
swords and serving-maids. She, laughing, replied to him: "It was

my fixed resolve never to love, and this I have kept throughout
my widowhood; but your honourable address, from the day you
first spoke to me, made me change my resolve and so love you
as you have loved me. It is true that honour always guiding me
would not allow my love to do that by which my good repute
might suffer hurt. But like as the hart, wounded unto death,
thinks in moving from one place to another to move from the ill
it carries with it, so did I fly from church to church, thinking to
escape that which was in my soul, but the proof of your perfect
love has made honour come to an agreement with it. Yet to the
end that I might be the more assured of placing my heart and
my love in a perfect man, I was fain to make this last proof of
you by means of my women. And I tell you that if, for the sake
of your life or aught else, I had found you fearful enough to get
under the bed, I was determined to rise and go into another
room, without ever having to do with you. But since I found in
you more beauty, grace, virtue, and bravery than I had been
advised of, and since fear has no power at all to touch your heart
or to chill your love towards me, I am resolved to cleave to you
for the rest of my days, for in no better hands could I put my life
and my honour than in him who in every way is without a
match." And all as if the will of man was unchangeable, they
promised and sware what lay not within their power—namely,
perpetual love, which cannot arise or dwell in a man's heart. And
only those women know this who have tried how long their passion lasts.

13 (XVII)

King Francis shows his courage that it is well approved.

There came to Dijon, in the duchy of Burgundy, a German
count named William, of the House of Saxe, which is so near
akin to the House of Savoy that of old they were one. This count,
being esteemed the bravest and most handsome gentleman in
Germany, having offered his service to the King of France, was
so well received of him that not only did he accept him as a follower, but kept him close at hand as a servant of the Body. Now

my lord de la Tremoille, governor of Burgundy, the same being
an ancient knight and loyal servant to the King, was always jealous and fearful of his master, and had spies on all hands, that he
might know the counsels of the enemies of the King, and so well
did he conduct matters that few things were hid from him. And
he was advertised by one of his friends that Count William had
received a sum of money, with assurance of more, to the intent
that he might in any way cause the King to be murdered.
Whereupon my lord de la Tremoille did forthwith advise the
King of it, and did not conceal it from his mother, Louise de
Savoye, who forgetting that she and this German were akin,
implored the King straightway to dismiss him. But the King
would have her speak no more of it, saying it was impossible for
so good and honourable a gentleman to have undertaken so evil
an enterprise. At the end of some time there came a second tidings concerning him to the same intent as the first, at which the
governor, burning with love for his master, demanded that he
should be sent from his service and banished the realm, or that
some manner of order should be taken with him. But the King
straightly charged him that he should make no sign, being well
persuaded that by some other means he should come to a
knowledge of the truth.

And one day, on which he was going a hunting, he took out
the best sword that he had, and bade Count William follow hard
after him; and after chasing the stag for some time, the King,
seeing that all his people were far off, and that the Count alone
was with him, turned aside from all the tracks. And when he saw
himself alone with the Count in the very depths of the forest,
drawing his sword he said to him: "Does this sword seem to you
both good to look upon and serviceable withal?" The Count,
handling the point, said he had seen none to overmatch it. "You
are in the right," said the King, "and methinks if a man was
resolved to kill me, and knew the strength of my arm and the
stoutness of my heart, and the goodness of this sword here, he
would think twice before having at me; nevertheless, I should
hold him for a pitiful scoundrel if we were all alone, without witnesses, and he durst not carry out what he durst conceive." To
which Count William, with an astounded countenance, replied:

"Sire, the wickedness of such an undertaking would be very great, but the folly of putting it into execution would be no less." The King, with a laugh, put back the sword into the sheath, and hearing the chase hard by, pricked after it as fast as he was able. When he was come up he spoke to no one on the matter, being assured that Count William, though a brave enough gentleman, was not competent for such an enterprise. But the Count, believing that he was found out or at the least suspected, came early on the next morning to Robertet, the King's treasurer, saying that he had considered the privileges and pay the King was willing to give him to stay in his service, and they did not suffice him for the half of a year. And if it was not the King's pleasure to give him double, he should be constrained to depart. And he prayed the said Robertet to ascertain as soon as might be the will of the King, who said that he could do him no better service than go to the King forthwith. And he did this willingly, since he had seen the advices of the governor. So when the King was awake he failed not to tell him what the Count had said, my lord de la Tremoille and Admiral de Bonnivet being present. But they knew not that which the King had done the day before. So with a laugh the King said: "You were desirous of dismissing Count William, and behold he dismisses himself! Wherefore tell him that, since he is not content with the estate to which he agreed when he entered my service, than which estate many a man of a noble house desires nothing better, it is reasonable that he seek his fortune somewhere else. And as for me I will put no let nor hindrance in his way, but shall be glad if he find a place according to his deserts." Robertet was as quick to carry back this reply to the Count as he had been to carry the Count's complaint to the King. And the Count said that, with his good pleasure, he was determined immediately to set forth. And as one whom fear makes to begone, it was not more than twenty-four hours from thence that he took leave of the King, as he was sitting at table, feigning to regret greatly that his poverty forced him away. Likewise he took leave of the mother of the King, who gave him leave as joyful as her welcome, when he came to her as a kinsman and a friend; and so returned he to his own land. But the King, perceiving his mother and his followers

astonished at this sudden parting, told them of the fright he had
given him, saying that though he were innocent of what was laid
against him, yet his fear was too great for him to stay with a master whose complexion he knew no longer.

14 (XVIII)
A notable case of a steadfast lover.

In one of the fair towns of France there lived a nobleman of an
illustrious house, who studied in the schools desiring to attain
the knowledge of the means by which men come to virtue and
honour. And although he was such a sound scholar that at the
age of seventeen or eighteen years he seemed to be a teacher
and an ensample to all the rest, natheless Love, amid all his
learning, made him go likewise to its lecture-hall. And for a better hearing and reception, it hid itself in the face and beautiful
eyes of the prettiest maid in all the countryside, who had come
up to town on some matter of law. But before that Love had
essayed to conquer him by the beauty of the lady, it had gained
her heart by showing to her the perfections that were in this
young lord; for in comeliness, grace, good sense, and pleasant
speaking, he had no rival in any sort or condition of men whatsoever. You who know the quick work this fire makes, when it
betakes itself to the extremities of the heart and fantasy, will
judge well that, with two subjects like these, Love never stopped
till it had them at its pleasure, and that it so filled them with its
shining light that their thoughts, words, and wishes were but of
this flame of Love. Youth, engendering in the gentleman fear,
made him pay his suit as gently as might be; but she, altogether
conquered by love, needed no pressing; natheless shame, which
always is companion to a maid, kept her some while without
declaring her mind. But at the end, the strong-place of her
heart, where honour dwelleth, was in such fashion brought to
the dust, that the poor maid agreed to that on which in truth
they had never disagreed. Yet, to make trial of the patience,
steadfastness, and love of her servant, she granted him what he
asked on a condition most hard to be observed, assuring him

that if he kept it she would love him with a perfect love, and if not she would have no more traffic with him. And this was her condition: she would be content to hold parley with him in a bed, the pair of them being clad alone in their shirts, if he would ask no more of her than kisses and sweet talk. And he, thinking no joy was there to be compared with the joy she promised him, agreed thereto. And when the evening was come, his promise was kept; in such sort that for all the good cheer she made him, and for all the temptations with which he was vexed, he would by no means depart from his oath. And though he thought his pains not less than those of purgatory, so strong was his love, and so assured his hope of the everlasting continuing of this their love, that he kept watch with patience and rose from beside her without doing her any wrong. The lady, as I believe, more astonished than delighted with this good faith, presently suspected either that his love was not so great as she had taken it to be, or that he had found her not so sweet as he had thought; and had no consideration to his honour, long-suffering, and faithfulness in the keeping of his oath.

This done she determined to make yet another trial of his love for her before she kept her promise. And to this intent she asked him to speak with a girl of her household, younger than herself and mighty pretty, and to hold love discourse with her, that those who saw him so often come to the house might think it was for the maid and not for the mistress. The young lord, well persuaded of being beloved even as he loved, altogether obeyed her commands, and constrained himself for love of her to make love to the girl. And she, seeing him of such pleasant speech and brave address, believed his lie more than another's truth, and loved him all as if she was verily beloved of him. And when her mistress saw that things were thus forward, and that all the same the gentleman ceased not to remind her of her promise, she granted him to come and see her an hour after midnight, and told him that she had tried so well his love and obedience towards her, that it was reasonable he should be rewarded for his long-suffering. One cannot doubt of the joy of this faithful lover at hearing of this, and at the appointed hour he failed not to be present. But the lady, to try the strength of his love, said

to the girl: "I am well advised of the love a certain lord bears
you, and I think your passion for him is not less. And I have
taken such pity on you two, that I am resolved to give you place
and leisure to parley together at your ease." At this the maid was
in such delight that she could not conceal her desire, saying she
would not fail her. In obedience therefore to the lady she
undressed herself and lay down all alone on a fine bed; the lady
leaving the door of the room open, and lighting it very brightly,
so that the girl's beauty might the more be manifested. And
feigning to go away she so shrewdly hid herself near the bed,
that no one might see her. Her lover, thinking to find her there
according to promise, at the appointed time entered into the
room as softly as he was able; and after that he had shut the door
and doffed his vesture and fur slippers, he got into bed thinking
to find there what he had desired. And he had no sooner
stretched out his arms to embrace her whom he thought his
mistress, than the poor girl, believing him entirely her own,
threw her arms round his neck, and spoke to him with such loving words and with so beautiful a face, that a holy hermit would
have dropped his beads at the sight of her. But when as much by
hearing as seeing he perceived who she was, love, which had
sent him to bed at such a rate, no less quickly got him up again,
when he found it was not she for whom he had borne so much.
And wrathful as much with the mistress as with the maid, he
said to her: "Not your folly, nor the maliciousness of her who has
put you there, can make me other than I am. But do you labour
to become an honest woman, for, by reason of me, you will
never lose your good name." And thus saying he went forth from
the room in a rage, and for a long time returned not to the place
where his mistress dwelt. But Love, who is never devoid of
hope, gave him good assurance that the greater the trials the
better the enjoyment. The lady, having seen and heard the passages between him and the maid, was so delighted and astonished at the greatness and steadfastness of his love, that she
wearied for the time of seeing him again, to ask his forgiveness
for all the evils with which she had afflicted him. And as soon as
she could find him she took such order with him that not only
did he forget his sorrows overpast, but deemed them happy,

inasmuch as they were turned to the glory of his steadfastness and the perfect assurance of his love. And of this love from that time forth he tasted the fruition as he had desired, without hindrance or weariness.

15 (XXI)

The steadfast and honourable love of Rolandine,
who after many sorrows at last finds happiness.

There was a Queen of France who in her household maintained many maidens of good and illustrious families. Amongst others there was one named Rolandine, who was the Queen's near kinswoman, but for some discontent she had conceived with her father she gave her not over-pleasant entertainment. This girl, not being of the prettiest or the ugliest, was yet so discreet and virtuous that several great personages had asked her in marriage, but met with a cold answer, for her father loved money so well that he made nothing of the advancement of his daughter, and the Queen her mistress, as I have said, held her in such small favour that they who were fain to gain her good grace asked not Rolandine of her. So by her father's neglect and the Queen's misliking the poor girl stayed a long while without being married. And being sad at heart on this account, not so much that she desired to be married as for shame that she was not, she gave herself up wholly to God, leaving behind her all the pomps and vanities of the Court, and her sole delight was in prayer and in the doing of needlework. So in this quiet manner of living her young years were past, and they were as well and virtuously spent as one could desire. Now there was at Court a young gentleman who carried on an exceeding noble coat the bar sinister, though as pleasant a comrade and as honest a man as any, but mighty poor, and for comeliness he had so little that none but she would have chosen him for a lover. For a long while he had lived without a mate, but since one unfortunate seeks out another, he addressed himself to Rolandine, seeing that their fortunes, complexions, and estates were all alike. And while they made complaint to one another of their mischances, they became great friends; and finding themselves to be partakers in the same lot, they sought one another out everywhere, and in this manner was engendered a great and lasting acquaintanceship between them. But those who had beheld Rolandine afore so retired that she spoke to no one, now seeing her incessantly with this gentleman, were mightily scandalised thereat, and told her gouvernante that she should not endure their long talks together. She therefore made remonstrance to Rolandine, telling her that all men took in bad part that she spoke so much to one who was not rich enough for a husband, nor handsome enough for a sweetheart. Rolandine, who had always suffered reproof for her austerity and not her worldliness, said to her gouvernante: "Alas, mother, you see that I cannot have a husband of like estate with myself, and as for those who are young and comely, I have always fled them, lest perchance I fall into the same pit into which others have fallen. And since I find, as you know, this gentleman to be a prudent man and a virtuous, and that his discourse is only on good and honourable things, what wrong have I done in consoling myself in my weariness to those who have spoken to you?" The poor old woman, who loved her mistress more than herself, said to her: "Mistress, I am well persuaded that you speak the truth, and that the treatment you have had of your father and the Queen is not according to your deserts. Yet, since men handle your honour in this fashion, were he your own brother, you would do well to separate yourself from him." Rolandine, weeping, replied to her: "Mother, I will do according to your counsel, but it is a strange thing not to have any matter of consolation in the world." The gentleman, as was his custom, came to talk with her, but she declared to him all that her gouvernante had said, and with tears implored him that he would be content not to hold parley with her until this rumour was overpast; and this at her request he did.

But during this estrangement, having both lost their consolation, they began to feel a torment that was new to both of them. She ceased not to pray to God, to go on pilgrimages, and to observe duly the fasts and days of abstinence; for love, till now unknown to her, made her so unquiet that she had not rest for a single hour. The gentleman was in no less pitiful case; but he,

who had already determined in his heart to love her and endeavour to get her for his wife, thinking both of love and the honour
he would have if he succeeded, conceived that he must seek
means of speaking with her, and, above all, of winning over the
gouvernante. This he did, making remonstrance to her of the
misery of her poor mistress, from whom they were fain to take
away all manner of consolation. At this the old woman wept, and
thanked him for the honourable friendship he had for her mistress. And they took counsel together how he might best speak
with her, and the plan was for Rolandine to often feign to be sick
of the megrims, in which noise is hurtful; and when her fellows
went into the Queen's chamber, they two could stay by themselves, and then he could talk with her. With this the gentleman
was quite content, and altogether ruled himself by the advice of
the gouvernante in such sort that when he would he talked with
his sweetheart. But this lasted not for a long while; for the
Queen, bearing no great love for her, asked what Rolandine did
in her room. And though one said it was by reason of her sickness, another would have it she stayed in her room because parley with the gentleman aforesaid made the megrims to pass
over. The Queen, who esteemed the venial sins of others in her
mortal, made seek her out, and strictly charged her that she
should not speak with this gentleman, unless it were in the presence or in the great hall. The girl made no sign, but answered:
"If I thought he was displeasing to you, I would never have spoken with him." Natheless she resolved within herself to search
out some other means of which the Queen should know nothing, and this she accomplished. For on Wednesdays, Fridays,
and Saturdays she fasted and stayed in her room with her gouvernante, and there had time, while her fellows supped, for
holding parley with him whom she began to love exceedingly.
And the more they were constrained to cut short their speech,
the more affection was there in it; for they took time by stealth
as does a robber something of great price. But the matter was
not kept so secretly that a servant did not see him go into her
room on a fast day, who told his tale in a quarter where it was
not concealed from the Queen. And she was so wroth thereat,
that no more durst the gentleman enter into the maid's room;

but so as not altogether to lose this blessing of speech, he often made pretence of going on a journey, returning at eventide to the castle church in the gear of a Grey Friar or a Jacobin, and so well disguised that none recognised him; and thither went Rolandine and her gouvernante. And he, perceiving the great love she bore him, feared not to say: "You see the risk in which, for your sake, I put my life, and that the Queen has forbidden us to speak together. And also consider of what sort is your father, who thinks not in any manner of marrying you. He has already refused many a good match, in such fashion that I know not any from far or near who can have you. I know well that I am poor, and that you cannot marry a gentleman of my estate; but if love and goodwill were accounted as great treasure, I should think myself the richest man in the world. God has given you riches, and you are in the likelihood of having still more, and if I were so happy as to be chosen by you, I would be your faithful husband, lover, and follower unto my life's end. But if you chose one of equal estate, a thing difficult for you, he would be to you as a master and would regard your goods more than yourself, and the beauty of others more than your virtuousness; and, while he enjoyed the usufruct of your wealth, he would not treat you as you deserve. The desire I have of this contentment, and my fear lest another possess himself of it, cause me to implore you that on the same day you make me happy and yourself the best satisfied and best entreated wife that ever was." Rolandine hearing the discourse that she herself had determined to hold with him, replied with a well-pleased face: "I am glad that you have made this beginning, for I have for a long time been resolved to speak with you to this intent, and have thought upon the matter for the two years in which I have known you, never ceasing to place before me all manner of conclusions both for and against. But since I confess that I wish to enter into this estate of matrimony, it is now full time that I begin and choose someone with whom I may live with a contented mind. I have not found one, be he rich, comely, or of noble blood with whom my heart and mind could be in such accord as with you; for I know that in marrying you I shall do God no displeasure, but rather follow his commands. As for my father, he has done so little for my good and so much to my hurt, that the law will have me marry and by no means lose mine inheritance. As for the Queen my mistress, I shall not make it a point of conscience to do her a pleasure and God a displeasure; since she has done nothing but hinder me from having any blessing I might have had in my youth. But to the intent that you may understand that my love is bottomed upon virtue and honour, you shall promise me that, if I take you in marriage, you will not endeavour the consummation thereof till that my father is dead or I bring him to consent." This promised willingly the gentleman, and they exchanged rings and kissed one another in the church before God, whom they had as witness to their promise; and between them there passed no other familiarity, save kissing.

This small contentment filled with joy the hearts of these two perfect lovers, and they were for some time without seeing but in full security of one another. Now there was no place in which glory might be gained to which the gentleman was not fain to go, since he could not account himself for a poor man, God having given to him so rich a wife; and while he was away she kept their perfect love so in her heart, that all others were as nothing to her. And although there were they who asked her in marriage, they had no answer from her but that, since she had lived such a long while unmarried, she had no wish ever to be married. This answer came to the ears of so many folk that the Queen heard thereof, and asked her wherefore she gave it. And Rolandine said that it was given from obedience to her, who had never desired her to be married to any man who could have made honourable provision for her; and that age and patience had made her resolve to content herself with her present estate. And to all who spoke to her on this manner she gave the same reply. But when the wars were over and the gentleman was returned to Court, she by no means spoke to him before other folk, but would go always to a certain church where, under pretext of confession, she would parley with him; for the Queen had charged both him and her that they should not speak to one another on pain of their lives, except it were in some great assembly. But honourable love, knowing nothing of such charges, was more ready to find means of speech than was the

enemy to spy it out; and he, concealing himself under the habit
of every order of monks he could think of, they continued in this
pleasant fashion till that the King went to his pleasure house
near Tours. In that place there was no church to which the
ladies could go on foot save only the one pertaining to the castle, and that so badly designed for their purpose that there was
no hiding-place or confessional in it in which the confessor
could not be clearly recognised. Natheless, if opportunity failed
them on one side, love found them other and easier, for there
came to Court a lady nearly related to the lover of Rolandine.
And she with the young prince her son were lodged in the King's
household, and the prince's room stood out beyond the rest of
the house, in such a manner that, from his window, it was possible to see and talk with Rolandine, for the windows were at the
angle where the two parts of the house joined one another. And
in this room of hers, that stood above the King's Hall, there were
lodged with her all the ladies who were her fellows. And she,
oftimes seeing the prince at his window, by her gouvernante
advertised her husband of it; whereupon, after well observing
the place, he feigned to take great delight in the reading of a
book concerning the Knights of the Round Table, which was in
the prince's room. And when all were gone to dinner he prayed
a body-servant to let him come and read, and to shut him up in
the room, and keep good watch over the door. The man, knowing him for a kinsman of his master and one to be trusted, let
him read as much as he would. On the other hand Rolandine
would come to her window, and that she might the longer stay
there, feigned to have a diseased leg, and dined and supped so
early that she went no more to dinner with the other ladies. She
likewise set herself to make a quilt of crimson silk, which she
fixed at the window, whereat she was fain to be alone, and when
she saw there was no one at hand she held parley with her husband, who answered her in such a voice that could not be heard
by others. And when she saw any folk she would cough and
make some sign to him, so that he might get him gone in good
time. They that played the spy on them were persuaded that all
love passages were over, for she never stirred from a room
wither of a certainty he could not come, since he was altogether

forbidden to enter it. But one day the prince's mother, being in her son's room, placed herself at the window where was the great book of Romances, and she had not been there a long while before one of Rolandine's companions saw her and spoke to her. The lady asked her how fared Rolandine, and the girl replied that she could see for herself if it were her pleasure, and made Rolandine come to the window in her nightcap. So, after speaking about her sickness, each went back to her own place. The lady, looking at the great book of the Round Table, said to the servant who had charge of it: "I marvel how young folk can waste their time in the reading of such folly!" The man answered that he marvelled still more that men of age and of repute for wisdom were exceedingly delighted with it; and as a matter for astonishment told her how the gentleman, her kinsman, stayed at the window four or five hours every day to read in this fine book aforesaid. Straightway the reason of it came into the lady's mind, and she charged the servant to hide himself close at hand and take account of what happened. This he did, and found this gentleman's book to be the window whither Rolandine came and spoke to him, and heard many a love-passage they thought to have kept altogether secret. On the morrow he bore this to his mistress, who sent for the gentleman, and after chiding him, forbade him any more to be in that place; and in the evening she spoke to Rolandine, threatening her that, if she continued in this foolish love, she would tell the Queen of all her doings. Rolandine, no whit affrayed, swore that after her mistress's forbidding her she had never spoken to him, let them say what they would, and she called her fellows and servants to witness that such was the truth. And for the matter of the window, she denied to have spoken there to the gentleman; but he, fearing the thing was made known, withdrew himself from the danger, and was a long time without returning to Court, but not without writing to Rolandine in such subtle fashion that, howsoever much the Queen might play the spy, there was not a week in which she did not twice get news of him.

And when a monkish messenger, who was the first he had used, failed him, he sent her a little page, now dressed in one colour and now in another. And he would stop at the doors,

through which all the ladies were wont to pass, and give her the
letters privily in the press. But one day, the Queen going into
the country, a certain one whose charge it was to look after this
affair, recognised the page and ran after him; but he, who was of
keen wit, suspecting that he would be searched, entered the
house of a poor woman who had her pot on the fire, and forthwith burnt up the letters. The gentleman followed him up and
stripped him quite naked, and thoroughly searched his vesture,
but found nothing, and so let him go. Whereupon the old
woman asked the gentleman why he had searched the boy. He
said to her: "To find certain letters which I thought he had carried." "By no means could you have found them," said the
woman, "so well were they hidden." "I pray you," said he, "tell
me in what slit they are hidden," having a good hope of getting
them back. But when he understood that the fire was the hiding
place, he knew the page to have been the keener of the two, and
made report of the whole matter to the Queen. And from
henceforth Rolandine's husband could no more avail himself of
the page; so he sent an old servant, who, forgetting the death
that he knew well the Queen threatened against those who
intermeddled with this matter, undertook to carry letters to
Rolandine. And when he was entered in unto the castle where
she was, he set himself to watch by a door at the foot of the
grand staircase whither all the ladies passed; but a servant who
before had seen him straightway knew him, and told the
Queen's master of the household, who presently came to seek
him and clap him up. But the messenger, prudent and wary, seeing they looked at him from far off, turned himself to the wall,
as if for a necessary occasion, and tearing up the letter into as
small pieces as he could, threw them behind a door. Forthwith
he was taken and searched in every way; but when they could
find nothing they asked him on his oath if he had not brought
letters, using with him all manner of threats and persuasions to
make him to confess the truth; but promising or threatening, it
was all one, and they none the wiser. Report of this came to the
Queen, and certain of the company were of the opinion that it
would be well to look behind the door near which he was taken;
and this being done they found that they sought—namely, the

pieces of the letter. Then was summoned the King's confessor, who, after putting the pieces in order on a table, read the letter at length; and so was brought to light the truth concerning the concealed marriage, for the gentleman called Rolandine nothing but *wife*. The Queen, who had no mind to cover her neighbour's misdeeds, as she ought to have done, made a great noise of it, and commanded that every way should be tried to make the poor man confess the truth of the letter; and when it was shown to him he could not deny it, but whatever they said or showed to him he would say no more. Those who had charge of him then led him to the bank of the river and put him in a sack, saying that he had lied to God and the Queen against the proven truth. He, who had rather lose his life than make accusation against his master, asked of them a confessor, and after easing his conscience as well as might be, he said to them: "Good sirs, I pray you tell my lord that I commend to him the life of my wife and children, for with hearty goodwill I give my life for his service. Now do your pleasure on me, for no word will I utter against my master. Thereupon, all the more to affright him, they threw him bound up in the sack into the river, calling to him: "Tell the truth and your life shall be spared." But perceiving that he answered them not a word, they drew him from the water and brought the report of it to the Queen, who said that neither the King her husband nor herself had such good fortune in their servants as a man who had not wherewithal to pay them. And she would fain have drawn him into her service, but he would by no means of his own will leave his master. Natheless, by the leave of the said master, he took service under the Queen, where he lived in happiness and good contentment.

And the Queen being acquainted with the truth of the marriage by the gentleman's letter, made summon Rolandine, and with a wrathful countenance calling her *wretch* in place of *cousin*, laid before her the shame she had done her father's house, her kinsfolk, and her mistress, in marrying without her leave or commandment. Rolandine, who for a long while had known the small love the Queen bore her, gave her as little in return. And since love was wanting between them neither had fear any place, and Rolandine thought likewise that this rebuke

before several persons did not proceed so much from love as
from a desire to do her an open shame, the Queen taking more
pleasure in chiding her than grief at seeing her in fault. So with
a face as glad and assured as the Queen's was wrathful and troubled, she replied: "Mistress, did you not plainly know your own
heart and the manner of it, I would set before you the ill-will
you have for a long time borne against my father and myself, but
this you know so well that it will not appear marvellous to you
that all the world has a suspicion of it; and as for me, I have felt
this intent of yours to my great hurt. For, if it had been your
pleasure to favour me as you do those who are not so near akin
as I, I should now have been married both to your honour and
mine, but you have left me as one altogether deprived of your
grace, so that all the good matches I might have made are
passed away before my eyes, by reason of my father's neglect
and the small account you make of me. At this I fell into such
despair, that if my health allowed of it, I had entered into the
religious life, and so escaped from the continual sorrows your
severity laid upon me. In this sad case one sought me out, who
would have been of as gentle blood as myself, if the love of two
persons were to be as much esteemed as the wedding-ring, for
you know that his father was before mine in precedency. And he
for a long while has courted me and loved me; but you, mistress,
who never pardon me any petty fault, nor praise me for any
good deed; although you well knew that it was not my custom to
listen to worldly love passages, and that I was altogether given
up to devotion; have found it a strange thing that I should speak
with a gentleman as unfortunate as myself, from whom I neither
wished nor sought anything except some matter of consolation.
And when I saw this consolation taken away from me, I was
resolved to take as much pains to gain it as you took to deprive
me of it; whereupon we promised each other marriage, and confirmed the promise with a ring. Methinks, therefore, you do me
great wrong to call me *wicked*, since in this great and perfect
love, in which I found the consolation I longed for, there passed
between us nothing worse than kissing, all else being deferred
by me till, by the grace of God, my father's heart should be
inclined to consent thereto. Sure am I that I have in no way

offended God nor my conscience, for I waited till the age of thirty years to see what you and my father would do for me, having kept my youth so chastely and virtuously that no living man can cast anything in my teeth. And using the reason given to me by God, seeing myself growing old, and despairing of finding a match according to my estate, I resolved to marry one according to my wish; not for the satisfaction of the lust of the flesh, since there has been no carnal consummation; nor for the lust of the eyes, since you know he is not comely; nor for the pride of life, he being poor and of small reputation. But I have taken account alone of the virtue that is in him, the which all men are constrained to laud and magnify; also of the great love he bears me, by reason of which I hope to find with him a life of quiet and good treatment. And after weighing duly both the good and the evil that may come of it, I have fixed on him who seems to me the best, and with whom I have determined for the last two years to pass the remainder of my days. And so steadfast is this my resolve, that not all the torments I may endure—no, not death itself—can turn me from it. Wherefore I pray you to excuse that which in truth is very excusable, and leave me to live in that peace which I hope to find with him."

The Queen, seeing her face to be so steadfast and her words so true, could not answer in reason, but, continuing in wrath to reproach her, at last fell to weeping, and said: "Wretch that you are, in place of humbling yourself before me, and repenting of your great fault, you speak dry-eyed and audaciously, and so make manifest the obstinacy and hardness of your heart. But if the King and your father will listen to me, they will put you in a place where you will be constrained to talk after another fashion." "Mistress," answered Rolandine, "since you accuse me of speaking audaciously, I will be silent, if it is not your pleasure that I should reply to you." And being commanded to speak, she said to the Queen: "It is not my part to speak audaciously and without due reverence to you who are my mistress and the greatest princess in Christendom; and this it was by no means my intent to do, but since I can call no advocate to speak for me, save the truth that is known only by me, I am constrained to tell it plainly and without fear, hoping that when you know it you

will not esteem me what it has been your pleasure to name me.
I am not afraid of any living creature hearing how I have kept
myself in this matter, since I know that I have thereby offended
neither God nor my honour. And since I am persuaded that He
who sees my heart is on my side, wherefore should I fear? And
having this Judge for me, shall I of His subjects be afraid? And
for what cause should I weep, since neither my conscience nor
my heart do at all reprove me?—nay, so far am I from repentance, that if I could make a new beginning I would do even as
I have done. But you, indeed, have good cause for weeping, as
much for the wrongs you did me in my youth as for that you now
reproach me before all for a thing which is rather to be imputed
to you than me. If I had justly offended God, the King, you, my
kinsfolk, and my conscience, I should be hard of heart if I did
not repent with weeping. But for so befitting and holy an agreement, in which no fault can be found save that you have too soon
blazed it abroad, showing thereby that you have a greater desire
for my dishonour than for preserving the good repute of your
house and kinsfolk, I by no means ought to weep; yet, mistress,
since such is your pleasure, I will not gainsay you; for whatever
pains you lay upon me, I being innocent, will take no less pleasure in the enduring of them than you in the inflicting.
Wherefore give what commands you please to my father, and I
am well assured that he will not fail you, and as far as my ill is
affected he will be altogether your creature; and as obedient to
your will he has hitherto neglected my good, so he will be quick
to obey you for my evil. But I have a Father in heaven, who, I
am assured, will give me patience to bear all your torments, and
in Him alone do I put my trust."

At this the Queen was still more wrathful, and commanded
that she should be taken out of her sight and put in a room by
herself, where she might have speech with no one. But she did
not deprive her of her gouvernante, by whose means she let her
husband know her case, and that which she thought it was best
for him to do. And he, thinking the deeds he had done in the
King's service might avail him something, came post haste to
Court and found the King a-hunting, and told him the truth of
the matter, entreating him to do so much for a poor gentleman

as to appease the Queen in such sort that the marriage might be consummated. The King replied nothing save: "Do you assure me that you have taken her to wife?" "Ay, sire," said the gentleman, "by word and gift alone; and if it please you, we'll make an ending to it." The King, lowering his head, and without saying a word more, returned forthwith to his castle, and when he was come thither gave charge to the captain of the guards that he should take the gentleman prisoner. Natheless, one of his acquaintance, who knew the King's intent by his visage, counselled him to get him gone and stay in a house hard-by; and if the King made search for him, as he suspected he would, he would presently let him know so that he might fly the realm; but if things were softened down he would send word for him to come back. And the gentleman, trusting in his friend, made such good speed that the captain of the guards could not at all find him.

The King and Queen took counsel together what they should do with this poor lady, who had the honour of being akin to them, and by the advice of the Queen it was determined that she should be sent back to her father, who was informed of the whole truth. But before she was sent they made several weighty doctors of the Church and Council hold parley with her, to the intent that since her marriage was a matter only of words, it could easily be dissolved by the agreement of both parties, this being the King's will on the matter, to preserve the honour of his house. Her reply was that in all things she was ready to obey the King save in cases of conscience, but those whom God hath joined together it is lawful for no man to put asunder. So she prayed them to tempt her no more, saying that if love and good-will, founded on the fear of God, are the true and sure bonds of marriage, she was so fast in bonds that neither fire, sword, nor water could burst them, but death alone, to whom and to no other she would give up her ring and her oath, and so entreated them to speak no more on't; for she stood so firm in her resolve that she had rather die and keep faith than live and break it. So these doctors aforesaid carried back to the King her answer; and when the King and Queen saw that there was no way to make her renounce her husband, they sent her back to her father in

such mean and pitiful sort that they who beheld her pass by
wept to see it. And though she was in fault, so grievous was the
punishment and so great her steadfastness, that this fault of hers
was commonly accounted as a virtue. And her father, being
advised of this her coming, would by no means see her, but
made bear her to a castle in a forest, the which he had aforetime
built for a reason well worthy to be told. And there he kept her
for a long while, saying that if she would renounce her husband
he would hold her for his daughter and set her free. All the same
she remained firm, and preferred to remain in the bonds both
of prison and marriage than to have all the freedom in the world
without her husband. And by the manner of her countenance
one would have judged her pains to have been most pleasant
pastimes, for she bore them for the sake of him whom she loved.

And as to men, what shall I say concerning them? Her husband, so deeply under obligation to her, fled to a country where
he had many friends, I would say Germany. And there he showed
well by the lightness of his disposition that not so much had he
paid court to Rolandine by reason of a true and perfect love, as
by reason of his covetousness and ambition. For he became
amorous of a German lady, and forgot his letters to her who
for his sake had borne so great tribulation. And whereas no ill-
fortune, however rigorous, had hindered them from writing to
one another, till this foolish and wicked love of his, so grievous
was it to Rolandine that she knew no rest. And seeing his letters
that they were cold and altogether changed from what they had
been, she suspected that some new love separated her husband
from her, and had done that which all the torments and pains of
her could not effect. But since perfect love bottoms not judgment upon suspicion, she found means to secretly send a servant
in whom she trusted, not to write or speak with her husband, but
to spy out his ways and discover the truth. And this servant, having returned from his journey, told her that of a surety he had
found him paying court to a German lady, and that the common
report was that he would endeavour to marry her, since she was
very rich. These tidings gave such sorrow to the heart of
Rolandine that she fell grievously sick, and they who knew the
reason of it told her, on behalf of her father, that after this great

wrong done her she would do right to renounce him, and strove to bring her to this opinion. But notwithstanding that she was in very great torment, yet in no way would she change her purpose, and showed in this last temptation the greatness of her love and virtue. For as love grew less on his side, so it grew more on hers, and when she knew that in her heart alone now dwelt the love that formerly was between the two, she was resolved to preserve it until the death of the one or the other. Wherefore the Divine Goodness, which is perfect charity and true love, had pity on her grief and her long-suffering, so that after a few days her husband died while courting another woman. And being well informed of this by those who had seen him laid in the ground, she sent to her father entreating him that he would come and speak to her. The father, who had never spoken to her since she was first put in bonds, went forthwith, and after having heard her just conclusions, in place of reproving her, or as he had often threatened, of killing her, he took her in his arms, and weeping, said: "My daughter, you are more in the right than I; for, if there have been any fault in this matter, it is I that am the chief cause thereof; but since God has so ordered it, I wish to make satisfaction for what has passed." And after that he had brought her to his house, he treated her as his eldest daughter, and she was asked in marriage by a prudent and virtuous gentleman who bore the arms and name of their house. And he held Rolandine, with whom he often talked, in such esteem that he gave her praise where others had but blame for her, since he knew her end and aim to have been virtue. Which marriage, being to the mind of the father, was before long concluded. It is true that a brother of hers, the sole heir of their house, would give her no portion, saying that she had disobeyed her father, and after his death entreated her in such sort that her husband, who was a younger son, and herself, had much ado to live. But God provided for them, since the brother who wished to keep all, by his sudden death, in a single day lost all, both of his and hers. So was she made heiress to a good and rich estate, in which, with her husband's love, she lived piously and honourably. And after having brought up two sons which God gave to them, she joyously rendered her soul to Him in whom she had always placed her trust.

16 (XXII)

How a wicked monk, by reason of his
abominable lust, was at last brought to shame.

In the town of Paris there lived a prior of the monastery of St. Martin in the Fields, of whose name I will make no mention for the friendship that I bore him. His life up to the age of fifty years was so austere, that the fame of his holiness was blazed abroad throughout the whole realm, in such wise that there was neither prince nor princess who did him not great honour when he came to see them. And no monastery was put into a state of reformation but that he had a hand in it; wherefore men called him the *father of true monkery*. He was made visitor of the great convent of The Ladies of Fontevrault; and was held by the nuns in such awe that, when he came among them, they all trembled for the fear they had of him. And to the end that they might soften his great severities, they entreated him all as if he had been the King, which at the first he refused; but at last, being hard upon his fifty-fifth year, he began to find the treatment he had at first despised mighty pleasant; and esteeming himself the one support of all monkery, desired to have a better care for his health than had been his custom. Wherefore such good cheer did he make him, that from a very lean monk he became an exceeding fat one; and changing his fare changed also his heart, so that he began henceforth to look upon faces with pleasure, which afore he had but done as matter of duty, and beholding the graces that the veil only made more desirable, began to covet them. So, to satisfy this covetousness, he used such means that at last from shepherd he turned wolf, and if among any of the nuns he found an innocent he failed not to deceive her. But after that he had for a long while continued in this wicked manner of living, the Divine Goodness, taking pity on the poor wandering sheep, would not longer endure the exaltation of this wretch, as you shall shortly see.

One day, as he held a visitation in a convent named Gif, hard-by Paris, it happened that while he confessed all the nuns, there came to him one called Marie Heroet, whose speech was so soft and pleasant that it gave good promise of a heart and countenance to match. So at the very hearing of her voice he conceived a passion for her which surpassed any he had for other nuns; and while he spoke he lowered his head to look at her, and saw such cherry lips that he could not restrain himself from raising her veil to see whether her eyes were to match, as indeed they were. And at this his heart was filled with a consuming fire, so that he left off to eat and drink, and the manner of his countenance was altered, though he was fain to conceal it. And when he was returned to his priory he found there no rest; wherefore his days and nights were spent in great disquietude, as he sought for means to accomplish his desire and do to her even as he had done to many others. But this he feared might be a difficult matter, inasmuch as he had found her prudent in speech, and of so keen a wit that he could have no great hopes; and on the other hand, he saw himself that he was old and ugly, and so was resolved to say nothing to her, but to strive to win her by fear. To which intent he soon afterwards went to the convent of Gif, and showed himself more austere a man than he had ever done, speaking wrathfully to all the nuns, and reproving one, that her veil was not low enough, another that she carried her head too high, and a third that she did him not reverence in the manner proper to a nun. In all these small matters so severe was he that they feared him as if he had been God sitting in assize. And he, having a defluction of rheum in the feet, grew so weary in visiting the usual places, that towards evensong-time, as was his design, he found himself in the dormitory. The abbess said to him: "Reverend Father, it is time to sing evensong." And he replied: "Go then, mother, to evensong, for I am so weary that I will remain here, not for rest, but to speak with Sister Marie, of whom I have heard a very bad report, for they tell me that she gossips like a woman of the world." The abbess, who was aunt to her mother, prayed him scold her heartily, and left her all alone with him, save for a young monk he had in his company. When he found himself alone with Sister Marie, he began by lifting her veil, and bade her look at him. She replied that her rule would not have her look at men. "'Tis well said, my daughter," said he, "but you must by no means consider us monks as men." Wherefore Sister Marie, fearing to be in fault through disobedi-

ence, looked him in the face, and found him so ugly that it
seemed to her more of a penance than a sin. The good father,
after discoursing some while on the great friendship he bore
her, would fain have put his hand on her breasts, but she, as was
her duty, repulsed him. At this enraged, he said to her: "Is it
befitting in a nun to know that she has breasts?" She replied: "I
know well that I have breasts, and that neither you nor any other
shall lay a hand upon them; for I am not so young and ignorant
as not to understand what is sin and what is not." And when he
saw that this manner of talk would not win her, he resolved to
try another, saying: "Alas! my daughter, I must declare to you
the necessity of my case—namely, that I have a sickness which
all the physicians deem incurable, unless I have pleasure of
some woman for whom I have a great love. For my part, I would
not, to save my life, do mortal sin, but when it comes to that I
am well assured that simple fornication is as nothing in comparison with self-murder. Wherefore, if you love my life, you will
both do good to your conscience and also to me." She asked him
what manner of pleasure he would have of her; to which he
answered that she could give her conscience into his keeping,
and that he would do nothing which could be imputed against
either of them. And to show her how to begin the pastime he
asked of her, he cast his arms around her and essayed to throw
her on the bed; but she, perceiving the wickedness of his intent,
so well defended herself with arms and voice that he could
touch nothing save her clothing. Then, seeing all his plans and
endeavours turned to nothing, as a madman not only wanting in
conscience but in natural reason, he drove his hand underneath
her dress, and so furiously scratched whatever he could touch
with his nails, that the poor girl, crying aloud, fell full length on
the ground in a dead swoon. At this cry the abbess came into the
dormitory, for she, while at evensong, recollected that she had
left this nun, her niece's daughter, alone with the good father; at
which her conscience taking some scruple, she left evensong
and listened at the door of the dormitory, and hearing her
niece's voice, pushed open the door that was held of the young
monk. Now when the prior saw the abbess come in, he showed
her the nun lying in a swoon, and said: "Without doubt, mother,

you did wrong in that you did not certify me of Sister Marie's complexion; for ignorant of her weakness, I when chiding her made her stand before me, and as you see she has swooned away." And while they were reviving her with vinegar and other medicaments proper to the occasion they found that her head had been hurt by the fall. And the prior, fearing lest she should tell her aunt the reason of it, spoke to her all apart, saying: "My daughter, I charge you, by your obedience and hope of salvation, that you by no means speak to any of what I have done to you, for you must understand that I was constrained by the vehemence of my love. But since I see you have no desire to love, I will speak to you no more on it, but I do assure you that, if you will consent, I will have you chosen abbess of one of the best convents in the kingdom." But her reply to him was to the intent that she would rather die in perpetual imprisonment than have any for lover save Him who died for her on the cross; affirming that with Him she had rather suffer all the evils that the world could give than be endowed with all its blessings without Him. And she would have no more talk of this kind from him, or else would tell the abbess of it; but if he kept silence so also would she. So went forth this wicked shepherd; but that he might show himself to be what he was not, and that he might again look upon her whom he loved, he returned to the abbess, and said to her: "Reverend mother, I pray you make all your nuns sing a *Salve Regina* to the honour of that virgin in whom I place my trust." And while this was being performed, the fox of a prior did nothing but weep, not for devotion but for regret that he had not gained his end. And all the nuns setting this down to his love for the Virgin Mary, esteemed him as an holy man; but Sister Marie, knowing his wickedness, prayed in her heart that he might be confounded, who held virginity in such contempt.

So went this hypocrite to St. Martin's, where the evil flame that was at the heart of him ceased not to burn day or night, nor to seek for some means of obtaining his desire. And since above all he stood in fear of the abbess, who was a virtuous woman, he sought means to send her away from her convent. Wherefore he betook himself to Madame de Vendosme, then living at La Fère, where she had built and founded a convent of the rule of

St. Benedict, calling it *The Mount of Olivet*. And the prior, as the
very prince of reformers, giving her to understand that the
abbess of the aforesaid Mount Olivet was not fit for the govern-
ing of so large a community, the good lady entreated him to find
her another whom she could meetly set over it. And he, asking
nothing better, counselled her to take the abbess of Gif as the
best that was in France, so Madame de Vendosme forthwith
sent for her, and made her abbess of the Convent of Mount
Olivet. And the prior of St. Martin's, who held the whole of
monkery in his hands, made choose abbess of Gif a woman to
his liking. This done, he went to Gif to try again a second time
if, by prayers or gentle persuading, he could gain Sister Marie
Heroet. But having no hope of success he returned in despair to
his priory of St. Martin, and there, to accomplish his ends and
to be avenged on her who had been so cruel to him, he caused
the relics that were at the aforesaid convent of Gif secretly to be
conveyed away by night, and accused the confessor of the convent, an old and good man, that he had stolen them, and for this
cause clapped him up in prison at St. Martin's. And whilst he
held him captive he stirred up two witnesses, who out of ignorance did what the prior ordered them, and they bore witness
that they had seen the said confessor and Sister Marie commit-
ting a foul and scandalous act in a garden; and this the prior was
fain to make the old man confess for truth. But he, knowing the
failings of the prior, entreated that he might be brought into
chapter, where before all the monks he would tell the truth of
the matter. The prior, fearing lest the confessor's justification
should be his condemnation, would by no means entertain this
request, and finding him not to be moved from his resolve,
entreated him so evilly in prison that some said he died there,
others that he was constrained to unfrock and quit the realm;
but howsoever this be no man saw him again.

So the prior, thinking to have Sister Marie altogether in his
hands, went to the convent, where the abbess, chosen by him to
this intent, opposed him in nothing. Thereupon he began to use
his authority as visitor, and made all the nuns, one by one, come
before him in a chamber after the manner of visitation. And
when it came to the turn of Sister Marie, who had lost her good

aunt, he said to her: "Sister Marie, you are advised of the matter of your accusation, and that for all your cloak of chastity you
are well known to be the very contrary thereto." But Sister
Marie, with a steadfast face, replied: "He that accuseth me let
him come before me, and you will discover if he persist in his
wicked position." He answered: "We have no need of further
witness, insomuch as the confessor has been found guilty." "I
esteem him too good a man," said she, "to have acknowledged
such a lie for truth; but, be it so, and let him come before me
that I may prove the contrary to his words." The prior, seeing
that in no manner could he affray her, said: "Forasmuch as I am
your spiritual father, and desirous that your honour be preserved, I put this before your conscience, and to your words I
will give belief. I therefore demand and conjure you, under pain
of mortal sin, that you tell me truly whether or no you were a
maid when you came hither?" She replied: "My age, father, that
was five years, should pass as a safe witness to my maidenhood."
"And since that time," said the prior, "have you not lost this
flower of your virginity?" She swore she had kept it safe, having
had no hindrance thereto but from him. To this he answered
that he could not believe it, and that the matter wanted proof.
"What proof," said she, "would be to your pleasure?" "The
same," said he, "as I use with others; for as I am visitor of souls,
so am I of bodies also. Your abbesses and prioresses have all
passed through my hands, wherefore fear not for your maidenhood but throw yourself upon the bed and lift your clothes over
your face." It was in wrath that Sister Marie replied to him: "You
have spoken in such wise of your wicked lust after me, that I am
persuaded you wish not to look for, but to take away my virginity; but understand that I will never consent thereto." Then he
said he would have her excommunicated, for that she had
refused him monastic obedience, and that he would shame her
in full chapter by the evil he wot of betwixt her and the confessor. But she, no whit afraid, answered: "He that knoweth the
hearts of His servants shall give me as much honour as you
before men shall give me shame. And since it has come to this,
I had rather you accomplished on me your cruelty than your
lust, for I know God, that he is a just judge." Forthwith was

gathered together all the chapter, and before them was brought
Sister Marie, kneeling on her knees, to whom the prior spoke
very dispiteously: "Sister Marie, it is to my displeasure that the
good admonitions that I have made to you are found altogether
of none effect, and that you are in such case that, contrary to my
custom, I am constrained to lay a penance on you. Now your
fault is, that your confessor, having been examined as touching
certain crimes imputed to him, confesses to have abused your
person in the place where the witnesses affirmed they had seen
him. Wherefore, since I have placed you in the honourable
estate of mistress of the novices, I ordain that not only shall you
be the last of all, but, kneeling on the ground, shall eat bread
and water before the sisters till your repentance be of a sort to
merit pardon." Sister Marie, being advertised by one of her fellows, who knew the whole matter, that if she answered in a fashion displeasing to the prior he would put her *in pace*—that is, in
perpetual imprisonment—patiently endured this sentence; raising her eyes to heaven, and praying Him, who had been her
resistance against sin, to be her patience against tribulation.
Furthermore, the prior of St. Martin's enjoined that, when her
mother or her kinsfolk might come to the convent, she should
not be suffered to speak with them, nor to write any letter to
them, save only such letters as were written in community.

So this wretched man went his way, and returned there no
more; and the poor maid was for a long time in the pitiful case
you have heard. But her mother, loving her above all her children, and seeing that she no more had any news of her, marvelled thereat, and said to one of her sons, the same being a man
of prudence and virtue, that she thought her daughter to be
dead, and that the nuns, so as still to have the yearly payment,
had concealed it from her. And she prayed him to hit upon some
means of seeing his sister, if she were yet alive, whereupon he
went forthwith to the convent, and was received with the accustomed excuse—namely, that it was now three years that his sister had not stirred from her bed. But with this he would not be
content, and swore if he did not see her that he would climb the
walls and take their convent by storm. Thereupon, in much fear,
they led his sister to the grate, but with the abbess following so

hard on her that Sister Marie could say nothing that was not fit
for her ears. But of her prudence she had put in writing all that
is set down here, with a thousand other devices of the prior for
her deception, of the which I omit relation, because of the
length of time thereto required. Yet I will not forget that, when
her aunt was abbess, thinking her refusal proceeded from his
ugliness, he had made her to be tempted by a young monk and
a handsome; hoping that, if she obeyed the monk for love, she
would do the same by him for fear. But the poor girl ran from
the garden, where the monk tempted her and used gestures so
shameful that I blush to remember, to the abbess, saying:
"Mother, they who come to visit us are no monks but rather devils!" Whereupon the prior, fearing to be discovered, said with a
laugh: "Doubtless, reverend mother, Sister Marie is in the
right." And taking Sister Marie by the hand, he said to her
before the abbess: "I had heard that Sister Marie spoke so well
and readily that she was esteemed worldly, and on this account
I constrained myself against the grain to address her after the
fashion that men of the world use with women, as I had found
it in books; for as to experience, I am as naked of it as the day I
was born. And deeming my ugliness and old age caused her to
make such virtuous answers, I charged a young monk of mine to
make love to her, whom you see she hath likewise virtuously
resisted. Wherefore, so good and prudent do I esteem her, that
I command that from henceforth she be first after you and mistress of novices, to the end that she may always increase more
and more in virtue."

This deed, and many more like to it, did the holy man, during
the three years in which he was amorous of the nun. And she, as
I have said, gave her brother through the grate the whole matter of this pitiful history. And it having been borne by him to her
mother, she in great despair came to Paris, where she found the
Queen of Navarre, only sister to the King, to whom she showed
the thing, saying to her: "Madam, put no more trust in these
hypocrites; I thought I had put my daughter hard-by Paradise,
or on the way to it, and lo! it is the road to hell, and she in the
hands of worse than devils, for the devils do but tempt us when
it is our pleasure to be tempted; and these, if love be wanting,

are fain to have us by force." At this the Queen of Navarre was
mightily distressed, for entirely had she put her trust in the prior
of St. Martin's, and had given into his hands the abbesses of
Montavilliers and Caen, her sisters-in-law. On the other hand
the greatness of the crime was an abomination to her, and filled
her with the desire of avenging the innocence of the poor girl,
in such sort that she made the matter known to the King's chancellor, the same being also legate, who summoned the prior to
appear in his court, and there was found no excuse at all in him,
save only that the number of his years was three-score and ten.
And to the Queen of Navarre he spoke, praying her, by all the
good she had ever wished to do him, and by all he had done for
her, and all he had wished to do for her, that she would be
pleased to make an end to this case, since he confessed and
declared that Sister Marie Hereoet was a very pearl of honour
and of maidenhood. The Queen of Navarre, hearing this, was so
astonished that she knew not what to reply to him, and so without a word left him there; and the poor man returned to his
monastery covered with shame, and from henceforth would see
no one, and only lived a year after. But Sister Marie Heroet,
esteemed according as she deserved for the virtues that God
had implanted in her, was removed from Gif, where she had suffered so much tribulation, and made abbess, by the King's man-
date, of Giy-juxta-Montargis. This convent she reformed, and
lived for the rest of her days as one fulfilled with the Spirit of
God, praising him always for that he had been pleased to give
back to her both honour and rest.

17 (XXIII)

How the lust of a Grey Friar made an honest
gentleman, his wife, and his child to perish miserably.

In the country of Perigord there was a gentleman who had so
great a devotion for St. Francis that he regarded all who wore
his dress as holy as the saint himself. And, to his honour, he had
appointed rooms in his house for the lodgment of the brethren,
by whose counsel he ruled all his affairs, even to the smallest,

thinking in this manner to make a safe journey through life. And one day it came to pass that his wife, who was both comely, wise, and virtuous, was brought to bed of a fine boy, the which increased much the more the love her husband had for her. And the better to make feast for her, his dear gossip, he had bidden his brother-in-law; and as the hour for supper drew nigh there came to the house a Grey Friar, whose name I will conceal for the honour of the order. At the coming of this his spiritual father, from whom he had no secrets, the gentleman was glad at heart, and, after some talk between his wife, his brother-in-law, and the monk, they set themselves at table for supper. And while they were at supper, the gentleman, looking upon his wife, in whom, indeed, there was enough beauty and grace to make her desired of her husband, began in a loud voice to question the holy father: "Father, is it of a truth a mortal sin in a man to lie with his wife after she has been in childbed?" The father, whose face and words altogether belied his heart, replied with a wrathful countenance: "Without doubt, sir, I esteem such to be one of the greatest sins that can be committed in the estate of marriage. And for what else was the ensample of the Blessed Virgin Mary, who would not enter the temple till the days of her purification were fulfilled, although she stood in no need of purification, but that you should abstain from this small delight? And this you should surely do, seeing that the good Virgin abstained from going to the temple, where was all her joy, to the end that she might obey the law. And besides this, the physicians say that the offspring of such delights stand in great jeopardy." And when the gentleman heard these words he was very sorry, since he had hoped the father would have given him leave; however, he spoke no more on it. The holy man, while he was talking, having had a cup too many, had looked at the dame, thinking within himself that if he was the husband he would not ask the leave of a spiritual father to lie with his wife. And as fire, beginning by little and little, at last sets the whole house aglow, the monk began to burn with such a flame of lust that on a sudden he determined to accomplish that desire he had carried for three years concealed in his heart.

So supper done, he took the gentleman by the hand, and,

leading him to the bed of his wife, said to him before her: "Since
I see, sir, the great love that is between you and the dame here,
which, conjoined to your youth, doth so much torment you, I
have compassion, and am minded to declare to you a secret of
our holy theology. This is, that the law, which, by reason of the
abuses and indiscretion of husbands, is thus rigorous, suffers
folk of good conscience like you to take some indulgence.
Wherefore, since before your people I uttered the law in its
severity, I will now not fail to show you, being a prudent man, its
softness also. Know, my son, that there are women and women,
just as there are men and men. In the first place, we must know
whether your dame here, it being now three weeks since she
was brought to bed, is freed from her effluxion of blood?" And
the lady replied that she was so. "Then," said the friar, "I give
you leave to lie with her, and take no scruple for it, but you must
promise me two things: firstly, that you speak to no man of it,
but come to her secretly; secondly, that you come not till two
hours after midnight, so that the dame's digestion suffer no hindrance through your play with her." All this the gentleman willingly promised, and confirmed his promise with an oath; and the
friar, knowing him to be rather a fool than a liar, was altogether
assured of him. And after some talk the holy man went to his
chamber, giving them good-night and his blessing; but before
going he took the gentleman by the hand, saying to him: "Come
you likewise, fair sir, and keep not your poor gossip any longer
awake." The gentleman kissed his wife, saying to her:
"Sweetheart, leave me the door of your room open." And this
the friar heard and understood very well, so each one went to his
chamber. But as soon as the father was in bed, he thought no
whit of sleep or rest, since, when all was quiet, about the
appointed hour for saying matins, he crept as softly as he could
to the room where the master of the house was expected, and,
finding the door open, entered in and put out the candle, and as
quickly as he could laid himself down beside her, speaking not a
word. The dame, thinking him to be her husband, said: "What?
sweetheart, you have ill kept the promise you made our confessor, not to come to me till two o'clock." The friar, more intent on
action than contemplation, and fearful lest he might be known,

thought chiefly of satisfying the wicked desire that for a long
while had corrupted his heart, and made her no reply, at which
the lady was much astonished. And when he saw the hour draw
near in which the husband was to come, he rose from beside the
dame, and returned to his room as speedily as might be.

And in like manner as the rage of concupiscence had taken
away from him all sleep, so fear, that always follows an evil deed,
would now let him take no rest, so he went to the houseporter,
and said to him: "My friend, your master has charged me to go
forthwith to our monastery, and there offer certain prayers on
his behalf; wherefore, prithee, give me my horse and open me
the door, so that no one may be advised of it, for this is a necessary occasion and a secret." The porter, knowing well that to
obey the friar was to do his master a service, secretly opened
him the door and sent him away. At that hour arose the gentleman, and seeing it was time for him to go to his wife, as the holy
father had appointed him, got up in his night-gear and went to
her, as was his right by the ordinance of God, without any leave
of man. And when she heard his voice speaking to her she marvelled greatly, and knowing not what had been done, said to
him: "Is this the promise you made to the good father to have a
care of your health and mine? And now not only did you come
to me before the appointed hour, but return again. I beseech
you think of it." The gentleman was so troubled to hear this that
he must needs say: "What means this discourse of yours? I know
of a truth that for three weeks I have not touched you, and you
reprove me for coming to you too often. If you still persist in this
you will make me think my company wearisome to you, and will
constrain me against my habit and wish to seek in other quarters
the pleasure which, by the law of God, I ought to have of you."
The lady thinking he was jesting with her, replied: "Beware lest,
thinking to deceive me, you be yourself deceived; for notwithstanding that you did not speak when you were with me the first
time, I know well enough that you were here." Then the gentleman perceived that they were both of them cozened, and he
swore a great oath that he had never come to her. At this the
dame was in such sadness, that with tears and lamentations she
besought him to make haste and discover who it could be, for in

the house there slept only her brother and the friar. Forthwith the gentleman, struck with suspicion of the friar, hastened to the chamber where he was lodged and found it empty. And to be more assured whether or no he had fled, he sent for the man who kept the gate and asked him if he knew what was become of the friar, and he told him the whole truth. The gentleman, certain of the friar's wickedness, returned to his wife's room, saying: "Of a surety, sweetheart, he who lay with you and played such pretty pranks is our good father confessor!" The dame, who had always loved her honour, was in such despair at this, that forgetting all humanity and womanly nature, she implored him on her knees to avenge her for this great wrong. Wherefore the gentleman forthwith mounted his horse and rode in pursuit of the friar.

The lady remained alone in her bed, having no counsel or consolation with her save her little child that was lately born. And falling to consideration of the dreadful thing that had come upon her, without making excuse for her ignorance, she esteemed herself as the most blameworthy and wretched of women. And then she, who had learned nothing of the friars save a confidence in good works, satisfaction for sin by austerity of life, fasts, and discipline, was altogether ignorant of the grace of God given to us through the merits of his Son, the remission of sins through his blood, the reconciliation of the Father to us by his death, the life given to sinners only by his goodness and compassion; and found herself so troubled by the enormity and weight of her sin, and the love she bore her husband and the honour of the line, that she not only turned away from the hope that every Christian ought to have in God, but even lost all commonsense. So, overcome by grief, driven by despair beyond all knowledge of her God and herself, like a woman enraged and distempered, she took a rope from the bed and with her own hands strangled herself. And still worse, being in the agony of this cruel death, her body, fighting against itself, made such a struggling that she pressed her foot upon the face of the little child, whose innocence could not save him from following in death his wretched mother. But dying, he cried so loudly that a woman who slept in the room rose in great haste and lighted a candle, and saw her mistress hanging strangled by the bed-cord, and the child choked under her feet. So in great affray she ran to the room where was lodged the brother of the lady, and led him to see this pitiful sight.

The brother, taking at this such grief as would befall a man who loved his sister with his whole heart, asked the serving-woman who had done this. She told him that she knew not, that no one had entered the room but her master, and he had but lately left it. Whereupon going to his brother's room and finding him not, he was assured that he was guilty, and taking his horse, without asking any more questions, chased after him, and met him on the road as he returned from pursuing the friar, in much grief at not having caught him. As soon as the brother saw the husband approaching, he began crying to him: "Villain and poltroon! have a care for yourself, for this day I trust to be avenged on you through God and my good sword." The gentle-man, who would have excused himself, found his brother-in-law's sword so near his body that he had enough to do to defend himself without making inquiry as to the matter in debate. And so many and such fierce blows did they give one another that they became feeble through loss of blood, and were constrained to sit down on the ground facing one another. And whilst they were taking their breath, the gentleman asked his brother-in-law: "What cause, my brother, has turned our great friendship into so fierce a fight?" To which the brother replied: "What cause has moved you to murder my sister, as good a woman as ever breathed? And so evilly, under colour of lying with her, to have strangled her with the bed-cord?" The husband hearing this, more dead than alive, went to his brother and, embracing him, said: "Is it possible that you have found your sister in the case you tell me?" And when his brother assured him that it was so, he said: "I pray you, brother, hear the cause for which I went forth from the house." And he told him all the story of the wicked Grey Friar, at which the brother was much astonished, and more grieved that for no reason he had assailed him. "I have done you wrong," he said, "forgive me." The gentleman replied: "If I had done you a wrong I have my punishment, for I am so deeply wounded that I hope not to escape death." So the

brother put him on his horse as well as might be, and led him
back to his house, where on the morrow he died, declaring and
confessing before all the kin of his brother-in-law that he himself was the cause of his own death. But his brother, to make satisfaction to justice, was counselled to go and ask for pardon of
King Francis, first of the name. Wherefore having made honourable burial for husband, wife, and child, he went on Good
Friday to Court to obtain this pardon, which he got from the
hands of Master Francis Olivier, the Chancellor of Alençon,
who afterwards, for his excellent endowments, was chosen by
the King to be Chancellor of France.

18 (xxv)

How a young Prince secretly had pleasaunce of the wife of a sergeant-at-law.

There lived in the town of Paris a sergeant-at-law, who stood in
greater esteem than any other of like estate, and being sought
out by all men, on account of the aptness of his parts, he became
the richest of all the brethren of the coif. But having had no children of his first wife, he was minded to see what he could do
with a second, and though his body was decayed, his heart and
hopes were as lively as ever. Wherefore he made choice of the
prettiest maid in the town, with a most excellent feature and
colouring, and a yet more excellent taille. Her he loved and
entreated as kindly as he was able, but nevertheless had no more
children of her than of his first wife, at the which she before
long grieved greatly. Wherefore her youth, that would not suffer
her to be weary, made her seek pastime otherwise than at home,
and she went to dances and feasts, but so openly and honourably
that her husband could not take it in bad part, for she was always
in the company of those in whom he had trust.

One day, when she was at a marriage-feast, a very great Prince
was there also, and he, in telling me the story, forbade me to make
mention of his name, but I will tell you this, that so brave and
comely an one there never was in the realm before, and I think
never will be again. So this Prince, seeing the dame that she was
young and pretty, was overcome with love, and spoke to her in

such words and so graciously that she deemed the discourse to
have been well begun. And she concealed not from him that she
had had for a long time in her heart the love for which he prayed,
and entreated him not to give himself the trouble of persuading
her to what Love at first sight had made her consent. And the
young Prince, having freely received a love well worth a long service, gave thanks to the god who was favourable to him. And from
that hour he forwarded matters so well, that they agreed together
as to the means of seeing one another, themselves unseen. At the
time and place appointed the young Prince failed not to present
himself, and, to preserve the lady's honour, he went to her in disguise. But not wishing to be known by the Roaring Boys who
coursed the town at night, he took with him some trusty companions, and at the beginning of the street where the lady lived he left
them, saying: "If you hear no noise within a quarter of an hour, get
you gone to your houses, and return again to fetch me about three
or four o'clock. This they did, and hearing nothing, returned
home. The young Prince went straight to the lawyer's house, and
found the door open, as had been promised him. But while he
was going up the stair he met the husband with a candle in his
hand, of whom he was seen before he was ware of him. But love,
which in straits of its own bringing about, finds wit and courage
also, made the Prince go up to master lawyer and say: "Master
sergeant, you are advised of the trust that I and my whole house
have always put in you, and that I hold you for one of my best and
most loyal servants. It has, therefore, come to my mind to visit you
here privily, as much to commend to you my occasion as to pray
you to give me to drink, of which I am in great need. And, prithee,
tell no one of the matter of my coming, since from here I must go
to a quarter where I am not willing to be known." The good
sergeant was mighty glad that the Prince did him so great honour
as to come thus secretly to his house, and led him to a room
whither he bade his wife set forth the best fruits and confections
she had, which she did with hearty goodwill, and after the best
sort she was able. And notwithstanding that her gear of a kerchief
and shawl made her look prettier than she was wont, the young
Prince appeared not at all to gaze at her or recognise her, but continued to talk with her husband on his occasions, which for a long

while had been in this lawyer's hands. And as the lady served the
Prince on her knees, while the sergeant was gone to a side table
for drink, she whispered him when he left the room to enter a
closet on the right hand, whither she would speedily come and
see him. When that he had drunken, the Prince thanked the
lawyer, who would have gone with him, but he assured him that
in the place whither he was going he had no need for company.
And turning to the wife, he said to her: "I would by no means take
from you your good husband, who is one of my most ancient servants. So happy are you in the having of him that you have good
cause to praise God, and to heartily obey this your husband, and
if you do not this you are worthy of all blame." With this virtuous
talk the Prince left them, and shutting the door after him so that
he might not be followed to the stair, entered into the closet. And
when her husband was asleep, my lady came there also, and led
him into a small room very bravely decked out, though, to speak
truth, there were no pictures in it as fine as he and she, in such
gear as it pleased them to put on. And there I doubt not she kept
in full all her promises.

From thence he departed at the hour he had advised his companions, whom he found in waiting at the appointed place. And
since this intercourse lasted a long time, the young Prince chose a
shorter way to go thither, the which passed through a religious
house. And such good interest did he make with the prior that
towards midnight the porter failed not to open the gate, and in like
manner did he at his return. And since the house of the lawyer was
hard-by he took no one with him. And though he led the life I tell
you, yet was this Prince in the love and fear of God; and though as
he went he would make no stay, yet on his return he never failed
to tarry a long while in prayer in the church; so that the monks,
who coming in and going out still saw him on his knees, had good
reason to think him one of the holiest men in the world.

Now it chanced that this Prince had a sister, who often went to
this monastery, and, loving her brother above the rest of mankind,
was accustomed to commend him to the prayers of all she knew to
be good men. And one day, as she was commending him affec-
tionately to the prior of the monastery, he said to her: "Alas! who
is this you commend to me? You speak to me of the one man

whose prayers I most desire, for if he is not good and holy I can
have no hope of being accounted for such. For what saith the
Scripture: 'Blessed is he who can do evil, and doeth it not.'" His
sister, who was desirous to know what proof the holy father had of
her brother's goodness, asked him so many questions that he told
her the secret after a very solemn fashion. "Is it not a thing worthy
of admiration," said he, "to behold a young Prince and a handsome
leave his pleasures and his rest to come and hear our matins? And
he comes not as a Prince, seeking the praise of men, but like a simple monk he comes all alone and hides himself in one of the side-
chapels. In truth, this piety of his so puts to shame me and my
monks that we are not worthy to be compared with him or to be
called 'religious.'" Hearing this, his sister knew not what to believe,
for though her brother were a worldly man he had great faith and
love of God, but as to his making observances of this sort she had
never suspected it of him. Wherefore she told him the good opinion the monks had of him, at which he could not restrain himself
from laughing in such wise that she, who knew him as well as her
own heart, was persuaded something was hidden under his devotion, and did not desist till he had told her the truth. And she has
made me put it here in writing, to the end that you, ladies, may
understand that neither the keenness of a lawyer nor the craft of
monks (the men most accustomed to cozen others) can in a case
of necessity hinder them from being deceived by them, whose
only experience is that they are deep in love.

19 (XXVI)

The love of an honourable and chaste woman for
a young lord, and the manner of her death.

There was in the time of King Lewis the Twelfth a young lord
named d'Avannes, son of my lord Albret, who was brother to
John, King of Navarre, with whom d'Avannes lived for the most
part. And he at the age of fifteen years was so comely and grace-
ful that he seemed made for nothing but love and admiration,
which indeed were given by all who saw him, and notably by a
lady living in the town of Pampeluna, in Navarre. And she being

married to a man of great riches lived with him after such a virtuous fashion that, though she was but twenty-three years of
age, her husband being hard on his fiftieth year, the manner of
her dress was more that of a widow than a married woman. And
no man ever saw her go to marriage or feast but that her husband went with her, for she put his goodness at so high a price,
that she preferred it to the beauty of all other men. And he on
his side, finding his wife to be thus prudent, was so assured of
her that he put into her hands all the charges of his house. So it
fell out that on a day the rich man and his wife were bidden to
a wedding among their kinsfolk, and thither also to do honour to
the marriage came my lord d'Avannes, who loved dancing as was
natural in one who therein excelled all the gallants of his time.
And after dinner, when the dances were beginning, the rich man
prayed d'Avannes to dance, who asked him whom he would that
he should lead out. He replied to him: "My lord, if there were a
prettier woman, and one more at my command than this wife of
mine, I would have you take her, but since it is not so be pleased
to dance with my wife." This the young prince did, being still so
young that he took more pleasure in the figures of the dance
than in the ladies' beauty. But his partner, on the contrary,
thought more of the grace and comeliness of d'Avannes than the
dance, but yet so prudent was she she made no appearance of
so doing. And when supper-time was come, my lord d'Avannes
bade farewell to the company and went home to his castle,
whither he had for fellow the rich man, riding upon his mule.
And as they fared upon the way the rich man said to him: "My
lord, you have this day done such honour to my kinsfolk and
myself that it would be great ingratitude in me if I did not put
myself altogether at your service. I know, my lord, that such as
you, who have severe and miserly fathers, often need more
money than do we plain folk, who by reason of our small household and good economy think of nothing but heaping up riches.
And God, having given me a wife according to my desire, has
not willed to make my paradise altogether in this world, since
He has not granted to me the joy that a father has in his children. I know, my lord, that it would not become me to adopt you
as a son, but if it were your pleasure to consider me as your ser-

vant and declare to me your small occasions, up to the sum of a
hundred thousand crowns of my substance, I will not fail to succour you in your necessities." At this offer d'Avannes was mightily pleased, for his father was all that the other had painted him,
and so thanked him, naming him his father by adoption.

From this time the rich man so loved my lord d'Avannes that
morning, noon, and night he ceased not to inquire if he needed
anything, and concealed not from his wife his devotion to the
service of the young lord, for which she did but love him all the
more, and henceforth d'Avannes had all things that he desired.
Often did he go and see the rich man, to eat and drink with him,
and when he found him not his wife gave him all he asked, and
moreover spoke to him so prudently, admonishing him to be
wise and virtuous, that he feared and loved her above all other
women. She, having the fear of God always before her eyes,
held herself content with sight and speech, wherefrom honourable and virtuous love draws its delight, and in such sort did
she that she gave him no cause to judge her love for him other
than a sisterly and Christian one. And while she kept her love
fast within her breast, d'Avannes, who by the rich man's aid went
always magnificently, came to his seventeenth year, and began
to seek out the ladies more than his custom had been. And
though he would fain have loved this prudent dame, yet the fear
he had lest he might lose her friendship, if he discoursed love-
talk with her, made him keep silence and seek his pastime in
other quarters.

So he addressed himself to a gentlewoman near Pampeluna,
who had a house in the town, and was married to a young man
whose sole delight was in horses, hounds, and hawks. And
d'Avannes began for love of her to give a thousand entertainments as tournaments, races, masks, banquets, and the rest, at all
of which he would have this young lady; but since her husband
was a man of fantastic complexion, and her father and mother,
knowing her to be both beautiful and gay, were jealous of her
honour, they all kept her so straitly that my lord d'Avannes could
get no more of her than a word snatched amid the dances. And
this, although he knew from the little talk they had had together,
that nothing was wanting to the plucking the fruit of their love

but a fit time and place. Wherefore he went to his good father
the rich man and told him that he had a great desire to go on a
pilgrimage to Our Ladye of Montserrat, and prayed him to keep
in his house all his retinue, since he was fain to go alone; and all
this was granted him. But the wife, who had within her breast
love, that great soothsayer, forthwith suspected the truth of the
journey, and could not refrain from saying to d'Avannes: "Sir, sir,
the Ladye you adore dwells within the walls of this town, so I
beseech you above all have a care for your health." He who
feared and loved her, blushed so red at this that, without speaking a word, he confessed the truth, and so set forth.

And when he had bought a pair of fine Spanish horses, he
dressed himself after the fashion of a groom, and so disguised his
face that none would have known him. The gentleman, husband
to his gay lady, seeing the two horses and d'Avannes leading them,
forthwith would buy them, and after that he had bought them,
looking at the groom who led them so well, asked him if he desired
to enter his household. My lord d'Avannes told him ay, and that he
was but a poor groom who had no craft save the care of horses, but
that he could do so well in this that his master would be mightily
pleased with him. Whereat the gentleman was very glad, and gave
him authority over all his horses; and when they were come to the
house, he told his wife he was going to his castle in the country,
and that he commended to her care the horses and the groom.
The lady, as much because she had no better pastime as to do her
husband a pleasure, went to see the horses, and looked upon the
new groom, who appeared to her somewhat well-favoured, but
she knew him not. He, perceiving that he was not known, did her
reverence in the Spanish fashion, and in kissing her hand squeezed
it so hard that she knew him; for many a time in dancing had he
played her this trick, and from that moment she thought of nothing save how she might best be able to speak with him apart. And
this she accomplished that same evening, for being bidden with
her husband to an entertainment she feigned to be sick and so
unable to go with him. He, not wishing to fail his acquaintance,
said to her: "Since you will not come, sweetheart, I pray you have
a care to my hounds and horses, so that they want nothing." This
charge his wife found mighty pleasant, but, making no sign, she

replied that since he would not employ her in greater matters, she would let him know by these smaller ones how she desired to do him pleasure. Hardly was her husband out of doors before she went down to the stable, where she found something amiss, and to take order with it she sent so many of the men one way and the other, that she remained at last alone with the head groom, and fearing lest someone should come upon them, said to him: "Begone to the garden and wait for me there in the summerhouse at the bottom of the alley." So quick was he to do her bidding that he had not leisure so much as to thank her. And when she had taken such order with the stables she went to the kennels, where she was so diligent to see that the hounds were well entreated that she appeared from mistress to have become maid; and afterwards, having returned to her room, found herself so weary that she lay down on the bed, saying she desired to rest. So all her women left her, except one whom she trusted, to whom she said: "Go to the garden and make come to me him you shall find at the bottom of the alley." The maid went and found there the groom, and led him forthwith to her mistress, who caused the wench to go outside and keep watch for her husband's coming. My lord d'Avannes, seeing himself alone with his mistress, doffed his groom's gear, took off his false nose and false beard, and not as a fearful groom but as the brave lord he was, without with your leave or by your leave, boldly got to bed with her, and was received as the prettiest man of his time should be received by the fairest and gayest lady in the land. There he stayed until the master returned, at whose coming, taking again his mask, he left the place he had won by his craftiness and guile. The gentleman, on entering his courtyard, perceived how diligent his wife had been to obey him, for which he heartily thanked her. "I do nothing but my duty, sweetheart," replied she. "True it is that if one did not keep watch over the varlets there would not be a hound that had not the mange, or a horse well fed and groomed; but now that I know their idleness and your wishes, you shall be better served than heretofore." The gentleman, who was fully persuaded he had chosen the best groom in the world, asked how he appeared to her. "I confess," answered she, "he does his duty as well as any you could find, but he needs our eyes upon him, since he is the sleepiest varlet I have ever seen."

So for some while the husband and wife lived in better agreement than they had before, he losing all his former jealousy, since in like manner as afore she had loved entertainments, dances, and assemblies, so now was she attentive to her household, contenting herself with wearing only a dressing-gown over her shift in place of taking four hours to deck herself out, as had been her custom. And for this she received praise from her husband and all men, who knew not that the stronger desire had cast out the weaker. Thus, under the cloak of hypocrisy and virtue, lived this young gentlewoman so voluptuously that reason, conscience, order, or measure found no more any place in her. But this the youth and delicate complexion of my lord d'Avannes could not bear any longer, insomuch that he grew so pale and thin that without a mask he were well disguised. Yet the mad love he bore this woman so blinded his senses that he strove to accomplish works too great for Hercules, until at last constrained by sickness, and advised to that intent by the lady, who liked him better sound than sick, he asked leave to return to his kin, which his master gave him with great regret, making him promise that when he was made whole he should come back to his service. And so d'Avannes went his way, and on foot, for he had but to journey the length of a street, and came to the house of the rich man, his father by adoption. And there he found the wife alone, whose virtuous love for him was not at all lessened by the reason of his journey. But when she saw him, that he was so thin and pale, she must needs say to him: "I know not, my lord, how it fares with your conscience, but your body hath not taken much benefit from this pilgrimage; and I strongly suspect that your travail by night hath done you more hurt than your travail by day, for if you had gone to Jerusalem on foot you would have come back more sunburnt, but not so thin and weak. Take good account of this one, and worship no more at such shrines, which, in place of raising the dead to life, bring the living almost to death. I could say more to you; but if your body has sinned it has been so shrewdly punished that I do not desire to add any new trouble." When d'Avannes heard this he was not less sorry than ashamed, and said to her: "Mistress, I have aforetime heard that repentance follows on sin, and I have well proved it to my sorrow. And I pray you to pardon my youth, that could not be punished save by making trial of the evil it would not before believe."

The dame, changing the matter of the discourse, made him lie down on a fair bed, where he stayed fifteen days, only living on restorative medicaments; and so well did the husband and wife keep him company that he always had the one or the other with him. And though he had done foolishly, even as you have heard, against the will and counsel of this prudent woman, yet this did not at all lessen the honourable love she bore him, for it was ever her hope that, after passing his youth in these evil ways he would cleanse them and love virtuously, and so should be all her own. And for the fifteen days he was in the house she talked with him to such purpose that he began to abhor the sin he had committed, and looking at this woman, whose beauty surpassed the strumpet's, and knowing more and more the graces and the virtues that were in her, he could contain himself no longer, but one day, as it grew dark, laying aside all fear, thus began: "Mistress, I know no better means of becoming as virtuous as you desire me to be than the being altogether in love with virtue: prithee tell me whether you will give me all the help and favour that lieth in you to this end?" The lady, very glad to hear him speak after this sort, answered him: "I promise you, sir, that if your love for virtue is as great as it ought to be in such a lord, I will help you in your endeavour to attain it unto the utmost of the power that God has given me." "Now, mistress," said d'Avannes, "be mindful of your promise, and understand that God, unknown of men save by faith, hath deigned to take our sinful fleshly nature upon Him, to the end that, in drawing our flesh to the love of His manhood, He might also draw our spirits to the love of His Godhead, and so has willed to use visible means, to make us love by faith the things that are invisible. In like manner, this virtue that I desire to love all my life is an invisible thing and only known by its effects, wherefore it is needful that it should take some bodily form that it may be known among men. And this it has done, clothing itself in your flesh as the most perfect it could find, wherefore I believe and confess that you are not alone virtuous but very virtue, which I, seeing it veiled beneath the most perfect body that ever was, desire to serve and honour all the days of my life, putting behind me all other vain and vicious love." The lady, who was both glad and astonished to hear him talk after this fashion, concealed her delight, and said to him: "My lord, I dare not reply to your theology, but since I am one that is slower to believe good than fear evil I beseech you cease this manner of talk; for if I believed it I should be but lightly esteemed of you. I am well assured that I am a woman, like any other, and imperfect, so that virtue would do a more wondrous thing in transforming me into it than in putting my form upon it, save only that it wished to be unknown in this world, for, under such covering as mine, it would stand in small peril of being revealed. But for all my manifold imperfections I none the less bear you as great an affection as any woman can, and love God and her honour, but this love shall not be manifested to you until your heart receive that patience required of a virtuous lover. And in that hour I shall know well what words to speak, but meanwhile think that you do not so much love your own good, yourself, and your honour, as do I." My lord d'Avannes, fearful, with tears in his eyes, strongly entreated her that, for surety to her words, she would kiss him, but this she refused, saying that for him she would not break the customs of the country. And while they were disputing as to this the husband came in, to whom said d'Avannes: "My father, so great has been the goodness of you and your wife towards me, that I beseech you always account me for your son." To this the good man willing agreed. "And for a surety of it," said d'Avannes, "grant me to kiss you." This he did. Afterwards he said: "If I were not in fear lest I should transgress the custom of the country, I would ask the same of your wife my mother." At this the husband commanded his wife to kiss him, which she did without any appearance of liking nor yet of misliking. And so the fire which words had kindled in the heart of this poor lord was increased much the more by the kiss as earnestly desired as, on her part, cruelly refused.

Then my lord d'Avannes went to the castle to see the King his brother, to whom he told very brave stories of his journey to Montserrat. And there he heard that the King was minded to go to Oly and Taffares, at which, by reason of the length of the journey, he fell into great sadness, and was resolved to try, before he set out with him, whether his lady bore him no better will than she appeared to do. To this intent he fixed his lodging in a house in the street where she lived, which house was an old wooden one, and in bad repair. And towards midnight he set it afire, the report of which was so noised abroad throughout the town that it came to the rich man, his father by adoption. And he asking from his window where was the fire, was told that it was the house of my lord d'Avannes, whereupon he went forthwith with all his household thither and found the young lord in the street clad only in his shirt. Filled with pity for him he took him in his arms, and, folding him in his robe, led my lord to his house as quickly as he was able, and said to his wife, who was in bed: "Here, sweetheart, is a prisoner for you, treat him as myself." No sooner was he gone than d'Avannes, who would have been mightily pleased to be treated as her husband, leapt lightly into the bed, hoping that the opportunity and the place would make this prudent dame change the manner of her discourse; but he found to the contrary, for as he got in at one side of the bed she got out at the other. And putting on her a loose robe, she sat at the bedside, and said to him: "Was it your thought, my lord, that opportunity could change a chaste heart? Trust me that as gold is refined in the furnace, so a chaste heart in the midst of temptation grows more steadfast and virtuous, and the more it is assailed by the heats of passion the more it is chilled. Wherefore be assured that, if my mind had been other towards you than I declared it to be, I should by no means have failed to find ways and means, of which, since I willed not to use them, I made no account. But I pray you, if you would have my affection continue towards you, put away not only the wish but the thought of ever finding me other than I am." In the midst of this parley her women came to her, whom she bade bring all kinds of sweetmeats, but for the time he knew not hunger nor thirst, in such despair was he at having failed in his undertaking, and fearing likewise that this manifestation of his desire towards her might take away all familiarity between them.

The husband, having taken order with the fire, returned and entreated d'Avannes to stay for that night in his house. And in such sort was that night passed of him, that his eyes were more employed in weeping than in sleeping, and very early in the morning he gave them farewell while they were in bed, and in kissing of the lady plainly saw that she took more pity for the sinner than anger for the sin, and thus was another coal added to the fire of his love. After dinner he set out with the King for Taffares, but before departing he went yet another time to say good-bye to his father and the lady, who, after the command of her husband, made no more difficulty in kissing him as her son. But be assured that the more her virtue hindered her eyes and face from making manifest the flame within, so much the more did it increase and become unbearable; in such wise that, not being able to endure the war in her heart between honour and love, the which she had always determined never to reveal, and having lost the consolation of seeing and speaking with him for whom she lived, she fell into a continuous fever. And the cause of this was a melancholic humour operating after such a fashion that the extremities of her body became altogether cold, whilst her inwards were in a perpetual heat. The physicians (who have not in their hands the health of men) because of an obstruction which rendered the extremities cold, began to be grievously afear'd for her, and spoke to her husband, counselling him to advertise his wife that she was in the hands of God, all as if they that were sound were not. The husband, loving his wife with a perfect love, was so sad at their words, that for consolation he wrote to d'Avannes, entreating him to come and see him, for he hoped the sick woman would be bettered by the sight of him. And as soon as he had received the letter, d'Avannes made no long tarrying, but came post haste to the house of his father by adoption, and on entering in thereto found the serving-men and serving-women sorrowing greatly, as was meet for such a mistress. At this my lord was so astonished that he stayed at the door, being as one who sees a vision, until he saw his father, who, as he embraced him, wept so sore that he was not able to speak so much as a word. And he led d'Avannes to the room where was the poor sick woman, and she, looking upon him with her languishing eyes, took him by the hand and drew him to her with all her feeble might. And as she kissed him and took him in her arms, she made marvellous lamentation, and said to him: "O,

dear my lord, the time has come to put an end to all concealment, and for me to confess what I have taken such toil to hide
from you. And it is this: if your love for me has been great,
believe me mine is no less: but my grief has been more grievous
than yours, since I have hidden my love against my heart and my
desire. For understand that God and my honour would never
have me declare it to you, since I feared to increase in you what
I was fain to diminish; but be assured that the *no* I have so often
said to you was so dolorous a word to me that it has brought
about my death. And with this I hold myself content, that God
hath given me the grace to die before the violency of my love
hath done shame to my conscience and good repute, for smaller
fires have brought higher houses to the dust. And again I am
content for that before I die I am able to declare to you my love
that it is equal to your own, save that the honour of men and the
honour of women are not like to one another. And I entreat you,
my lord, henceforth to fear not to address yourself to the most
noble and the most virtuous ladies, for in such hearts dwell the
strongest passions and the most wisely governed; and the grace,
comeliness, and virtue that are in you will not let your love be in
labour for nothing. I crave no prayers of yours to God for me,
since I know the gates of paradise are not shut to true lovers,
and since love is a fire that punishes lovers so well in this life that
they are set free from the sharp torment of purgatory. Farewell,
my lord; I commend into your hands my husband, and pray you
tell him the truth concerning me, that he may know in what
manner I have loved my God and him, and come no more
before mine eyes, since henceforth I would fain think of nothing but of gaining those promises given me by God or ever the
world was made." Thus speaking, she kissed him, and clung to
him as best she could with those feeble arms; and the lord,
whose heart was as dead with pity as hers with grief, without
power to say a single word, went from her sight to a bed that was
in the room, and there several times swooned away.

And after this the lady called her husband, and when they had
parleyed one with the other in seemly sort she commended
d'Avannes to his care, assuring him that after himself he was the
most beloved of her; and, kissing her husband, she bade him

farewell. Then was borne to her the Holy Sacrament of the
Altar, after that she had taken extreme unction, both of which
she received with the joy of one sure of salvation. And seeing
that her eyes waxed dim, and her strength abated, she said with
a loud voice: *"In manus tuas, Domine, commendo spiritum
meum."* At this cry my lord d'Avannes raised himself from the
bed, and, pitifully looking upon her, saw her give back with a
gentle sigh her glorious soul to Him from whom it had come.
And when he saw her to have passed, he ran to the dead body,
which when living he had approached with fear, and fell to kissing and throwing his arms round it in such wise that hardly
could he be drawn away, whereat the husband marvelled
greatly, for he had never thought him to have loved her in this
manner; and saying to him: "My lord, it is too much," he led him
away. Then after for a long time lamenting her together,
d'Avannes told him all the passages of their friendship, and that
till she was nigh a-mort she had never shown him any sign save
of great severity. At this the husband grieved all the more for her
he had lost, and throughout his whole life did service to my lord
d'Avannes. But he, from this time, being now only eighteen
years old, went to Court, where he lived a long while without
wishing to see or speak with any woman, for the grief he had for
his mistress; and for more than ten years he wore black.

20 (xxx)

A man takes to wife one who is his own sister and daughter.

In the time of King Lewis the Twelfth, and while a lord of the
house of Amboise, nephew to Georges the legate of France, was
legate of Avignon, there lived in the land of Languedoc a gentlewoman of better than four thousand ducats a-year, whose
name I will conceal for the love I bear her family. And she, when
the mother of an only son, became a widow very early, and, as
much for the sake of her husband as her son, determined never
to marry again. And to fly the occasion of so doing, she would
thenceforth only see devout folk, thinking that the opportunity
makes the sin, though the truth is that the sin will find an oppor-

tunity. So this young widow gave herself entirely to the service of God, fleeing all worldly assemblies, in such sort that it was only as matter of duty that she would be present at weddings, or hear the organs playing in church. And when her son was come to the age of seven years she chose a man of holy life for his schoolmaster, so that by him he might be disciplined in all piety and devotion. But when her son's years were fourteen or fifteen, Nature, who keeps a school in the heart, finding him full-fed and exceeding idle, taught him lessons somewhat different to his tutor's, so that he began to look upon and lust after the things he thought fair, and among the rest a wench who slept in his mother's chamber. But of this they had no suspicion, for they held him but as a child, and in that house was heard nothing but godly talk. The young gallant began to pester the girl in privity, and she told her mistress of it, who loved and esteemed her son so much that she thought the girl told it to make her hate him; but so strongly did she affirm the truth to the gentlewoman, that at last she said: "If I find him to be as you say, he shall by no means lack chastisement; but if this accusation of yours is no true one, have a care to yourself." And that she might by experience know the truth of the matter she commanded the wench to fix him a time and place to go to bed to her—namely, midnight, in the room of her mistress, where she slept all alone in a bed by the door. The girl obeyed this command, and when the evening drew nigh the gentlewoman lay down in the servant's bed, determined, if she spoke the truth, to take such order with her son that he would never again lie with a woman without having it in remembrance.

And while she pondered wrathfully over this, her son came to bed to her, and she, for all that she saw him come, would not believe that he had in his mind to do any shameful deed, and so delayed speaking to him till that she had for certain some sign of his evil intent. For she would not be convinced by small things that his was a criminal desire, but so great was her long-suffering, and so frail her nature, that her anger was converted into an abominable delight, and she forgot that she was his mother. And even as water that has been kept back by force rushes the more vehemently when it is let go, so was her boasting in the constraint she put on her body turned unto her shame, for when she had descended the first step to dishonour she found herself on a sudden at the bottom of the ladder. And in that night she was made great with child by him whom she would have kept from fouling others. No sooner was this sin accomplished than the tooth of conscience began to gnaw her with such remorse that her whole life was one repentance, and so sharp was it at the first that, rising from beside her son, who always thought he had had the wench, she went into her closet, and there calling to mind the goodness of her design and the wickedness of her act, passed all the night in weeping and lamentation. But in place of humbling herself and considering the frailty of our carnal nature, which without the help of God does nothing that is not sin, she endeavoured by her own tears and by her own power to make satisfaction for the past, and by her forethought to avoid all evils in the future. So she always made the occasion an excuse for her sin, and made no account of her own wickedness, for which God's grace was the sole relief, and thought so to order herself as never to sin any more after that fashion. And as if there were but one sin that could bring to pass her damnation, she put out all her strength to flee from that alone. But the pride that was rooted in her heart, which the conviction of her sin should have plucked out, increased more and more, so that in avoiding one pitfall she fell into many others. And on the morrow, very early, as soon as it was light, she sent for her son's tutor, and said to him: "My son is near that age when it is no longer fit for him to be at home. I have a kinsman, named Captain Monteson, who is with my lord the grandmaster of Chaumont across the mountains, and he will be well content to take him into his company. To which end take him thither this very hour, and so that I may not sorrow the more have a care that he come not to me to say farewell." So saying she gave him the monies necessary for the journey, and the young man set out that very morning, for, after enjoying his sweetheart, he desired nothing else than to go to the wars.

For a long while the gentlewoman continued to be very sad and melancholic, and, were it not for the fear of God, she would many a time have desired the unhappy fruit that was in her

womb to perish. She made a pretence of sickness, to the end
that she might go in a cloak, and thereby conceal that she had
sinned. And when the time drew near for her to be delivered,
she pondered within herself that there was none in the world
whom she so trusted as her bastard brother, to whom she had
given much of her substance, and she told him her ill-hap, but
named not her son as the author of it. So she prayed this brother
to give her his aid, and a few days before her time he would have
her take a change of air, saying that she would get back her
health in his house sooner than in any other place. Thither she
went, and with a mighty small following, and found there a mid-
wife come as if for her brother's wife, who knew her not, and
one night delivered her of a fine maid child, whom the gentleman gave to a nurse under the name of being his own. And
when his sister had stayed with him a month, she returned
whole to her house, and there lived in stricter sort than before,
keeping fasts and austere observances. But her son having come
to manhood, there being no longer any war in Italy, sent to his
mother entreating her to permit him to come back to his own
home. She, fearing to fall again into the same ditch, was fain not
to grant him leave, but at last so strongly did he press her that
she, having no reason to assign against his coming, gave way. Yet
she would by no means have him appear before her till that he
had taken to wife one he heartily loved, telling him to take no
thought for her substance so long as she came of gentle blood.
During this time the bastard brother, seeing the girl that was in
his charge growing up into a perfect beauty, thought fit to put
her in some house a long way off, where she should be
unknown, and, using his mother's counsel, he gave her to
Catherine Queen of Navarre. And the girl, being now twelve or
thirteen years old, was so comely and good withal, that the
Queen of Navarre had a great liking for her, and was very
desirous that she should be honourably married to one of high
estate. But, by reason of her poverty, she had many lovers, but
no husband. It fell out that one day the gentleman who was her
unknown father, having journeyed across the mountains, came
to the house of the Queen of Navarre, where, as soon as he saw
his daughter, he loved her. And since he had leave from his

mother to marry whomsoever he would, he made no inquiries concerning her, save as to whether she was of gentle blood, and being told that it was so, he asked her in marriage of the Queen, who gladly gave him her, since she knew the gentleman that he was rich and also handsome, and of a noble house.

And when the marriage was consummated, he wrote to his mother, saying that henceforth she could not deny him her house, seeing that he would bring with him as pretty a daughter-in-law for her as one would wish to see. The gentlewoman, having inquired with whom he had allied himself, found it was the very daughter of herself and him, and fell thereby into such grievous despair that she was like forthwith to have died, since the more she put hindrances in the path of her sin the further it journeyed onwards. And, knowing not what else to do, she went to the legate at Avignon, and to him confessed the greatness of her sin, and asked counsel as to the manner in which she should order herself. The legate, to satisfy her conscience, sent to several weighty doctors of the schools, to whom he opened the affair, without naming the persons. And their counsel was that the gentlewoman should never say a word of it to her children, for as to them, since they were in ignorance, they had done no sin, but as to herself all her life should be spent in penance. So the poor woman went back to her house, and soon her son and daughter-in-law arrived there. And so great was their love towards one another that never were there husband and wife who loved one another better, or were more nearly allied; for she was his daughter, his sister, and his wife; and he was her father, her brother, and her husband. And this love of theirs always continued, so that the poor gentlewoman, of her great repentance, could not see them so much as kiss without going apart to weep.

21 (XXXI)

The horrid and abominable lust and murder of a Grey Friar, by reason of which his monastery and the monks in it were burned with fire.

In one of the lands subject to the Emperor Maximilian of Austria there stood a monastery of Grey Friars, the which was in great esteem. And hard-by it was the house of a gentleman, who bore the monks such goodwill that he shared with them all his goods, so as to have a part in the benefit of their fasts and austerities. And among them there was a tall and comely friar whom this gentleman had chosen for his confessor, and such power had he to give commands in the house as had the master of it. Now this friar, seeing the gentleman's wife that she was fair, and likewise a good and prudent woman, became so amorous of her that he lost not only his appetite for food and drink, but his very reason. And one day, thinking to bring the matter to a conclusion, he went all alone to the house, and finding not the master, asked the dame whither he had gone. She told him he was gone to a place where he must needs stay three or four days, but that if he had need of him she would send an express messenger. He answered no, and began to come and go about the house, as a man who has some urgent matter in his brain, and when he was gone out of her room, she said to one of her two women, for she had no more: "Go after the good father and discover what it is he desires, for his face is the face of one who is not well pleased." The serving-maid went to the courtyard where he was, and asked if he needed anything, whereupon he answered that he did, and drawing her into a corner took a dagger he had in his sleeve and drove it through her throat. No sooner was this done than there came into the yard a serving-man on horseback, who had gone to get the rent of a farm. And when he stood on the ground the friar saluted him, and as he put his arms round him stabbed him in the back of the throat with the dagger, and shut the castle gate. The lady, seeing her maid did not return, was astonished she stayed so long with the friar, and said to the other: "Go see what hinders your fellow that she does not come." Straightway she went, and as soon as the monk saw her he took her apart and did to her as he had done to her fellow. And perceiving himself to be alone in the house he went to the dame and told her that for a long while he had lusted after her, and that the hour was come in which she needs must do his will. She, who would never have suspected him, said: "I am assured, father, that if I had so wicked an inclination you would cast the first stone on me." The monk replied: "Come hither and you shall see what I have done." And when she beheld her two women and the serving-man lying dead, she was in such affright that she stood as a statue without uttering a word. Then this evil man, who did not wish to have her only for an hour, would not take her by force, but said: "Mistress, be not afraid, you are in the hands of the man who of all the world loves you best." So saying he doffed his habit, having under it a small one, the which he gave to the dame, telling her if she would not put it on he would lay her among them she saw dead before her eyes.

She, already more dead than alive, resolved that she would feign to obey him, both to save her life and because she would gain time wherein she hoped her husband might return. And, the friar so charging her, she began as slowly as she was able to take off her headdress, and when it was done he, not regarding the beauty of her hair, hastily cut it off. Next he made her take off all her clothes save her shift, and clothed her in the small habit, putting on him again the large one he was accustomed to wear; then as soon as might be he set forth from the house, leading with him the little friar he had so long lusted after. But God, who has compassion on the innocent in tribulation, regarded the tears of this poor dame in such sort that her husband, having accomplished his affairs sooner than he thought to have done, returned to his house by the same road as went his wife. But when the friar saw him afar off he said to her: "Behold, I see your husband drawing near. I know that if you look upon him he will take you from my hands, wherefore walk on before me, and by no means turn your head towards him, for if you make but a single sign I will have my dagger in your throat before he can deliver you from me." While he said this the gentleman drew near and asked whence he came. He replied: "From your house, where I have left the dame in good case, and waiting for you."

The gentleman passed by and saw not his wife, but a servant he had with him, who was always wont to talk with the friar's companion, who was called Brother John, began calling to his mistress, thinking her to be his friend. The poor woman, who dared not turn her eyes on her husband, answered him not a word, but the servant crossing the road to see her face to face, the lady, without saying anything, made him a sign with her eyes that were full of tears. So the man followed after his master and said to him:

"Sir, I crossed the road and saw the friar's companion, who is by no means Brother John, but altogether is like to the dame your wife, and her eyes are most pitiful and full of tears." The gentleman told him he dreamed, and made no account of it, but the servant persisting, asked leave of him to go back and see if matters were as he thought, whilst his master waited for him on the road. The gentleman gave him his leave, and waited for whatsoever news he might bring him. But when the friar heard the servant behind him calling out Brother John, he suspected the lady was known, and came to meet him with a great club of iron which he carried, and gave the servant with it such a blow that he fell from his horse to the ground, and leaping upon his body the monk forthwith cut his throat. The gentleman, seeing his servant fall from afar off, thought it to be from some mischance, and ran back to succour him. And as soon as the monk saw him he smote him with his club in like manner as he had smitten the servant, and threw him to the earth, and leapt upon him. But the gentleman being strong and powerful, threw his arms round the friar in such sort that not only did he get no hurt but forced the dagger from his fist, which his wife took and gave to her husband, and with all her might held the friar by his hood. And the gentleman gave him several blows with the dagger, till at last he entreated forgiveness and confessed the evil he had done. But the gentleman having no mind to kill him, prayed his wife go to the house and fetch his people and a cart wherein to put the friar. This she did, taking off her monkish dress and running to the house with her shaven head in her shift alone. Presently came all the servants to the aid of their master, and to lead away the wolf he had taken prisoner, and finding him in the road where he had been captured they bound him and clapped him up in the house. And the gentleman, after some time, made take him to the Emperor in Flanders, where he was lawfully tried, and confessed his wickedness. And by his confession, and proof made by commissioners on the spot, it was found that a great number of women of gentle blood and comely wenches had been borne to that monastery by the same means as the monk had used with the dame, and in this he had had good success but for the grace of Our Lord, who always succours them that put their trust in Him. And the goods in the monastery that

were stolen, and the comely women that were therein, were taken
out of it, and the monks having been shut up were burned
together with it, for a perpetual memory of this evil deed. And by
this we may learn that there is nothing more dangerous than love
when it is bottomed upon vice, as in like manner there is nothing
more kindly and praiseworthy than it when it has its habitation in
a virtuous heart.

22 (XXXII)

The notable manner in which a gentleman
punished his wife whom he had taken in adultery.

King Charles, the Eighth of his name, sent into Germany a gentleman named Bernage, lord of Sivray, near Amboise, who to
make good speed spared not to journey by day or night, and so
one evening came very late to a house and asked there for lodging. At this great difficulty was made, but when the master
understood how great a king he served, he entreated him not to
take in bad part the churlishness of his servants, since, by reason
of certain kinsfolk of his wife, who were fain to do him a hurt, it
was necessary that the house should be under strict ward. Then
the aforesaid Bernage told him the reason of his embassage,
which the gentleman offered to forward with all his might, and
led him into his house, where he honourably lodged and entertained him.

It was now supper-time, and the gentleman brought him into
a large room, bravely hung with tapestry work. And as the meats
were set upon the table there came a woman from behind the
tapestry, of a most surpassing beauty, but her head was shorn
and the rest of her body was clothed in black gear of the
German fashion. After that the gentleman had washed his hands
with Bernage, water was borne to the lady, who when she had
washed her hands sat herself down at the bottom of the table,
without a word from her or to her. My lord de Bernage looked
at her very attentively, and she seemed one of the comeliest
women he ever had beheld, save that the manner of her countenance was pale and melancholic. And when she had eaten a

little she asked for drink, and this was brought her by a servant in a most marvellous vessel, I would say a death's-head with the eyes closed up with silver, and so from this she drank three or four times. And her supper having come to an end she washed her hands, and with a reverence to the lord of the house she returned behind the tapestry without a word to anyone. Bernage was so astonished to see so strange a case that he fell into a thoughtful melancholy, which being perceived of the gentleman, he said to him: "I know well that you marvel within yourself at what you have seen done at this table; and for that I judge you to be an honourable man, I will not conceal the affair from you, to the intent that you may not think there is so great cruelty in me without a weighty cause. The lady you have seen is my wife, whom I loved as man never loved before, so much indeed that to wed her I forgot all fear and brought her here by force against the will of her kinsfolk. And she in like manner gave me so many evident proofs of her love that I would have risked ten thousand lives to bring her here as I did, to the delight of the pair of us, and we lived awhile in such quietness and contentment that I esteemed myself the most fortunate gentleman in all Christendom. But while I was away on a journey made for the sake of my honour, she so far forgot her virtuousness, her conscience, and the love she had for me, that she fell in love with a young gentleman whom I had brought up in my house, and this I perceived upon my coming home. Yet I loved her so well that I was not able to distrust her till experience gave belief unto my eyes, and with them I saw what I feared more than death. Then was my love turned to madness and my trust to despair; and so well did I play the spy upon her that one day, feigning to go out, I hid myself in the room which is now her dwelling-place. And very soon after she saw me go, she went away and made the young man come to her, and him I beheld handling her in such fashion as belonged to me alone. But when I saw him get upon the bed beside her, I came forth from my hiding-place, and, taking him between her very arms, there put him to death. And since the offence of my wife seemed to me so great that death would not suffice for her punishment, I appointed one that I deem is much more bitter than death to her: namely, to shut her up in the room where she had her greatest pleasures of him she loved more than me, where I have set all the bones of her lover in an aumbry, as a precious thing and worthy of safe keeping. And to the end that in eating and drinking she may not lose the memory of him, I have made serve her at table, with the head of that villain in place of a cup, and this in my presence, so that she may see living him whom she has made through her sin a mortal enemy, and dead for love of her him whom she preferred before me. And so at dinner and supper she beholds the two things which should most make her to despair; the living enemy and the dead lover; and all through her own sin. For the rest, I treat her as myself, save that she goes shorn, for an array of hair doth not belong to a woman taken in adultery, nor the veil to an harlot. Wherefore her hair is cut, showing that she has lost the honour of virginity and purity. And if it be your pleasure to see her, I will take you there."

To this Bernage willingly agreed; and they went down the stair and found her in a fine room, sitting alone before a fire. Then the gentleman drew a curtain that was before a high aumbry, and in it were hanging all the bones of the dead man. Bernage had a great desire to speak with the lady, but for fear of the husband durst not do it. He perceiving this, said to him: "An it please you to say anything to her, you shall see how admirably she talks." Forthwith Bernage said: "Mistress, your long-suffering and your torment are alike great. I hold you for the most wretched of all woman." The lady, with tears in her eyes, graciously yet most humbly answered him: "Sir, I confess my sin to be so great that all the ills the lord of this place (for I am not worthy that I should call him husband) can bestow upon me, are as nothing compared with my sorrow that I have done him a displeasure." So saying she fell to weeping bitterly; and the gentleman took Bernage by the arm and led him away. And very early on the morrow he went on to execute the charge given him of the King. But, in bidding the gentleman farewell, he could not refrain from saying to him: "Sir, the love I bear you, and the honour and privity you have used towards me in this your house, constrains me to tell you that, in my opinion, seeing the repentance of your poor wife, you should have compassion on her.

Furthermore, you being still young have no children, and it would be a great pity that such a brave line as yours should come to an end, and they for whom, perchance, you have no great love, should be your heirs." The gentleman, who had resolved never again to speak to his wife, thought for a long while on what my lord de Bernage had said to him, and finding him to be in the right, promised that if she continued in her humble repentance he would one day have compassion on her. And so Bernage went forth on his embassage. And when he was returned to the King his master, he told him the whole matter, which the prince, having made inquiry, found to be as he had said. And among other things, Bernage having spoken of the lady's beauty, the King sent his painter, John of Paris, thither, that he might draw her to the life. This he did, and with the consent thereto of the husband, who, beholding her long repentance, and having a great desire for children, took pity on his wife, who with such humbleness had borne her punishment, and, taking her back to him, had of her many brave children.

23 (XXXIII)

The hypocrisy of a parson, who having got his sister
with child concealed it under the cloak of holiness.

When the Count Charles of Angoulême, father to King Francis, and a faithful prince and a God-fearing, was at Cognac, it was told him that in a village hard-by Cherves there lived a maid so austerely that it was matter of admiration, and yet for all that she was big with child. Of this she made no concealment, assuring all people that she had never known a man, and that she knew not how she came to be in such case, save it were the work of the Holy Ghost. And the people readily believed this thing, and among them she was accounted for a second Virgin Mary, since all knew that from her youth up she had been so good and prudent that there never had been displayed in her so much as a sign of worldly lust. Not only did she fast on the days appointed by the Church, but many other days in the week from her own devotion. Whenever there was any service at the church she would never stir from it; wherefore her life was in such repute among the common folk that men came as to a miracle to behold her, and happy was he that could touch her garment. The parson of the parish was her brother, a man in years, and very austere, loved and esteemed by his parishioners as an holy man. And he used such rigorous treatment with his aforesaid sister, that he clapped her up in a house and kept her there, and this was taken of all the people in very bad part, and so great was the noise of it that, as I have told you, it came to the ears of the Count. He, seeing the people to be blinded by some error, and desiring to enlighten them, sent a Master of Requests and an almoner, two exceeding honest men, that they might make discovery of the truth. And they went to the place and informed themselves of the matter with their utmost diligence, addressing themselves to the parson, who, so weary was he of it, prayed them to be with him when he made out the truth, and this he hoped to do on the morrow.

And early in the morning the parson sang mass, his sister being present on her knees, and to say truth mighty big. And at the end of mass, the parson took the *Corpus Domini,* and before all said to his sister: "Wretch that thou art, behold Him who suffered for thee his Death and Passion, before whom I adjure thee, tell me if thou art a maid, the which thou hast oftentimes assured me." She answered boldly that she was. "How then can this thing be, that thou art great with child and still a maid?" She answered him: "I can give no reason, save it be the grace of the Holy Ghost, who doeth in me according to his pleasure; but I cannot deny the grace of God given to me, whereby I am still a maid, and never have I wished to be married." Then her brother said to her: "I give thee the precious Body of Jesus Christ, the which thou wilt take to thy damnation if the truth is other than thou hast said. And of this they who are here present on behalf of my lord and Count are witnesses." The girl, who was nearly thirteen years of age, swore with this oath: "I take the Body of Our Lord here present to my damnation, before you, sirs, and you, my brother, if ever a man has touched me any more than you." So saying she received the Body of Our Lord. The Master of Requests and the almoner, beholding this, went away in con-

fusion, believing that under such an oath there could not be
deceit. And they made report of the matter to the Count, being
fain that he should believe even as they believed. But he who
was a wise man, after having well thought on the matter, made
them tell him the very words of the oath. Thereupon he said:
"She spoke the truth and so deceived you; for she said that never
man had touched her any more than her brother, and I am persuaded that it is her brother that has got the child, and would
fain cover his wickedness under this monstrous deceit. But we,
believing one Jesus Christ to have come, wait not for another.
Wherefore get you gone and clap the parson in gaol, and I am
assured he will confess the truth." And the thing was done even
as he had commanded, not without remonstrance from many,
for that they put that good man to open shame. But so soon as
the parson was taken he made confession of his wickedness, and
of how he had counselled his sister to talk in the manner she had
done, so as to cover the life they had led together, not only
because the excuse was an easy one, but that thereby they might
have honour of all men. And when his wickedness was laid
before him, in that he had taken the very Body of Our Lord for
her to swear upon, he replied that he had not been so bold, but
had taken an unconsecrated and unblessed wafer. The report of
this being brought to the Count of Angoulême, he commanded
that justice be done upon them after the accustomed manner.
So they waited till the girl was brought to bed, and after that she
was delivered of a boy the brother and sister were burned alive
together, whereat all the people marvelled greatly, who had seen
under the cloak of holiness so monstrous a deed, and under so
pious and praiseworthy a life a most hateful crime.

24 (XXXV)

Of a rare case of spiritual love, and a good cure for temptation.

In the town of Pampeluna there lived a fair and virtuous lady, as
chaste and devout as any in the land. So well did she love and
obey her husband that he entirely put his trust in her: at divine
service and at hearing of sermons she was always to be found,

and would persuade her husband and children to go there with
her. And on a certain Ash-Wednesday, she having come to the
age of thirty years, when ladies are content to put by the name of
fair for that of discreet, she went to church to take the ashes
which are for a memorial of death. And the preacher was a Grey
Friar, a man held by all the people as holy on account of the great
goodness and austerity of his life, which, though it had made him
to be thin and pale, yet hindered him not from being as comely
a man as one could desire to see. The lady listened to his sermon,
with eyes fixed upon his venerable person, and eyes and mind
ready to hear what he said. And the sweetness of his words
passed through her ears even unto her soul; and the comeliness
and grace of his body passed through her eyes and smote her so
at heart, that she was as one in a dream. When the sermon was
finished she was careful to look at what altar the preacher was to
say mass, and there she presented herself to take the ashes from
his hand that was as fine and white as any lady's. And to this hand
the devout woman paid more attention than to the ashes it gave
to her. So being assured that this manner of spiritual love and
certain pleasures she felt therein could do her conscience no
harm, she failed not to go every day and hear the sermon, taking
her husband; and so great praise did both of them give the
preacher that at table or elsewhere they spoke of nought else.
Then did this fire named spiritual become so carnal that it burnt
up first the heart and next the whole body of this poor lady; and
as she was slow to feel it, so swift was it to spread, and, before she
knew she was in love, she felt all love's delights. And as one altogether surprised by Love her enemy, she resisted none of his
commands; but it was sore grief to her that the physician for all
her sickness was not so much as ware of it. Wherefore, setting
aside all fear of showing her foolishness to a man of wisdom, and
her wickedness and vice to a man of virtue and goodness, she set
down as softly as she could the love she bore him in a letter, and
gave it to a little page, telling him what he had to do, and above
all enjoining him to have a care lest her husband should see him
going to the Grey Friars. The page, seeking for the shortest way,
passed through a street where was his master sitting in a shop;
whereupon the gentleman, seeing him go by, came out to dis-

cover whither he was going, and when the page saw him, much affrighted, he hid himself in a house. At this his master followed him, and taking him by the arm asked whither he went, and finding no sense or meaning in his excuses, and the face of him terrified, he threatened to beat him shrewdly if he would not say whither he was going. The poor page said to him: "Alas, sir, if I tell you the dame will kill me"; so the gentleman, suspecting that his wife was treating for some commodity in which he should have no share, assured the page that if he told the truth he should have no evil but rather all good, but if he lied he should be put in gaol for life. The little page, so as to have the good and avoid the evil, told him the whole matter, and showed him the letter his mistress had written to the preacher, which gave the husband as much astonishment as anger, since he had altogether trusted his whole life in his wife's faithfulness, and had never found in her any fault. But being a prudent man, he concealed his wrath, and entirely to discover what his wife was minded to do, he counterfeited a reply as if the preacher had written it, thanking her for her goodwill towards him, and declaring that on his side there was no less. The page, having sworn to conduct the matter discretely, carried to his mistress the counterfeited letter; and so great gladness did it give her that her husband plainly perceived the manner of her countenance to be altered, since in place of being thin, as is fitting in the Lenten Fast, she was fairer and more ruddy than in the Carnival.

And now it was Mothering Sunday, yet did she not cease to send the preacher by letters her mad ravings, nor for the matter of that during Passion and Holy Week. For it seemed to her, when he turned his eyes to that part of the church where she was, or spoke of the love of God, that love of her was at the bottom of it; and as far as her eyes could tell him her mind, she did not spare them. And to all these her letters the husband failed not to reply after the same sort, and after Easter he wrote to her in the preacher's name praying her to devise some means of speaking with him privily. She, who for this hour waxed weary, counselled her husband to go see some lands he had in the country, to which he agreed, and went and hid himself in the house of one of his acquaintance. The lady failed not to write to

the preacher that the time was come for him to see her, since
her husband was in the country; and the gentleman, willing to
sound his wife's heart to the very bottom, went to the preacher,
praying him for the love of God to lend him his habit. But the
monk, who was a good man and an honest, told him his rule forbade him, and by no means would he lend it for masquerading
in; yet the gentleman, assuring him that he would make no ill
use of it, and that it was necessary to his wellbeing, the friar, who
knew him for a good and devout man, lent it him. And putting
the habit on him, and drawing the hood over his face so that his
eyes could not be seen, the gentleman got him a false beard and
a false nose like to the friar's, and with cork in his shoes made
himself of the fitting height. In this gear he betook himself,
when evening was come, to his wife's room, where she awaited
him with much devotion. And the poor fool stayed not for him
to come to her, but, as a woman out of her wits, rushed to throw
her arms around him. He, with his face lowered, so as not to be
known, began to draw away from her, making the sign of the
cross, and saying the while only one word: "Temptation! temptation!" The lady said: "Alas, father, you are in the right, for
there is none stronger than what comes from love. But since you
have promised to be the cure, I pray you now we have time and
leisure to have compassion upon me." So saying she strove by
force to throw her arms around him, but he, flying round the
room, making great signs of the cross, cried all the while:
"Temptation! temptation!" But when he saw she pressed him
hard, he took a stout stick he had under his habit, and so
entreated her with it that her temptation was overcome, and he
not known of her. This done he forthwith gave back the habit to
the preacher, assuring him he had done him a great kindness.

And on the morrow, making a pretence of returning from
afar, he came to his house and found there his wife in bed, and,
as if he knew it not, asked what ailed her, and she replied that it
was a rheum, and, moreover, that she could not stir hand nor
foot. The husband, though exceeding desirous to laugh, feigned
to be much grieved; and, as a matter of consolation, told her he
had bidden the good preacher to sup with them that very
evening. But to this she instantly answered: "Be it far from you,

sweetheart, to ask such folk hither, for they work ill in every house they enter." "Why, sweetheart, how is this?" said the husband; "you have always mightily praised this man. I, for my part, think that if there be a holy man on this earth it is he." The lady replied: "They are good at the altar and in the pulpit, but in houses they are Anti-Christ. Prithee, sweetheart, let me not see him, for with this my sickness it would be the very death of me." The husband said: "Since you wish it not you shall not see him, but for all that he must sup with me." "Do as you will," said she, "so long as I do not see him, for I hate the monks like the devil." The husband, having given the good monk his supper, said to him as follows: "Father, I esteem you so beloved of God that He will not refuse you anything you ask Him, wherefore I entreat you have compassion on my poor wife, who these eight days hath been possessed of an evil spirit, in such sort that she endeavours to bite and scratch whomsoever she sees. Of cross or holy water she makes no account, but I firmly believe that if you put your hand on her the devil would come out; and this I pray you to do." The good father said: "My son, to a believer all things are possible. Do you steadfastly believe that the goodness of God refuses no grace to him who asks it faithfully?" "I do believe it, father," answered the gentleman. "Be then also assured, my son," said the friar, "that God is able to do what He wills, and is as all-mighty as He is good. Let us go, then, strengthened by faith, to resist this roaring lion, and snatch from him his prey, that God hath won for Himself by the blood of His dear Son, Jesus Christ." So the husband led the good man to the room where his wife lay on a small bed; and she, thinking she saw him who had beaten her, fell into great astonishment and wrath; but for that her husband was also present, lowered her eyes and was dumb. Then said the husband to the holy man: "While I am with her the devil no longer tormenteth her, but as soon as I am gone forth, do you cast holy water upon her, and you will see the evil spirit do his work." So saying he left the friar alone with his wife, but stayed by the door, so as to observe the fashion of their discourse. And when she saw herself alone with the friar, she began as one mad, to cry out at him, calling him wretch, villain, murderer, deceiver. The good father, thinking that of a very truth she was possessed of an evil spirit, would have taken her by the head to say his exorcisements over it, but she scratched and bit him in such wise that he was fain to parley with the devil from afar; and while he cast the holy water on her very plentifully, said many a devout orison. And the husband, thinking him to have done his duty, entered the room and thanked him for the pains he had taken, and as he came in his wife ceased her cursing and abuse, and for fear of her husband, kissed the cross with much meekness. But the holy friar, who had seen her before so furiously enraged, firmly believed that by his prayer to Our Lord the devil had come out of her, and went his way praising God for this mighty work. The husband, seeing his wife to have been well chastised for her brainsick folly, would not declare to her what he had done; for he was content to have conquered her desire by his wisdom, and to have taken such order with her that she mortally hated what aforetime she had loved, and so gave herself up more than before to her husband and her household.

25 (XXXVI)

How the president of Grenoble came to make his wife a salad.

There lived in the town of Grenoble a president, whose name I will not tell you; I say only that he was no Frenchman. He had a mighty pretty wife with whom he lived in great love and contentment. But she, finding her husband grow old, took for her lover a young clerk named Nicolas; and when he would go in the morning to the Justice Hall, the aforesaid Nicolas came into his room and took his place. And this was perceived by a servant of the president, the same having been in his household for thirty years, and from the loyalty he bore his master he could not refrain from advertising him of it. The president, for that he was a wise man, would not lightly believe this thing, telling the man he was desirous of putting contention between him and his wife, and that if the truth were as he said, he could easily show it to be so, but if he did not evidently prove it, he should be esteemed as one who had contrived a lying tale to put enmity betwixt him and his wife. The man assured him that he should

see it to be true with his own eyes; and one morning as soon as
the president was gone to court, and Nicolas was in the room,
this servant sent one of his fellows to tell his master to come
quickly, while he himself kept watch upon the door lest Nicolas
should sally out. And as soon as the president saw one of his servants making signs at him, feigning sickness, he left the bench
and came hastily to his house, where he found his old follower
at the door of the room, who strongly affirmed to him that
Nicolas was within, having scarce entered. And his lord said to
him: "Stir not from this door, for you know well that there is
none other incoming or outgoing to the room, save only a small
closet, and I alone have the key of it." Then he entered the room
and found his wife and Nicolas in bed together, of whom the
clerk in his shirt, throwing himself on his knees before him,
asked forgiveness, and his wife on the other hand fell to weeping. Then said the president: "Though the deed you have done
is such as you yourself can judge it to be, yet I am not willing
that on your account my house be dishonoured and the daughters I have had of you brought to shame. Wherefore I charge
you weep no more, and hear what I shall do; and do you,
Nicolas, hide yourself in my closet and make no sound." When
it was thus done he opened the door and calling his old serving-
man, said to him: "Didst thou not assure me that thou wouldst
show me Nicolas and my wife together, and on thy word I am
come hither in danger of putting this poor wife of mine to death,
and have found nothing of what thou didst tell me? I have
searched through this room as I will make plain to thee," and so
saying he made the man look under the beds and in every quarter. And when he found nothing, all astonished he said to his
master: "Needs must be that the devil has carried him away, for
I saw him come in, and though he went not out at the door, I am
persuaded he is not here." Then said his lord to him: "Thou art
a very wicked servant who wouldst fain put enmity between me
and my wife; wherefore I bid thee begone, and for all that thou
hast done for me, I pay thee what I owe thee, and more also, but
go quickly, and beware that I see thee not in the town after this
day." And the president gave him payment for five or six years
in advance, and knowing that he had been a faithful servant,

hoped to advantage him in more. But when the man had gone out weeping, the president made Nicolas come forth from the closet, and having opened his mind to him and his wife on the wickedness they had wrought together, he forbade them to let any know of it. To his wife he gave command to array herself more bravely than she had been accustomed, and to go frequently to assemblies, dances, and entertainments. And he would have Nicolas live more merrily than he had afore, but that as soon as he should whisper in his ear, *Begone!* he should beware of being found in the town three hours after. And thereupon he returned to the Justice Hall and made no sign, but for two weeks and a day, against his custom, set himself to make feast for his neighbours and acquaintance. And after the feast he would have music for the ladies to dance thereto. And on the fifteenth day, seeing that his wife danced not at all he commanded Nicolas to lead her out, which he, thinking his past sins to have been forgotten, did most joyously. But when the dance was finished, the president, making pretence of giving him some charge as to his household concernments, whispered in his ear: "Begone, and return no more!" So went Nicolas, sorry enough to lose his mistress, but yet most glad to have saved himself alive. And when the president had set firmly in the heads of his kinsfolk and his acquaintance, and all the country side, the great love he bore his wife, one fine Mayday he went into his garden and gathered herbs and made a salad therefrom. And such herbs were they that his wife did not live more than twenty-four hours after the eating of them; whereat he made such an appearance of grief that none suspected him to have been the occasion of her death; so he avenged him on his enemy and preserved the honour of his house.

26 (XXXIX)

In what manner my lord of Grignaulx exorcised an evil spirit.

A certain lord of Grignaulx, Esquire of the Body to Anne Duchess of Brittany and Queen of France, returning to his house, from which he had been absent more than two years,

found his wife at another demesne hard-by. And when he would
know the reason of this, she told him there was a ghost in their
house that tormented them so much that none could live in it.
My lord de Grignaulx, who put no belief in such fantasies, told
her that he feared it not, were it the very devil, and so brought
his wife to the house. And at nighttime he made light many can-
dles to see the ghost more clearly, and after watching a long while
to no purpose, fell asleep. But on a sudden he was wakened by a
mighty buffet on the cheek, and he heard a voice crying aloud:
Brenigue, Brenigue, and this was the name of his grandmother.
Then he called his wife who lay beside him to light a candle, the
which were all put out, but she durst not rise from the bed.
Straightway he felt the quilt pulled from off him, and heard a
great noise of tables, trestles, and stools falling all about the
room; and it ceased not all through the night. And he was more
troubled in that he had lost his rest than for fear of the ghost, for
he by no means believed it to have been such, and the next night
he determined to take Master Goblin a prisoner. So a little after
he was come to bed he made a great pretence of snoring loudly,
and put his hand open near his face. And while he waited he
knew that something was approaching him, and so snored all the
more. At this the ghost, taking heart, gave him a mighty buffet,
whereupon my lord de Grignaulx took his hand from his face and
seized it, crying to his wife: "I have the ghost." And she rose and
lighted a candle, and they found it was the maid that slept in
their room, who falling on her knees entreated forgiveness, and
promised to tell the truth. And this was that she had for a long
while loved a serving-man of the house, and so had undertaken
this brave mystery, thereby to drive from the house the master
and mistress, so that they, who would have had all the care of it,
should have means of entertaining one another, which indeed
when they were all alone they by no means failed to do. My lord
de Grignaulx, who was a somewhat surly man, commanded that
they should be beaten in such sort that they would never forget
the ghost, and this having been done, they were driven away.
And thus was the house freed from the ghostly torments that had
plagued it throughout two whole years.

27 (XL)

Wherein is given the cause wherefore Rolandine's
father made build the castle in the forest.

The father of Rolandine, who was entitled the Count of
Jossebelin, had several sisters, of whom some were married to
exceeding rich men, and the rest were nuns, save one who lived
in his house unmarried, though beyond compare she was prettier than all the others. And so well was she beloved of her
brother that he preferred before her nor wife nor children. And
she was asked in marriage by many of good estate; but her
brother, for fear of the separation, and loving too well his
money, would not listen to them. So she passed some time without being wed, living virtuously in her brother's house. Now
there lived there also a young and comely gentleman, who having been brought up by the Count from his childhood, so grew
in comely stature and virtuousness of living, that he bore a
peaceful rule over his master, in such sort that when he had any
charges for his sister, it was ever the young gentleman that gave
them. And with such familiarity did the Count use him that
evening and morning would he send him to his sister, so that by
this frequent converse together a great love was engendered
between them. But since he feared for his life if he should haply
offend his master, and she had no less fear for her honour, they
had in this love of theirs none other contentment save words
only. And the lord of Jossebelin would often say to his sister that
he wished the gentleman was richer, and of as good a house as
she, for he knew no man he would have liked better for his
brother-in-law. So many times did he say this, that the lovers,
having taken counsel together, judged that if they were to wed
he would readily pardon them. And Love, that easily believes
what it wishes, made them to suppose that nothing but good
could come of it; and so on this hope their marriage was solemnised and consummated, and none knew thereof but a priest
and certain women.

And after that they had lived for some years in the delight that
a married pair can have together, as one of the bravest in all

Christendom, and bound by the greatest and most perfect love, Fortune, that hated to see two persons so much at their ease, stirred up an enemy against them, who spying out the lady, perceived her great happiness in her husband, but yet knew not that they were married. And this man came to the lord of Jossebelin, saying that the gentleman in whom he had so great trust went too much into his sister's room, and at hours in the night when it was not meet for men to enter therein. And this the Count at the first would not believe, for the trust he had in his sister and the gentleman; but the enemy, as one who loved the honour of his house, so many times repeated it, that at last a watch was put, and so shrewd a one that the poor folk, suspecting nothing, were surprised. For one evening the lord of Jossebelin was advertised that the gentleman was in his sister's room, and presently going thither he found them, blinded by their love, in bed together. Wrath took away speech, and drawing his sword he ran at the gentleman. But he, being agile in body, fled from him in his shirt, and not able to escape by the door let himself down by a window into the garden. The poor lady threw herself on her knees before her brother, and said to him: "O sir, save my husband's life, for indeed I have wed him, and if there be any fault punish me alone, for he married me at my desire." Her brother, beside himself with wrath, only replied to her: "If he be a hundred times your husband, yet will I punish him as a wicked servant who hath deceived me." So saying he set himself at the window and cried with a loud voice to kill him, and so it was done straightway by his command and before the eyes of him and his sister. But she, beholding this piteous sight, and knowing that prayers were of no avail, spoke to her brother as a mad woman, saying: "Brother, I have nor father nor mother, and am come to an age at which I can marry according to my pleasure, and so chose one whom oftentimes you have said you were fain had been my husband. And for that I did by your counsel a thing I could by the law have done without your consent, you have made kill the man for whom you had a great liking. And since no prayers of mine could prevent his death, I entreat you by all your love towards me to make me in this hour a fellow with him in death, as I have been in all his other chances. And so you will both satisfy your cruel and unjust anger, and give rest to the body and soul of her who nor can nor will live without him." Her brother, though he was in such a rage as almost took away his reason, yet had such pity on his sister that, without granting or refusing her prayer, he left her. And after that he had well considered the deed he had done, and understood that the gentleman had married his sister, he would have been heartily glad not to have committed such a crime. But for the fear he had lest his sister should demand vengeance and justice on him, he made build for her a castle in the midst of a forest, whither he placed her, and forbade any to speak with her.

And after some time, to satisfy his conscience, he essayed to win her back to him, and made some talk about marriage; but she sent word to him that he had given her so ill a breakfast that she wished not to sup off the same meat, and that she had a good hope to live in such wise that he would have no second husband of hers to put to death, and that she hardly thought he would forgive another, since he had used so evilly the man for whom he had such a liking. And though she was weak, and had not the power to avenge herself on him, yet she trusted in Him who is the true judge and suffers no evil deed to go unpunished. And with His love alone she intended to pass the remainder of her days in her retreat. This she did, and stirred not from the place till her death, living in such patience and austerity that men came from all parts to her sepulchre as to that of a saint. And from the time she died her brother's house came to such a ruinous condition that of six sons he had not one that was left alive, for they all perished miserably; and at last the heritage passed, as you have heard in another tale, to his daughter Rolandine, who was kept in the prison that was made for her aunt.

28 (XLII)

How the virtuousness of a maid endured against all manner of temptation.

In one of the fairest towns in Touraine there lived a lord of an illustrious house who had been brought up there from his earliest youth. Of his perfections, graces, comeliness, and great virtues, I say nothing; but know that in his time he had no match. Being at the age of fifteen years, he took more pleasure in hunting than looking at the ladies; but one day while he was in church he saw a young girl, the same having been when she was a child brought up in the castle where he lived. And after the death of her mother, her father married again, wherefore she went to Poitou with her brother. And she, whose name was Frances, had a bastard sister, whom her father loved greatly, and married to the prince's chief butler, and he kept her in as good estate as any of the family. And when her father died he left Frances as her heritage the lands he had near the said town, on which account she came to live hard by her demesne. But for that she had yet to marry, and was under sixteen years, she was unwilling to live alone in her house, and so went to lodge with her sister, the butler's wife. And the young prince seeing this girl that for a light brunette she was pretty, and of a grace that passed her condition of life, for she more resembled a gentlewoman or great lady than a townswoman, looked for a long while at her, and never before having been in love, felt an unwonted pleasure in his heart. And when he was returned to his castle, he made inquiry about the girl he had seen at church, and remembered that in her youth she came to play at dolls with his sister, whom he reminded of her. And his sister sent for her and entreated her kindly, praying her to come often to the castle, which she did when there was a marriage feast or great assembly, and with such goodwill did the young prince behold her, that he knew he was deep in love. And perceiving her poor and mean estate, he hoped easily to gain his desire, but having no means of speaking with her, he sent a gentleman of the bedchamber to her to do his business for him. And she who was a good woman, fearing God, told the gentleman that she did not believe his master, so brave and good a prince, would divert himself by looking upon so poor a thing as herself, since in his castle there were fair ladies enow without seeking for them in the town, and she professed not to doubt that he had spoken of his own authority without his master's commandments. And when the young prince heard this reply, love that strives the more where it is strongly opposed, set him more hotly on this enterprise than before, so he wrote a letter praying Frances to

believe entirely what the gentleman had said to her. She, knowing well how to read and write, read his letter through, but let the
gentleman entreat her as he would, made never any reply to it,
saying that it pertained not to one of such low degree to write to
such a prince, and asked him not to think her so foolish as to
believe his master had such love for her. And she said that if he
hoped, by reason of her poor estate, to have her for his pleasure,
he deceived himself, for she had a heart no less honourable than
the greatest princess in Christendom, and esteemed all the treasures of the world as nothing compared with her honour and her
conscience, entreating him not to hinder her in the keeping of
them safe, since she would rather die than change her mind. This
answer the young prince found by no means to his taste, natheless he still loved her, and failed not to place his seat by hers at
the church where she went to hear mass, and during the service
fixed his eyes on her alone. And when she perceived this she
changed her place and went into another chapel, not to fly the
sight of him, for she had not been a reasonable creature if she
loathed to look at him, but because she feared his seeing her, and
did not esteem herself worthy of being loved honourably and for
marriage, and would not, on the other hand, be loved wantonly
for his pleasure. And when she saw that, in whatsoever part of
the church she sat herself, the prince made sing mass at an altar
hard by, she would no longer go to this church, but went always
to one as far off as she was able. And when there was feasting at
the castle, she would no more go there, though the prince's sister often sent for her, but she excused herself for that she was
sick. The prince, seeing that he was not able to speak with her,
took counsel with his butler, and assured him of great gain if he
would help him in this matter, which the butler promised willingly as much to do his master a pleasure as for the hope of a
reward. And, day by day, he told the prince what she said and
did, but that above all she fled every occasion of seeing him. So
the great desire he had of speaking with her at his ease made him
light upon another device. That was, that one day he took his
great horses, of which he began well to understand the manage-
ment, into the town square in front of his butler's house, where
lived Frances. And after making his paces and leaps where she

could easily see them, he let himself fall from his horse into the mud, and so softly that he did himself no hurt, but yet made enough complaint, and asked if there were no house where he might change his raiment. Each one offered his house, but a certain man said that the nearest and the best was his own butler's, which was forthwith chosen. He found the room bravely decked out with tapestry, and there stripped himself to his shirt, for all his clothes were fouled with the mud, and so lay down in a bed. And when he saw that all his people, save the gentleman of the bedchamber, were gone to get him fresh clothes, he called his host and hostess, and asked them where was Frances. And they had enough to do to find her, for so soon as she saw the young prince come into the house she went and hid herself in the most secret place that was in it. Natheless, her sister found her, and bade her fear not to parley with so good and virtuous a prince. "What, sister," said Frances, "do you, whom I hold as my mother, wish me to go speak with a young lord, of whose intent toward me I am, as you know, by no means ignorant?" But her sister made so many remonstrances with her, and promised so often not to leave her alone with him, that she went with her, with so pale and sad a face, that she was more fit to move compassion than concupiscence. And when the young prince saw her near his bed, he took her by her cold and trembling hand and said: "Do you think me to be so villainous a man, Frances, and so cruel a fantastic, that I eat the women I look upon? You know that in whatsoever place it was possible I have sought out to see and speak to you, and have had therein but poor success. And to do me a greater wrong you have fled the churches where I was wont to see you at mass, to the end that I might have no more delight from sight than from speech. But all that you have done hath availed you nothing, for I ceased not till I came here in the manner you saw, and have risked my neck, in tumbling of my own will off my horse, so as to have the delight of speaking to you at my ease. Wherefore, prithee, Frances, since with so great toil I have won this opportunity, let it not be for nought, but by the greatness of my love let me win yours." And when for a long while he had awaited her reply, and saw that her eyes were full of tears and fixed on the ground, he drew her as near to him as he could

and would have thrown his arms about her and kissed her; but
she said to him: "No, my lord, that which you seek for you can
never have, for though compared with you I am but a poor
worm, yet so dear do I hold my honour that I would rather die
than see it diminished for any pleasure this world can give me.
And the fear I have of them who have seen you come here, lest
they suspect the truth, has made me thus to tremble and to be
afraid. And since it has been your pleasure to do me the honour
of speaking to me, you will pardon me if I speak also to you in the
manner my honour requires of me. I am not so foolish nor so
blind, my lord, that I do not see the beauties and the graces that
God hath given you, and her who shall possess the body and the
love of such a prince I deem the happiest in the world. But what
is all this to me? for not to me nor to my estate does it pertain,
and the very desire thereof would be the utmost folly. And what
reason can I give for your addressing yourself to me, save that the
ladies of your household (whom you love, if beauty and grace be
beloved of you) are so virtuous that you dare not ask nor hope
that of them which the smallness of my condition makes you
hope to have of me? And sure am I that if from a woman like to
myself you got that you asked, it would serve as good matter of
entertainment for two hours and more with your mistress, to tell
her the conquests you achieved over one who is of the weakest.
Wherefore be pleased, since God hath not made me a princess,
to be your wife, nor of an estate to be your mistress and sweetheart, not to put me in the number of the poor unfortunates,
since I think you are and desire you may always be one of the
happiest princes in all Christendom. And if you are fain to have
women of my condition for your pastime, you will find enough in
this very town, beyond compare prettier than I, who will not give
you the trouble of so long a wooing. Be content, then, with them
that will gladly sell their honour to you, and trouble no more her
that loves you better than herself. For if God this day required
either your life or mine, I should hold myself happy to offer up
mine to save yours; since it is no want of love that makes me fly
your presence, but rather too great a love for your conscience
and mine, for I love my honour better than my life. I desire to
remain, my lord, if it please you, in your good grace, and all my

life I will pray God for your health and wealth; and true it is that
the honour you have done me will make me to be more
esteemed among my own sort of people; for what man of my own
rank would I look upon after I have talked with you? So my heart
shall be at large, save that it shall always pray God for you, and
no other service can you have of me." The young prince, hearing
this honest answer, was by no means pleased thereat, but yet was
not able to esteem her less good than she was. He did all that was
in his power to make her believe he would never love any other
woman, but so wise was she that such an unreasonable thing
could have no place in her understanding. And whilst they were
thus talking together, though it was often told him that his
clothes were come from the castle, in such delight and ease was
he that he bade answer he slept; even till it was suppertime, at
which he durst not fail his mother, who was one of the most prudent and most severe dames in the world. So the young prince
went his way, esteeming more than ever the virtue of the maid.
And he often spoke concerning her to the gentleman of his bedchamber, who, thinking gold would avail more than love, counselled him to offer the maid a good sum for doing him a kindness.
The young prince, whose treasurer was his mother, had not
much money for his privy pleasures, and so borrowed, making up
altogether five hundred crowns, and sent them to the girl, praying her to change her mind. But when she saw the gift, she said
to the gentleman: "I pray you tell my lord that I have a heart so
virtuous that if by any means I could be compelled to obey his
desires, the beauty and the grace that are in him would have ere
this made a conquest of me; but since against my honour they are
as nothing, all the gold in the world is much less. Wherefore take
it back to him, for I prefer honest poverty to all the substance in
the world." The gentleman, hearing this stiff reply, thought she
might be won by severity, and threatened her with the authority
and might of his master. But she, laughing a good deal, answered
him: "Make a dreadful thing of him to the maids that know him
not, for I am well assured that he is too good and virtuous for
such discourse to come from him, and I am persuaded he will
deny it altogether when you tell it him. But though he were the
man you say, no death nor torment could move me, for, as I have

told you, since love has not turned my heart, not all the ills nor
all the goods you can give me can stir me one step from my position." The gentleman, who had promised that he would gain her,
carried back these tidings in a wondrous rage, and would have his
master pursue her in every possible manner, telling him it would
be a blot on his honour to have failed in winning a woman of her
estate. The young prince, not willing to use any dishonourable
means, and fearing also lest the affair should be commonly
reported, and so should come to his mother's ears, who would be
very wrathful with him, durst undertake nothing, till the gentleman showed him so easy a way, that he thought to have her at
last. And to put it into execution he spoke to his butler, who,
determined to do his master any fashion of service, asked his wife
and his sister-in-law to come and see their vintages in a house he
had near the forest, to which they agreed. And when the
appointed day was come he advertised the young prince of it,
who was resolved to go all alone with the gentleman, and made
hold his mule ready for them to set out when the time should
draw near. But it was God's will that on that day his mother was
decking a most admirable cabinet, and for her help she had all
her children with her, and so the young prince diverted himself
with her till the hour was passed. But the butler had made his
wife feign sickness in such sort that when he and his sister-in-law
were on horseback, she on the crupper behind him, his wife
came to tell him she could not come. And when he saw that the
hour in which the prince should have come was gone by, he said
to his sister-in-law: "I do suppose we can return to the town."
"And what stops us?" said Frances. "Why," said the butler, "'tis
my lord, for whom I am waiting, since he promised me he would
come." When his sister heard his wickedness, she said: "Wait not
for him, brother, for I am assured he will not come to-day," so her
brother believed her and took her home. And when they got to
the house she showed her great anger, telling him he was the
devil's servant, and did more than his master bade him, for she
knew the scheme was invented by the gentleman and himself
and not by the young prince, whose money he had rather gain by
aiding him in his follies than do the duty of a good servant, but
since she knew him for such an one she would no longer tarry in

his house. Thereupon she sent for her brother to take her to his own country, and straightway left the house of her sister. The butler, having failed in his undertaking, went to the castle to hear on what account the prince had not come, and he had not gone far before he met him on his mule with the gentleman in whom he trusted. And he asked the butler: "Is she still there?" who told him all that had been done. The young prince was very sorry to have failed in this last and extreme means of gaining her, but, seeing no cure for it, sought her out in such wise that he met her in an assembly whence she could not fly from him, and spoke bitterly to her for that she had been so cruel towards him, and spoke bitterly to her for that she had been so cruel towards him, and was now leaving her brother's house. But she answered that she could live in no worse house nor one more perilous for her, and told him he was fortunate in his butler, insomuch as he served him not only with his body and his substance, but also with his soul and his conscience. And when the prince saw he could do nothing more, he determined to pester her no longer, and esteemed her greatly all his days. And a servant of the prince, seeing the goodness of the maid, was fain to have her to wife, but she would by no means consent without the leave and command of the prince, in whom she had placed all her affection, and this she made report to him. So by his goodwill the marriage was concluded, and she lived all her life in great repute, the prince doing her many a good turn.

29 (XLIII)

Of a woman who was willing to be thought virtuous, but yet had secret pleasure with a man.

In a mighty fine castle there dwelt a great princess, and one possessed of much authority, and she had a lady in her household named Jambicque, the same being very haughty. And this lady had used her mistress in such sort, that she did nothing without taking her counsel on the matter, since she held her for the most prudent and virtuous lady that she knew. And so wrath was this Jambicque against light love, that when she saw any gentleman amorous of one of her fellows, she would reprove them sharply, and give such an account of them to her mistress, that they often were publicly rebuked, wherefore in that household she had a larger share of fear than love. For herself, she spoke to no man, save haughtily and in a loud voice, and in such wise that she was reputed as a mortal enemy to all love, though her secret inclinations were altogether very amorous. For there was a gentleman in the household of her mistress for whom she had so great a desire that she could scarce bear it, but yet her love for her honour and repute made her quite to conceal her liking for him. And when she had endured this passion for a good year, not willing to ease herself, as other lovers do, with looks and words, it kindled such a flame in the heart of her, that she was fain to seek for the last cure for love-sickness, thinking she would do better to satisfy her lust and have God only for a witness, than tell it to any one who might reveal it to all.

And having resolved upon this it fell out that she was in a room that looked upon a terrace, and saw walking thereon him she loved so well, and after gazing on him so long that the day drew to an end and it became dusk, she called to her a little page, and showing him the gentleman, said: "Mark well that man yonder with the doublet of crimson satin and the cloak of lynx-fur. Go tell him that one of his acquaintance would speak with him in the garden gallery." And so soon as the page was gone, she went through the closet of her mistress and came to the gallery, having put on her low hood and her half-mask, and when the gentleman had come, she straightway shut the two doors by which they might be taken unawares. And without taking off her mask she threw her arms round him, and spoke as low as she could, saying: "For a long time, sweetheart, my love towards you hath made me desire to find time and place for seeing you, but fear for my honour has been so great that it has constrained me, against my will, to conceal for awhile my passion. But at last the strength of love has overcome fear, and by the knowledge I have of your honour, if you will promise me to love me and to speak of me to no one, nor to inquire who I am, I give you good assurance that I will be your true and faithful mistress, and will never love any other but you. But I had rather die than you should know who I am." The gentleman promised all she asked him, and this easily made her be as civil, that is, not to refuse anything he was fain to take. The hour was between five and six in the winter, so he had no sight at all of her, but touching her dress he found it was of velvet, that in those days was not worn every day, save by ladies of noble and illustrious houses. And as for her underclothing, as far as he could judge by feeling it, all was in good case, neat, and well cared for. So he took pains to give her the best entertainment he was able, and she on her side did no less. And one thing the gentleman perceived very plainly, that she was a married woman.

She would have returned forthwith to the place from whence she came, but he said to her: "I greatly esteem the kindness you have done to me who deserve it not, but still more shall I esteem that I am about to ask you. So satisfied am I with the favours I have had that I pray you conceive that I hope for a continuance thereof; but in what manner shall I obtain this, since I know not who you are?" "Trouble not yourself," said the lady, "but be assured every evening I will send word to you, but take heed that you be on the terrace where you were before. And if it is told you to be mindful of your promise, understand by that that I am waiting in the gallery, but if the talk is of going to meat, either begone or come into our mistress's room. And above all I desire you never to seek to know me, save you wish our friendship to be broken in twain." So with this the lady and gentleman parted, each on his several way. And for a long time their love passages endured, and he knew not who she was, whereat he fell into great pensiveness, musing within himself on the matter, for he surely thought there was no woman in the round world who would not fain be seen as well as loved. And he feared she was an evil spirit, having heard of some senseless preacher that no one can look the devil in the face and love him; and by reason of this fear he resolved to ascertain who it was that entreated him so kindly, and one time she sent for him he took in his hand a piece of chalk, with which, while he threw his arms round her, he made a mark on her back by the shoulder without her perceiving him. No sooner was she departed than the gentleman ran round to the chamber of his mistress and set himself at the door, to look at the shoulders of the ladies who came in. Among the rest he saw Jambicque enter the room, gazing so proudly about her, that he was afraid to look at her like the rest, being quite persuaded that she was not his mistress. But as she turned he saw on her shoulder the mark of his white chalk, whereat he was so astonished that he could scarce trust his eyes. Yet having well regarded her figure, he found it none other than the one he had touched, and in like manner with the face of her, and so of a surety he knew that she it was. And at this he took no small contentment to think that a woman who was reputed never to have had a lover, but rather had refused many an honest gentleman, should have chosen him. But love, that never continueth in one stay, would not let him live thus restfully any longer, and put in him such vain-boasting and idle hope, that he was resolved to make his love known to her, thinking that when she was discovered, her love for him should be all the more increased. And so one day, when the princess was walking in the garden, and Jambicque in an alley by herself, he seeing her alone went up to talk with her, feigning to do so for the first time. "Mistress," said he, "'tis a long while since I have carried my affection for you in my heart, fearing to make it manifest lest it should do you a displeasure; and am come thereby to such a pass that I can keep my pain a secret no longer and still live; for I truly believe man never loved you as do I." Jambicque would not suffer him finish his discourse, but broke in mighty wrathfully: "Have your seeing or hearing ever told you that I had sweetheart or lover! Marry! I think not, and I marvel you dare talk in this fashion to an honest woman like me, since this house had held you long enough for you to know that I love my husband and none other, wherefore have done or beware for yourself." The gentleman at this piece of deceit could not refrain from laughing, and said to her: "You are not always so cruel as now, and what profits it to use this concealment? Is not perfect love better than imperfect?" Jambicque replied: "I have no love for you, perfect nor imperfect, save as one of my mistress's servants; but if you cease not this manner of talk, I shall surely have such a hatred for you as will be to your mischief." But the gentleman persisted in his discourse, and said: "And where is the good cheer you make me when I cannot see you? Wherefore do you deprive me of it now when the noonday shows me your beauty and your perfect grace?" Jambicque, with a great sign of the cross, replied to him: "Either you have lost your reason, or you are the greatest of all liars, for never in my life to my knowledge have I made you better or worse cheer than I do now, so prithee tell me what is your intent." Then the poor gentleman, thinking to have the vantage over her, told the place where they had met, and the mark of chalk whereby he knew her; and at this so hot was her anger that she told him he was an evil man, and had contrived this abominable lie against her, for which she would labour to bring him to repentance. He, knowing how well she stood with her mistress, would have appeased her, but to no purpose, for furiously leaving him she went up to the princess, who left all others to talk to Jambicque, since she loved her as herself. And finding her to be so wrathful, she asked the cause of it, which Jambicque, by no means willing to conceal, told, and all the talk of the gentleman, and so little to his advantage that the princess bade him that very evening begone to his house, without speaking to any one, and to stay there till that she sent for him. And this he did in great haste, for fear lest some worse thing should befall him. And so long as Jambicque dwelt with the princess, the gentleman did not return to court, and never heard any more tidings of his mistress, who had so well kept her promise that in the hour in which he sought to find her he should lose her.

30 (XLV)

How a tapestry-maker gave a wench the Innocents, and his
pleasant device for deceiving a neighbour who saw it done.

In the town of Tours there lived a man of very subtile and keen wit, who was tapestry-maker to the late Duke of Orleans, son of King Francis the First. And though he by the hap of sickness was become deaf, yet was his understanding not diminished, for in his trade he had no match for keenness, and so in other matters, and you shall see how good a care he could have for himself. He had to wife an honest woman with whom he lived in great peace and quietness, fearing much to do her a displeasure, whilst she for her part only sought to be obedient to him in all things. But notwithstanding the great love he bore her, so charitable was he, that he would often give to neighbouring women what belonged only to his wife, and this as secretly as he was able. Now they had in their household a serving wench of a very pretty figure, of whom this tapestry-maker became amorous. Yet, fearing lest his wife might come to know of it, he often made pretence of chiding and rebuking her, saying she was the idlest wench he had ever seen, and that he marvelled not at it, since her mistress never beat her. And one day when they were talking about giving the Innocents, the tapestry-maker said to his wife: "It were mere charity to give them to that idle wench of yours, but it must not be from your hand, for it is too feeble, and your heart too pitiful; but if I made use of mine, we should perchance be better served than we are now." His poor wife, suspecting nothing, prayed him to do execution on her, confessing she had neither heart nor strength for the business; so the husband, who accepted the charge with mighty goodwill, playing the stern executioner, made buy the sharpest rods that could be found, and, to show his great desire not to spare her, put them in pickle, so that his wife had more pity for the wench than suspicion of her husband. So Innocents Day being come, master tapestry-maker rose very early in the morning, and went up on high to the room where the wench slept all alone, and there gave her the Innocents, but in a different fashion from that he had spoken of with his wife. The wench fell amain to weeping, but it availed her nothing; natheless, for fear lest his wife should come up he began striking the rods which he held in his hand against the bedstead, till he had got the bark off them and had broken them; and thus broken he carried them down to his wife, saying: "I believe, sweetheart, that your maid will have some remembrance of the Innocents." And when the master was gone from the house the poor wench came and threw herself on her knees before her mistress, and told her that he had done her the greatest wrong that a man might do a maid. But the mistress, thinking that this was on account of the beating he had given her, would not let her finish her discourse, but said: "My husband has done well, for it is more than a month I prayed him to do so; and if he pressed hard on you I am well content thereat. But whatever he did set it down to none but me, and even as it is he has not done as much as he ought to have done." The wench, seeing her mistress approve of the affair, thought it could not be the great sin she had conceived, since so good a woman had been the occasion of it, and henceforth durst say no more on the matter. But the master, seeing his wife as content to be deceived as he was to deceive, determined to give her often matter for contentment, and took such order with the wench that she wept no more at having the Innocents. For a long while he continued this manner of living, without his wife perceiving anything of it, till there was a great fall of snow; and just as he had given her the Innocents in his garden on the grass, so he wished to give her them upon the snow. And one morning, before any in the house were awake, he took her in her shift to make the sign of the crucifix upon the snow, and there they pelted one another, but did by no means forget the game of the Innocents. And this was seen by a neighbour of theirs, who had set herself at a window looking straight upon the garden, to see what weather it was; but seeing this wickedness she waxed so wrathful that she resolved to tell her good gossip, to the end that she might no longer be deceived by such a bad husband, nor served by such a wicked wench. The tapestry-maker, after these brave diversions, looked all around him to discover if any saw them, and perceived his neighbour at the window, at which he was sore troubled. But he, knowing how to colour tapestry of any device, thought he would so colour this matter that their neighbour would be as much deceived as his wife. And as soon as he had got back to bed, he made his wife rise in her shift, and took her to the garden as he had taken the wench, and played a long while with her in the snow as he had done with the other, and gave her the Innocents just as he had given them to the other; and afterwards they both went to bed together. When this good wife was going to mass, her neighbour and dear gossip did not fail to seek her out, and with great zeal but without saying any more entreated her to send away her serving-maid, for that she was a very bad and dangerous wench. But she would not do this before she knew wherefore her neighbour held her in such ill-fame, and at last she told her how she had seen the wench that morning in the garden with her husband. The good woman fell to laughing heartily, and said: "Why, dear gossip, 'twas myself." "What, gossip? She was in her shift; at five o'clock in the morning." The good woman replied: "Faith, gossip, 'twas myself." The other continued her discourse: "They pelted one another with snow, maybe on the breasts, maybe on certain still more privy parts." The good woman said: "Why, dear gossip, 'twas myself." "But gossip, I saw them afterwards doing on the snow a thing that was not pretty nor seemly." "Gossip," said the good woman, "I have told you, and I tell you again, 'twas myself and none other who did all you mention, for my good husband and myself do use to play thus privily. Prithee, then, be not scandalized thereat, for you know we are bound to do our husband's pleasure." So her neighbour went her way, more desirous of having such a husband than she had been before wishful of exposing him to her good gossip. And when the tapestry-maker returned home his wife told him the whole story. "Consider then, sweetheart," replied he, "that if you had not been an honest woman and of a good understanding, we should a long while ago have been divided the one from the other; but I hope God will keep us in this love of ours to His glory and our contentment." "Amen, sweetheart," said the good woman, "and I hope that on my side you will never find any fault."

31 (XLIX)

A pleasant case of a gentlewoman that had three lovers
at once, and made each to believe himself the only one.

In the days of King Charles—I say not which, for the sake of her of whom I am about to speak, and whose name I will not give you—there came to Court a Countess of a very illustrious house, but a foreigner. And because whatsoever is new is pleasant, this lady, at her coming, as much for the novelty of her dress as for its great richness, was looked upon by all; and though she was none of the prettiest, yet she had such a daring grace and such a weighty manner of speaking that none durst approach her save the King, who loved her exceedingly. And that he might parley with her the more privily, he gave certain charges to the Count her husband, the which kept him a long while away, and during this time the King and his wife entertained one another right merrily. So several gentlemen about the Court, knowing their master to have had good treatment at her hands, made bold to speak to her, among others one Astillon, a hardy man and of a brave address. And in the beginning she held herself gravely towards him, threatening to tell the King his master, whereby she thought to make him afraid; but he, who was not accustomed to dread the threats of great warriors, made but small account of hers, and pressed her so hard, that she granted him to parley with her alone, showing him the manner wherein he should come to her room. In this he failed her not, yet to the end that the King might have no suspicion, he prayed leave of him to go on a journey, and set out from Court, but on the first day left all his people, and returned by night to obtain the promises made to him by the Countess. She discharged them in full, and so satisfied was he thereat, that he was well pleased to stay five or six days shut up in a closet without going forth from it, and his meat there was only strengthening medicaments. But during the eight days he was clapped up in this closet there came one of his companions, whose name was Durassier, to make love to the Countess, who received him in the same manner as she did the first: in the beginning with stern and haughty discourse, that grew softer every day, and when the time came for her to set free her prisoner she put another in place of him. And while Durassier was there, another courtier named Valnebon did in like manner as his fellows had done, and after this two or three others had a share in the pleasant prison.

And this fashion of living lasted a long while, and so subtilely was it ordered, that none of them suspected his fellow, for though each knew of the other's love, yet each thought that he alone got what he asked, and mocked his fellow for that he had failed in so rare a quest. But one day, as the aforesaid gentle-

men were feasting and making merry together, they fell to talking of the chances of war, and the prisons they had been in. And
Valnebon, who had hardly been able to conceal from his fellows
his great good fortune, began to say: "I know nothing of your
prisons, but for my part I, for the love I bear one in which I
have been, will speak well of it all my days, and of others also
for the sake of it; for I esteem no delight in the world equal to
that of being a prisoner." Astillon, who had been the first prisoner, suspected what prison it was, and said to him: "Valnebon,
what gaoler or gaoleress was it that entreated you so kindly, and
whose prison-house is it that you love so well?" Valnebon
replied: "Whosoever the gaoler might be, so pleasant was my
captivity that I would it had lasted longer, for never was I better treated or more content." Durassier, a man of few words,
knowing very well that the talk was of the prison which he had
shared with the rest, said to Valnebon: "On what meats were
you fed in this prison you praise so much?" "On what meats?"
said Valnebon. "His Sacred Majesty hath not better nor more
invigorant." "But still I am fain to know," said Durassier, "if
your gaoler made you work well for your bread?" Valnebon,
suspecting he was understood, could not refrain from saying:
"Gadsfish! had I then fellows where I thought to have been
alone?" Astillon, seeing plainly how he had shared his fortune
with the rest, said with a laugh: "We have all been under one
master and in one fellowship from our youth, wherefore if we
have been fellows in good luck, we ought to rejoice thereat. But
to know if the matter be as I deem it is, I pray you give me leave
to interrogate and do you confess the truth, for if it have fallen
out as you suppose, it will be as pleasant a case as was ever written and imprinted in a book." They all swore to tell the truth, if
his questions were such as they could not deny. He said: "I will
tell you my hap, and do you answer yea or nay whether yours
was like unto it." They all agreed, and so he began: "I prayed
leave of the King to go on a journey." All made answer: "So we."
"When I was distant two leagues from Court, I left my people
and rendered myself prisoner." All made answer: "So we." "I
abode there seven or eight days, and lay in a closet, where I was
fed but on restorative medicaments, and the most opiparous

fare I have ever eaten; and at the end of the eighth day they that kept the prison enlarged me, weaker by far than when I came." "My captivity," said Astillon, "began and ended on such and such a day." "Mine," said Durassier, "began on the very day that yours came to an end, and lasted to such a day." Valnebon, losing all patience, began to swear and to say: "'Sblood! from what I hear I was the third, while I thought to have been the first and the only captive, for I went in and came out on such and such a day." The other three who were at the board swore to the due order of their several captivities. "Since this is as it is," said Astillon, "I will make interrogation as to the estate of our gaoleress: is she married and her husband in a far country?" All answered that this was she. "Well," said Astillon, "to put us quite out of our pain, I, who was the first on the roll, will be likewise the first to name her; 'tis the fair Countess, who was so haughty that when I won her love, I was as if I had overcome Cæsar. To the devil with the strumpet that made us win her with such toil, and deem ourselves happy in that we had gained her! Sure there never was the like of her; for, whilst she had one in her closet, she was fooling another, so as never to be without pastime. I had rather die than see her get off scot free. All asked as to what manner of punishment she should receive, and affirmed themselves ready to give it her, and one would have the King, who accounted her a goddess, advertised of the affair. "By no means," said Astillon; "we have power sufficient to avenge us on her, without calling in the King our master. Let us find out tomorrow when she goes to mass, and let each carry an iron chain around his neck, and when she goes into the church we will give her a befitting salutation."

This counsel was found good by all, and each one got for himself an iron chain. And when morning was come, all clothed in black, with their chains about their necks in place of collars, they went and made search for the Countess as she went to church. And so soon as she saw them thus mournfully arrayed, she fell to laughing, and said to them: "Whitherwards go ye, most dolorous folk?" "Mistress," said Astillon, "we come to accompany you as your prisoner, bound to do your service." The Countess, feigning to understand nothing of this, answered: "You are none of my prisoners, and I know not wherefore you are bound to do my service more than other men." Then Valnebon came forward and said: "Since we have so long time eaten your bread, we should be mighty ungrateful if we did not your service." She put on an appearance of not understanding aught of this, supposing that thereby she would dumbfounder them, but they pursued her with their discourse in such wise that she knew that the whole matter was discovered. And straightway did she find means to cozen them afresh, for having quite lost her honour and conscience, she, despite their endeavour, refused to be at all shamefaced; but as one who had rather pleasure than all the honour the world can give, received them none the worse nor changed her countenance towards them, and so astonished were they at this that the confusion with which they would have covered her was turned upon their own heads.

32 (LII)

How an apothecary's prentice gave two gentlemen their breakfast.

Hard-by the town of Alençon there lived a gentleman named my lord de la Tireliere, who came one morning from his house to the town on foot, as much because it was no long distance as for that it was freezing hard enough to split the stones, on which account he had not left at home his great cloak lined with fox-skin. And when he had done his business, he lit upon a lawyer named Antony Bacheré, who was of his acquaintance, and after some talk of his affairs, said to him that he was desirous of finding a good breakfast, but it must be at another's charges. And while they spoke to this effect they sat them down before an apothecary's shop, where the apprentice heard their discourse, and resolved forthwith to provide them with a breakfast. So he went out from his shop to a certain street in the town, where all men performed their occasions, and found there a mighty lump of ordure, frozen so hard that it was like to a small loaf of refined sugar; straightway he wrapped it in brave white paper, as he was accustomed to do with his drugs that they might be an admiration to men, and hid it in his sleeve. And as he passed before the gentleman and the lawyer he let this fine sugar-loaf fall near them as if by mischance, and entered into a house whither he feigned to be carrying it. My lord de la Tireliere, thinking it was a sugar-loaf, hasted to pick it up, and so soon as he had done so the knave of an apprentice returned searching and asking for his sugar on every side. The gentleman, who conceived he had admirably cozened him, went quickly with his fellow to a tavern, saying: "The charges of our breakfast are provided for by master apprentice." When he was in the inn he called for good bread, good meat, and good drink, being persuaded that he had wherewithal to pay; but when as they ate they began to grow warm, the sugar-loaf began to thaw and filled the room with its own peculiar stink. Whereat he that bore it in his bosom began to chide the serving-maid, saying: "You of this town are the beastliest folk I ever have seen, for either you or your children have strown all the floor with filth." The serving-maid answered: "By St. Peter, but there is no filth in this house, unless you have brought it in with you." On this they arose for the great stink that was in their nostrils, and stood hard-by the fire, where the gentleman, drawing a handkerchief from his breast, found it all besmeared with the melted sugar. And when he opened his great-cloak lined with fox-skin, it was altogether spoilt, and he had nought to say to his fellow but: "The rogue we thought to deceive hath paid us well for it!" And having discharged their reckoning they went out as sad as they had come in glad, thinking to have cozened the knave of an apprentice.

33 (LIII)

How a lady by too close concealment was put to shame.

Once upon a time King Francis the First was at a fine castle whither he had gone with a small following for the sake of hunting, and also to get some rest from affairs of state. In his following was one called the Prince of Belhoste, as honourable, virtuous, and prudent a man as any at Court, and married to a wife of somewhat low condition. Yet he loved her and treated her as well as any husband could treat his wife, and altogether trusted her, and when he fell into love with any other woman he concealed it not from her, knowing she thought only as he did. Now this prince conceived a great affection for a widow lady named Madame de Neufchâtel, who passed for as pretty a woman as was to be seen: and if the Prince of Belhoste loved her well, his wife did the like, often bidding her to dinner, and found her to be so discreet and virtuous, that in place of being wrathful with her husband, she rather rejoiced to see him do his suit in so good and honourable a quarter. This friendship lasted a long while, and was of such sort that in all the affairs of Madam de Neufchâtel the prince employed himself as if they had been his own; and his wife did no less. But by reason of her beauty her favour was earnestly sought by many great lords and gentlemen; some craving love alone, and others the wedding ring also, for beside her comeliness she had much riches. Among the rest there was one young gentleman called my lord des Cheriots, who pressed her so hard, that he failed not to be at her levee and couchee, and as far as was in his power he kept by her side all the whole day. Now this was not pleasing to the Prince of Belhoste, since he thought a man of his small estate and mean address did not deserve so good and kindly a reception: wherefore he often made remonstrance with the lady. But she, being a true daughter of Eve, excused herself, saying she held parley with all men, and their love would be the more concealed that she spoke to one as much as to another. But at the end of some time my lord des Cheriots pressed his suit so well that, more for his importunity than for any love she bore him, she promised marriage, praying him not to make her declare the same till that her daughters were wed. Henceforth, without fear or scruple, the gentleman went to her room at all hours as he was minded, and only a bedchamber woman and gentleman were privy to the matter. The prince, seeing the gentleman grow more and more familiar in the house of her he loved, took it in so bad part that he could not refrain from saying to the lady: "I have always prized your honour, even as that of mine own sister, and you know the honourable passages that have been between us, and the contentment I have had in the loving of a lady as discreet and virtuous as you are: but if I conceived that another, who deserves it not, had gained by his importunity that which I would not crave from you against your inclination, this would be a grievous weight for me to bear, and to you a great dishonour. I dare tell you this because you are young and comely, and hitherto have been in good repute: and now you begin to be in ill-fame, for though he be no match for you in house, nor substance, far less in authority, wit, and address, yet it would have been better for you to have married him than to have made all men suspicious. Wherefore, prithee tell me whether or no you are resolved to have him for a lover, since I will be no fellow of his, and will leave him to you altogether, and rid myself of the goodwill I have borne you." The poor lady fell to weeping, for fear lest she should lose his friendship, and swore to him she had rather die than wed the gentleman of whom he spoke; but so importunate was he that she could not keep him out of her room when all other folk entered it. "Of that," said the prince, "I do not speak, for I can come there then as well as he, and all can see what you do; but it is reported to me that he goes to you after your couchee, the which I esteem so indiscreet, that if you continue this manner of living and do not declare him for your husband, you will be esteemed the most scandalous of all women." She swore to him that she held him neither as a lover nor a husband, but the most importunate gentleman that ever was. "Since it is so, and he wearies you," said the prince, "be assured that I will rid you of him." "What!" said she, "would you then kill him?" "Not so, not so," answered the prince, "but I will make him understand that the house of His Most Sacred Majesty is not the place to bring shame upon ladies: and I swear by the love I bear you, that if after my words he will not cleanse his ways I will cleanse them for him in such wise that others shall take example by him." Thereupon he went out, and failed not at the door to light upon my lord des Cheriots, to whom he spoke after the same sort, assuring him that the first time he found him there after the accustomed hour for gentlemen to speak with ladies, he would give him such a fright as he would never forget, and that her kinsfolk were too noble for him to play with her in this fashion. The gentleman swore he had never been in the room except with others, and gave him leave, if he found him there, to entreat him as evilly as he was able. But some time after, believing the prince to have forgotten the matter, he went to see his lady in the evening and stayed with her somewhat late. And the prince told his wife that Madam de Neufchâtel had a grievous rheum, wherefore she prayed him to go see her for the two, and to make her excuses for not going, since she was kept to her room by a necessary occasion. So the prince waited until after the King's couchee, and then went to see the lady; but, as he began to mount the stair, a servant came down, who when he asked how his mistress did, replied that she was a-bed and asleep. The prince went down the stair thinking that he lied to him, wherefore he looked behind him and saw the servant returning at great speed whither he came. The prince then sauntered in the courtyard by the door to see if the servant would come back or no, and a quarter of an hour after he saw him coming down the stair again, and looking all around to see who was in the courtyard. From this he suspected that my lord des Cheriots was in the room with the lady, and durst not come down for fear of him, which made him persist to walk about the courtyard. But he called to mind that in the lady's room there was a window, not over high and looking on a garden, and thinking of the saw: *He who is not able to pass through the door may leap through the window,* instantly beckoned to a servant he had with him and said: "Go into the garden behind the house, and if you see a gentleman come down from a window, as soon as he shall put foot to earth, draw your sword and clash it against the wall, and cry aloud: "*Slay, slay!* But beware you touch him not at all." So the servant did as his master had bidden him, and the prince walked in the courtyard till it was about three hours after midnight. But when my lord des Cheriots heard that the prince was still in the courtyard, he determined to get away by the window, and after having first thrown out his cloak, with the aid of his good friends he leapt into the garden. And so soon as the servant saw him he failed not to clash his sword, and cried aloud: "*Slay, slay!*" at which the poor gentleman, taking him for his master, was so grievously afeared that, without a thought of his cloak, he fled away as speedily as he could. And he lit upon the bowmen of the watch, who were mightily astonished to see him thus running, but he durst not tell them anything, and only prayed them to open him the gate, or to lodge him with them till the morrow: and this they did, for as to the gate they had not the keys of it. In that hour the prince came to bed, and finding his wife asleep he awoke her, saying: "Guess what hour it is." She replied: "Since I went to bed I have not heard one stroke of the clock." He said: "It is three hours past midnight." "Where then," said his wife, "have you been? I fear greatly your health will suffer for it." "Sweetheart," answered the prince, "waking will never hurt me, when thereby I keep them that would deceive me from sleeping." So saying he fell to laughing heartily, and his wife asked him the cause wherefore he did it, which he told her, and showed her the wolfskin cloak that his servant had brought. And after they had made merry at the expense of the poor couple they fell into a pleasant sleep, while the two others passed the night in fear and trembling lest their passages should be revealed to all. But the gentleman, knowing he could not hide the matter from the prince, came on the morrow to his levee, entreating him not to make it manifest, and to give him back his cloak. The prince made pretence of his being ignorant of the whole affair, and kept so well his countenance that the gentleman was altogether at a loss. But at last he talked to him after another fashion than he had looked for, telling him that if he went again to the lady's room he would tell the King, and make him to be banished from the Court.

34 (LV)

How a widow sold a horse for a ducat and a cat for ninety and nine.

In the town of Sarragossa there lived a rich merchant, who seeing his death draw nigh, and that he could no longer keep what perchance he had gathered together by evil means, thought that if he made God a small present, it would be in some sort a satisfaction for his sins; as if God would sell his grace for money. And when he had set his house in order, he said that he devised his fine Spanish horse to be sold at the highest price that could be got, and the money given to the poor; praying his

wife not to fail, so soon as he was dead, to sell the horse and dis-
tribute the money according to his desire. And when the burial
of him was at an end, and the first tears had fallen, the wife,
who was no more of a fool than other women of Spain, went to
a servant who had likewise heard his master's pleasure, and said
to him: "It seems to me that the loss of the husband I loved so
well is enough for me to bear, without also losing his substance.
Yet I would in nowise disobey his will, but rather do it after a
more perfect manner, for the poor man, misled of the covetous
priests, thought to do God a great service by giving, after his
death, these monies, of which in his life he would not have
given a single ducat in a case of extreme necessity, as you well
know. Wherefore I am of opinion that we do what he charged
us at his death, and after a better fashion than he would have
done himself had he lived five days longer; but not a single soul
must be privy to the matter." And when she had the servant's
promise to keep it secret she said to him: "You shall go sell the
horse, and to them that ask how much, you shall answer a
ducat; but I have a mighty serviceable cat which I am minded
to put into the market, and you must sell it together with the
horse for ninety-nine ducats, and so the cat and the horse will
bring the hundred ducats that my husband would have taken
for the horse alone." The servant forthwith did as he was commanded of his mistress, and as he led the horse through the
market place, holding the cat under his arm, a gentleman who
had afore seen the horse and desired to have it, asked the price
thereof. The servant replied a ducat. The gentleman said:
"Prithee do not mock me." "I do assure you," said the man, "it
will cost you but a single ducat. It is true you must buy the cat
along with it, of which the price is ninety-nine ducats."
Straightway the gentleman, thinking it was a reasonable bar-
gain, paid him one ducat for the horse, and ninety and nine for
the cat, as it was asked of him, and bore away his commodities.
The servant, on the other hand, took the money to his mistress,
which she received right merrily, and failed not to give the one
ducat that was the price of the horse to the poor beggars, as her
husband had enjoined, and kept the ninety and nine for herself
and her children.

35 (LVI)

Of a cozening device of an old friar.

It was told to a French lady in Padua that in the bishop's prison there was a friar, and seeing that all men made a jest of him, she asked the reason of it. And she was told that this friar, an old man, was confessor to an honourable and devout lady who for some time had been a widow, and had one only daughter whom she loved so much that her care was but to heap up riches for her and to find her a good match. And perceiving her daughter to be growing of age, she incessantly troubled herself to find her a husband who could live with them in peace and quietness; that is to say, she would have a man with a good and honest conscience. And since she had heard a foolish preacher declare that it is better to do wrong by the counsel of the doctors of the Church than do right by the inspiration of the Holy Ghost, she addressed herself to her confessor, a man then stricken in years, a doctor in theology, esteemed of good life by all the town, assuring herself that with his counsel and prayers she would not fail to gain peace and quietness for herself and her daughter. And on her earnestly entreating him to choose a husband for her daughter, and such a man as he knew would be befitting for a maid that loved God and her conscience, he replied that first of all he must implore the grace of the Holy Ghost with prayer and fasting, and then, God confirming his understanding, he would hope to find what she wanted. So the friar went apart to ponder the matter, and hearing from the lady that she had got together five hundred ducats to give her daughter's husband, and would feed, lodge, and clothe the pair, he bethought him that there was a young friar of his acquaintance, of a good figure and pleasant countenance, to whom he would give the maid, the house, and an assured maintenance, and keep the five hundred ducats as an easement for his unspeakable covetousness. And having spoken to the young friar he agreed with him, and returned to the lady, saying: "I steadfastly believe that God hath sent me his angel Raphael, as he did to Tobit, to find a perfect husband for your daughter, for I do assure you I have in my house the bravest gentleman in all Italy, who, having several times seen your daughter, is mightily pleased with her, and this very day, while I prayed, God sent him to me, and he declared the desire he had for this marriage; and I, knowing his house and lineage, and that he comes of a very notable stock, promised him to speak with you on the matter. It is true that one thing, and one only, is not as it should be with him; that is, that, wishing to save a friend whom another would have killed, he drew his sword for to part them; but it fell out that his friend killed the other, and so he, though he struck no blow, is fled from his town, since he was present to the murder and drew his sword. And, by the counsel of his kinsfolk, he has hidden himself in this town in the habit of a scholar, and remains here unknown till his friends have brought the matter to a conclusion, which he hopes will be no long time. Wherefore the marriage must be done secretly, and you must be content for him to go during the day to the public lecture, and sup and lie here every night." To this the good woman answered: "I deem your words, father, to be spoken greatly to my advantage, for at the least I shall have by me that I desire most of all things." Then the friar brought in his fellow, clad in a crimson satin doublet, and altogether very brave, so that as soon as he was come the betrothal was performed, and on the last stroke of midnight mass was sung and they were married. Then they went to lie together, but at the dawn of day the bridegroom said to his wife that he must begone to the college if he would remain unknown, and, taking his doublet and his long robe, together with his coif of black silk, he bade farewell to his wife, who was still in bed, and promised to take his supper with her every evening, but she must not look for him at dinner. So he went his way and left his wife, she esteeming herself the most fortunate of women, in that she had met with such a good match. But the young married friar returned to the old father confessor, and gave him the five hundred ducats according to their agreement, and in the evening supped with her who took him for her husband, and in such wise did he obtain her love and that of her mother-in-law that they would not have changed him for the greatest prince in the world.

This manner of living endured for some time, but since God has compassion on them that are deceived through no fault of

their own, he put it into the hearts of the mother and daughter
to go to hear mass at the Grey Friars' Church of St. Francis,
where likewise they would see their good confessor who had
provided the one with so dutiful a son-in-law, and the other with
so brave a husband. And it chanced that, not being able to find
the confessor, or any other of their acquaintance, they were
pleased to wait his coming, and in the meanwhile to hear high
mass, which was then beginning. And as the daughter gazed
with attentive eyes on the holy mysteries being performed at the
altar, when the priest turned him to the people to say the
Dominus vobiscum, she was struck with a great astonishment,
for it seemed to her that the priest was either her husband or
the express image of him. But she said not a word, and waited
till he should turn a second time, looking upon him more carefully, and doubted not that he was the man. Wherefore she
touched her mother, who was in a devout contemplation of the
mysteries, and said to her: "Alas! alas! mother, who is that I see?"
Her mother asked her who it was. "'Tis my husband that is now
singing mass, or the one man in the world who is altogether like
to him." Her mother, who had not carefully looked upon him,
said: "I entreat you, daughter, let no such imaginations enter
your brain, for 'tis a thing plainly impossible that these holy men
should devise such a cozening device, and you will sin grievously
against God if you put faith in this fantasy." Natheless the
mother did not omit to look upon him, and when he turned him
at the *Ite missa est* she clearly perceived that never were twin
brothers more like to one another than this priest to her son-in-
law. Yet so simple was she that she would fain have said: "Save
me, O God, from believing mine own eyes!" But since it
touched her daughter she would not leave the matter thus in
darkness, and resolved to know the truth of it. And when the
time was come in the evening for the husband to return, the
mother said to her daughter: "Now, if you are willing, we can
know the truth concerning your husband, for as soon as he is
bedded I will come in, and do you snatch off his coif from
behind so that he perceive you not, and we shall see if he has a
tonsure like him who sang mass." As it was resolved, so it was
done, for when that evil husband was in bed the old dame came

in, and while she took him by the hands, as if in jest, her daughter snatched off his coif and left him with his fine tonsure, whereat the two women were mightily astounded. But forthwith they called the servants that were in the house, and made them take him and keep him fast in bonds till the morning, and no excuse or talking at all availed him. And on the morrow the lady sent for her confessor, feigning to have some great secret for his ear, so he came in great haste, and she made take him like the young friar, reproaching him with the deceit he had used toward her. And after this they were haled before the judges, and these, if they were honest folk, would by no means let them escape unpunished.

36 (LX)

How a man, for putting too great trust in his wife, fell into much misery.

In the town of Paris there lived so good-natured a man, that he would have thought it a sin to believe one was lying with his wife, though he had seen it with his eyes. And he was married to a very wicked woman, whose wickedness he never perceived, but treated her as if she was as good as any in the world. But one day, when King Lewis the Twelfth was in Paris, his wife left him for one of the songmen of the aforesaid prince; and when the King went away and she could see her lover no more she determined to forsake her husband and follow him. To this the songman agreed, and took her to a house he had at Blois, where they lived a long while together. The poor husband, finding his wife to have wandered away, sought for her on every side, and at last it was told him that she was with the songman; and willing to recover his lost sheep, that he had so badly guarded, he wrote her many letters, praying her to return, and saying he would take her back again if she would from henceforth live virtuously. But his wife, who had such delight in the singing of her songman that she had forgotten her husband's voice, made no account of all his kindness, but mocked him; wherefore he grew angry and let her know that he would get her by the laws ecclesiastical, since in no other way she would return to him. And she, fearing lest if the law should deliver her into his hands, she and her songman would fare badly, devised a plot well worthy of her. And, dissembling sickness, she sent to certain honourable women of the town asking them to visit her, and this they did gladly, hoping through sickness to draw her from her wicked life, and to this intent each one did make unto her most seemly remonstrances. Then she, feigning to be grievously sick, wept and bewailed her sins in such sort that all present had compassion on her, steadfastly believing that she spoke from the bottom of her heart. And seeing her thus redeemed and repentant, they set them to console her, saying that God was not so terrible as the preachers for the most part declared, and that he would never refuse his pity. Thereupon they sent for a good and discreet man to hear her confession; and on the morrow came the parson to administer the Holy Sacrament, the which she received so devoutly that all the honourable women of the town who were present wept to see her, praising God that of His goodness He had pity on this poor soul. Afterwards, feigning she could eat no more, the parson gave her extreme unction, which she received with pious signs, since scarcely now could she speak; for such was her pretence. So she remained a long time, seeming little by little to lose sight, and hearing, and all the other senses, whereat all present fell to crying aloud *Jesus!* And since night was near at hand, and the ladies lived afar off, they all left her, and while they were going from the house it was told them she was gone, and saying a *De Profundis* for her, they returned each one to her own house. The parson inquired of the songman where he would that she should be buried, who answered that she had charged him to bury her in the cemetery, whither it would be good to carry her at night. So the poor wretch was made ready for burial by a servant that took care to do her no hurt, and then with brave torches she was borne to the grave the songman had made. But when the corpse passed before the houses of those women who had been present at the giving of extreme unction, they all came out and followed her to the grave, and soon both priest and women left her with the songman, who, so soon as he saw the company at some little distance, together with the servant took out of the grave his sweetheart more alive than ever, and brought her privily to his house, where he kept her a long while in hiding.

Her husband, who pursued after her, came to Blois and craved justice, and there he found that she was dead and buried in the estimation of all the ladies of the town, who told him the manner of her end. At this the honest man was very glad; that her soul was in paradise, and he was quit of her wicked body. In this contentment he went back to Paris, where he took to wife a young and pretty woman of good repute and a notable house-wife, of whom he had several children; and they lived together for fourteen years and upwards; but at last Fame, that can keep nothing hid, advertised him his wife was not dead, but alive and with the wicked songman. And the poor man concealed this so long as he was able, dissembling that he knew of it, and desiring to believe it was a lie. But the affair was told to his wife, a dis-creet woman, and she was so anguished thereat, that she was like to die of grief; and had it been possible for her, with a safe conscience, to hide this mischance, she would willingly have done it, but it was not so, for the bishop's court presently took order with them, and in the first place put them asunder till the whole truth should be known. So was this poor man constrained to eschew the good and ensue the evil, and came to Blois, a little after the coronation of King Francis the First. And there he found Queen Claude and the Regent, before whom he made his plaint, asking her that he would have fain not received; but needs must he take her, wherefore he was mightily pitied of all the company. And when his wife was brought before him, for a long time she stiffly maintained she was not his wife, the which he would have gladly believed if he could. She, more sad than sorry or ashamed, told him she had rather die than return to him, and this was good news for her poor husband. But the ladies, before whom she made her wicked pleadings, con-demned her to return, and used such threats with the songman, that he was forced to tell his mistress, and indeed she was an ugly woman enough, to go back to her husband, since he would have no more commerce with her. So, since she was obliged, the poor wretch returned to her husband, and was more kindly entreated of him than she had deserved.

37 (LXI)

Of the shamelessness and impudency of a certain woman
who forsook her husband's house to live with a canon.

Hard-by the town of Autun there dwelt a lady, tall, fair, and of as
goodly a feature as I have ever seen. And she was wed to an honest gentleman somewhat younger than herself, who loved and
entreated her so well that she had good reason to be satisfied
with him. Some space of time after they were married he
brought her with him to Autun where he had some business, and
while he pleaded in the court his wife went to church to pray to
God for him. And she resorted so much to this holy place that a
rich canon grew amorous on her, and paid his suit to such purpose that the poor wretch submitted to him, of which her husband had no suspicion, taking more thought for his substance
than for his wife. But when she must needs depart thence and
return to her home, seven long leagues from Autun, she grieved
sore, though the canon promised he would often come and see
her. This he did, feigning to go on a journey, and the road always
led past the gentlemen's house, and he, not being altogether foolish, perceived his intent, and took such order that when the
canon came there he found the wife no more, for the husband
made her to bestow herself so secretly that there could be no
parley between them. She, not ignorant of her husband's jealousy, gave no sign that it was displeasing to her, natheless she
resolved to effect something, for to lose the sight of her divinity
seemed to her as hell. So one day, on the which her husband was
away from the house, she so dealt with the servants that she was
left alone; and forthwith taking what was needful, and with no
fellow save her brainsick rapture, she fared forth on foot to
Autun. There she arrived not too late to be recognised of her
canon, who kept her privily in his house for better than a year, for
all the excommunications and citations procured by her husband; and he, having no other remedy, made complaint to the
bishop, who had as good an archdeacon as there ever was in
France. And such diligent search did he make for her through all
the canon's houses that he found her that was lost and clapped
her into prison, condemning the canon to a sharp penance. The

husband, being advised that by means of the good archdeacon and several other honest folk she was recovered, was content to take her back on her oath that from henceforth she would live virtuously, which the good man easily believed, for he loved her greatly. And being received again into his house, she was entreated as honourably as afore, save that her husband gave her two ancient bedchamber women, one of whom was always with her. But however kindly he might use her, the wicked love she had for the canon made her deem all rest as torment; and though she was a mighty pretty woman, and he a strong burly man, of a sanguine complexion, yet they had no children, for her heart was ever seven long leagues from her body. Yet this she dissembled so well that her husband conceived that all that was past was forgotten of her as it was forgiven of him. But when she saw that her husband loved her as greatly as ever, and had no suspicions, she craftily feigned to fall sick, and so persisted in her cozenage that he was exceeding afraid, sparing nothing to succour her. Natheless she played her part so well, that he and all his house thought that she was sick unto death, and growing by slow degrees weaker and weaker; and she, seeing him to be as sorry as he should have been glad, prayed him to give her authority to make her will, and this he willingly did, weeping the while. And having power to devise, though she had no children, she gave to her husband all that she was able, asking his pardon for her offences against him; then the parson being come she confessed and received the holy Sacrament of the altar with such devotion that all wept to see so glorious an end. And when it was evening she prayed her husband to send for extreme unction, since she grew so feeble that she scarce hoped to take it alive; so he sent with all haste for the parson, and she, by her great humility in the reception of it, made all present to praise her. So, having discharged these holy mysteries, she said to her husband, that God having given her grace to receive all the rites of Holy Church, she was so quieted in her mind that she would fain rest awhile, and prayed her husband to do the like, and indeed with all his weeping and watchings he stood in sore need thereof. And when her husband and all his people with him were gone out, the two old women who had guarded her so long in health, not fearing now to lose her, save by death, went to sleep at their ease. And so soon as she heard them snoring, she arose in her shift and went out of the room, listening whether any one in the house was stirring; and having her loins girded and her staff in her hand, she sallied forth by a little garden gate that was not shut, and while it was night, in her shift alone and with bare feet, she made her pilgrimage to the saint at Autun, who could raise her from death to life. But since it was a long journey she could not accomplish the whole space of it before the day began to dawn. Then looking all along the road she saw two horsemen riding furiously, and, thinking it was her husband who sought her out, she hid her body in a marshy place, with her head amidst the rushes, and as her husband chased by he said to his servant, in a manner of despair: "Alas! the wicked woman! Who would have thought that, under the holy sacraments of the church, she would have concealed so foul and abominable a deceit!" The servant replied: "Since Judas, who received the same bread as she, feared not to bewray his master, do not esteem it a strange thing for a woman to do the like." Then her husband passed on; and his wife tarried amidst the rushes, more glad to have deceived him than when she esteemed herself as a slave in her good bed at home. The poor husband made search through all the town of Autun, but he perceived that of a certainty she was not entered therein, wherefore he went back making great complaint of her and his loss, and threatening her with nothing less than death if he found her. But of this she had no fear in her mind, no more than she had of the cold in her body, though the place and the season should have sufficed to make her repent of this her damnable pilgrimage. And if we knew not how the fire of hell burns up them that are filled with it, we should justly find it a marvellous thing that this wretched woman, coming out of a warm bed, was able to stay a whole day in the bitter cold. Yet she lost not heart for the journey, but so soon as it was night fared forth again upon her way; and when they were about to shut the gates of Autun this pilgrim arrived there, and went straight to the shrine of her saint, who scarcely was able to believe that it was she, so astonished was he at the sight of her. But when he had made careful examination of her he found that she had flesh and bones, which a spirit hath

not, and so assuring himself that she was no phantom, from
henceforth they were in such good accord that they lived
together fourteen or fifteen years. And though for some time she
abode with him privily, at last she lost all fear, and worse than
this, gloried to have such a sweetheart, so that she set herself in
church higher than most of the honest women in the town, the
wives of officers and other folk. And by the canon she had children, notably a daughter who was married to a rich merchant,
and after so magnificent a sort that all the women in the town
murmured at it, but had not authority to take any order in the
matter. Now it came to pass that at this time Queen Claude, wife
of Francis the First, passed through Autun, having in her following the Regent, mother to the King, and also her daughter the
Duchess of Alençon. And the Queen had a servant, named
Perrette, who came to the aforesaid Duchess, and said to her:
"Mistress, hear me, I entreat you, for so you will do better than
to go to the service at the church." The Duchess willingly gave
ear to her, knowing she would not say aught that was not good,
so Perrette forthwith told her how she had taken to her a little
girl to help in the washing of the Queen's linen; and on asking her
the news of the town, she spoke as touching the grief of the honest women to see the canon's strumpet thus going before them,
and made some relation of the woman's life. And the Duchess
went presently to the Queen and the Regent, and recounted to
them this history, and they, without any form of law, cited this
poor wretch before them, who by no means hid herself away. For
her former shame was changed into boasting that she kept the
house of so rich a man, and no whit afraid or shamefaced, she
came into the presence of the aforesaid ladies, who marvelled at
this impudency, so that at first they knew not what to say. But
afterwards the Regent remonstrated with her in such sort as
should have made a woman of any understanding weep. But she
did none of this, and with unspeakable audacity answered them:
"I pray you, ladies, touch not mine honour, for, praised be God,
I have lived with the canon so honestly and virtuously that no living soul can cast anything in my teeth. And let no one think that
I do anything against the will of God, since for these three years
past he hath not known me, and we dwell together as chastely

and lovingly as two little angels, and never a thought nor a word betwixt us to the contrary. And whosoever shall sunder us will commit a great sin, insomuch as the good man, who is hard on his eightieth year, cannot live without me, who am but forty-five." You can conceive what fashion of discourse the ladies used with her, and the remonstrances which they made; but for all that her heart was not softened by their words, nor by her own years, nor for the company she was in. And to humiliate her the more they sent for the good archdeacon of Autun, who condemned her to a year's imprisonment on bread and water. Then the ladies sent for her husband, who, by reason of their exhortations, was content to take her back, after that she had performed her penances. But being a prisoner, and advised that the canon was resolved to be altogether quit of her, she thanked the ladies for that they had thrown the devil from her back, and repented her so heartily, that her husband, in place of waiting for a year, came and asked her of the archdeacon in a fortnight, and they lived in perfect peace and contentment ever after.

38 (LXVI)

A lord and lady sleeping together were mistaken by an old dame for a
prothonotary and a servant maid, and were sharply reproved of her.

During the year in which my lord of Vendôme espoused the Princess of Navarre, the King and Queen their father and mother having been feasted at Vendôme, went into Guienne with them. And tarrying in the house of a gentleman, in the which were many fair maids, they danced for so long a time in this good company, that the bridegroom and his bride grew weary, and went to their chamber. There they threw them on the bed in their clothes, the doors and windows being shut, and no one remaining with them. But in the midst of their slumbers they were awakened by the opening of a door, and my lord of Vendôme, drawing the curtain, looked to see how it was, supposing it to be one of his friends endeavouring to take him by surprise. But in the stead thereof he beheld entering in a tall old bedchamber woman, who for the darkness of the room knew

them not, but seeing them mighty close to one another, fell to
crying: "Ah! thou nasty wanton strumpet, 'tis a long time that I
have suspected thee for what thou art, but for want of proof have
not told my mistress! Now are thy wanton ways so manifest, that
I am determined to cloak them no more. And thou, apostatical
wretch, who hast brought such shame upon this house, by leading the poor wench astray, were it not for the fear of God, I
would beat thee soundly where thou liest. Arise, in the name of
the devil, arise, for it seemeth as if there were no shame in thee!"
My lord of Vendôme and his Princess, to make this discourse last
the longer, hid their faces against one another, and laughed so
heartily that they could not speak a word. But the old woman,
perceiving that for all her threats they would not budge an inch,
came near to them to have them forth by the arms. Then she
knew both by their faces and their dress that they were not what
she sought for; and recognising them, threw herself on her
knees, entreating them to pardon her for disturbing their rest.
But my lord of Vendôme, willing to learn somewhat more on the
matter, arose incontinent, and would have the old woman tell
him for whom she had mistaken them. This at first she would not
confess, but having obtained their oath never to reveal it, she
declared it was a girl of the house, on whom a prothonotary was
amorous; and said she had watched them a long while for her displeasure that her mistress put her trust in a man that would bring
this shame upon the house. With this she left the Prince and
Princess with closed doors, as she had found them, and they
were mighty merry over the case. And though they told the story
again, yet they would never name the persons concerned in it.

39 (LXVII)

How a woman trusted in God amidst the lions.

Captain Robertval once made a sea voyage, with certain vessels
over which he was set by the King his master, to the island of
Canada, where he was determined, if the air of the country
should be found wholesome, to abide, and to build towns and
mansions; and as to the beginning he made all men are advised

of it. And that Christianity might be spread abroad throughout the land, he took with him all manner of mechanicals, amongst whom there was one so vile, that he betrayed his master, and put him in danger of being taken by the folk of the country. But God willed that his undertaking was brought to light before any hurt could befall the captain, who made seize this wicked traitor, and would have punished him according as he had deserved. And this had been done were it not for his wife, who, having followed her husband through all the dangers of the sea, would not leave him to perish, but by her tears and lamentations worked so with the captain and all his company, that as much for pity of her as for the services she had done him, he granted her desire. And this was for the husband and wife to be left on a little island in mid-ocean, where dwelt no people, but only ravening wild beasts; and it was likewise granted that they should take thither such things as were needful to them. So the poor folk, finding themselves all alone amid the fierce brutes, had no help but in God, who had always been the steadfast hope of the wife; and she, gaining from Him all her consolation, carried for her safe-guard, comfort, and nourishment the New Testament, in which she read without ceasing. And as to temporals, she and her husband laboured to build them as good a house as they were able, and when the lions and other beasts came near to devour them, the husband with his arquebuss, and she with stones, made so stout a defence, that they not only kept them at a distance, but very often killed some that were good provaunt; so with such meats and the herbs of the island they lived some time, after their bread had failed them. At length the husband could no more bear with such victuals, and for the water he drank became so swollen that, after a few days, he died, having no ser-vant nor consoler save his wife, who was to him both parson and physician; thus passed he from that wilderness to the heavenly country. And his poor wife, left alone, buried him in the earth as deeply as she could, but yet the beasts straightway smelt him out and came to devour the flesh of him; and she in her little hut shot at them with her arquebuss, so that her husband's body should not have such a sepulture. So living as to her body the life bestial, as to her soul the life angelical, she spent her time in reading of the Scriptures, in prayers and in meditations, having a joyful and contented mind within a body that was shrunken away and nigh amort. But He who never forsaketh His own, and who, when there is no hope in man, showeth His strength, did not allow that the virtue he had set in this woman should be hid from men, but willed rather that it should be made manifest unto His glory. So at the end of some time one of the ships of the armament passing by the island, the folk that were in it saw a smoke that put them in mind of them that had been left there, and they determined to see how God had dealt with them. The poor woman, seeing the ship draw near, went down to the strand, where she was when they came. And after praising God for it, she brought them to her hut, and showed them what manner of victuals she had eaten during her stay; the which would have passed their belief, had they not known that God can as well feed His servants in a wilderness as at a prince's feast. And since she could not abide in such a place, they took her with them to Rochelle, whither after their voyage they came, and made known to all that dwelt therein her faithfulness and patient long-suffering. And on this account she was received by all the ladies with great honour, and they with goodwill gave her their daughters that she might teach them to read and write. And in this honest craft she earned a livelihood, always exhorting all men to love Our Lord and put their trust in Him, setting forth by way of example the great compassion he had shown towards her.

40 (LXX)

In the which is shown the horrid lust and hatred of
a Duchess, and the pitiful death of two lovers.

In the Duchy of Burgundy there was a Duke, an honourable and excellent prince, who had a woman to wife from whose beauty he took such contentment, that he made no account of her complexion, only striving to do her pleasure, the which affection she very craftily feigned to return to him. Now the Duke had in his household a gentleman, so fulfilled with all the

graces that are to be looked for in a man, that he was beloved of
the whole house, and notably by the Duke, who from his childhood had reared him near his person; and seeing him so virtuous took a great liking for him, and from time to time trusted
him with such of his occasions as were fitting to his youth. The
Duchess, whose heart was not inclined towards chastity, not
contenting herself with the love her husband had for her and
the kindness he used in their conversation, looked often upon
this gentleman, and found him so mightily to her taste that she
grew to love him with a love that passed all reason. And of this
she did every day endeavour to inform him, by sweet and pitiful
looks, conjoined with a passionate manner of feature and much
sighing. But he, who had made virtue his sole delight, could not
conceive of vice in a lady who had such small temptation
thereto; so that the languishing eyes and sheepish looks of this
poor wanton brought her no harvest save a mad despair. And
this one day pricked her so shrewdly, that, forgetting she was a
woman to be entreated and yet to refuse, and a princess who
should be adored of such servants and yet have them in disdain,
took upon her the spirit of a man far gone in love, to ease her of
this fire she could no longer bear. So when her husband was at
the council board, whither the young man by reason of his age
did not yet go, she made him a sign to come to her; and this he
did, thinking she had some charge to lay upon him. But taking
him by the arm, as a woman who is weary of too much idleness,
she led him to a gallery, and then said to him: "I marvel that you
who are handsome, young, and full of grace, have lived so long
in this company and yet have never loved." And looking upon
him as pleasantly as she was able, she stopped short, and he
answered: "Madam, if I were worthy that your highness should
look down on me, it would be more a matter of astonishment to
see one so unworthy as I am, offer his service and be refused
and mocked." The Duchess, hearing this discreet reply, loved
him more than ever, and protested that there was not a lady in
the Court who would not deem herself happy to have him for a
lover, and that he might well essay such an undertaking, for he
would without doubt bring it to an honourable completion. The
gentleman kept his eyes lowered all the while, not daring to look

upon her face, that was hot enough to have melted an icicle, and just as he would have excused himself, the Duke came to require the Duchess at the council board on some affairs that concerned her; and with great regret she went thither. But the gentleman made no sign that he had understood the words she had spoken to him, whereat she vexed sore, not knowing wherefore he kept silence, save it were on account of foolish fear, of which she deemed him to have too much. A few days after, seeing that he made no account of her speech, she resolved to put from her the thought of fear and shame, and open her mind to him, being persuaded that a beauty like to hers could get none but a good reception; natheless it would have been greatly to her liking to have had the honour of being entreated. But she let honour go for the sake of pleasure, and having several times made trial of discourse like to what had gone before, and getting no reply to her taste, she one day took him by the sleeve, and said she would speak with him on certain weighty matters. The gentleman, humbly and reverently as was befitting, followed her to a deep window recess whither she had gone; and when she perceived that none in the room could see them, in a trembling voice, halfway betwixt desire and fear, she went on with her former discourse, chiding him that he had not yet chosen any lady in the company, and assuring him that on whomsoever the lot might fall she would give him her help so that he should be entreated kindly. He, not less troubled than astonished at her words, replied: "Madam, my heart is such that, were I once refused, I should have no more joy in the world, and I know myself to be so lowly that there is not a lady of the Court who would deign to accept me as her lover." The Duchess, blushing, for she thought he was well-nigh won, swore to him that she knew the prettiest of all her ladies would gladly have him, and render him perfectly content with her. "Alas! mistress," said he, "I do not suppose there is a woman of this company so blind as to be well affected towards me." The Duchess, perceiving he would not understand her, drew up the veil a little from before her passion, and for the fear his virtuousness gave her, proceeded by manner of interrogation, saying to him: "If Fortune had so favoured you that it was I who bore you this goodwill, what then would you reply?" The gentleman at the hearing of this thought he was dreaming, and falling on his knees, said to her: "Madam, when it please God that I have both the favour of the Duke my master, and of yourself, I shall deem myself the happiest man in the world, for 'tis all I ask in return for my loyal service, who more than any other am under obligation to lay down my life for you. And I am persuaded that the love you bear to my lord Duke is conjoined with such chastity and nobleness of heart, that not only I, who am but a worm of the earth, but the greatest prince and most gallant gentleman in Christendom would be altogether unable to break asunder the union between you two. And as for me, my lord hath brought me up since I was a child, and hath made me to be what I am; wherefore I would rather die than have any thoughts unbecoming in a faithful servant towards any wife or daughter or sister or mother of his." The Duchess would hear no more, but seeing herself in danger of being disgracefully refused, she broke on a sudden into his words, saying to him: "O boastful and foolish one, who would have you do so? Think you that the very flies in the air love you for your beauty? But if you were so daring as to address yourself to me, I would show you that I nor love nor wish to love other than my husband, and all the talk I have had with you has been but a pastime for me, that I might know your mind, and make a mock of you, as I do with foolish lovers." "Madam," said the gentleman, "I have believed and do believe that all this is as you say." Then without listening for more she went hastily away, and seeing that her ladies followed her, entered her closet and grieved beyond all telling. For on the one side love, wherein she had failed, made her very sorrowful, and on the other hate, both against herself for her folly and against him for his wit, brought such fury upon her, that one hour she was fain to lay violent hands on herself and die, the next she would live to be avenged on him she accounted her mortal enemy.

After that she had wept a long while she feigned to be sick, so that she should not sup with the Duke, the young gentleman being commonly in waiting at supper-time. The Duke, who loved his wife better than himself, came to see her; but so as the better to gain her end, she told him that she thought she was

great with child, and for that cause had a defluction of rheum in
the eyes, the which was great pain to her. So passed two or three
days, the Duchess still keeping to her bed, so sad and melancholic that the Duke plainly perceived that there was something
else besides her greatness to be mourned for. And he came to
lie with her at night, and made her as good cheer as he was able,
but for all that she ceased not to sigh continually. Then he said
to her: "Sweetheart, you know I love you even as my life, and
that when yours fails mine will not endure; wherefore, if you
would keep me whole, I pray you tell me the cause of all your
sighing, for I do not believe that the reason you have given is
sufficient." The Duchess, seeing her husband to be minded
towards her as she would have wished him, conceived that the
time was come to take vengeance on her enemy, and throwing
her arms about her husband wept, and answered him: "Alas, my
lord, my greatest grief is to see you cozened of them that be so
deeply pledged to guard your substance and honour." Hearing
this, the Duke was very desirous to have the interpretation
thereof, and besought her to tell him the truth without fear. And
after several times refusing, at last she said: "Henceforth, my
lord, I shall never wonder if strange peoples make war on
princes, when they that are most of all indebted to them dare
such a deed that the loss of goods is as nothing in comparison. I
speak with respect to such a gentleman (and here she named
him by his name), who having been fed by your hand, and
entreated more as a son than a servant, has dared this miserable
deed; namely, to lay siege to the honour of your wife, with which
is bound up the honour of your house and lineage. And though
by looks he hath long striven to acquaint me with his wicked
intent, yet my heart, that takes account of none but you, perceived nothing; wherefore at the last he made it known to me by
word of mouth. And to him I made a reply befitting mine estate
and chastity, natheless I do so hate him, that I cannot endure to
behold him, for which reason I have stayed in my chamber and
lost the pleasure of your company. So I beseech you, my lord,
keep no longer this pest near your person; for after such a crime,
fearing lest I tell you of it, he may well do worse. This then is the
cause of my grief, and methinks it is meet and right that you

should forthwith take order with it." The Duke, who on the one hand loved his wife and esteemed that a great injury had been done him, and on the other hand loved his servant, whose faithfulness he had tried so well that he could hardly believe this lie for truth, was in great perplexity and wrathfulness. And he went to his chamber, and charged the gentleman no more to appear before him, but to begone to his lodging and tarry there for some time. He, not knowing the reason, was sorely vexed, thinking that he had deserved the very contrary to this ill treatment, and well assured of his thoughts and deeds, sent a fellow of his to speak to the Duke and carry a letter to him. Wherein he humbly besought him, that if by bad report he was estranged from his presence, he would be pleased to grant a suspension of judgment until he had heard from his lips the truth of the matter, for it would be found that in no respect had he done aught worthy of his displeasure. Having seen this letter the Duke's anger was somewhat appeased, and he privily sent for him to his room, and with a wrathful countenance said to him: "I never thought that my trouble with your nurture when you were a child should have been converted to repentance for having so far advanced you. But now you have sought to do me a worse thing than to take away my goods or my life; to bring shame on the honour of her who is the half of me, and so to make my house and lineage a byword for ever. And you can conceive that such a wrong pricks me so at heart, that were I not in doubt as to whether it is the truth or no, you would have been by now at the bottom of the moat, that I might deal to you a privy punishment for a privy crime." The gentleman was no whit stumbled at this discourse, for his innocency gave him a firm and constant speech, and craved to be informed who was his accuser, since such slanders should be answered with sword rather than a word. "Your accuser," said the Duke, "hath no arms save her chastity, for I will have you know that it is my wife and none other who made this thing manifest to me, and prayed to be avenged on you." The poor gentleman, hearing the crafty wickedness of the Duchess, yet would not accuse her, but answered: "My lord, my lady can say what she will; you know her better than I, and that I have never been with her alone, save

one time when she spoke but very little with me. Your judgment
is as sound as any prince in the world, wherefore, my lord, I
entreat you declare whether you have ever seen aught on my
face that engendered any suspicion. For this fire of love cannot
be kept secret a long while and not be discovered of them that
are afflicted with the same disease. And I entreat you, my lord,
to believe two things of me: the one, that I am so loyal to you
that were your wife the prettiest of all women, yet love would
have no power to bring a stain on my honour and fidelity; the
other, that even were she not your wife, she is the last woman on
whom I should grow amorous, and there is many another that
would come before her in my heart." At the hearing of these
truths the Duke began to soften, and said: "I assure you that I
too never believed it; wherefore come into my presence again,
and if it be discovered that the truth is with you, I will love you
better than I ever did; and on the other hand your life is in my
hands." For this the gentleman thanked him, submitting to all
manner of pains and penalties if there should be found any fault
in him.

The Duchess, seeing the gentleman in waiting as was accustomed, could not patiently bear it, but said to her husband: "You
will get but your deserts, my lord, if you are poisoned, since you
put more trust in your mortal enemies than in your friends."
"Prithee, sweetheart, trouble not yourself as to this matter, for if
I find that the truth is even as you have told me be certain that
he will not live four-and-twenty hours after; but he hath so
sworn to the contrary effect, that I, not having perceived myself
any fault in him, cannot believe it without some sure proof." "In
good faith," she said, "your kindness makes his wickedness the
greater. What more proof would you have than to see a man like
him remain so long and not be reported to be in love? Trust me,
my lord, that without the great desire he had to be my lover, he
would have found a mistress before now; for never did a young
man live in such a company in this manner, without aiming at so
high a mark that he was content with the mere hope of attaining thereto. And since you are persuaded that he is telling you
the truth, put him to the oath as to his love, for if he loves
another I am content that you should credit him; but if not

believe that I speak the truth." The Duke found the conclusions
of his wife good, and took the gentleman with him to the chase,
and said to him: "My wife still persists in her judgment concerning you, and gives me a reason that makes me very suspicious—namely, that so comely and young a man was never
before seen without a sweetheart for any length of time, and this
doth cause me to believe that your intent is as she affirms, and
that the expectation you have of her doth give you so much contentment, that you have no thought for other women.
Wherefore as a friend I entreat you, and as a master charge you
to tell me, whether you love any lady or no." The poor gentleman, to whom this secret was as dear as life, was nevertheless
constrained, by reason of his lord's jealousy, to confess that of a
truth he loved a woman whose beauty was so great that the
comeliness of the Duchess and the ladies of her Court was but
ugliness in comparison. But he besought him never to require
her name at his hands, since the love betwixt him and his sweetheart was of such sort that none could do it a hurt save the one
who first made it known. The Duke promised not to press him
as to this matter, and was so content with him, that he showed
him more kindness than ever he had before. This the Duchess
very plainly perceived, and with her wonted craft set herself to
find out the cause thereof. And the Duke concealed it not from
her, whereby to her lust of vengeance was conjoined a bitter
jealousy, that made her entreat the Duke to require his sweetheart's name of the gentleman. For she would have him believe
'twas all a lie, and the best means to discover it would be to
demand proof of the story, and if he could not name her he
esteemed so beautiful it would be exceeding foolish to put any
trust in his words. The poor lord, whose mind was swayed by his
wife at her pleasure, went forth and walked all alone with the
gentleman, telling him that he was in greater trouble than afore,
for he strongly suspected that he had given him this excuse to
prevent the discovery of the truth; wherefore he prayed him to
declare the name of her he loved so much. The gentleman
entreated him not to be the occasion of his doing such a sin
against his mistress—namely, to break the promise he had made
and kept for so long awhile, and cause him to lose in a day that

he had preserved for more than seven years; and said he had rather die than do this wrong to her who was so faithful to him. The Duke, finding that he was not willing to tell him, grew most furiously jealous, and said to him: "Choose then one of two things: either tell me the name of your mistress or be banished from the lands over which I have authority, and if I find you in them eight days after, I will put you to a cruel death." If ever grief took hold on the heart of faithful lover, then did it on this poor gentleman, who might well say *Angustiae sunt mihi undique,* since on the one hand if he told the truth he would lose his sweetheart if she came to know that he had broken his promise; and on the other, if he told it not, he would be banished from the lands wherein she dwelt, and would no more have the means of seeing her. So, pressed hard on either side, there came a cold sweat upon him as one who is dying of a broken heart, which being seen of the Duke, was esteemed by him a proof that the gentleman's only mistress was his own wife, and he thought that, because he was not able to name any other, he was in such piteous case, wherefore he harshly said to him: "If your words were true, you would have none of this difficulty to declare her name, wherefore I believe that your sin is torment- ing you." The gentleman, pricked by this speech, and driven by his love for his master, resolved to tell him the truth, being per- suaded that he was so honourable a man that he would on no account reveal it. So throwing himself on his knees before him, with clasped hands, he said: "My lord, both what I owe you, and the great love I bear you, do more urge me than any fear of death; for I see you in such imagination and false judgments concerning me, that to set you at rest I am determined to do what no torment could have compelled me. And I entreat you, my lord, to swear and promise, on your faith as a Christian prince, never to reveal the secret that, as it is your pleasure, I am constrained to make known to you. Forthwith the Duke swore all the oaths he could call to mind that never by his lips, his pen, or his countenance, would he reveal this thing to any living soul. The young man, being assured of so virtuous a prince, straight- way put the first stone to the building of his woes, and said to him: "It is seven years ago, my lord, that, knowing your niece the

Lady of Vergier was a widow and had no kindred, I set myself to
gain her favour. And since I came not of a house that I should
wed her, I was content to be received as a lover, and this was
granted me. And it has pleased God that hitherto our passages
have been ordered so discreetly, that we two alone are advertised of them, and now, my lord, you also are of our privity, and
in your hands I put my life and my honour, entreating you to
keep our secret, and to make no less account of your niece, for
I think in the round world there is none to be compared to her."
At this the Duke was glad, for knowing the great beauty of his
niece, he made no doubt she was more pleasant than his wife,
but yet could not understand how such a matter should be con-
ducted without ways and means, and so prayed the gentleman
tell him how he visited her. The gentleman showed him how his
lady's chamber opened out to the garden, and how, on the
appointed day, she would leave a little door open through which
he passed, and waited till he heard the barking of a little dog,
that his mistress sent into the garden when all her women were
asleep. Then he went in and talked with her all the night, and,
before he set forth, she set him a day on which to see her again,
and he never failed to keep the appointment without some
urgent cause preventing him. The Duke, who was mighty
inquisitive, and who in his time had been a hot gallant, as much
to satisfy altogether his suspicions as to hear more of so strange
a case, prayed him the next time he visited his mistress to take
him also, not as a master but as a companion. The gentleman,
having gone thus far, granted him his desire, telling him that
very day was appointed for their meeting, whereat the Duke was
in such delight as he would not have exchanged for a kingdom.
And feigning to go to rest in his closet, he made bring two horses
for him and the gentleman, and all the night they fared upon
their way from Argilly, where dwelt the Duke, to La Vergier.
And leaving their horses without the park, the gentleman led
the Duke into the garden by the little door, praying him to
remain behind a walnut-tree, where he could judge whether his
tale were true or no. He had not been in the garden a long while
before the dog began to bark, and the gentleman walked to the
tower, where his lady failed not to come out to him, and with a

kiss said it seemed a thousand years since she had seen him last, and then they entered the tower together and shut the door upon them. The Duke, having seen the whole mystery, was more than satisfied, and had not to wait there long, for the gentleman told his mistress that he must return earlier than was his wont, for that the Duke was going a-hunting at four of the clock, and he dared not fail to be with him. The lady, who preferred honour before pleasure, would by no means keep him from his duty, for the thing of which she made most account in their virtuous love was that it was secret from all men. So the gentleman set forth at one hour after midnight, and the lady, in her mantle and kerchief, went some way with him, but not so far as she wished, for he made her turn back lest she should see the Duke, with whom he returned as he had come to the castle of Argilly. And as they were upon the way the Duke swore continually to his servant never to reveal the secret; and so loved and trusted him that there was no one at Court more in his favour, whereat the Duchess became mightily enraged. But the Duke straitly charged her never more to speak on this matter, for he knew the truth and was pleased with it, inasmuch as the lady was more loveable than she. At this the Duchess was so cut to the heart that she fell into a sickness more grievous than a fever; and the Duke going to see her and console her, could effect nothing if he would not tell her the name of the Beloved Lady, and she used such importunity with him that he went from her room, saying: "If you talk to me again after this sort, we will part from one another." These words made the sickness of the Duchess to increase, and she feigned to feel the child moving in her womb, whereat the Duke rejoiced so much that he came to lie with her. But at the moment in which she perceived him to be most amorous on her she turned away from him saying: "I beseech you, since you have no love for wife nor child, leave us to die together." And with these words she poured forth such tears and lamentations that the Duke was in great fear lest she should miscarry; wherefore, taking her between his arms, he entreated her to tell him her desire, since all things were in common between them. "Alas, my lord," she replied, weeping, "how can I hope that you will do for me a thing at all difficult when you refuse that which is most easy and reasonable—namely, to tell me the mistress of the most wicked servant you ever had in your house? I thought that you and I were but one heart, one soul, and one flesh, but since you hide from me your secrets, I am persuaded I am to you as a stranger and one not akin. Alas! my lord, you have told me many a secret and weighty matter, of which you have never heard that I spoke; you know by such sufficient trial that my will is altogether your own, that you ought not to doubt that I am more you than myself. And being you have sworn to tell no other the secret of the gentleman, you will not break your word in telling me, for I am not and cannot be other than yourself: I have you in my heart, I hold you in my arms, and your child, in whom you live, is in my womb; and yet I cannot have your heart, as you have mine! But the more I am loyal and faithful to you, the more are you cruel and severe with me; and this it is that makes me a thousand times a day to desire, by a sudden death, to deliver your child from such a father, and myself from such a husband. And this I hope I will fall out soon, since you prefer a faithless servant before such a wife as I am to you, and before the mother of your child, that will without doubt perish, since I cannot learn of you what I greatly desire to know." So saying she threw her arms about her husband and kissed him, watering his face with her tears and lamenting in such wise, that the good prince, fearing lest he should lose his wife and his child together, determined to tell her the whole truth. But before he did so, he swore to her that if ever she revealed it to a living soul she should die by his hand, to which she agreed and accepted the penalty. Then the poor cozened husband told her all that he had seen from beginning to end, at which she feigned to be pleased, but in her heart was very wrath. Natheless, for fear of the Duke, she dissembled her passion as well as might be.

And it came to pass that on a great feast-day the Duke held his court, bidding to it all the ladies of the land, and amongst the rest his niece. And the dances having begun, each gladly did his duty therein; but the Duchess being in torment to see the beauty and grace of the Lady of Vergier, could neither rejoice with the rest nor so much as conceal her spleen. For having made all the ladies to sit around her, she began to discourse concerning love, and perceiving that the Lady of Vergier said nothing, she asked her with a heart black with jealousy: "And is it possible, fair niece, that your beauty is without a friend or follower?" "Mistress," replied the Lady of Vergier, "my beauty hath not gained me such; for since the death of my husband I have willed to have no lovers save my children, with whom I am content." "Fair niece, fair niece," replied the Duchess with an abominable spitefulness, "there is no love so secret as not to be revealed, nor little dog so well trained and instructed whose bark cannot be heard." I leave to your imagination, ladies, what pain the poor Lady of Vergier felt at her heart, hearing a thing so long concealed made thus manifest to her great shame; her honour, so carefully guarded and so woefully lost, was a torment to her, but still more her suspicion that her lover had broken his promise, the which she had never looked for except he were to love some lady prettier than she, who by her enchantments should cause him to make all known to her. Yet so great was her prudence that she made no sign, and replied laughing to the Duchess that she understood not the language of the beasts. But under this wise concealment her heart was so full of sadness that she arose, and, passing through the chamber of the Duchess, entered a closet whither the Duke, as he walked up and down, saw her go in. And when she found herself in a place where she thought to be alone, she let herself fall upon a bed as one who swoons away, so that a lady who was lying by the bedside to rest herself, arose and looked through the curtain to see who it was; and finding it was the Lady of Vergier who thought herself alone, she durst not do anything, but kept still and listened to what she said. And the poor lady with a dying voice began her plaint, saying: "Ah, hapless one! what word is this that I have heard? What sentence of death hath been passed upon me? What final judgment have I received? O my beloved, my beloved, is this the reward of my chaste and honourable affection? O heart of me, what dangerous choice hast thou made; for the most loyal the most faithless, for the truest a deceiver, for the most secret a scandalous man? Alas! can it be that this thing that was hidden from the eyes of all men hath been revealed to the Duchess? My little dog that was the only help of our long love was too well taught; it

was not thou that hath discovered me, but he whose voice can be
heard above the barking of the dog, and whose heart is more
thankless than the heart of the beast. He it was who, against his
oath and promise, hath made manifest our happy life that did hurt
to none, and endured for many a year. O my beloved, my beloved,
who alone art in my breast, in whom alone I live, was it needful
for thee to declare thyself my mortal enemy, and to cast my honour to the four winds, my body to the earth, and my soul to its
eternal rest? Hath the Duchess, then, so great beauty that it hath
changed thee as did the beauty of Circe? Art thou, then, become
from virtuous vicious, from good evil, and from a man a ravening
beast? O my love, my love, though thou hast broken thine oath,
yet will I keep mine. Never more will I see thee, after that thou
hast noised our love abroad; but since I cannot live without the
sight of thee, I submit willingly to mine anguish, and seek no cure
for it either in reason or in medicine; for death alone shall bring
it to a close, and be sweeter to me than to tarry in the world without love, without honour, or delight. Nor war nor death hath
taken my lover from me, nor sin nor fault of mine hath robbed me
of mine honour or contentment; 'tis cruel chance that rendereth
him who of all had most cause for gratitude ungrateful, and
maketh me to receive the contrary to what I have deserved. Ah,
my lady Duchess, what delight it was to mock me and my little
dog; enjoy, then, that which belongs alone to me. Make her to be
a jest who thought, by concealment and virtuous loving, to be
freed from all such jesting. How hath this word pierced through
my heart, that I redden with shame and grow pale with jealousy.
Alas! my heart, 'tis time thou wast no more. Love burneth thee as
with fire, jealousy and wrong are on thee as a frost of death, and
sorrow and shame will not have me give thee any comfort. Alas!
poor soul, that for adoring the creature forgot the Creator, thou
must return into the hands of Him from whom an idle love drew
thee awhile away. Be of good courage, O my soul, for thou shalt
find a kinder Father than was the lover who made Him to be forgotten. O God, my creator, true and perfect love, by whose grace
my love was unspotted from sin, save that of loving too much, I
entreat Thee of Thy mercy receive the soul of her who repenteth,
for that she hath broken Thy first and most righteous command-

ment. By the merits of Him whose love passeth all understanding, pardon the sin that I by too great love have committed, for in Thee alone do I put my trust. And farewell, O my lover, whose name doth break my heart." And forthwith she fell backward, and her face became white as death, her lips blue, and her extremities cold. And at that moment her lover came into the hall, and saw the Duchess dancing amid the ladies, and looked on every side for his mistress, but not seeing her, entered the chamber of the Duchess. There he found the Duke sauntering up and down, who, guessing his intent, whispered in his ear: "She is gone into that closet, and methinks she looked somewhat sickly." The gentleman asked if it was his pleasure that he should go after her, and the Duke prayed him to do so. And when he was come into the closet he saw the Lady of Vergier standing at the threshold of death, and he threw his arms about her and said: "What ails you, sweetheart? Would you leave me, then?" The poor lady, hearing that voice she knew so well, took a little strength, and, opening her eyes, looked on him who was the cause of her death, but upon that look love and sorrow swelled so within her that with a pitiful sigh she gave up her soul to God. The gentleman, with scarce more life in him than the dead woman, asked of the lady that was by the bed after what sort this sickness had come upon her. And she told him all the words that she had heard. Then he knew that the Duke had revealed the secret to his wife, and, embracing the body of his sweetheart, he for a long while watered it with tears, saying thus: "O traitorous and wicked lover that I am, wherefore has not the punishment of my treachery fallen upon me, and not upon her who is innocent? Wherefore did not thunder from heaven overwhelm me on the day that my tongue revealed the secret of our virtuous love? Wherefore did not the earth open and swallow me up, faithless that I am? O tongue, mayest thou be punished as was the tongue of the rich man who in hell lifted up his eyes being in torment. O heart, too, fearful of death and banishment, mayest thou be torn for ever of eagles as was the heart of Ixion.* Alas! my love, the woe of woes, and the bitterest of all

---

*There appears to be some confusion here between Ixion (who was bound to a wheel) and Prometheus (whose *liver* was torn by a *vulture*).

woes, hath overtaken me. Thinking to keep you, I have lost you
for ever; thinking to live with you a long while in virtuous contentment, I cast my arms about your dead body; and dying, you
were displeased with me, my heart, and my tongue. O most loyal
and faithful of all women, I do condemn myself for the most dis-
loyal, fickle, and unfaithful of all men. Would that I could impute
the blame to the Duke, in whose promise I trusted, hoping
thereby to prolong our days in happiness, but alas! I should have
known that none could keep my secret better than myself. The
Duke was more justified in that he revealed it to his wife than I
who revealed it to him. I accuse myself alone of the greatest
wickedness that ever fell out between lovers. Would that I had
endured to be cast into the moat, as he threatened me; then, my
love, you would be still alive, and I should have met with a glorious death, in keeping of the law of love. But I broke my promise
and remain alive, and you, by reason of your perfect love, are
dead; for the purity of your heart could not bear to know the
wickedness of your lover, and suffer you to live. O God, why hast
thou made me man, with love so light and heart devoid of knowledge? Why madest Thou not me the dog that served his mistress
faithfully? Alas! my little friend, my joy at your bark is turned to
bitter grief for that another has heard it. Yet, dear sweetheart, neither the love of the Duchess nor of any other woman could make
me vary, though several times in her wicked craftiness she prayed
and entreated me; but my folly hath overcome me, who thought
by it to establish our love for ever. Yet though I was foolish, none
the less am I worthy of blame, for I revealed the secret of my mistress, and I broke my promise to her, and for that alone I see her
dead before mine eyes. Alas! sweetheart, will death be more cruel
to me than thee, whose love hath ended thy life? I believe that it
will not deign to touch my wretched, faithless heart, for life with
dishonour and the recollection of what by mine own fault I have
lost will be harder to bear than ten thousand deaths. And if any,
by malice or mischance, had slain you, forthwith would my sword
been in my hand to avenge you; so it is right that I should not pardon that murderer who is the cause of your death by a more
wicked deed than the stroke of a sword. And if I knew a more
infamous executioner than myself, I would pray him to put to

death your traitorous lover. O love, by my love that was without
knowledge I have done you a displeasure, thus it is that you will
not succour me as you succoured her who kept all your laws. Nor
is it befitting that I should die so honourable a death, but rather
that mine own hand should slay me. Since with my tears I have
washed your face, and since with my tongue I have besought your
forgiveness, now with my hand I will make my body like to yours,
and send my soul whither you are, for I know that a virtuous love
hath no end in this world nor in the next." And then rising from
beside the body, he drew his dagger, and like a madman dealt
himself a violent blow therewith, and, falling back, took his sweetheart in his arms and kissed her in such wise that there seemed to
be in him more of love than death. The lady, seeing the blow, ran
to the door and called for help; and the Duke, hearing the cry, and
fearing for them that he loved, came the first into the closet, and,
beholding the pitiful pair, essayed to draw them apart, so that the
gentleman, if it were possible, might be saved. But he held his
sweetheart so firmly, that till he was dead they could not be sun-
dered. Yet hearing the voice of the Duke speaking to him, and
saying: "Alas! what is the cause of this?" with a terrible look he
replied to him: "My tongue and yours, my lord." So saying, he
gave up the ghost, with his face close to that of his mistress. The
Duke, desiring to know more, constrained the lady to tell him
what she had heard and seen, and this she did, sparing nothing.
Then the Duke, knowing that he himself was the cause of it,
threw him on the dead lovers, and with tears and very sorrowful
lamentations, and ofttimes kissing them, asked pardon for his sin.
And after, in furious fashion, he arose, and drew the dagger from
the gentleman's body; and as a wild boar, wounded by a spear,
rushes madly against his enemy, so went he to seek her out who
had wounded the very depths of his heart. And he found her
dancing in the hall, more gay than she was wont to be, for the
thought that she had avenged her on the Lady of Vergier. So the
Duke took her in the middle of the dance, and said to her: "You
took the secret upon your life, and upon your life fall the punishment." So saying, he seized her by the hair, and struck her with
the dagger through the throat, whereat all the company were
astonished, and each thought the Duke was beside himself. But

having fulfilled his intent, he gathered together into the hall all his servants, and recounted the honourable and pitiful history of his niece, and the evil his wife had done to her, and all present wept at the hearing of it. And the Duke ordained that his wife should be buried in an abbey that he had founded, in part for satisfaction of his sin in putting her to death; and he made build a fair sepulchre where the bodies of his niece and the gentleman were laid together, with an epitaph showing forth their tragical history. And the Duke led an armament against the Turks, wherein God so favoured him that he gained both honour and profit, and found when he returned that his eldest son was fit to take the lordship upon him, and so, leaving all, he became a monk in the abbey where the bodies of his wife and the two lovers were buried, and there with God passed happily the remnant of his days.

A CATALOG OF SELECTED
DOVER BOOKS
IN ALL FIELDS OF INTEREST

A CATALOG OF SELECTED DOVER
BOOKS IN ALL FIELDS OF INTEREST

CONCERNING THE SPIRITUAL IN ART, Wassily Kandinsky. Pioneering work by father of abstract art. Thoughts on color theory, nature of art. Analysis of earlier masters. 12 illustrations. 80pp. of text. 5⅜ x 8½.　　　　0-486-23411-8

CELTIC ART: The Methods of Construction, George Bain. Simple geometric techniques for making Celtic interlacements, spirals, Kells-type initials, animals, humans, etc. Over 500 illustrations. 160pp. 9 x 12. (Available in U.S. only.)　　　　0-486-22923-8

AN ATLAS OF ANATOMY FOR ARTISTS, Fritz Schider. Most thorough reference work on art anatomy in the world. Hundreds of illustrations, including selections from works by Vesalius, Leonardo, Goya, Ingres, Michelangelo, others. 593 illustrations. 192pp. 7⅛ x 10¼.　　　　0-486-20241-0

CELTIC HAND STROKE-BY-STROKE (Irish Half-Uncial from "The Book of Kells"): An Arthur Baker Calligraphy Manual, Arthur Baker. Complete guide to creating each letter of the alphabet in distinctive Celtic manner. Covers hand position, strokes, pens, inks, paper, more. Illustrated. 48pp. 8¼ x 11.　　　　0-486-24336-2

EASY ORIGAMI, John Montroll. Charming collection of 32 projects (hat, cup, pelican, piano, swan, many more) specially designed for the novice origami hobbyist. Clearly illustrated easy-to-follow instructions insure that even beginning papercrafters will achieve successful results. 48pp. 8¼ x 11.　　　　0-486-27298-2

BLOOMINGDALE'S ILLUSTRATED 1886 CATALOG: Fashions, Dry Goods and Housewares, Bloomingdale Brothers. Famed merchants' extremely rare catalog depicting about 1,700 products: clothing, housewares, firearms, dry goods, jewelry, more. Invaluable for dating, identifying vintage items. Also, copyright-free graphics for artists, designers. Co-published with Henry Ford Museum & Greenfield Village. 160pp. 8¼ x 11.　　　　0-486-25780-0

THE ART OF WORLDLY WISDOM, Baltasar Gracian. "Think with the few and speak with the many," "Friends are a second existence," and "Be able to forget" are among this 1637 volume's 300 pithy maxims. A perfect source of mental and spiritual refreshment, it can be opened at random and appreciated either in brief or at length. 128pp. 5⅜ x 8½.　　　　0-486-44034-6

JOHNSON'S DICTIONARY: A Modern Selection, Samuel Johnson (E. L. McAdam and George Milne, eds.). This modern version reduces the original 1755 edition's 2,300 pages of definitions and literary examples to a more manageable length, retaining the verbal pleasure and historical curiosity of the original. 480pp. 5⁵⁄₁₆ x 8¼.　　　　0-486-44089-3

ADVENTURES OF HUCKLEBERRY FINN, Mark Twain, Illustrated by E. W. Kemble. A work of eternal richness and complexity, a source of ongoing critical debate, and a literary landmark, Twain's 1885 masterpiece about a barefoot boy's journey of self-discovery has enthralled readers around the world. This handsome clothbound reproduction of the first edition features all 174 of the original black-and-white illustrations. 368pp. 5⅜ x 8½.　　　　0-486-44322-1

STICKLEY CRAFTSMAN FURNITURE CATALOGS, Gustav Stickley and L. & J. G. Stickley. Beautiful, functional furniture in two authentic catalogs from 1910. 594 illustrations, including 277 photos, show settles, rockers, armchairs, reclining chairs, bookcases, desks, tables. 183pp. 6½ x 9¼. 0-486-23838-5

AMERICAN LOCOMOTIVES IN HISTORIC PHOTOGRAPHS: 1858 to 1949, Ron Ziel (ed.). A rare collection of 126 meticulously detailed official photographs, called "builder portraits," of American locomotives that majestically chronicle the rise of steam locomotive power in America. Introduction. Detailed captions. xi+ 129pp. 9 x 12. 0-486-27393-8

AMERICA'S LIGHTHOUSES: An Illustrated History, Francis Ross Holland, Jr. Delightfully written, profusely illustrated fact-filled survey of over 200 American lighthouses since 1716. History, anecdotes, technological advances, more. 240pp. 8 x 10¾. 0-486-25576-X

TOWARDS A NEW ARCHITECTURE, Le Corbusier. Pioneering manifesto by founder of "International School." Technical and aesthetic theories, views of industry, economics, relation of form to function, "mass-production split" and much more. Profusely illustrated. 320pp. 6⅛ x 9¼. (Available in U.S. only.) 0-486-25023-7

HOW THE OTHER HALF LIVES, Jacob Riis. Famous journalistic record, exposing poverty and degradation of New York slums around 1900, by major social reformer. 100 striking and influential photographs. 233pp. 10 x 7⅞. 0-486-22012-5

FRUIT KEY AND TWIG KEY TO TREES AND SHRUBS, William M. Harlow. One of the handiest and most widely used identification aids. Fruit key covers 120 deciduous and evergreen species; twig key 160 deciduous species. Easily used. Over 300 photographs. 126pp. 5⅜ x 8½. 0-486-20511-8

COMMON BIRD SONGS, Dr. Donald J. Borror. Songs of 60 most common U.S. birds: robins, sparrows, cardinals, bluejays, finches, more—arranged in order of increasing complexity. Up to 9 variations of songs of each species.
Cassette and manual 0-486-99911-4

ORCHIDS AS HOUSE PLANTS, Rebecca Tyson Northen. Grow cattleyas and many other kinds of orchids—in a window, in a case, or under artificial light. 63 illustrations. 148pp. 5⅜ x 8½. 0-486-23261-1

MONSTER MAZES, Dave Phillips. Masterful mazes at four levels of difficulty. Avoid deadly perils and evil creatures to find magical treasures. Solutions for all 32 exciting illustrated puzzles. 48pp. 8¼ x 11. 0-486-26005-4

MOZART'S DON GIOVANNI (DOVER OPERA LIBRETTO SERIES), Wolfgang Amadeus Mozart. Introduced and translated by Ellen H. Bleiler. Standard Italian libretto, with complete English translation. Convenient and thoroughly portable—an ideal companion for reading along with a recording or the performance itself. Introduction. List of characters. Plot summary. 121pp. 5¼ x 8½. 0-486-24944-1

FRANK LLOYD WRIGHT'S DANA HOUSE, Donald Hoffmann. Pictorial essay of residential masterpiece with over 160 interior and exterior photos, plans, elevations, sketches and studies. 128pp. 9¹/₄ x 10¾. 0-486-29120-0

THE CLARINET AND CLARINET PLAYING, David Pino. Lively, comprehensive work features suggestions about technique, musicianship, and musical interpretation, as well as guidelines for teaching, making your own reeds, and preparing for public performance. Includes an intriguing look at clarinet history. "A godsend," *The Clarinet,* Journal of the International Clarinet Society. Appendixes. 320pp. 5⅜ x 8½.   0-486-40270-3

HOLLYWOOD GLAMOR PORTRAITS, John Kobal (ed.). 145 photos from 1926-49. Harlow, Gable, Bogart, Bacall; 94 stars in all. Full background on photographers, technical aspects. 160pp. 8⅜ x 11¼.   0-486-23352-9

THE RAVEN AND OTHER FAVORITE POEMS, Edgar Allan Poe. Over 40 of the author's most memorable poems: "The Bells," "Ulalume," "Israfel," "To Helen," "The Conqueror Worm," "Eldorado," "Annabel Lee," many more. Alphabetic lists of titles and first lines. 64pp. 5³⁄₁₆ x 8¼.   0-486-26685-0

PERSONAL MEMOIRS OF U. S. GRANT, Ulysses Simpson Grant. Intelligent, deeply moving firsthand account of Civil War campaigns, considered by many the finest military memoirs ever written. Includes letters, historic photographs, maps and more. 528pp. 6⅛ x 9¼.   0-486-28587-1

ANCIENT EGYPTIAN MATERIALS AND INDUSTRIES, A. Lucas and J. Harris. Fascinating, comprehensive, thoroughly documented text describes this ancient civilization's vast resources and the processes that incorporated them in daily life, including the use of animal products, building materials, cosmetics, perfumes and incense, fibers, glazed ware, glass and its manufacture, materials used in the mummification process, and much more. 544pp. 6¹⁄₈ x 9¹⁄₄. (Available in U.S. only.)
0-486-40446-3

RUSSIAN STORIES/RUSSKIE RASSKAZY: A Dual-Language Book, edited by Gleb Struve. Twelve tales by such masters as Chekhov, Tolstoy, Dostoevsky, Pushkin, others. Excellent word-for-word English translations on facing pages, plus teaching and study aids, Russian/English vocabulary, biographical/critical introductions, more. 416pp. 5⅜ x 8½.   0-486-26244-8

PHILADELPHIA THEN AND NOW: 60 Sites Photographed in the Past and Present, Kenneth Finkel and Susan Oyama. Rare photographs of City Hall, Logan Square, Independence Hall, Betsy Ross House, other landmarks juxtaposed with contemporary views. Captures changing face of historic city. Introduction. Captions. 128pp. 8¼ x 11.   0-486-25790-8

NORTH AMERICAN INDIAN LIFE: Customs and Traditions of 23 Tribes, Elsie Clews Parsons (ed.). 27 fictionalized essays by noted anthropologists examine religion, customs, government, additional facets of life among the Winnebago, Crow, Zuni, Eskimo, other tribes. 480pp. 6⅛ x 9¼.   0-486-27377-6

TECHNICAL MANUAL AND DICTIONARY OF CLASSICAL BALLET, Gail Grant. Defines, explains, comments on steps, movements, poses and concepts. 15-page pictorial section. Basic book for student, viewer. 127pp. 5⅜ x 8½.
0-486-21843-0

THE MALE AND FEMALE FIGURE IN MOTION: 60 Classic Photographic Sequences, Eadweard Muybridge. 60 true-action photographs of men and women walking, running, climbing, bending, turning, etc., reproduced from rare 19th-century masterpiece. vi + 121pp. 9 x 12.   0-486-24745-7

ANIMALS: 1,419 Copyright-Free Illustrations of Mammals, Birds, Fish, Insects, etc., Jim Harter (ed.). Clear wood engravings present, in extremely lifelike poses, over 1,000 species of animals. One of the most extensive pictorial sourcebooks of its kind. Captions. Index. 284pp. 9 x 12.   0-486-23766-4

1001 QUESTIONS ANSWERED ABOUT THE SEASHORE, N. J. Berrill and Jacquelyn Berrill. Queries answered about dolphins, sea snails, sponges, starfish, fishes, shore birds, many others. Covers appearance, breeding, growth, feeding, much more. 305pp. 5¼ x 8¼.   0-486-23366-9

ATTRACTING BIRDS TO YOUR YARD, William J. Weber. Easy-to-follow guide offers advice on how to attract the greatest diversity of birds: birdhouses, feeders, water and waterers, much more. 96pp. 5³⁄₁₆ x 8¼.   0-486-28927-3

MEDICINAL AND OTHER USES OF NORTH AMERICAN PLANTS: A Historical Survey with Special Reference to the Eastern Indian Tribes, Charlotte Erichsen-Brown. Chronological historical citations document 500 years of usage of plants, trees, shrubs native to eastern Canada, northeastern U.S. Also complete identifying information. 343 illustrations. 544pp. 6½ x 9¼.   0-486-25951-X

STORYBOOK MAZES, Dave Phillips. 23 stories and mazes on two-page spreads: Wizard of Oz, Treasure Island, Robin Hood, etc. Solutions. 64pp. 8¼ x 11.
0-486-23628-5

AMERICAN NEGRO SONGS: 230 Folk Songs and Spirituals, Religious and Secular, John W. Work. This authoritative study traces the African influences of songs sung and played by black Americans at work, in church, and as entertainment. The author discusses the lyric significance of such songs as "Swing Low, Sweet Chariot," "John Henry," and others and offers the words and music for 230 songs. Bibliography. Index of Song Titles. 272pp. 6½ x 9¼.   0-486-40271-1

MOVIE-STAR PORTRAITS OF THE FORTIES, John Kobal (ed.). 163 glamor, studio photos of 106 stars of the 1940s: Rita Hayworth, Ava Gardner, Marlon Brando, Clark Gable, many more. 176pp. 8⅜ x 11¼.   0-486-23546-7

YEKL and THE IMPORTED BRIDEGROOM AND OTHER STORIES OF YIDDISH NEW YORK, Abraham Cahan. Film Hester Street based on *Yekl* (1896). Novel, other stories among first about Jewish immigrants on N.Y.'s East Side. 240pp. 5⅜ x 8½.   0-486-22427-9

SELECTED POEMS, Walt Whitman. Generous sampling from *Leaves of Grass*. Twenty-four poems include "I Hear America Singing," "Song of the Open Road," "I Sing the Body Electric," "When Lilacs Last in the Dooryard Bloom'd," "O Captain! My Captain!"–all reprinted from an authoritative edition. Lists of titles and first lines. 128pp. 5³⁄₁₆ x 8¼.   0-486-26878-0

SONGS OF EXPERIENCE: Facsimile Reproduction with 26 Plates in Full Color, William Blake. 26 full-color plates from a rare 1826 edition. Includes "The Tyger," "London," "Holy Thursday," and other poems. Printed text of poems. 48pp. 5¼ x 7.
0-486-24636-1

THE BEST TALES OF HOFFMANN, E. T. A. Hoffmann. 10 of Hoffmann's most important stories: "Nutcracker and the King of Mice," "The Golden Flowerpot," etc. 458pp. 5⅜ x 8½.   0-486-21793-0

THE BOOK OF TEA, Kakuzo Okakura. Minor classic of the Orient: entertaining, charming explanation, interpretation of traditional Japanese culture in terms of tea ceremony. 94pp. 5⅜ x 8½.   0-486-20070-1

FRENCH STORIES/CONTES FRANÇAIS: A Dual-Language Book, Wallace Fowlie. Ten stories by French masters, Voltaire to Camus: "Micromegas" by Voltaire; "The Atheist's Mass" by Balzac; "Minuet" by de Maupassant; "The Guest" by Camus, six more. Excellent English translations on facing pages. Also French-English vocabulary list, exercises, more. 352pp. 5⅜ x 8½. 0-486-26443-2

CHICAGO AT THE TURN OF THE CENTURY IN PHOTOGRAPHS: 122 Historic Views from the Collections of the Chicago Historical Society, Larry A. Viskochil. Rare large-format prints offer detailed views of City Hall, State Street, the Loop, Hull House, Union Station, many other landmarks, circa 1904-1913. Introduction. Captions. Maps. 144pp. 9⅜ x 12¼. 0-486-24656-6

OLD BROOKLYN IN EARLY PHOTOGRAPHS, 1865-1929, William Lee Younger. Luna Park, Gravesend race track, construction of Grand Army Plaza, moving of Hotel Brighton, etc. 157 previously unpublished photographs. 165pp. 8⅞ x 11¾. 0-486-23587-4

THE MYTHS OF THE NORTH AMERICAN INDIANS, Lewis Spence. Rich anthology of the myths and legends of the Algonquins, Iroquois, Pawnees and Sioux, prefaced by an extensive historical and ethnological commentary. 36 illustrations. 480pp. 5⅜ x 8½. 0-486-25967-6

AN ENCYCLOPEDIA OF BATTLES: Accounts of Over 1,560 Battles from 1479 B.C. to the Present, David Eggenberger. Essential details of every major battle in recorded history from the first battle of Megiddo in 1479 B.C. to Grenada in 1984. List of Battle Maps. New Appendix covering the years 1967-1984. Index. 99 illustrations. 544pp. 6½ x 9¼. 0-486-24913-1

SAILING ALONE AROUND THE WORLD, Captain Joshua Slocum. First man to sail around the world, alone, in small boat. One of great feats of seamanship told in delightful manner. 67 illustrations. 294pp. 5⅜ x 8½. 0-486-20326-3

ANARCHISM AND OTHER ESSAYS, Emma Goldman. Powerful, penetrating, prophetic essays on direct action, role of minorities, prison reform, puritan hypocrisy, violence, etc. 271pp. 5⅜ x 8½. 0-486-22484-8

MYTHS OF THE HINDUS AND BUDDHISTS, Ananda K. Coomaraswamy and Sister Nivedita. Great stories of the epics; deeds of Krishna, Shiva, taken from puranas, Vedas, folk tales; etc. 32 illustrations. 400pp. 5⅜ x 8½. 0-486-21759-0

MY BONDAGE AND MY FREEDOM, Frederick Douglass. Born a slave, Douglass became outspoken force in antislavery movement. The best of Douglass' autobiographies. Graphic description of slave life. 464pp. 5⅜ x 8½. 0-486-22457-0

FOLLOWING THE EQUATOR: A Journey Around the World, Mark Twain. Fascinating humorous account of 1897 voyage to Hawaii, Australia, India, New Zealand, etc. Ironic, bemused reports on peoples, customs, climate, flora and fauna, politics, much more. 197 illustrations. 720pp. 5⅜ x 8½. 0-486-26113-1

THE PEOPLE CALLED SHAKERS, Edward D. Andrews. Definitive study of Shakers: origins, beliefs, practices, dances, social organization, furniture and crafts, etc. 33 illustrations. 351pp. 5⅜ x 8½. 0-486-21081-2

THE MYTHS OF GREECE AND ROME, H. A. Guerber. A classic of mythology, generously illustrated, long prized for its simple, graphic, accurate retelling of the principal myths of Greece and Rome, and for its commentary on their origins and significance. With 64 illustrations by Michelangelo, Raphael, Titian, Rubens, Canova, Bernini and others. 480pp. 5⅜ x 8½. 0-486-27584-1

PSYCHOLOGY OF MUSIC, Carl E. Seashore. Classic work discusses music as a medium from psychological viewpoint. Clear treatment of physical acoustics, auditory apparatus, sound perception, development of musical skills, nature of musical feeling, host of other topics. 88 figures. 408pp. 5⅜ x 8½.   0-486-21851-1

LIFE IN ANCIENT EGYPT, Adolf Erman. Fullest, most thorough, detailed older account with much not in more recent books, domestic life, religion, magic, medicine, commerce, much more. Many illustrations reproduce tomb paintings, carvings, hieroglyphs, etc. 597pp. 5⅜ x 8½.   0-486-22632-8

SUNDIALS, Their Theory and Construction, Albert Waugh. Far and away the best, most thorough coverage of ideas, mathematics concerned, types, construction, adjusting anywhere. Simple, nontechnical treatment allows even children to build several of these dials. Over 100 illustrations. 230pp. 5⅜ x 8½.   0-486-22947-5

THEORETICAL HYDRODYNAMICS, L. M. Milne-Thomson. Classic exposition of the mathematical theory of fluid motion, applicable to both hydrodynamics and aerodynamics. Over 600 exercises. 768pp. 6⅛ x 9¼.   0-486-68970-0

OLD-TIME VIGNETTES IN FULL COLOR, Carol Belanger Grafton (ed.). Over 390 charming, often sentimental illustrations, selected from archives of Victorian graphics—pretty women posing, children playing, food, flowers, kittens and puppies, smiling cherubs, birds and butterflies, much more. All copyright-free. 48pp. 9¼ x 12¼.
0-486-27269-9

PERSPECTIVE FOR ARTISTS, Rex Vicat Cole. Depth, perspective of sky and sea, shadows, much more, not usually covered. 391 diagrams, 81 reproductions of drawings and paintings. 279pp. 5⅜ x 8½.   0-486-22487-2

DRAWING THE LIVING FIGURE, Joseph Sheppard. Innovative approach to artistic anatomy focuses on specifics of surface anatomy, rather than muscles and bones. Over 170 drawings of live models in front, back and side views, and in widely varying poses. Accompanying diagrams. 177 illustrations. Introduction. Index. 144pp. 8⅜ x11¼.   0-486-26723-7

GOTHIC AND OLD ENGLISH ALPHABETS: 100 Complete Fonts, Dan X. Solo. Add power, elegance to posters, signs, other graphics with 100 stunning copyright-free alphabets: Blackstone, Dolbey, Germania, 97 more—including many lower-case, numerals, punctuation marks. 104pp. 8⅛ x 11.   0-486-24695-7

THE BOOK OF WOOD CARVING, Charles Marshall Sayers. Finest book for beginners discusses fundamentals and offers 34 designs. "Absolutely first rate . . . well thought out and well executed."—E. J. Tangerman. 118pp. 7¾ x 10⅝.   0-486-23654-4

ILLUSTRATED CATALOG OF CIVIL WAR MILITARY GOODS: Union Army Weapons, Insignia, Uniform Accessories, and Other Equipment, Schuyler, Hartley, and Graham. Rare, profusely illustrated 1846 catalog includes Union Army uniform and dress regulations, arms and ammunition, coats, insignia, flags, swords, rifles, etc. 226 illustrations. 160pp. 9 x 12.   0-486-24939-5

WOMEN'S FASHIONS OF THE EARLY 1900s: An Unabridged Republication of "New York Fashions, 1909," National Cloak & Suit Co. Rare catalog of mail-order fashions documents women's and children's clothing styles shortly after the turn of the century. Captions offer full descriptions, prices. Invaluable resource for fashion, costume historians. Approximately 725 illustrations. 128pp. 8⅜ x 11¼.
0-486-27276-1

HOW TO DO BEADWORK, Mary White. Fundamental book on craft from simple projects to five-bead chains and woven works. 106 illustrations. 142pp. 5⅜ x 8.
0-486-20697-1

THE 1912 AND 1915 GUSTAV STICKLEY FURNITURE CATALOGS, Gustav Stickley. With over 200 detailed illustrations and descriptions, these two catalogs are essential reading and reference materials and identification guides for Stickley furniture. Captions cite materials, dimensions and prices. 112pp. 6½ x 9¼. 0-486-26676-1

EARLY AMERICAN LOCOMOTIVES, John H. White, Jr. Finest locomotive engravings from early 19th century: historical (1804–74), main-line (after 1870), special, foreign, etc. 147 plates. 142pp. 11⅜ x 8¼. 0-486-22772-3

LITTLE BOOK OF EARLY AMERICAN CRAFTS AND TRADES, Peter Stockham (ed.). 1807 children's book explains crafts and trades: baker, hatter, cooper, potter, and many others. 23 copperplate illustrations. 140pp. 4⅝ x 6.
0-486-23336-7

VICTORIAN FASHIONS AND COSTUMES FROM HARPER'S BAZAR, 1867–1898, Stella Blum (ed.). Day costumes, evening wear, sports clothes, shoes, hats, other accessories in over 1,000 detailed engravings. 320pp. 9⅜ x 12¼.
0-486-22990-4

THE LONG ISLAND RAIL ROAD IN EARLY PHOTOGRAPHS, Ron Ziel. Over 220 rare photos, informative text document origin (1844) and development of rail service on Long Island. Vintage views of early trains, locomotives, stations, passengers, crews, much more. Captions. 8⅞ x 11¾. 0-486-26301-0

VOYAGE OF THE LIBERDADE, Joshua Slocum. Great 19th-century mariner's thrilling, first-hand account of the wreck of his ship off South America, the 35-foot boat he built from the wreckage, and its remarkable voyage home. 128pp. 5⅜ x 8½.
0-486-40022-0

TEN BOOKS ON ARCHITECTURE, Vitruvius. The most important book ever written on architecture. Early Roman aesthetics, technology, classical orders, site selection, all other aspects. Morgan translation. 331pp. 5⅜ x 8½. 0-486-20645-9

THE HUMAN FIGURE IN MOTION, Eadweard Muybridge. More than 4,500 stopped-action photos, in action series, showing undraped men, women, children jumping, lying down, throwing, sitting, wrestling, carrying, etc. 390pp. 7⅞ x 10⅝.
0-486-20204-6 Clothbd.

TREES OF THE EASTERN AND CENTRAL UNITED STATES AND CANADA, William M. Harlow. Best one-volume guide to 140 trees. Full descriptions, woodlore, range, etc. Over 600 illustrations. Handy size. 288pp. 4½ x 6⅜. 0-486-20395-6

GROWING AND USING HERBS AND SPICES, Milo Miloradovich. Versatile handbook provides all the information needed for cultivation and use of all the herbs and spices available in North America. 4 illustrations. Index. Glossary. 236pp. 5⅜ x 8½.
0-486-25058-X

BIG BOOK OF MAZES AND LABYRINTHS, Walter Shepherd. 50 mazes and labyrinths in all—classical, solid, ripple, and more—in one great volume. Perfect inexpensive puzzler for clever youngsters. Full solutions. 112pp. 8⅛ x 11. 0-486-22951-3

PIANO TUNING, J. Cree Fischer. Clearest, best book for beginner, amateur. Simple repairs, raising dropped notes, tuning by easy method of flattened fifths. No previous skills needed. 4 illustrations. 201pp. 5⅜ x 8½. 0-486-23267-0

HINTS TO SINGERS, Lillian Nordica. Selecting the right teacher, developing confidence, overcoming stage fright, and many other important skills receive thoughtful discussion in this indispensible guide, written by a world-famous diva of four decades' experience. 96pp. 5⅜ x 8½. 0-486-40094-8

THE COMPLETE NONSENSE OF EDWARD LEAR, Edward Lear. All nonsense limericks, zany alphabets, Owl and Pussycat, songs, nonsense botany, etc., illustrated by Lear. Total of 320pp. 5⅜ x 8½. (Available in U.S. only.) 0-486-20167-8

VICTORIAN PARLOUR POETRY: An Annotated Anthology, Michael R. Turner. 117 gems by Longfellow, Tennyson, Browning, many lesser-known poets. "The Village Blacksmith," "Curfew Must Not Ring Tonight," "Only a Baby Small," dozens more, often difficult to find elsewhere. Index of poets, titles, first lines. xxiii + 325pp. 5⅝ x 8¼. 0-486-27044-0

DUBLINERS, James Joyce. Fifteen stories offer vivid, tightly focused observations of the lives of Dublin's poorer classes. At least one, "The Dead," is considered a masterpiece. Reprinted complete and unabridged from standard edition. 160pp. 5$\frac{3}{16}$ x 8¼. 0-486-26870-5

GREAT WEIRD TALES: 14 Stories by Lovecraft, Blackwood, Machen and Others, S. T. Joshi (ed.). 14 spellbinding tales, including "The Sin Eater," by Fiona McLeod, "The Eye Above the Mantel," by Frank Belknap Long, as well as renowned works by R. H. Barlow, Lord Dunsany, Arthur Machen, W. C. Morrow and eight other masters of the genre. 256pp. 5⅜ x 8½. (Available in U.S. only.) 0-486-40436-6

THE BOOK OF THE SACRED MAGIC OF ABRAMELIN THE MAGE, translated by S. MacGregor Mathers. Medieval manuscript of ceremonial magic. Basic document in Aleister Crowley, Golden Dawn groups. 268pp. 5⅜ x 8½. 0-486-23211-5

THE BATTLES THAT CHANGED HISTORY, Fletcher Pratt. Eminent historian profiles 16 crucial conflicts, ancient to modern, that changed the course of civilization. 352pp. 5⅜ x 8½. 0-486-41129-X

NEW RUSSIAN-ENGLISH AND ENGLISH-RUSSIAN DICTIONARY, M. A. O'Brien. This is a remarkably handy Russian dictionary, containing a surprising amount of information, including over 70,000 entries. 366pp. 4½ x 6⅛. 0-486-20208-9

NEW YORK IN THE FORTIES, Andreas Feininger. 162 brilliant photographs by the well-known photographer, formerly with *Life* magazine. Commuters, shoppers, Times Square at night, much else from city at its peak. Captions by John von Hartz. 181pp. 9¼ x 10¾. 0-486-23585-8

INDIAN SIGN LANGUAGE, William Tomkins. Over 525 signs developed by Sioux and other tribes. Written instructions and diagrams. Also 290 pictographs. 111pp. 6⅛ x 9¼. 0-486-22029-X

ANATOMY: A Complete Guide for Artists, Joseph Sheppard. A master of figure drawing shows artists how to render human anatomy convincingly. Over 460 illustrations. 224pp. 8⅜ x 11¼. 0-486-27279-6

MEDIEVAL CALLIGRAPHY: Its History and Technique, Marc Drogin. Spirited history, comprehensive instruction manual covers 13 styles (ca. 4th century through 15th). Excellent photographs; directions for duplicating medieval techniques with modern tools. 224pp. 8⅜ x 11¼. 0-486-26142-5

DRIED FLOWERS: How to Prepare Them, Sarah Whitlock and Martha Rankin. Complete instructions on how to use silica gel, meal and borax, perlite aggregate, sand and borax, glycerine and water to create attractive permanent flower arrangements. 12 illustrations. 32pp. 5⅜ x 8½.   0-486-21802-3

EASY-TO-MAKE BIRD FEEDERS FOR WOODWORKERS, Scott D. Campbell. Detailed, simple-to-use guide for designing, constructing, caring for and using feeders. Text, illustrations for 12 classic and contemporary designs. 96pp. 5⅜ x 8½.
                                                        0-486-25847-5

THE COMPLETE BOOK OF BIRDHOUSE CONSTRUCTION FOR WOOD-WORKERS, Scott D. Campbell. Detailed instructions, illustrations, tables. Also data on bird habitat and instinct patterns. Bibliography. 3 tables. 63 illustrations in 15 figures. 48pp. 5¼ x 8½.   0-486-24407-5

SCOTTISH WONDER TALES FROM MYTH AND LEGEND, Donald A. Mackenzie. 16 lively tales tell of giants rumbling down mountainsides, of a magic wand that turns stone pillars into warriors, of gods and goddesses, evil hags, powerful forces and more. 240pp. 5⅜ x 8½.   0-486-29677-6

THE HISTORY OF UNDERCLOTHES, C. Willett Cunnington and Phyllis Cunnington. Fascinating, well-documented survey covering six centuries of English undergarments, enhanced with over 100 illustrations: 12th-century laced-up bodice, footed long drawers (1795), 19th-century bustles, 19th-century corsets for men, Victorian "bust improvers," much more. 272pp. 5⅜ x 8¼.   0-486-27124-2

ARTS AND CRAFTS FURNITURE: The Complete Brooks Catalog of 1912, Brooks Manufacturing Co. Photos and detailed descriptions of more than 150 now very collectible furniture designs from the Arts and Crafts movement depict davenports, settees, buffets, desks, tables, chairs, bedsteads, dressers and more, all built of solid, quarter-sawed oak. Invaluable for students and enthusiasts of antiques, Americana and the decorative arts. 80pp. 6½ x 9¼.   0-486-27471-3

WILBUR AND ORVILLE: A Biography of the Wright Brothers, Fred Howard. Definitive, crisply written study tells the full story of the brothers' lives and work. A vividly written biography, unparalleled in scope and color, that also captures the spirit of an extraordinary era. 560pp. 6⅛ x 9¼.   0-486-40297-5

THE ARTS OF THE SAILOR: Knotting, Splicing and Ropework, Hervey Garrett Smith. Indispensable shipboard reference covers tools, basic knots and useful hitches; handsewing and canvas work, more. Over 100 illustrations. Delightful reading for sea lovers. 256pp. 5⅜ x 8½.   0-486-26440-8

FRANK LLOYD WRIGHT'S FALLINGWATER: The House and Its History, Second, Revised Edition, Donald Hoffmann. A total revision—both in text and illustrations—of the standard document on Fallingwater, the boldest, most personal architectural statement of Wright's mature years, updated with valuable new material from the recently opened Frank Lloyd Wright Archives. "Fascinating"—*The New York Times*. 116 illustrations. 128pp. 9¼ x 10¾.   0-486-27430-6

PHOTOGRAPHIC SKETCHBOOK OF THE CIVIL WAR, Alexander Gardner. 100 photos taken on field during the Civil War. Famous shots of Manassas Harper's Ferry, Lincoln, Richmond, slave pens, etc. 244pp. 10⅝ x 8¼.   0-486-22731-6

FIVE ACRES AND INDEPENDENCE, Maurice G. Kains. Great back-to-the-land classic explains basics of self-sufficient farming. The one book to get. 95 illustrations. 397pp. 5⅜ x 8½.   0-486-20974-1

A MODERN HERBAL, Margaret Grieve. Much the fullest, most exact, most useful compilation of herbal material. Gigantic alphabetical encyclopedia, from aconite to zedoary, gives botanical information, medical properties, folklore, economic uses, much else. Indispensable to serious reader. 161 illustrations. 888pp. 6½ x 9¼. 2-vol. set. (Available in U.S. only.)   Vol. I: 0-486-22798-7   Vol. II: 0-486-22799-5

HIDDEN TREASURE MAZE BOOK, Dave Phillips. Solve 34 challenging mazes accompanied by heroic tales of adventure. Evil dragons, people-eating plants, blood-thirsty giants, many more dangerous adversaries lurk at every twist and turn. 34 mazes, stories, solutions. 48pp. 8¼ x 11.   0-486-24566-7

LETTERS OF W. A. MOZART, Wolfgang A. Mozart. Remarkable letters show bawdy wit, humor, imagination, musical insights, contemporary musical world; includes some letters from Leopold Mozart. 276pp. 5⅜ x 8½.   0-486-22859-2

BASIC PRINCIPLES OF CLASSICAL BALLET, Agrippina Vaganova. Great Russian theoretician, teacher explains methods for teaching classical ballet. 118 illustrations. 175pp. 5⅜ x 8½.   0-486-22036-2

THE JUMPING FROG, Mark Twain. Revenge edition. The original story of The Celebrated Jumping Frog of Calaveras County, a hapless French translation, and Twain's hilarious "retranslation" from the French. 12 illustrations. 66pp. 5⅜ x 8½.
0-486-22686-7

BEST REMEMBERED POEMS, Martin Gardner (ed.). The 126 poems in this superb collection of 19th- and 20th-century British and American verse range from Shelley's "To a Skylark" to the impassioned "Renascence" of Edna St. Vincent Millay and to Edward Lear's whimsical "The Owl and the Pussycat." 224pp. 5⅜ x 8½.
0-486-27165-X

COMPLETE SONNETS, William Shakespeare. Over 150 exquisite poems deal with love, friendship, the tyranny of time, beauty's evanescence, death and other themes in language of remarkable power, precision and beauty. Glossary of archaic terms. 80pp. 5³⁄₁₆ x 8¼.   0-486-26686-9

HISTORIC HOMES OF THE AMERICAN PRESIDENTS, Second, Revised Edition, Irvin Haas. A traveler's guide to American Presidential homes, most open to the public, depicting and describing homes occupied by every American President from George Washington to George Bush. With visiting hours, admission charges, travel routes. 175 photographs. Index. 160pp. 8¼ x 11.   0-486-26751-2

THE WIT AND HUMOR OF OSCAR WILDE, Alvin Redman (ed.). More than 1,000 ripostes, paradoxes, wisecracks: Work is the curse of the drinking classes; I can resist everything except temptation; etc. 258pp. 5⅜ x 8½.   0-486-20602-5

SHAKESPEARE LEXICON AND QUOTATION DICTIONARY, Alexander Schmidt. Full definitions, locations, shades of meaning in every word in plays and poems. More than 50,000 exact quotations. 1,485pp. 6½ x 9¼. 2-vol. set.
Vol. 1: 0-486-22726-X   Vol. 2: 0-486-22727-8

SELECTED POEMS, Emily Dickinson. Over 100 best-known, best-loved poems by one of America's foremost poets, reprinted from authoritative early editions. No comparable edition at this price. Index of first lines. 64pp. 5³⁄₁₆ x 8¼. 0-486-26466-1

THE INSIDIOUS DR. FU-MANCHU, Sax Rohmer. The first of the popular mystery series introduces a pair of English detectives to their archnemesis, the diabolical Dr. Fu-Manchu. Flavorful atmosphere, fast-paced action, and colorful characters enliven this classic of the genre. 208pp. 5³⁄₁₆ x 8¼.   0-486-29898-1

THE MALLEUS MALEFICARUM OF KRAMER AND SPRENGER, translated by Montague Summers. Full text of most important witchhunter's "bible," used by both Catholics and Protestants. 278pp. 6⅝ x 10.   0-486-22802-9

SPANISH STORIES/CUENTOS ESPAÑOLES: A Dual-Language Book, Angel Flores (ed.). Unique format offers 13 great stories in Spanish by Cervantes, Borges, others. Faithful English translations on facing pages. 352pp. 5⅜ x 8½.

0-486-25399-6

GARDEN CITY, LONG ISLAND, IN EARLY PHOTOGRAPHS, 1869–1919, Mildred H. Smith. Handsome treasury of 118 vintage pictures, accompanied by carefully researched captions, document the Garden City Hotel fire (1899), the Vanderbilt Cup Race (1908), the first airmail flight departing from the Nassau Boulevard Aerodrome (1911), and much more. 96pp. 8⅞ x 11¾.   0-486-40669-5

OLD QUEENS, N.Y., IN EARLY PHOTOGRAPHS, Vincent F. Seyfried and William Asadorian. Over 160 rare photographs of Maspeth, Jamaica, Jackson Heights, and other areas. Vintage views of DeWitt Clinton mansion, 1939 World's Fair and more. Captions. 192pp. 8⅞ x 11.   0-486-26358-4

CAPTURED BY THE INDIANS: 15 Firsthand Accounts, 1750-1870, Frederick Drimmer. Astounding true historical accounts of grisly torture, bloody conflicts, relentless pursuits, miraculous escapes and more, by people who lived to tell the tale. 384pp. 5⅜ x 8½.   0-486-24901-8

THE WORLD'S GREAT SPEECHES (Fourth Enlarged Edition), Lewis Copeland, Lawrence W. Lamm, and Stephen J. McKenna. Nearly 300 speeches provide public speakers with a wealth of updated quotes and inspiration–from Pericles' funeral oration and William Jennings Bryan's "Cross of Gold Speech" to Malcolm X's powerful words on the Black Revolution and Earl of Spenser's tribute to his sister, Diana, Princess of Wales. 944pp. 5⅜ x 8⅜.   0-486-40903-1

THE BOOK OF THE SWORD, Sir Richard F. Burton. Great Victorian scholar/adventurer's eloquent, erudite history of the "queen of weapons"–from prehistory to early Roman Empire. Evolution and development of early swords, variations (sabre, broadsword, cutlass, scimitar, etc.), much more. 336pp. 6⅛ x 9¼.

0-486-25434-8

AUTOBIOGRAPHY: The Story of My Experiments with Truth, Mohandas K. Gandhi. Boyhood, legal studies, purification, the growth of the Satyagraha (nonviolent protest) movement. Critical, inspiring work of the man responsible for the freedom of India. 480pp. 5⅜ x 8½. (Available in U.S. only.)   0-486-24593-4

CELTIC MYTHS AND LEGENDS, T. W. Rolleston. Masterful retelling of Irish and Welsh stories and tales. Cuchulain, King Arthur, Deirdre, the Grail, many more. First paperback edition. 58 full-page illustrations. 512pp. 5⅜ x 8½.   0-486-26507-2

THE PRINCIPLES OF PSYCHOLOGY, William James. Famous long course complete, unabridged. Stream of thought, time perception, memory, experimental methods; great work decades ahead of its time. 94 figures. 1,391pp. 5⅜ x 8½. 2-vol. set.
Vol. I: 0-486-20381-6   Vol. II: 0-486-20382-4

THE WORLD AS WILL AND REPRESENTATION, Arthur Schopenhauer. Definitive English translation of Schopenhauer's life work, correcting more than 1,000 errors, omissions in earlier translations. Translated by E. F. J. Payne. Total of 1,269pp. 5⅜ x 8½. 2-vol. set.   Vol. 1: 0-486-21761-2   Vol. 2: 0-486-21762-0

MAGIC AND MYSTERY IN TIBET, Madame Alexandra David-Neel. Experiences among lamas, magicians, sages, sorcerers, Bonpa wizards. A true psychic discovery. 32 illustrations. 321pp. 5⅜ x 8½. (Available in U.S. only.) 0-486-22682-4

THE EGYPTIAN BOOK OF THE DEAD, E. A. Wallis Budge. Complete reproduction of Ani's papyrus, finest ever found. Full hieroglyphic text, interlinear transliteration, word-for-word translation, smooth translation. 533pp. 6½ x 9¼. 0-486-21866-X

HISTORIC COSTUME IN PICTURES, Braun & Schneider. Over 1,450 costumed figures in clearly detailed engravings–from dawn of civilization to end of 19th century. Captions. Many folk costumes. 256pp. 8⅜ x 11¾. 0-486-23150-X

MATHEMATICS FOR THE NONMATHEMATICIAN, Morris Kline. Detailed, college-level treatment of mathematics in cultural and historical context, with numerous exercises. Recommended Reading Lists. Tables. Numerous figures. 641pp. 5⅜ x 8½. 0-486-24823-2

PROBABILISTIC METHODS IN THE THEORY OF STRUCTURES, Isaac Elishakoff. Well-written introduction covers the elements of the theory of probability from two or more random variables, the reliability of such multivariable structures, the theory of random function, Monte Carlo methods of treating problems incapable of exact solution, and more. Examples. 502pp. 5⅜ x 8½. 0-486-40691-1

THE RIME OF THE ANCIENT MARINER, Gustave Doré, S. T. Coleridge. Doré's finest work; 34 plates capture moods, subtleties of poem. Flawless full-size reproductions printed on facing pages with authoritative text of poem. "Beautiful. Simply beautiful."–*Publisher's Weekly.* 77pp. 9¼ x 12. 0-486-22305-1

SCULPTURE: Principles and Practice, Louis Slobodkin. Step-by-step approach to clay, plaster, metals, stone; classical and modern. 253 drawings, photos. 255pp. 8⅛ x 11. 0-486-22960-2

THE INFLUENCE OF SEA POWER UPON HISTORY, 1660–1783, A. T. Mahan. Influential classic of naval history and tactics still used as text in war colleges. First paperback edition. 4 maps. 24 battle plans. 640pp. 5⅜ x 8½. 0-486-25509-3

THE STORY OF THE TITANIC AS TOLD BY ITS SURVIVORS, Jack Winocour (ed.). What it was really like. Panic, despair, shocking inefficiency, and a little heroism. More thrilling than any fictional account. 26 illustrations. 320pp. 5⅜ x 8½. 0-486-20610-6

ONE TWO THREE . . . INFINITY: Facts and Speculations of Science, George Gamow. Great physicist's fascinating, readable overview of contemporary science: number theory, relativity, fourth dimension, entropy, genes, atomic structure, much more. 128 illustrations. Index. 352pp. 5⅜ x 8½. 0-486-25664-2

DALÍ ON MODERN ART: The Cuckolds of Antiquated Modern Art, Salvador Dalí. Influential painter skewers modern art and its practitioners. Outrageous evaluations of Picasso, Cézanne, Turner, more. 15 renderings of paintings discussed. 44 calligraphic decorations by Dalí. 96pp. 5⅜ x 8½. (Available in U.S. only.) 0-486-29220-7

ANTIQUE PLAYING CARDS: A Pictorial History, Henry René D'Allemagne. Over 900 elaborate, decorative images from rare playing cards (14th–20th centuries): Bacchus, death, dancing dogs, hunting scenes, royal coats of arms, players cheating, much more. 96pp. 9¼ x 12¼. 0-486-29265-7

MAKING FURNITURE MASTERPIECES: 30 Projects with Measured Drawings, Franklin H. Gottshall. Step-by-step instructions, illustrations for constructing handsome, useful pieces, among them a Sheraton desk, Chippendale chair, Spanish desk, Queen Anne table and a William and Mary dressing mirror. 224pp. 8⅛ x 11¼. 0-486-29338-6

NORTH AMERICAN INDIAN DESIGNS FOR ARTISTS AND CRAFTSPEOPLE, Eva Wilson. Over 360 authentic copyright-free designs adapted from Navajo blankets, Hopi pottery, Sioux buffalo hides, more. Geometrics, symbolic figures, plant and animal motifs, etc. 128pp. 8⅜ x 11. (Not for sale in the United Kingdom.) 0-486-25341-4

THE FOSSIL BOOK: A Record of Prehistoric Life, Patricia V. Rich et al. Profusely illustrated definitive guide covers everything from single-celled organisms and dinosaurs to birds and mammals and the interplay between climate and man. Over 1,500 illustrations. 760pp. 7½ x 10⅛. 0-486-29371-8

VICTORIAN ARCHITECTURAL DETAILS: Designs for Over 700 Stairs, Mantels, Doors, Windows, Cornices, Porches, and Other Decorative Elements, A. J. Bicknell & Company. Everything from dormer windows and piazzas to balconies and gable ornaments. Also includes elevations and floor plans for handsome, private residences and commercial structures. 80pp. 9⅜ x 12¼. 0-486-44015-X

WESTERN ISLAMIC ARCHITECTURE: A Concise Introduction, John D. Hoag. Profusely illustrated critical appraisal compares and contrasts Islamic mosques and palaces–from Spain and Egypt to other areas in the Middle East. 139 illustrations. 128pp. 6 x 9. 0-486-43760-4

CHINESE ARCHITECTURE: A Pictorial History, Liang Ssu-ch'eng. More than 240 rare photographs and drawings depict temples, pagodas, tombs, bridges, and imperial palaces comprising much of China's architectural heritage. 152 halftones, 94 diagrams. 232pp. 10¾ x 9⅞. 0-486-43999-2

THE RENAISSANCE: Studies in Art and Poetry, Walter Pater. One of the most talked-about books of the 19th century, *The Renaissance* combines scholarship and philosophy in an innovative work of cultural criticism that examines the achievements of Botticelli, Leonardo, Michelangelo, and other artists. "The holy writ of beauty."–Oscar Wilde. 160pp. 5⅜ x 8½. 0-486-44025-7

A TREATISE ON PAINTING, Leonardo da Vinci. The great Renaissance artist's practical advice on drawing and painting techniques covers anatomy, perspective, composition, light and shadow, and color. A classic of art instruction, it features 48 drawings by Nicholas Poussin and Leon Battista Alberti. 192pp. 5⅜ x 8½. 0-486-44155-5

THE MIND OF LEONARDO DA VINCI, Edward McCurdy. More than just a biography, this classic study by a distinguished historian draws upon Leonardo's extensive writings to offer numerous demonstrations of the Renaissance master's achievements, not only in sculpture and painting, but also in music, engineering, and even experimental aviation. 384pp. 5⅜ x 8½. 0-486-44142-3

WASHINGTON IRVING'S RIP VAN WINKLE, Illustrated by Arthur Rackham. Lovely prints that established artist as a leading illustrator of the time and forever etched into the popular imagination a classic of Catskill lore. 51 full-color plates. 80pp. 8⅜ x 11. 0-486-44242-X

HENSCHE ON PAINTING, John W. Robichaux. Basic painting philosophy and methodology of a great teacher, as expounded in his famous classes and workshops on Cape Cod. 7 illustrations in color on covers. 80pp. 5⅜ x 8½. 0-486-43728-0

LIGHT AND SHADE: A Classic Approach to Three-Dimensional Drawing, Mrs. Mary P. Merrifield. Handy reference clearly demonstrates principles of light and shade by revealing effects of common daylight, sunshine, and candle or artificial light on geometrical solids. 13 plates. 64pp. 5⅜ x 8½. 0-486-44143-1

ASTROLOGY AND ASTRONOMY: A Pictorial Archive of Signs and Symbols, Ernst and Johanna Lehner. Treasure trove of stories, lore, and myth, accompanied by more than 300 rare illustrations of planets, the Milky Way, signs of the zodiac, comets, meteors, and other astronomical phenomena. 192pp. 8⅜ x 11. 0-486-43981-X

JEWELRY MAKING: Techniques for Metal, Tim McCreight. Easy-to-follow instructions and carefully executed illustrations describe tools and techniques, use of gems and enamels, wire inlay, casting, and other topics. 72 line illustrations and diagrams. 176pp. 8¼ x 10⅞. 0-486-44043-5

MAKING BIRDHOUSES: Easy and Advanced Projects, Gladstone Califf. Easy-to-follow instructions include diagrams for everything from a one-room house for bluebirds to a forty-two-room structure for purple martins. 56 plates; 4 figures. 80pp. 8¾ x 6⅜. 0-486-44183-0

LITTLE BOOK OF LOG CABINS: How to Build and Furnish Them, William S. Wicks. Handy how-to manual, with instructions and illustrations for building cabins in the Adirondack style, fireplaces, stairways, furniture, beamed ceilings, and more. 102 line drawings. 96pp. 8¾ x 6⅜. 0-486-44259-4

THE SEASONS OF AMERICA PAST, Eric Sloane. From "sugaring time" and strawberry picking to Indian summer and fall harvest, a whole year's activities described in charming prose and enhanced with 79 of the author's own illustrations. 160pp. 8¼ x 11. 0-486-44220-9

THE METROPOLIS OF TOMORROW, Hugh Ferriss. Generous, prophetic vision of the metropolis of the future, as perceived in 1929. Powerful illustrations of towering structures, wide avenues, and rooftop parks–all features in many of today's modern cities. 59 illustrations. 144pp. 8¼ x 11. 0-486-43727-2

THE PATH TO ROME, Hilaire Belloc. This 1902 memoir abounds in lively vignettes from a vanished time, recounting a pilgrimage on foot across the Alps and Apennines in order to "see all Europe which the Christian Faith has saved." 77 of the author's original line drawings complement his sparkling prose. 272pp. 5⅜ x 8½. 0-486-44001-X

THE HISTORY OF RASSELAS: Prince of Abissinia, Samuel Johnson. Distinguished English writer attacks eighteenth-century optimism and man's unrealistic estimates of what life has to offer. 112pp. 5⅜ x 8½. 0-486-44094-X

A VOYAGE TO ARCTURUS, David Lindsay. A brilliant flight of pure fancy, where wild creatures crowd the fantastic landscape and demented torturers dominate victims with their bizarre mental powers. 272pp. 5⅜ x 8½. 0-486-44198-9

Paperbound unless otherwise indicated. Available at your book dealer, online at **www.doverpublications.com**, or by writing to Dept. GI, Dover Publications, Inc., 31 East 2nd Street, Mineola, NY 11501. For current price information or for free catalogs (please indicate field of interest), write to Dover Publications or log on to **www.doverpublications.com** and see every Dover book in print. Dover publishes more than 500 books each year on science, elementary and advanced mathematics, biology, music, art, literary history, social sciences, and other areas.